Rafaella

A treacherous temptress
who knew every man's
hidden shame and secret desire.

RAFAELLA

On the surface, life had all the lazy elegance of
Southern gentility—from morning rides through
the green coolness of vast plantations to moonlit
balls in white-columned mansions. But underneath
its crinolined respectability, Natchez seethed with
ruthless greed and ambition, with unbridled lusts
and unspeakable desires, with bloody conflict between slave and master.

Bantam Books by George McNeill

RAFAELLA
THE PLANTATION

Rafaella

George McNeill

A Bernard Geis Associates Book

BANTAM BOOKS
TORONTO · LONDON
NEW YORK

RAFAELLA
A Bantam Book / November 1977
2nd printing
3rd printing
4th printing

ISBN 0-553-10945-6

Published simultaneously in the United States and Canada

Bantam Books are published by Bantam Books, Inc. Its trade-
mark, consisting of the words "Bantam Books" and the por-
trayal of a bantam, is registered in the United States Patent
Office and in other countries. Marca Registrada. Bantam
Books, Inc., 666 Fifth Avenue, New York, New York 10019.

Prologue
Cairo. March 1, 1811

From his hiding place in the tower, Salhan Rahdi watched the Sultan's troops defile the heaped headless corpses of his countrymen with wine and urine. Rahdi looked out into a small, dusty square near the Citadel, which overlooked Cairo. He saw a group of old men smoking pipes of *kef* and staring as the soldiers beheaded a man.

Another man was dragged into the square. Rahdi gasped. The man was Mustapha, his best friend!

Two soldiers forced Mustapha to a palm tree. One of them laughed to see him stumble. Three other soldiers lounged against a wall. One held a razor, another a long cord, the third a whip.

Bile rose in Rahdi's throat. He knew what would happen to his friend. Mustapha's stomach would be slit open. The cord would be tied to his intestines and to the tree. Then Mustapha would be driven around the tree and forced to disembowel himself.

Rahdi climbed to his feet and grabbed his scimitar. He stumbled down the tower's steep stairs, almost blind with pain from a festering flesh wound.

As he neared the square, he smelt death. His arm ached from the weight of his scimitar. His thoughts were crazed, desperate. In one day, his life, his whole world, had been devastated.

Rahdi was a young Mameluke, one of the white slave elite who had ruled Egypt for hundreds of years. But the Sultan, Muhammed Ali, had tricked the Mamelukes into riding in procession through the Citadel. Then he had locked all the gates and his troops had opened fire on them.

Hundreds of Mamelukes were killed at once. Rahdi had been wounded, escaped, fled. He had been hunted, seen his home burned. All around the Citadel were the rotting corpses of Mameluke princes. Now the Sultan's troops were hunting down the rest, ravaging Mameluke palaces and slaughtering their families.

For a time, Rahdi had found refuge in the home of a friendly British silk merchant. But now. . . He swayed, propped himself against a palm tree on the edge of the square. He had little strength left. And if he did reach Mustapha? Then what? He could only hope to kill them both before he was overpowered by the soldiers.

He began to run, using his scimitar as a cane. Again his shocked mind wandered, this time to the mystery of his origin. He knew that, like many Mamelukes, his parents had been Christians, with the fair skin and light hair and eyes that set off the Mamelukes from the Egyptians. He also knew that he had been born in the Balkans, but he did not know whether he had been kidnapped in a raid or sold by his parents.

Mustapha's first scream was high-pitched. Rahdi moved toward the sound, his faltering steps in rhythm with his friend's screams. But his strength failed suddenly. He stumbled, fell beneath a fig tree. There he lay, wet with dew and his own blood, and prayed that he would die before he was discovered.

Book
I

1.

New Orleans. September 1836

Alain LeBeau had watched a hundred duels here beneath the live oaks of Lower City Park. But he had never seen so curious a swordsman as Wyman Ridgeway.

In the month since his arrival in New Orleans, Ridgeway had fought three duels and become the scandal of a city whose social life was built around a rigid code of chivalry that often left a dozen men each week dead or wounded from sword or pistol.

Ridgeway won his duels easily. He never killed an adversary. Nor was he content to draw blood and end the affair. In his first duel he took out one of his opponent's eyes. In the second he cut off a man's thumb. And last Thursday he had sliced off the tip of Carlton Swift's nose.

LeBeau drank brandy from a silver flask and asked himself how Ridgeway would cripple Simon Domingeaux, the bald, sweating lawyer who was choosing his rapier. Poor Domingeaux. The lawyer must have cursed himself a hundred times for laughing when an opera performance caused Ridgeway to break into tears. Domingeaux would double his curses, LeBeau knew, if he learned that Ridgeway had cried, not from the pathos, but from the ludicrous intent of the composer.

As the two men advanced and retreated with a ringing clash of rapiers, LeBeau looked past them and saw a girl hiding behind an oleander bush. She was an incredibly lovely girl of perhaps seventeen, with dark eyes and pale oval face framed by dark hair. LeBeau

3

was surprised to see a woman at a duel, but he shrugged it off and turned back to the duel.

The duel was going as LeBeau had expected. Domingeaux was outclassed. After a brief initial advance, he had been forced to retreat a dozen paces, though Ridgeway fenced with an obvious boredom and did not press his advantage.

Then Ridgeway straightened from his slouch. His rapier thrust and feinted in mocking ways that had Domingeaux stumbling backward as he lost all sense of strategy and parried with desperate slashes.

Ridgeway's rapier flashed past Domingeaux's blade and sliced off the man's right ear and neatly impaled it as it fell.

He walked over and presented the ear to Domingeaux's second.

2.

Rafaella Blaine found the evening at Miss Delma's quite ordinary compared to her experiences in the salons of Europe. As usual, the men flattered her and begged for dances. And, as usual, the women were jealous of a seventeen-year-old girl who was beautiful, educated, and dressed in the height of European fashion.

After an hour in the hot salon, a room crowded with furniture, potted palms, and two hundred people, Rafaella's only salvation from boredom was her pleasure in noting the way women hovered about her father.

This pleasure soon faded, and Rafaella became petulant at the thought that, however bored she might be, at least New Orleans was a city of some sophistication. What would she find to amuse her in a place like Mississippi among cousins who lived on a plantation a hundred miles from nowhere? Oh, well, there was that city called Natchez, but it was certainly no Paris and not even comparable to New Orleans.

Rafaella smiled dutifully as the Spanish consul told her about his recent adventures in Mexico. She found his story dull and his Spanish inferior.

She had just excused herself from the consul and taken another glass of sherry when she saw Miss Delma talking to a man from the duel, the one who drank from a silver flask. Rafaella suspected that the man had seen her and hoped he had the discretion not to mention her presence.

The man moved a few steps. Behind him was the man who had fought the duel, the handsome man who had sliced off his opponent's ear!

Rafaella stood impatiently, sipping her sherry, while Miss Delma introduced the two men to her guests. Finally, Miss Delma led the men, along with her father, to Rafaella.

"Miss Blaine, may I present Mr. Alain LeBeau, Mr. Wyman Ridgeway," Miss Delma said. "Gentlemen, this is Miss Rafaella Blaine, Mr. Blaine's daughter."

Rafaella accepted their bows with a smile. LeBeau she dismissed at once, a dark-haired young man with a handsome but weak face and blue eyes that seemed watered from too much whiskey.

But Wyman Ridgeway was quite something else. He was tall and his black hair was greying and he was the handsomest man Rafaella had ever seen—except for her father, of course. She was fascinated by his grey eyes. He stood to her side, his left hand resting on his hip, in the same arrogant pose he had assumed during the duel.

"Mr. Ridgeway is the scandal of New Orleans," Miss Delma said. She laughed. "Why, just this evenin', from what I understand, his rapier took the measure of that pompous attorney Mr. Domingeaux."

"Do you approve of dueling, Miss Delma?" LeBeau asked.

"In a civilized society dueling is inevitable," Miss

5

Delma said. She sipped from a glass of Madeira. "There will always be fools who insult gentlemen and there will always be gentlemen who must defend their honor." She smiled. "Or that of a lady."

"And you, Miss Blaine?" LeBeau asked. "How do you . . . see the practice of dueling?"

Rafaella turned to LeBeau. He had obviously seen her and was letting her know it. She was infuriated.

"Why, Mr. LeBeau, dueling is as natural as honor or cowardice or slavery," she said. "And you, sir, do you duel with the same skill as Mr. Ridgeway?"

He hesitated before speaking, and Rafaella knew she had been right to take the attack. She did not let him reply.

"Though I suppose there are some men who never duel," she said. "They only watch and drink."

"Touché!" LeBeau said. His self-mocking smile placated Rafaella.

"And you, sir," Rafaella said to Ridgeway. "I assume you approve of dueling and don't hold with those who call it an unforgivable sin."

"I believe that boredom is the only unforgivable sin, Miss Blaine," Ridgeway said.

"What are your views on dueling, Mr. Blaine?" LeBeau asked.

"I suppose I accept the inevitability of the practice, sir," Blaine said.

"Oh, Daddy!" Rafaella said. "I've heard you speak eloquently on the subject, and you yourself carry a scar from a duel of honor—"

Rafaella bit off the sentence. She regretted the words she would never have spoken if not for the sherry and an impulse to impress Wyman Ridgeway. She had promised her father she would never mention his scar. He said he had received it in a secret duel in which he killed an aristocratic and influential man.

"My daughter is quite grown-up in most matters," Blaine said. "But it seems that when I allow her to drink sherry, her romantic nature takes over from her common sense and she fabricates stories."

Rafaella was startled by her father's words. He never rebuked her in public.

"I understand you're returning to Natchez day after tomorrow, Mr. LeBeau," Miss Delma said. "How do you find life upriver after living in New Orleans?"

"I suppose Natchez has its compensations," LeBeau said. "But I'm eager to return to New Orleans. I'll only remain upriver long enough to dispose of my late aunt's property."

"I'm glad I made the decision to move down here from Natchez," Miss Delma said. "At my age one grows weary of constant travel on a steamboat."

"Did you find a buyer for your plantations and niggers?" LeBeau asked.

"Yes, a man from North Carolina bought my plantations. And my nephew, Lawton Deavors, is buyin' my niggers. I'm quite fortunate that Lawton needs my people. We Deavorses never sell our niggers out of the family. I brought ten of them down here with me, but find I don't need that many. So I'm thinkin' of givin' Rayford his freedom."

"Of course, the nigger's yours to do with as you wish, Miss Delma," LeBeau said. "But I'm afraid I disapprove of manumission."

"So do I," Rafaella said. "How can a nigger not be a slave? Why, any race that's enslaved . . . the condition of servitude becomes its natural mode, and it would take centuries for it to pass."

"You're quite articulate and passionate on the matter of slavery, Miss Blaine," Ridgeway said. "And you, Mr. Blaine? Do you share your daughter's vivid opposition to freeing slaves?"

"Rafaella and I think alike on most matters, sir," Blaine said.

Rafaella looked at her father. Why did he remain so quiet, so insufferably dull, when he could be so articulate and entertaining?

"And you, Mr. Ridgeway?"

Several men had gathered around them, and Rafaella

saw that they were all looking at Ridgeway, eager to hear what he had to say.

"Oh, I believe all black men should be enslaved," Ridgeway said. He glanced around and smiled. "And, of course, any number of white men, as well."

"But that's scandalous talk, sir!" a fat man said.

"What's scandalous, sir?" Ridgeway asked. "Certainly you're not opposed to the institution of slavery."

"No, course not," the man said. "The institution of nigger slavery. But the other . . ."

"Well now, how about the other, sir?" Ridgeway said. "I've met some niggers in my day who were more outstanding than some white men. Why enslave the better man and not the inferior?"

The man's face turned a deep red. Sweat glistened on his forehead. "But sir, our nation is founded on the principle of freedom and equality for . . . for white men. Do you dispute that, sir?"

"Freedom may well be the prerogative of the white man. But equality, sir? What a droll idea! You have only to look around to see how absurd the concept is."

The man glanced around and saw his reflection in a mirror.

3.

Rafaella savored the tension. She could sense that an explosive moment was rapidly approaching. Ridgeway's audacity pleased her so much she could have kissed him right there, and damn the scandal such behavior would cause. If there was one more insult, surely it would have to lead to a duel.

Rafaella looked into his grey eyes and imagined Wyman Ridgeway fighting a duel for her honor. The thought excited her.

But Miss Delma defused the situation with an amusing story. Rafaella could have strangled the woman.

The fat man muttered something about strange ideas and gratefully changed the subject. He and most of the other men quickly drifted away.

The conversation grew tedious, and Ridgeway covered a yawn with his hand when Miss Delma began to talk of the Deavorses' recent trouble up in Natchez. Rafaella also put her hand to her mouth, pretending to yawn. She was disappointed that Ridgeway did not seem to notice.

Miss Delma had been talking about the family trouble since Rafaella and her father first arrived from Italy two weeks earlier. Rafaella could not have cared less that a relative named Lavon Deavors had murdered his brother, Athel; that Lavon had tried all kinds of despicable ways to drive Athel's family off their plantation; that Lavon and Athel's son Tillman had both died in a terrible fire . . .

Really, how primitive, almost Biblical, Rafaella told herself. And now another of Athel's children, Lawton, was master of the plantation, called The Columns.

"Yes, my wretched nephew, Lavon, would have ruined the family and destroyed The Columns if he'd had his way," Miss Delma was saying. "But enough of this talk. The gods and good fortune intervened. The gods, good fortune—and Mr. LeBeau, I might add."

"I did very little, really," LeBeau said.

"No, sir, you did a great deal," Miss Delma said. "Why, if Mr. LeBeau hadn't agreed to sell Lawton a vital piece of land adjacent to The Columns, Lavon would have bought that land—he owned every other parcel around the place—and then he would have isolated the plantation. We Deavorses will be forever grateful for that, Mr. LeBeau."

"It was my pleasure and privilege, Miss Delma," LeBeau said. "I could never refuse a request from Lucinda, an old friend."

Rafaella was intrigued by the smile that passed between LeBeau and Ridgeway.

"Mr. LeBeau, I'm tempted to ask a favor of you," Miss Delma said. "The Blaines are going up to Natchez in three days, and I wonder if I might prevail on you to meet their boat and see that they get to The Columns without difficulty."

"It would be my pleasure," LeBeau said. He turned to Blaine. "Are you visiting Natchez on business, or is it a holiday?"

"We plan to settle there," Blaine said. "My late wife's father recently passed away and left us a plantation near Natchez."

"Then Wyman and I look forward to welcoming you and being of what assistance we can," LeBeau said.

"I would greatly appreciate that, sir," Blaine said. "We arrive on the *Yazoo Queen* this coming Thursday."

"I've written Lawton that you're coming, Mr. Blaine," Miss Delma said. "He'll be delighted to see you and offer you the hospitality of The Columns. And as executor of the estate, I'm sure he'll make certain no silly probate court delays your taking title to the plantation. There's little of the family left, I'm afraid, and I was always so fond of Rafaella's late mother and her parents . . ."

Miss Delma was interrupted by sharp thunder. The talk turned to the possibility of a tornado.

"Please excuse me, but I must leave," Ridgeway said abruptly. "Thank you for your hospitality, Miss Delma. Good night, Alain . . . Miss Blaine . . . Mr. Blaine . . . a pleasure to meet you."

Good-nights were returned. And Ridgeway left rather abruptly, for all his smiles and gracious bows.

"I quite like your new friend, Mr. LeBeau," Miss Delma said. "Despite his unorthodox views. But do you really know anything of the man?"

"Very little, I'm afraid," LeBeau said. "Wyman comes from a prominent North Carolina family. He once sat in the House of Representatives. He arrived here a month ago and has fought four duels and left each adversary badly crippled. He never speaks of himself."

Rafaella heard the voices but not the words, for her excitement had taken a new and dreadful turn as

Wyman Ridgeway removed his left hand from his hip and walked away.

The left hand was withered. Rafaella grimaced. She detested deformity. Cripples were as despicably low as slaves, in her opinion.

4.

Rafaella had traveled on grand boats in Europe, but she had never seen a boat as splendid as the *Yazoo Queen*.

Her cabin was a vast room with powder blue wallpaper. The curtains were red velvet and the carpet a blue Persian of intricate geometrical design. Statues of gods and goddesses stood on marble pedestals about the room, and the chandelier was reflected in tall gold-leaf mirrors.

The dining room was so large Rafaella could not recognize her own father at the far end. Lunch consisted of eleven courses, served on English bone china from silver trays and dishes, attended by thirty stewards dressed in blue and gold. A ten-piece orchestra serenaded the diners, who ate amid mounds of fresh flowers.

Rafaella had explored the seemingly endless corridors, the salons, the bars, the gambling rooms, and now she stood on the promenade deck and leaned against the white filigree railing. Behind her, two tall funnels sent up swirls of grey smoke. To her right, at the rear of the boat, two enormous wheels churned through the water.

The *Yazoo Queen*'s elegance had put Rafaella in gay spirits, for a time. But her father's melancholy was beginning to depress her. She leaned against the rail and tried to counter the depression by thinking of Wyman Ridgeway.

Ridgeway was handsome, mysterious, audacious.

She thought it romantic that he crippled but never killed his opponents. In those few minutes at Miss Delma's she had given full rein to her excitement. He had stirred her imagination as few men ever had.

And then she had discovered he was deformed!

She would cringe to see that hand again. She shivered at the thought of that hand holding her while they danced or of it touching some intimate part of her body. Yet the repulsion was tinged with a different kind of excitement which she did not understand.

She wondered if he had been born with a withered hand. Or had it happened in an accident? Or a battle? Was his hand the reason he left each adversary crippled, to avenge himself against fate?

Ridgeway seemed interested in virtually nothing except dueling. She wondered what it would take to end his boredom. She smiled. She was certain she could make the man take an interest in a more pleasant activity.

Rafaella was perspiring. She *hated* to perspire. At least there's some wind, she told herself. But a moment later the wind brought up an odor from the bottom deck. She paused and looked down the stairs to the deck, which housed the slaves and the poor whites who took deck passage.

The odor was strong, the smell of dozens of people crammed together in the damp heat. Surely those whites are no better than slaves, she told herself. Perhaps Ridgeway was right. The odor was making her ill, but she paused another moment before walking away.

Rafaella brushed perspiration from her forehead and began to circle the deck. On the second circuit she found her father at the rail and joined him. They stood together and looked into the water for several minutes without speaking. Then Rafaella tried to amuse him with light conversation, but nothing would help. He was deep in one of his moods.

"I just hate it when you won't tell me what's wrong," she said. "I always tell you what's wrong when

I feel melancholy, Daddy. I don't want us to have any secrets from each other. Now please, tell me what it is."

"Oh, I'm just a bit anxious about the estate, Raffles," he said. "After all, I'm not an American citizen. I'm unfamiliar with the probate laws in Mississippi. And we don't really know what this Lawton Deavors is like, or how he feels about us."

"Miss Delma assured us there will be no problem," Rafaella said. "Just some silly formalities in court. We have every right to that estate, after all. And our cousin Lawton practically owns the county. What could go wrong? Or is there something I don't know, Daddy?"

"Oh, no, no, Raffles," he said. "Stop thinking I have some romantic secrets I'm not revealing. But you're right. Miss Delma did assure us there will be no difficulty. I promise to stop brooding. I feel better already. I always feel better after I talk to you, Raffles."

He kissed her cheek. They stared at each other a moment as he pulled away.

"The same is true for me," she said.

When he smiled, she returned the smile, not the enigmatic smile on the corners of her lips, the smile that she knew intrigued and excited men. This was a full, deep, sincere smile that creased her dimples.

Yet Rafaella did wonder if her father was telling her everything. He had been brooding and acting strangely since they decided to leave Rome.

"Lovely Rafaella," he said. "Shall we go into the salon for tea? I could use something a little stronger myself."

"I don't think so, Daddy," she said. "I'm perspiring and I'm so hot. I want to go take a long, long bath and . . . change my clothes."

"Perhaps I'll take a sherry," he said, looking down at the water. "One sherry . . ."

"All right, Daddy," she said.

Rafaella kissed her father's cheek. His flesh was feverish. His breathing was heavy, erratic.

As Rafaella walked slowly down the deck, her own

cheeks began to glow and her breathing quickened.

Rafaella was taking down her long, black hair when she heard her father enter his cabin, which was adjacent to hers. She glanced around at the connecting door, which was open, just a crack, then down at the tub of steaming water.

Slowly, she unfastened her dress and took it off. She posed in her boots and petticoats, then pirouetted several times, admiring her reflection in the mirror. Her heart was fluttering. She saw that her cheeks were red.

She bent down and tested the water. Her full breasts nearly spilled from her tight-laced bodice. As she bent over further, her pink nipples hardened and she touched them in turn, smiling to herself at the excitement that flowed through her body.

Her cheeks were hot now, and she dabbed moisture from her forehead before she sat down to unlace her boots. As she removed each boot, she held her leg high for five seconds, ten seconds . . . She squeezed her thighs together, then spread them . . .

She backed to the tub and removed her petticoats and slowly lowered herself into the water. She began to bathe her damp, tingling body very slowly and deliberately, rubbing soap over her breasts and nipples, her stomach, between her thighs . . .

Although she would never have admitted it, Rafaella was well aware that her father was watching her through the crack in the door. Her skin was rosy all over from the heat of the bathwater, and she knew she looked her prettiest and most provocative.

It was a game they had played many times, in hotel rooms from Rome to New Orleans, and it was part of the very nature of her developing sexuality.

Sighing gently, she squirmed a bit in the tub, then raised one finger. She extended it, then deliberately poked it down in the water, down between her legs and into herself.

She gasped, and heard an answering exclamation,

muffled but unmistakable. He was aware of everything she did. She writhed a bit, splashing water out of the tub, then she withdrew her finger . . .

5.

The Blaines accepted Captain Rossi's invitation to sit at his table for dinner, but Roger Blaine complained of a headache and excused himself after the fish course. Rafaella was left with the captain, a planter named Bayson Hodges, and two elderly spinsters who giggled at everything and never said a word.

Over dessert, Hodges mentioned that he was going upriver to search for two slaves who had disappeared from his plantation.

"Why did the niggers run away?" Rafaella asked.

"Hellfire—pardon, ladies—they didn't run away," Hodges said. "Some Yankee abolitionist was seen in town the day 'fore they disappeared. I'm sure he took my niggers away. It's been a week and they haven't been seen around and I learned that Yankee was from up in Ohio, and that's where I'm headed."

"A white man helped the niggers escape?" Rafaella asked.

"Yes, Miss Blaine, sure did," Hodges said.

"That's difficult to believe," Rafaella said. "Surely such conduct isn't common here."

"Common as bugs," Hodges said. "These criminals are the scourge of our society, let me tell you. Now they've got themselves organized, call themselves the Underground Railroad. What could be lower than a man who runs against his own race? Such a man should be flogged and thrown under the jail."

"I quite agree with you about such men," Rafaella said. "They should be most severely punished. Or *they* should be made slaves and put to doing field work like niggers. Yes, such men, and any number of other criminal and inferior white men, they should become slaves, and their children after them. And their children."

For the first time, the two women did not giggle. They looked at each other. Hodges and Rossi exchanged glances.

"For a moment there we thought you were serious, Miss Blaine," Hodges said.

"But I *am* serious, Mr. Hodges," Rafaella said. "Surely some white men give up any pretense to being free men by their criminal conduct, their stupidity, their beastlike behavior."

"Now who put those unlikely ideas into your head, young lady?" Captain Rossi said.

"But, sir, they're most *likely* ideas," she said. She paused to sip her wine and thought of the comments of Wyman Ridgeway that so scandalized his listeners.

They were waiting for her to continue, not without some apprehension. Rafaella took a bit more wine and smiled. "We can agree, I think, that slavery has always existed, that it is a most natural state for some men, that it is justified in the Bible . . ."

"Yes, yes, of course," Hodges said. "But . . . but it's nigger slaves in the Bible."

"No sir, Mr. Hodges," she said.

"Or Jews, then," he said. "The Egyptians enslaved the Jews. But, miss, there haven't been any white men who were slaves."

"Why, Mr. Hodges," she replied in a rather pedantic voice, "how can you say that? Throughout history, white men have been enslaved! The Greeks and Romans had white slaves. And in our present day the Arabs hold any number of white-skinned slaves—"

A steward interrupted her.

"Pardon, miss," he said. "I got a message for the cap'n. Cap'n, sir, mate on the bridge, he send his compliments, say the *Louisville* comin' up on our side mighty fast, like she gone pass us."

Captain Rossi threw his napkin down on the table and stood up.

"Hell will freeze over—pardon, ladies—before the

Louisville passes the *Yazoo Queen*. I'll go to the bridge myself. Boy, tell the engineer I want full steam up. Tell him to get a tub of lard ready."

"Yessir," the steward said. He hurried away.

"Miss Blaine, ladies, Mr. Hodges, please excuse me," Captain Rossi said. "But we beat the *Louisville* in a race last month and damn it—excuse me, ladies—it seems they want to challenge us again. I must go and make sure we leave them far downriver. The owner of the *Yazoo Queen* is aboard, and he'll expect a winning race out of us."

Word of the impending race had evidently already circulated throughout the dining salon. Men shouted encouragement as the captain walked through the huge room. The level of discussion rose sharply and bets were made. People began to stream from the room. The two women left the table, giggling and whispering, their heads bobbing together.

"What did the captain mean about a tub of lard?" Rafaella asked.

"Trick some of these captains have, Miss Blaine," Hodges said. "Pour a tub of lard in the boiler, gives the boat a real spurt. But kind of risky, to my way of thinkin'."

6.

The wind lashed Rafaella's hair into her eyes as she watched the *Louisville* glide even with the *Yazoo Queen*. Above her on the bridge the captain was shouting instructions to his frantic crew.

"The lard!" Captain Rossi shouted. "Get that damn lard into the boiler or I'll have your hide!"

The wheels churned faster. Black smoke poured from the funnels. The boat bumped and shook over the water. Rafaella had to grip the rail with both hands.

She heard a rumbling sound from the lower deck and

asked herself what kind of noise the slaves could be making. Then she realized it was not the Negroes. The rumbling came from the engines. And a white mist was rising from the back of the boat.

The *Yazoo Queen* spurted ahead of the *Louisville*. The passengers clapped and shouted. Everyone looked up at Captain Rossi. He smiled and began to raise his hand to acknowledge their salutes.

The captain's hand got no higher than his chest. A geyser of steam shot into the air. The boat began to wobble, then bump violently. The rumbling was deafening.

Captain Rossi disappeared. A woman screamed. The back of the boat was enveloped in the hissing steam. People fled down the deck, away from the engines. Rafaella was thrown against the rail.

A tall man with grey-streaked red hair and beard was herding passengers toward the front of the boat. Rafaella fought free of the crowd and headed back toward her suite.

The red-headed man grabbed her arm and pulled her forward.

"Go for'd!" he shouted. "Damn thing may explode!"

"My father!" she cried. "He's in our suite . . . back there . . . He may have taken a sedative."

"Nothing you can do now," the man said. "He'll get out."

Rafaella pulled free of his grip and ran through the crowd, which now included slaves streaming from the lower deck.

"You little fool!" the man shouted. "Come back!"

Rafaella gained the inside of the deck, and somehow her desperation gave her the strength to move against the tide of people. She was oblivious to the rumbling, to the hissing steam, to the man's warnings. No fear of explosion could overcome the greater fear for her father.

The man caught her at the stairs that led to the cabin deck. Again he grabbed her arm. She tried to pull free. He held her. She kicked and scratched but she could not pull away. The boat shook violently. The hissing steam became a terrible scream, and Rafaella was enveloped in a hot mist.

"You'll get us both—"

The man bit off the words as Roger Blaine hurtled from the stairway. Rafaella pulled free. Blaine shoved the man backward with both hands. Startled, the man attempted to grapple with Blaine but succeeded only in ripping off half his sleeve. Blaine slammed a fist into the man's face.

"Daddy, stop!" Rafaella screamed. She ran to his side. "Stop! He was only trying to help me."

Blaine glanced at Rafaella. His hand fell to his side. A lurch of the *Yazoo Queen* nearly shook all three of them from their feet. Now even more bitter-smelling clouds of steam rose up around them, and Rafaella began to cough and choke. The temperature of the air rose rapidly. It was more than hot, it was scalding. She gasped for air and shut her eyes to protect them.

"Daddy!" she whimpered.

"Oh, my God," Blaine exclaimed. "Oh, God!"

"What is it?" Rafaella demanded.

"Don't look!" Blaine said.

"Where?" Her voice rose in panic. "Oh, Daddy! It's too hot!"

"Both of you!" the red-headed man ordered. His voice was deep with authority. "This way!"

The heat was like boiling water scalding and suffocating. It was in front of them, then all around them, like a tidal wave. Rafaella opened her eyes despite her father's warning just as she heard the screams that rent the air and were more horrible than anything she had heard before in her life.

Somewhere deep in the hold of the *Yazoo Queen* an engine had exploded, killing the crewmen and passengers nearby. Steam and fire and flying debris had injured scores more, including the passengers of the lowest decks, and some of them had now climbed and clawed their way up to the open deck.

A man stood before Rafaella. His shirt was charred

tatters, his bare chest bright red, and his eyes rolled back in his head. Behind him a black woman staggered blindly. Her mouth was open in one continuous scream and all the hair on her head had been singed and hung in burnt wisps. Her eyebrows were missing. "Ten men dead!" a voice screamed.

"Oh, Daddy!" Rafaella shrieked.

"Don't look," Blaine begged, but it was the stranger who seized both Blaines and forcibly dragged them away, steering them into a side entrance to the main passageway.

Rafaella was choked with sobs, but Blaine regained some composure when the three of them were safely inside the galleyway.

"I am sorry for assaulting you, sir," he said. "At first I thought you were attacking my daughter." He had one arm around Rafaella, and she had hidden her face in his sleeve.

"I understand," the man said. He held a handkerchief against his bleeding nose. His face was red and streamed with sweat. "No apology necessary. But, please, take your daughter to her cabin at once. Such a horrible sight."

"Yes, of course. We do thank you, sir. I'm in your debt. Oh! I'm Roger Blaine."

"Carter Ramsey, sir! May we meet again, under far better circumstances!"

Crewmen burst into the galleyway and ran out toward the decks as Blaine turned away with Rafaella. "Come this way, my dear," Blaine said, but as Rafaella moved to obey, she lifted her eyes for a last look at Ramsey and intercepted his gaze.

Ramsey was staring at her father's bare shoulder. Her father realized it at the same moment Rafaella did, and he stiffened. It seemed to her that the look on his face was one of distress. She knew that he never willingly displayed his dueling scar, but she had never understood why. To her, it was a mark of great honor.

Before either man could speak, though, the press of the crowd separated them, and Rafaella gave herself up to the relief of her father's protective arm. Even as she closed her eyes, an image of the scalded people flashed before her eyes again and she shuddered.

Her legs trembled as she allowed herself to be led down the gangway to her cabin.

Later that evening, Rafaella sat alone in the salon and drank sweet tea. She was upset and annoyed. She cursed the tea and Carter Ramsey in language that would have appalled the other women in the salon had she spoken aloud. As it was, the other women were already shocked that a young lady would appear alone.

Heads turned as Rafaella slammed her cup into the saucer.

She told herself she would have to leave. Never in her life had a man failed to show up—and promptly—for a rendezvous with her. Ramsey himself had proposed it, with a note delivered to her cabin. Of course he had invited her father, too, but Rafaella had decided to meet him alone. She had gone to considerable trouble to arrange it, lying to her father about needing to rest after the trauma of seeing the burned people.

A steward came to her table. "Miss Blaine?" he asked.

Rafaella looked up. "Yes?"

He handed her an envelope. She ripped it open. The message was written in a small, elaborate hand: "Please excuse my rudeness, Miss Blaine. Urgent business prevents me from meeting you today. I beg your forgiveness and look forward to seeing you and your father again soon. Your humble servant, Carter Ramsey."

As she read the note, Rafaella felt her mind go black with rage and humiliation. How dare he? She felt pain, and with it a powerful urge to inflict worse pain on someone else. For a moment she struggled to calm her anger; then she gave in to it and dismissed the steward with a gesture.

Her knee knocked against the table when she stood

up to leave, and a pitcher of cream overturned onto the carpet. She felt as if all eyes were on her, but she ignored them and rushed out of the room with a rustle of her yellow silk dress.

"Stupid oaf," she muttered as she swept along the galleyway. "These country people have no manners, no manners at all."

But as she reached the open doorway to the gambling salon on the port side, she saw that Ramsey's gaff was not exactly one of etiquette. She recognized him at once; his tall, red-headed, elegantly slim figure in a bright blue waistcoat was bent over a game of billiards. And clinging to his arm was a florid yellow-haired woman in a tight red dress with outrageous décolletage.

Rafaella gasped and her eyes filled with tears. Her first instinct was to hide, and she jumped away from the open doorway, back into the dimness of the galleyway. It was a direct insult! There was no excuse for this, no apology would be acceptable; but now she must retreat, retreat to recover her composure and . . .

"Raffles! My dear, what are you doing here?"

"Oh, Daddy!" It was too soon for another blow. Rafaella was too nonplussed to react to the embarrassing coincidence of being confronted by her father —and he was not alone. Instead she gave in to tears.

"You should never have left your suite, my dear," Blaine said, not altogether sympathetically. "You know you needed to rest after the shock of that explosion."

Ignoring him, Rafaella stared at the woman on her father's arm. She bore an uncanny resemblance to Rafaella—the same pale oval face, the same cloud of soft, dark hair. But of course the woman was older, much older.

"Who are you?" Rafaella demanded.

"Excuse me, Miss Richardson. Dear, this is Miss Sylvia Richardson. Miss Richardson, this is my daughter, Rafaella."

"So difficult," cooed the slim brunette, "so difficult to raise a child alone. Especially a girl. Dear Mr. Blaine, how I admire you!"

22

"Oh, shut up!" Rafaella snapped.

"Rafaella! I'm ashamed of you. Apologize at once!" Blaine said, but Rafaella had fled.

Her eyes were streaming with tears and she was angry enough to kill.

7.

LeBeau stood at the edge of a blood-stained pit in which two bull terriers were fighting. Polemen in ragged clothes made bets with top-hatted dandies and passed around jugs of Monongahela whiskey. The men's guttural sounds matched those of the animals. There was a shout. One dog gripped the other's lower jaw and pulled away flesh and teeth.

LeBeau retreated from the pit. The heat and the stench of blood and sweat made him nauseous. He walked along a wooden sidewalk covered with brackish water and fishheads. Why had he agreed to meet Ridgeway down here? It was a repulsive and dangerous place. This area extended from the Natchez docks along the Mississippi River for over half a mile beneath bluffs that rose some two hundred feet to the parks and mansions of the city.

On the mud flats beneath the bluffs were shacks and lean-tos. And out here in the river, laced together by the rotting wooden sidewalks, were hundreds of taverns, whore-barges, gambling dens, cock-fighting pits, and the hovels of the river's criminal flotsam.

Even New Orleans, famed for all varieties of sin and depravity, had nothing to equal Natchez-Under-the-Hill.

Even with a pistol in his fob, LeBeau felt uneasy. He vowed he would not come down again.

Then he heard the familiar spinet.

He walked faster. A minute later he entered a long red barge and turned right, into the parlor. It was a huge room decorated with red plush hangings and lit by silver chandeliers and candles in silver holders on the walls between mirrors. Black waiters in red and silver outfits served champagne to men who lounged on black velvet couches and talked to the mulatto whores in red dresses.

At the far end of the room, a young woman with glowing almond skin played the spinet.

The barge madame said that Ridgeway had not yet arrived. LeBeau sat down on a couch by the door and sipped champagne.

LeBeau drained one of many glasses of champagne and decided to allow himself one more. If Ridgeway hadn't arrived by the time he finished, he would have to meet the Blaines without him.

A warm, pleasant drunkenness came over LeBeau as he settled back against the couch and thought how well his life was going. He had inherited all his aunt's property in Adams County and was making a fortune selling it. His new friend, Ridgeway, kept him amused and joined in his revels and adventures. And because of the Blaines and Miss Delma, he had sent a note out to The Columns and been invited to Lucinda's own doorstep.

This barge had been owned by Lavon Deavors. The man had murdered his brother, become that most detestable of traitors to his class, a slave dealer, and he had even owned a whore-barge.

LeBeau smiled. For one of the state's oldest and most prominent families, the Deavorses seemed to be literally going to hell. Well, he would certainly help one of them to make that journey soon.

Lavon might have been a foul man, LeBeau told himself, but if it were not for Lavon's attempt to buy that land, he would not now be on his way to collect a debt from Lucinda Deavors.

LeBeau opened his eyes and sat up. Damn Ridgeway, he muttered. Where in hell could he be?

LeBeau pulled himself up from the couch. He cursed Ridgeway again as he left the barge.

The wooden sidewalk back to the dock was down, wrenched apart by two drunken polemen who were fighting with knives in the water, so LeBeau headed back along the mud path beneath the bluffs.

The heat was intense, and the filth and stench made his stomach churn. He held his handkerchief to his nose. His mellow drunkenness was burning away in the sun.

As LeBeau neared the docks, he saw a white man with a wooden stub for a left arm herding half a dozen shackled Negroes into a building. A notice on the door indicated that the man was a slave trader who had just received a fresh shipment of Negroes from Virginia.

Some greedy bastard is rushing the slave-selling season, LeBeau told himself. October to May was the usual season, and it was unprofitable to march slaves down in this late-summer heat.

A steamboat whistle interrupted his thoughts. He walked faster and kicked at a dog that darted in front of him.

LeBeau was surprised to find Ridgeway standing in front of the *Yazoo Queen* with the Blaines.

LeBeau apologized to the Blaines for being late. Ridgeway apologized for not meeting LeBeau.

"I was detained by some unfortunate business that will also prevent me from accompanying you today," Ridgeway said.

The Blaines' luggage was loaded into a wagon. Captain Rossi, seeking to make amends, sent down drinks and trays of refreshments. LeBeau sipped a cool gin fizz and watched the usually sophisticated Rafaella attack a lemon ice with the messy enthusiasm of a child.

Finally the wagon was loaded. They hired a carriage, said good-bye to Ridgeway, and set off.

Alain pulled out his silver flask. He offered it to Blaine, who declined. The brandy was hard to swallow in such heat, and LeBeau wished he had more champagne or another gin fizz.

He felt betrayed by Ridgeway and suspicious about his sudden business obligation. He assumed it was a duel, since Ridgeway never had any other business, but if so, why hadn't Ridgeway told him?

Yes, Ridgeway was certainly strange and unpredictable, but what could one expect from a crippled man?

LeBeau settled back in the carriage. The Blaines didn't seem interested in conversing, so he looked at the countryside.

The few plantations were many miles apart, and some stretches of road still harbored bandits and slave rustlers.

LeBeau took out his handkerchief and dabbed his face. He closed his eyes and sighed. Four more damned hours of this hot, silent misery.

8.

Lucinda looked past the ashes of the old barn to the dark, fast-moving clouds on the horizon above the swamp. All day the air had been hot and damp, but in the past few minutes it had taken on a strange new quality.

The clouds raced through the sky, but there was not a hint of a breeze on the ground. Yet the leaves were rippling.

When she had passed through the slave quarters earlier, she had heard the people muttering about a "heinous tornado."

Lucinda prayed they would be spared a tornado. Neither the family nor the people deserved such punishment from nature after what they had endured at the hands of Lavon Deavors.

Nothing could undo the suffering or bring back the

dead, but slowly life at The Columns was returning to normal. Time heals grief. And the doctor said Cellus should be on his feet soon. Cellus had been brutally whipped and branded by Lavon's slave patrol. Like the rest of the family, Lucinda was very fond of the ageless black man who helped Lawton run the plantation.

Yes, she told herself, if the rain let up this would be a fine autumn. The cotton crop promised to be magnificent. And Lawton had a bold, exciting plan to buy up land and clear it all the way down to the Mississippi River.

The sound of hammering caught her attention. Four slaves were putting up the beams for a new barn. Ed, the hostler, looked down from his ladder and waved.

Lucinda returned his wave, then strolled toward the house. She hesitated at the back steps and looked down the long, open gallery that divided the house. She wondered if Lawton and Joleen were still talking in the parlor. If so, she did not want to interrupt them.

Lawton and Joleen were the only family left now, and Lucinda knew how desperately Lawton wanted Joleen to stay on the plantation, no matter what she had done in the past.

Lucinda decided to walk through the vegetable garden. The ground was muddy. On an impulse she removed her shoes and pulled her skirt above her ankles. She was delighted at the feel of the cool mud oozing between her toes. She hadn't done this in years. She glanced over her shoulder. Lawton would disapprove. But she smiled and continued her walk, plucking silk from the ears of corn.

Although she tried again to reassure herself that their troubles were over, she was obsessed by the knowledge that she still had one enormous debt to pay.

And Alain LeBeau would soon arrive to collect that debt. The thought made her tremble.

At a time when Lavon had owned every land parcel adjacent to The Columns except the parcel that Alain was about to inherit from his aunt, Lucinda had traveled to New Orleans and begged him to sell Lawton the land. LeBeau had refused, despite their friendship of many years, and said he intended to sell the land to Lavon. He rejected every offer she had made. Finally, she had nothing left to offer but herself.

LeBeau had accepted that offer. They had made a bargain on their oaths. When LeBeau inherited the land he would sell it to Lawton. And when this was done, when the land title actually changed hands, Lucinda would surrender her body to LeBeau.

Lawton now owned the land.

LeBeau was coming out to The Columns now, and he would expect Lucinda to keep her word.

No man but Lawton had ever so much as kissed her. She had tried to think of some way to extricate herself from her oath. But she remembered many times during their schooldays when someone angered LeBeau or denied him something he wanted. His retaliation was always dreadful. There was nothing of which he wasn't capable, particularly if drunk. If she went back on her oath he might well ruin her marriage.

Lightning began to streak the sky. The thunder was so loud it frightened Lucinda. She began to shake all over.

She brushed a gnat from her eye and turned back toward the house. In the end, she told herself bitterly, she had no choice but to give LeBeau what she had promised.

Lawton slapped at a mosquito as he watched Joleen walk from the parlor. He poured a glass of whiskey but hesitated with his hand on the glass. The last thing he needed was whiskey so early in the day.

He looked out at the dark clouds. The people were certain a tornado would form by nightfall. Lawton refused to believe it. No tornado had ever struck The Columns. He supposed he should take some precautions, but there was no storm shelter and he had no idea what to do. If Cellus were well, he would know.

The talk with Joleen had upset Lawton. She was in

a strange, nervous mood that was quite unlike her. And she refused to discuss her problems.

Lawton only hoped Joleen was keeping her promise to refrain from dangerous activities, especially anything involving the Underground Railway. When she agreed to stay on for a while and let Aaron return to Ohio alone, she and Lawton had agreed on a truce: she would do nothing illegal while living at The Columns, and Lawton would not discuss the matter.

He was determined that eventually he *would* bring up the matter, that somehow he would alter her attitudes about slavery. But he feared that if he ended the truce, Joleen would try to leave The Columns. He didn't know if he could stop her. So the truce stayed in effect. Or at least he had observed it so far.

Lawton walked out into the front yard. There was no wind, but the leaves of the azalea and oleander bushes were rustling. And the air had an odd quality.

On the horizon to his right he saw the first of the slaves coming in from the fields. He thought of his plan to expand the plantation all the way down to the Mississippi River. He had already authorized his lawyer to acquire the necessary land. The only problem was clearing that snake-and-panther-infested swampland. He was reluctant to let his people undertake such a dangerous project. In any case, the project must wait until after the harvest.

Lawton turned his thoughts to their guests, these cousins who had inherited Price Deavors's plantation and were arriving this evening with Alain LeBeau. Lawton welcomed the opportunity to offer his hospitality to a man who had proved such an ally at a crucial time, but he was not pleased to be named executor of an estate that consisted of some six hundred acres and ninety slaves.

Price's only child, a daughter named Sarah, had run off to Italy, as Lawton understood it, and she had married an English silk merchant named Roger Blaine. Sarah had died many years ago, and now Blaine and his daughter, Rafaella, were coming to claim the estate.

Aunt Delma's notes had assured Lawton that the Blaines were respectable people. "Our kind of people, dear," she had written. "And, of course, they're family."

Well, he would certainly do what was required of him, he told himself.

Lawton heard a galloping horse on the road. He looked up. It was Filch, his senior driver.

Filch dismounted and wiped sweat from his face with the back of his hand.

"You ride like somethin' vigus is chasin' you, Filch," Lawton said.

"No sir, nothin' like that," Filch said. "But I was just down in the swamp. Somethin' got two more piglets, Mist' Lawton."

"Dammit! Was it the panther?"

"I'm pretty sure it was," Filch said.

"Damn! That makes six piglets in less than a week, Filch. Well, come tomorrow, we're goin' to do somethin' about it. We'll take the dogs and hunt down that cat. Oh, hell. There are guests arrivin' this evenin' . . ."

"You want me to take some of the boys and do it?"

"No, our guests will just have to understand. Joleen and Lucinda can entertain them. It's goin' to be a dangerous day's work. I want to be along. Let's see now. Pick out three boys to handle the dogs. We'll have an early breakfast and go into the swamp at first light."

"All right, Mist' Lawton," Filch said. "I'll tend to it."

"And Filch," Lawton said, "I'm worried about the weather. I want somebody on watch in the quarters all night. If there's any sign of a tornado, at the first sign we have to get the people out of the quarters and away from the buildings and trees."

"I'll tend to that, too," Filch said. "I was goin' to mention it. Everythin' sure points to a tornado."

Filch rode away. Lawton felt indecisive. He wasn't sure when his guests would arrive and he had work to do. He began to pace between the oleander and azalea bushes. The first fireflies were out. A lone honeybee seemed lost in the approaching dusk and buzzed irresolutely from flower to flower.

There was a sudden commotion from the quarters. Lawton heard screams and shouts. He ran around the side of the house.

The funnel of a tornado was cutting through the swamp.

9.

The tornado pirouetted through the swamp like a graceful but demented ballerina. The funnel's erratic path toward the quarters spread panic among the people. There was no storm cellar, and no one knew which way the wind column would zigzag the next moment.

The slaves darted about in panic, three hundred people running on three hundred paths. Mothers ran to the nursery for their children, but some children fled their own parents. Only a few had the presence of mind to prostrate themselves in ditches.

At first, Lawton stumbled about with the same panic his people showed. He started for the house, pivoted and ran toward the quarters, turned back to get his wife and sister.

Lucinda was upstairs, in her bathtub. She held her body rigid as she let the mud soak from her feet. When she heard the first screams from the quarters, she began to tremble and climbed from the tub. Florine, her maid, threw a robe about her shoulders and led her out into the hall.

Joleen was sitting in a steaming tub, also, but her body was relaxed. She let the hot water and her soapy fingers caress her breasts and thighs in ways she had learned as a girl.

It took several seconds for the pandemonium from the quarters to break through the haze of her sensual pleasure. When Joleen realized what the screams meant, she was out of the tub and into a robe in an instant. She met Lucinda and Florine in the hall and they ran to the stairs, where they encountered Lawton.

"Get outside!" he shouted. "Tornado!"

Lawton led the women out of the house. He told them to lie flat in a ditch beside the road. He was running toward the quarters when he realized the shouts and screams had died down. The slaves were no longer darting about. The funnel was gone. It had disappeared into the swamp. The sky was brightening.

Lawton escorted Joleen and Lucinda back to the house. He calmed the people in the quarters. Then he and Filch walked down to the swamp.

They stared at the tornado's work, then at each other. Lawton shook his head. The funnel had touched down a few yards out into the fields, then reversed itself and cut back into the swamp. The wind had cleared a wide zigzag path, tearing up massive oaks by the roots and sweeping away impenetrable tangles of bush and vine and moss as though they were weeds.

Lawton heard a rattling sound to his left. He froze. Then slowly he moved his head to the left. The rattlesnake was coiling up, striking blindly at the cotton plants, then writhing on the ground. Lawton also saw a frantic copperhead and two cottonmouth moccasins. And on an uprooted cotton plant was the deadliest of all, a striped coral snake.

Lawton and Filch began to back away from the snakes. They glanced about at each step. Finally they were several yards from the nearest snake.

"Tornado done panicked 'em," Filch said. "Never seen nothin' like this. It done drove 'em plum crazy, Mist' Lawton. Destroyed their nests, their cover. No tellin' what they liable to do now. They mighty *vigus* this way."

"You better get several boys," Lawton said. "And some guns from the house. Come back here and kill every snake you find. Stay here till they're all dead. I don't care if it takes all night."

Lawton and Filch hurried back to the house. The frenzied snakes upset Lawton, but he was more disturbed at his own reaction to the threat of a tornado. Simply because a storm had never struck the plantation, he had ignored the obvious signs and taken no precautions at all.

Lawton was depressed by the time he reached the house. He was about to go into the parlor and brood over a glass of whiskey, but as he climbed the steps he heard a carriage approaching.

Most Adams County families would have considered the supper at The Columns elaborate. For the Deavorses, a table of roast beef, cured and green hams, fried turkey and pheasant, trout and catfish, roast sweet potatoes, fried peas, crowder peas, turnip greens, corn bread, and three kinds of pie was normal. The Blaines and Alain LeBeau found the food overabundant, rather bland and curious.

After supper, everyone moved to the broad white-columned front porch to carry on the polite but strained art of conversation among strangers.

Rafaella was telling an anecdote about a bald Roman princess when a shot interrupted her. Everyone looked around. Lanterns were moving toward the house. It was an eerie sight, those slaves' lanterns in the dark, as though the fireflies that lit the oleander blossoms had grown obese.

"What's happenin', Filch?" Lawton called.

"Found a copperhead here, Mist' Lawton," Filch said.

"So near the house?" Lawton asked. "All right, Filch. Bring the boys in closer and make sure you kill 'em all before you quit."

"The snakes won't come right to the house, will they, Lawton?" Lucinda asked.

"I doubt it," Lawton said. "But they're so crazed after the storm you can't tell. In any case, Filch and the hands'll make sure they're all dead."

"I thought it was against the law for a slave to use a gun," Rafaella said.

"I suppose it is," Lawton said. "I mean, it's written

33

down in the law books. But on a plantation like The Columns, out here away from everything and everybody, it's pretty common. For somethin' like tonight, killin' the snakes. Or in the mornin', when we go after the painter I mentioned at supper."

"I wonder if I might join that hunt," Blaine said. "I enjoy a good shoot and I haven't been hunting in a long while."

"Well, if you wish, I suppose so," Lawton said. "But this is no social kind of hunt. It could be dangerous, huntin' a painter that size."

"Oh, Daddy's not afraid of any old panther," Rafaella said. "Why, he's hunted more dangerous game than that. In Africa. Daddy, tell them about hunting crocodiles in Africa—"

"Rafaella, that's enough now," Blaine said. "You're letting your imagination get the better of you. I've certainly never hunted any game as dangerous as panther. But I can assure you, sir, that I'm quite an adequate shot and can take care of myself."

"All right, then," Lawton said. "We're goin' to have an early breakfast and start out at first light."

Lawton and Blaine began to discuss hunting. Their hunting talk isolated them from the others. Lucinda and LeBeau drifted away with their gossip about New Orleans. Joleen and Rafaella found themselves in conversation. And they quickly decided they did not like each other.

LeBeau drained his glass and poured himself another brandy. The carefree, self-mocking tone of his voice had changed in the last five minutes. Now his voice was nasty and his words were slurred. Lucinda knew he was bored with their idle talk, and when he got drunk and bored he often became reckless.

She knew he expected her to arrange for the privacy they needed to discuss their business, but she had no experience in such tactics and had no idea what to do or say. The silence between them lasted a full minute.

Lucinda heard Roger Blaine saying, "No, I've hunted

in England . . ." And Rafaella, "Unthinkable to even consider giving a slave his freedom, under any circumstances. Why, it would take a thousand years of freedom for the qualities of slavery to disappear . . ."

LeBeau was gulping his brandy. His blue eyes had narrowed as he stared at Lucinda.

"Yes, that's a lovely painting by Mr. Audubon," Lucinda said, abruptly raising her voice so everyone could hear. "Let's go into the parlor and I'll show it to you."

"I've looked forward to seeing the painting since Miss Delma mentioned she had given it to you," LeBeau said.

Lucinda stumbled twice as they walked toward the parlor.

10.

Lucinda stared intently at Audubon's lifelike pheasant in a thorn thicket and tried to control her erratic breathing. LeBeau touched her hand. She jerked it away as though burned.

He laughed. "You should take something for those nerves, Lucinda," he said. "Though I believe I have the ideal remedy for such a condition. I've been waiting all evening for you to give me the opportunity to offer my prescription."

"Spare me your foul wordplays, Alain," she said.

"And spare me your preaching, Lucinda," he said. "I am what I am, as you well know, and I make no apologies. And don't forget, my dear, you made the offer to me quite freely in New Orleans. I didn't coerce you."

"I was desperate, Alain," she said. "We all were. I was afraid Lawton would lose The Columns if you sold that land to Lavon."

"Yes, and I was quite specific in what I told you

then, Lucinda," he said. "I had already agreed to accept the offer of Lavon's agent. I didn't know your husband and had not the slightest interest in him or his plantation. Nor do I care anything about right and wrong. As I made clear, Lucinda, I felt no obligation to you at all. I only do favors for those who give me something I want. You knew I had always wanted you, and so you offered yourself to me."

"You were quite eloquent on the subject, Alain," she said.

"I want to make certain that you remember how our conversation went," he said. " 'I'll surrender my body to you.' Those were your very words, Lucinda. And why should it be such a terrible price for you to pay? We were once fond of each other, and I've always lusted after you."

"Please, Alain," she said. "I can do without such talk!"

"Of course, Lucinda," he said. "What is there to say? It's only a matter of logistics. I'm sure you know me too well to try and back out of your promise now that the land is yours."

"I know you only too well, Alain," she said. "So let's settle the matter here and now!"

"Oh, I'm quite willing," he said. "Though the floor will be hard on your delicate body. And I might find it amusing when the sounds of our passion bring in the others from the porch, but I should think you'd be embarrassed."

Lucinda's cheeks grew warm. "You know what I mean, sir," she said. "Set a time and place."

"A time and place," he said. "Discreet, of course . . ."

He walked out into the gallery and headed for the back. She had no choice but to follow down the gallery to the back steps.

"As you know, I must leave The Columns tomorrow," he said. "I can return after business on some of my nearby property. That would be in four, perhaps five, days. You can invite me to stay here again. Nothing could seem more natural."

"Not here at The Columns, Alain!" she said.

He moved down the steps. Again she followed.

"Of course, not here at the house," he said. "We'll go riding. Just the two of us. Two old friends. There's nothing but wilderness around here. We can easily find cover in some pleasant grove."

"I suppose that's all right," she said. "We can do that. Now, we must join the others. We have nothing further to discuss, sir."

"As you wish," he said. "But I hope by the time I return you've recovered from this feisty mood, Lucinda. It makes you less than appealing. Since it's inevitable, you might as well show some enthusiasm for it. I rather think you will when the time comes."

"I can assure you, sir, that I . . ."

Something brushed Lucinda's foot. She glanced down. A small, striped snake was writhing across her boot. She shivered. Her knees nearly buckled. But she knew a sudden movement could be fatal.

LeBeau had also seen the snake. He, too, forced himself to stand still.

Someone with a lantern moved around the corner of the house. It was Filch. He approached them slowly, then lowered the lantern to the ground.

Filch raised a rifle to his shoulder, but he had to hold his fire because the snake still writhed across Lucinda's boot. She bit her lips until she tasted blood. Her stomach contracted. Bile rose in her throat.

A minute later the snake crawled from her boot. Filch fired. The snake splattered into bits of skin and blood.

Lucinda turned and collapsed. Filch helped her up. The others ran down the gallery. Lawton took Lucinda in his arms. She cried and shook violently several times. Then she lay still against Lawton.

"It was a coral snake, sure 'nough," Filch said. "Never seen one in the yard this way."

"Isn't that snake especially poisonous?" Rafaella asked.

"Sure is, Miss," Filch said. "Poison don't go to your

blood, like rattlers and them others. Goes right to the nerves. One of them little fellas gets you, you'd be dead, sure 'nough."

"Enough of that talk!" Lawton said. He lifted Lucinda up and helped her along the gallery.

"It's similar to a cobra's poison," Rafaella told Joleen as they followed the others to the porch. "A nerve poison. If I wanted to kill someone with a snake, I think I'd choose a coral snake."

"I think we've all had enough talk about snakes for one night," Joleen said.

"Oh, not me," Rafaella said. "I find them fascinating creatures. Many religions consider snakes the source of all mystery, all knowledge, according to my tutor. The ancient Egyptians, for instance. And Queen Cleopatra ended her life with the bite of an asp against her breast, after her defeat by the Romans."

11.

The dogs went wild when they picked up the panther's scent. The slaves had trouble holding them back until Lawton gave the order to let them run into the forest. Blaine, Filch, and three field hands followed Lawton and the dogs.

The hunt was torturous from the beginning. Low-slung limbs and thorn-vines slapped at the riders. One slave was knocked to the ground by a sycamore limb. Both Lawton and Blaine bled from thorn cuts, but nothing disturbed Blaine. Lawton was impressed with the man's ability on horseback.

After an hour, Lawton caught his first glimpse of the biggest panther he had ever seen. The dogs chased the big cat into a vine-tangled grove of water oaks. They were no longer barking. Their sounds were high-pitched, eerie, blood-hungry.

When the men dismounted, Lawton told the field

hands to stay with the horses. He and Blaine and Filch inched their way into the grove. Tall trees and clusters of moss blocked out much of the sunlight. The dogs had stopped whining. The silence was ominous. A twig cracked. Lawton swung around, his finger on the trigger. He saw nothing but mottled leaves rippling in the wind. Then a dog whined. They all began to bark and snap. Something was running over dry leaves, unseen in the deep shadows. Despite the heat, a chill raced up Lawton's spine.

The men inched forward to a clearing surrounded by huge oaks where the dogs were running in circles. A spotted dog raised his nose and sniffed. The other dogs moved to his side, all sniffing. They began to growl, then to bay at the tallest oak tree.

Filch touched Lawton's shoulder and pointed high in the oak. Lawton looked up, and slowly the panther's snout showed among the leaves. Lawton glanced at Blaine. He should give his guest the first shot. But this was no time for manners.

Lawton raised his rifle. He sighted on the cat and squeezed the trigger.

The panther jumped an instant after Lawton fired. It hit the ground running and vanished in the shadows, with the dogs only a few feet behind.

Lawton took a rifle from Filch and led Filch and Blaine into the shadows. He saw sunlight reflected on the drops of red blood among the dry leaves.

They were stalking a wounded panther.

The dogs ran ahead in the endless, maddening shadows. They yelped and barked and howled. The men followed the dogs.

Once they heard awful screams and howls and found the spotted dog with its throat ripped open. One of the cat's ears was impaled on the dog's teeth. Fur was matted to the blood-wet leaves.

"Can't go much further in that shape," Filch said.

Five minutes later they found the dogs running in erratic patterns beneath a grove of sycamore trees. The dogs growled deep in their throats. They sniffed, ran from tree to tree, looking up. The wounded panther was up there somewhere, leaping from limb to limb. It could be in front of them, behind them . . .

Lawton saw the cat as it sprang from a limb to the ground at his left, and as he jerked his rifle up he knew his shot would be too late. The panther charged directly at him.

Blaine pivoted and fired almost without aiming. His bullet caught the animal full in the chest and dropped it in its tracks.

The dogs fell on the bleeding carcass. Filch tried to drive them away but they snapped at him.

"Let 'em have it," Lawton said. He turned to Blaine. "That was some shot, sir. I owe you my life."

"A lucky shot," Blaine said.

"A true shot," Lawton said. "I'm in your debt, sir." He turned to lead the men back to the horses, but he found his legs could barely support him, and he had to stop after a few yards and recover from his fright.

The shortest way back to The Columns took the party through a corner of the swamp. They had ridden for half an hour, but now they led their weary horses beside a slime-filled bayou. The dogs had been dragging themselves along, panting and whimpering, but here their attitude changed. They raised their heads. They sniffed the air. They strained against the leashes.

The men stopped and watched the dogs. Something was out there beyond the bayou, something that was beginning to drive the dogs into a frenzy.

"Some animal, I reckon," Lawton said. "Maybe another painter."

"Maybe," Filch said. "But them dogs, they all tuckered out, Mist' Lawton. Take somethin' pretty special to get 'em riled up like this. You want 'em turned loose?"

"No, no, I don't think so," Lawton said. "We've done enough huntin' for one day, Filch."

They started off again. They came to the end of the

bayou and into a muddy bog. Their boots creaked in the mud, made sucking sounds when pulled free. The growth became so thick Lawton had to send one of the field hands ahead to cut a path. Now it took two men to hold back the dogs.

Suddenly, there was a clearing. Every tree, bush, and vine had been violently uprooted. Then they understood. They had come on the tornado's path.

Lawton thought of snakes just an instant before he heard the first rattle and saw the rattler striking frantically at a moss-lined stump. There were king snakes, queen snakes, roadrunners, garter snakes, copperheads, moccasins, and coral snakes. Some lay coiled tightly and darted out their tongues. Others writhed about, coiling and uncoiling.

"Let's get away from here!" Lawton said. "I'd rather walk through the swamp than take a chance with these snakes."

"Reckon that's what got the dogs started?" Filch asked. "Yet it don't seem . . . Wait a minute, Mist' Lawton. Look yonder! To your right down there!"

"Yes, I see it," Lawton said. "Looks like some kind of buildin' was blown down. And Lord . . . is that a body?"

Lawton told the slaves to keep the dogs on leash. He and Filch and Blaine moved forward very slowly, killing two copperheads.

The body was that of a black man. His skull had been crushed by an oak limb. A few feet away lay another black man. His fingers were curled around a rifle. There were puncture marks on his arm and hand. Nearby were two moccasins with their heads blown off.

All around the men lay the ruin of a log building.

"They're runaway slaves," Lawton said. "Slave finds some excuse, runs off and hides in the swamp, usually wanders back, or a patrol arrests him after a few days. But these . . . they seem to have built some kind of fort. And one of them was armed."

"Runaway slaves . . . armed . . . a fort," Blaine said. "A nasty business. Nasty and threatening."

"Yes, this place isn't far from The Columns," Lawton said. "There's constant po' white talk of nonexistent slave uprisin's, and the patrols overreact far too often. But niggers outnumber us four to one here in Adams County. Just last month some runaways fought a pitched battle with a patrol near Rodney. And none of us can forget the Nat Turner massacre up in Virginia."

"And your own niggers?" Blaine asked.

"Except for one man we've never had any trouble," Lawton said. "I wonder now . . . these renegades . . . it's not only the danger they pose. They could sneak onto the plantation and influence my own niggers with their ideas. Some Yankee abolitionist could have . . . I wonder if any of my people . . . Filch!"

"No, sir, Mist' Lawton," Filch said. "I haven't seen or heard nothin' in the quarters. I'd bet a pretty these fellas, they done stayed well clear of us. So don't you go frettin' none 'bout nobody on the place bein' involved. Not nobody at all."

"I hope not," Lawton muttered. "Christ, I hope not!" He stared at Filch but couldn't say what he wanted because of Blaine. "We'll talk later. Come on. Let's get home. I want to notify the sheriff."

But the sheriff was secondary to Lawton. His greatest concern was that Joleen had broken their truce and again become involved in the Underground Railroad.

12.

Lawton stood on the front porch and watched Lucinda and LeBeau ride away. He had cautioned them not to ride beyond the plantation, but LeBeau had laughed and joked about "some ragtag nigger army."

"Besides, the sheriff and the patrols and their nigger dogs have flushed out every runaway for twenty miles around," LeBeau said. "The area has never been safer from fugitive slaves."

LeBeau had returned to The Columns the previous day, and after a long evening of whiskey and talk, Lawton decided he had no use for the man, despite his gratitude about the land. Lawton judged LeBeau cynical, opinionated, lazy, malicious, a drunk, and totally amoral. And Lawton sensed how deeply Lucinda was disturbed by her old friend.

Thank God he's leaving tomorrow, Lawton told himself. He was sick of guests, even the Blaines.

But the Blaines might be at The Columns for a long while.

For the afternoon after the Blaines' arrival, Lawton had received an express letter from a Mr. Anson, who had been Price Deavors's New York attorney. Anson wrote that he was leaving for Natchez the next day. He said that he was bringing vital information and that on no account should the estate be awarded to the Blaines before his arrival.

Lawton couldn't imagine what the problem might be. He dreaded telling Blaine. But Blaine had reacted calmly when Lawton said probate would be delayed because of some minor legal technicalities.

Lawton deeply resented being involved in this matter, though he was fond of Blaine. The harvest had started, and he had no time for Yankee lawyers and probate courts. He even dreaded the party he was giving to introduce the Blaines.

Lawton walked into the yard and snatched off an oleander leaf. Dammit, he muttered. On top of everything else, there were his fears about Joleen. She had denied any involvement with the runaways in the swamp. When Lawton pressed the issue, she became angry and accused him of breaking their truce. She threatened to take the next boat to Ohio. This frightened him. He had become dependent on Joleen, if only for the supportive family feeling so diminished by his parents' death. He begged her to stay and swore that he did trust her.

But he really didn't trust Joleen. Not only had her abolitionist activities jeopardized everyone at The Columns, but she had lied again and again. What if she were lying now?

Lawton couldn't understand how Joleen had ever let Aaron turn her against her own people. Joleen, his little sister, an abolitionist! She was determined to go against all family tradition and free her slaves. At times Lawton became so angry he felt like ordering her out of the house!

He tried to imagine what had happened to change her so. Memories came as he walked the lawn, memories of a younger, innocent Joleen. Another memory followed, of the summer when childhood between them ended . . .

"Oh, here you are!"

Lawton turned, his mind filled with guilty memories. Rafaella stood in the door. She was stunning in a yellow silk dress, though Lawton thought the dress was cut rather low for a girl of her age.

"Is there anything you'd like?" he asked.

"Oh, nothing in particular," she said. "Daddy is taking his siesta but I'm not the least bit sleepy."

"Then I'll have some lemonade sent out here and we can talk."

"I'd really like that," she said.

Rafaella walked to the kitchen with Lawton, and he realized that she was wearing a perfume with a musky, disturbing scent.

For nearly an hour, Lucinda and LeBeau had been riding into the woods, away from The Columns. The day was warm and the air was heavy with moisture. They had not exchanged a half-dozen words, and Lucinda was so anxious and apprehensive that she felt nearly sick. Sweat soaked into her cotton riding dress and ran down her face, mixing with her tears. She struggled to hide her feelings from LeBeau, but she knew her eyes were red from crying, and she was afraid all her emotions were written on her face.

She had never in her life been in a position like this one—never even dreamed that she would be. It was terribly wrong—fearful, like all things unknown, and yet far worse. Alain LeBeau was such a strange man—so sophisticated and so unscrupulous. God only knew what he would demand of her . . . and, of course, anything he might ask was in violation of her moral beliefs and against everything she'd been brought up to believe.

"Oh, damn!" she thought, choking on tears, "dear God, what am I doing here?" She had never made love with anyone but her husband, never even thought of it, or wanted to, and yet . . . it had seemed the only way of dealing with LeBeau, at the time. She had promised him his way in order to save The Columns. She had promised out of desperation, and now, not like a gentleman, LeBeau had come back out to The Columns and made it clear that he intended to collect.

She felt dirty at the prospect. Dirty and sinful and scared. What would it be like with LeBeau? What might he demand? She'd heard stories about sex all her life, but Lawton had always been tender and gentle. LeBeau was obviously a different sort of man . . . and not in a romantic way at all. LeBeau was forceful and ironic and blunt and rough. He was not a gentleman, she had thought over and over again, not a gentleman . . .

"Surely we've come far enough," he called to her. She saw that he was drinking from a silver flask. He had been drinking brandy all day.

Lucinda closed her eyes for a minute, praying that she would wake up safely at home in her bed, or in a tub of hot water that would wash her clean from all this. But when she opened her eyes again, LeBeau was still there, grinning at her. His smile frightened her anew.

"Yes," she said. "I suppose we've come far enough."

They reined the horses in and dismounted in a grove of loblolly pines. LeBeau held out a hand to Lucinda, but she rejected help and struggled out of the saddle

45

by herself. She stood stiffly beside her mount, struggling for composure, staring down at the brown pine needles.

"Well, Lucinda, you're hardly the picture of passion," LeBeau said. He took a long gulp of brandy. "But you are beautiful, nevertheless. I've always thought so."

Lucinda felt herself flush. The man was repulsive. She could smell liquor on his breath.

"Yes, you are quite lovely," LeBeau said. "Here, look at me."

She looked up. "What's this?" he asked. "Those lovely blue eyes all red from crying? What a shame. Here, drink some brandy. It'll put you in the proper mood . . ."

"No amount of brandy will put me in the mood for you," Lucinda said. She set her jaw and looked at the ground again.

"Why, Lucinda! Where is your sense of honor?" he asked. "Obviously you and I have different ideas of keeping a bargain. Is this what I am to get for my land? A stiff, red-eyed woman?"

"I'm here, aren't I, Alain?"

"Oh, yes, my dear . . ."

"I can force my physical being to surrender to you," she said. "I gave you my word of honor, and I intend to keep my word, but I can't force my spirit, my feelings . . ."

"Even though you know how much I've always wanted you, Lucinda?" He laughed and she felt more confused than ever. "How desirable I've always found you . . . your skin so pale and freckled, so soft looking. I've wanted you for years."

Lucinda felt an emotion she didn't understand. "Wanted me?" she said in an excited voice. "Me and every other woman you've ever laid eyes on! Just how many women have you had, Alain? And did any one of them have the slightest feeling for you?"

Their eyes met. Lucinda was even more surprised than LeBeau by her sudden outburst. LeBeau's lips quivered as he raised the flask to them. His eyes frightened Lucinda. They were dark and threatening.

"I wouldn't know about such feeling," he said. "I suppose I've had hundreds of women. Whenever I needed one. I buy them as I need them, just as I bought you, Mrs. Deavors. But what the hell have I bought? Looks as if I've made a bad purchase!"

Lucinda hadn't known it was possible to feel more humiliated, but now she did. He was talking about her as if she were a common prostitute.

"Look at you!" he said. "Eyes red! Trembling! Mousy one minute and insulting the next. I've never seen you look less womanly. Goddamit, I wonder if you're capable of giving me any pleasure at all!"

He drained the flask and reached to take another from his saddlebag. Lucinda was afraid to be with him if he became any more intoxicated, but more afraid that he would ride back to the plantation in a drunken rage and confront Lawton with some awful lies . . . or worse, with the truth.

"Please don't drink any more, Alain," she begged. "I'm sorry. I shouldn't have said what I did. I'm very nervous. Try to understand . . . I've never been with anyone but my husband, and . . . oh, what's the use of trying to explain!"

"Here, drink some brandy," he said. "Go on, dammit, take some!"

Lucinda took the flask. She had difficulty forcing down a swallow, but the ones that followed went down easier. At his insistence, she took two more gulps and felt the liquor like fire in her throat, then her stomach, then her head. She flushed redder, and a drop of the brandy fell from the corner of her mouth and wet the front of her pale green dress. Even the smell of the stuff made her dizzy.

"Well?" LeBeau asked. "Less nervous?"

"I . . . I think so," she said.

"Have a bit more. I want to get my money's worth."

She bit her lip in a flash of anger, then took a long draught of brandy. Although she had never been drunk before, she knew that she was quite drunk now. She looked up to see LeBeau grinning at her.

"Can you do it?" he asked. "Can you arouse me?"

"Oh!!!" she cried out. She hated him, how she hated him, and yet . . . she was ashamed that he found her so wanting in sexual attractiveness. No man had ever said such a thing to her before.

"Undress, Lucinda, I want to look at you."

Her fingers unfastened the buttons at her wrists, then moved to her throat. They were shaking.

"Let me help," he said. She felt sick as she endured his probing fingers. Her body was rigid. He pulled open the buttons on the front of her bodice, then reached inside and took hold of one nipple through her cotton lace chemise. She trembled. His touch horrified her, and yet she could not stop herself from groaning out of some awful excitement.

His fingers caressed her body, moving over her flesh as if it were a piece of sculpture as he removed the rest of her clothing.

Finally, she was naked except for her chemise. LeBeau stepped back from her and smiled.

"Lift up the chemise," he said.

Slowly, reluctantly, she raised the flimsy garment over her thighs and higher. She had never before stripped in front of a man. With tight fists, she held the chemise over her vagina, protecting the last bit of her body. Her nails dug through the sheer batiste and into her palms.

"Turn around slowly," he said.

She obeyed him, her face burning as she turned.

"Now drop it, slowly, that's right . . ."

Lucinda dropped the chemise to the ground. She looked at her own body, afraid to look at LeBeau. She was stark naked. She had never felt so lewd, so humiliated, so vulnerable!

She could not look at him, or even at the trees and bushes surrounding them. They all seemed to have eyes. People were watching, the whole county would know what she was doing. . . She moved her hands to cover her body.

"No!" LeBeau ordered. She dropped her hands to her sides.

"Yes, you're a pretty woman, Lucinda," he said. "Though a bit skinny for my taste. I like a woman's breasts to be more than acorns, though I must admit your little red nipples are appealing enough. I like the freckles on your breasts and thighs. And then there's that pretty red bush down there. . ."

She winced. How could she endure another second of such nasty talk?

"Bush on fire . . ." LeBeau murmured. His hand reached for the thick tangle, and Lucinda gasped as she felt his rough fingers. Lawton had never touched her so, so hungrily, so masterfully.

It'll soon be over, she thought, closing her eyes. Less roughly, he lowered her to the ground and she felt the prickle of dry pine needles on her bare back. The brandy had both numbed her and excited her, and when she looked up at LeBeau, the sky behind his head seemed to swim and the branches of the pine trees above were like a dark canopy.

LeBeau indolently stroked her breasts and nipples while he drank more brandy. When he offered her more, she shook her head, but he leaned forward, and when he kissed her, his mouth was full of the liquor and she tasted it.

His tongue was rude and probing—it seemed so large that it filled her whole mouth, choked her. When it touched the back of her throat she growled, half in fear, but half, also, in some other spirit.

"Alain!" she gasped. He—and the liquor—had aroused her to a point where she was both totally responsive and almost totally passive. She felt she could not fight back any more if her life depended on it. She felt every inch of his body with every inch of hers— felt it come alive, felt it respond. "Alain!" she cried in astonishment.

His mood was otherwise. He seemed to grow more forceful, even angry. He was naked and his penis was huge and hard. He stroked her body lazily. She closed her eyes. Her nipples were so tight and sensitive that they ached. One of his fingers was teasing her vagina, and she groaned as she became aware of dampness there.

Without thinking she opened her thighs, doubled her legs at the knees, ready to receive him, while she grasped his buttocks.

But LeBeau was pulling from her body. She opened her eyes as her knees tried to lock around his thighs. Her nails dug into his back. But he rolled free and drank from his flask.

"Alain, what . . ."

"You simply fail to arouse me, Lucinda," he mumbled. "Too skinny, too awkward, unable to control yourself. Look at you!" He touched her sore nipples.

"But I . . . Alain . . . What can I do? Please, Alain, don't humiliate me this way . . . Don't do this to me . . ."

"Do you want me?" he asked. She sucked in her breath as he fondled her breasts. "Tell me you want me . . . inside you, Lucinda."

Lucinda's nostrils flared and there was a sting of hatred and rebellion, but her body betrayed her at once. She shuddered and licked her lips and tasted the sweat pouring down her cheeks.

She closed her eyes again. "Yes, I want you, Alain . . . I want you . . . inside me . . ."

"Then you may have me," he said. "But in a way that I prefer and that I'll teach you to like . . ."

Suddenly he picked her up in his arms as if she were a child and turned her over. She was dizzy.

She had no idea what was going on. She knew only that she was helpless and very hungry to be caressed and cuddled.

Instead, she found herself lying face down in the pine needles, sprawled out. He was on top of her, his weight tremendous, pinning her so that she couldn't move.

"Alain, what . . ." she tried to ask, but her wind was pressed out of her by the thing he was doing to her . . . a thing she could not have imagined, had never heard of, and could not bear . . .

"It's about all you're good for," LeBeau muttered. His voice was strange, wild. She screamed as she tried to move and couldn't, tried to cry out, for help, tried to comprehend . . .

He entered her with one incredibly painful thrust, and she screamed again. She felt as if she were being ripped apart. The invasion, the violation was intolerable . . . unimaginable. And yet he kept on, kept moving, kept thrusting, kept rocking into her, arousing waves of pain that extended to every part of her body.

"No, no, no, no, no," she gurgled, deep in her throat. Would it never end? She would die soon . . . she hoped.

And then it was over. He gave one last thrust and groaned, and she felt heat and wetness and then, like a benediction, she felt her own orgasm ripple throughout her vagina and entire lower body, felt it soothe her and drain her and leave her wrecked.

"To hell with you!" LeBeau mumbled. He stood up and pulled on his pants in one rapid motion. Lucinda still lay there.

LeBeau reached for his flask. When he found it empty, he hurled it against a tree trunk.

"Oh, oh," Lucinda gasped. She forced herself to roll over and look up at him. He was swaying above her, his eyes wild, his mouth twisted. His image swam in her misted, sensation-strained eyes.

"Don't think this is the last, Lucinda," he threatened her. "This is not the seal of our bargain. This is just a taste of what is to come. Maybe next time you'll do better at arousing me."

He turned and staggered toward his horse.

Lucinda sat up. She could not rise. "My God, Alain! Don't go back to the house . . . like that . . . don't tell anyone, please! I'll do anything you ask! I'll meet you again, I promise!"

"Damn right you will!" he swore.

LeBeau mounted his horse and galloped into the bushes.

Lucinda lay back, trembling and crying. Pine needles stuck to her damp skin.

"Lawton would kill you . . ." The words trailed off. Her throat contracted. She began to cough. The effort set off further waves of orgasm, all over her body. She had never felt like this before. I'll kill you for doing this to me, she wanted to say, but the words would not come out.

Then she thought of LeBeau's arriving at The Columns without her. He was drunk and angry enough to do anything.

Lucinda fumbled into her clothes. She was crying hysterically as she lurched toward her horse.

13.

Rafaella rode through the cotton fields, past a hoe gang of women clearing weeds from the tall, ripening cotton plants. A thin black girl stood nearby with a water jug balanced on her head. Rafaella returned the girl's smile.

There were slaves all the way to the horizon. Lawton had said that he had three hundred slaves and over fifteen hundred acres in cotton. The estate of Price Deavors was much smaller, only ninety slaves and six hundred acres. But cotton was making a fortune for everyone, and Rafaella was confident that she and her father would soon expand their plantation and make their own fortune.

That was, if Lawton let them have their plantation. No matter what her father said, she wouldn't accept Lawton's explanation of legal technicalities.

They were the only heirs to the estate and had documents to prove it. The Deavorses were so influential in the county that Rafaella was certain the judge would do whatever Lawton asked. She knew Lawton too well, even in this short time, to suspect he had an ulterior motive in the delay. He seemed almost insufferably honest, and besides, with all his wealth, why would he want the Price Deavors estate?

What made her even angrier was her father's refusal to discuss the matter. He brushed off her questions, saying that he trusted Lawton and reminding her that probate was complicated.

Rafaella knew she might be building up her resentment at the delay out of all proportion, but it wasn't only the delay.

There had been a shadow on the closeness with her father ever since that day on the padwheeler when Carter Ramsey had snubbed her and her father had insulted her with that woman—what was her name? It didn't matter. Rafaella didn't care to remember the woman's name, but she could never forget the shock of what she saw later that night.

She had retreated to her suite, nearly wild with frustration and resentment, suffering from a severe headache.

It's not just the woman, she had thought over and over again as she lay in bed. And it wasn't just that Carter Ramsey, damn him to hell, had stood her up. Worse was the implication that she was too young, too immature, too much of a child, too powerless to matter. Ramsey had referred to her father in his note—as if she shouldn't have agreed to meet him alone in the first place. And that woman with her father—that dark-haired tramp—had called her a child to her face!

It had been a hot night, and Rafaella's bed had soon been wet with tears and perspiration. She was suffering from her headache and unable to sleep when she heard noises coming from her father's adjoining room.

Nothing could have kept her from creeping to the door to investigate. Dizzy with pain and dread, she had peeked through a chink in the door and she had seen them together in there, her father and that stupid woman.

The recollection shot a bolt of fury through her entire body.

It had not been the first time Rafaella had spied on her father with a woman, but she had never been as close as that night on the *Yazoo Queen,* close enough to hear the sucking, slapping sounds, to hear the woman cry out in passion, to hear her own father emit sounds like a growling animal. She had seen them coupled, seen them bobbing up and down, her father lying on top of Miss Sylvia Richardson—yes, that was her name—she had even been able to smell the perspiration and the odd, nose-wrinkling stench of sex.

For several days after that, Rafaella could not bring herself to speak more than a few words to her father, but finally she was touched by his embarrassed misery and gave in to his entreaties for forgiveness. He had sworn, and she knew, that no woman meant anything to him at all. She was his only love. She believed it wholly.

But the incident had tainted something. It had spoiled their love and intimacy in a way that only time could repair, more on her father's part than on hers, for he hadn't been himself ever since. He was gloomy. He seemed distracted and melancholy all the time, as if he had worries he could not discuss with her. And she could not believe that it was only the delay over probate that was causing his melancholy.

Rafaella decided that she would confront her father this very afternoon and demand the truth.

To raise her spirits, Rafaella thought of the glorious life she and her father would soon lead. He would be the most sought-after man in the county. He would dally with beautiful women and allow them to fulfill his needs. But of course he would never marry one of them.

And she would blossom into the most beautiful and desirable woman in the whole South! Her father would love her even more. He would become more dependent on her. She would love him beyond reason, and all her fantasies would come true.

Rafaella rode faster and cursed the heat. What good were her fantasies so long as they had to depend on these cousins? Damn that Lawton! She had worn her most appealing dress and her expensive Persian perfume. He ordered lemonade, treated her like a child, and refused to discuss the Price Deavors estate.

Lawton was really something of a bumpkin, she told herself. Though she couldn't deny she found him quite handsome with his blonde hair and blue eyes and dimples. He was tall and strong and a fine horseman. And it was impressive that at twenty-five he ran such a huge plantation without even an overseer.

She felt sure he would soon be enthralled by her, but that time on the porch had been wasted. She wished now that she had followed Lucinda and LeBeau. Their ride was probably innocent enough, but there was always the hope of finding them in some deliciously compromising situation.

Rafaella smiled as she thought of spying on them in the woods. She loved to spy on people. Her fantasies drifted from Lawton to Carter Ramsey. She wasn't certain how, but someday she would see him again and she would make him suffer, far worse than the suffering he had inflicted on her. She knew her power with men. She could have any one of them, any way she wanted, and Carter Ramsey would find that out!

Rafaella dismounted at the barn. She felt restless and mischievous, and she decided that if her father was honest with her, she would reward him by spending a long time in her bath.

Rafaella had started up the stairs when she noticed that the parlor door was closed. She pressed against the door. She could make out Lawton's voice but she could not hear what was being said.

She went out to the front porch. A carriage was tied to the hitching post, and an elderly black man was sitting under a sycamore tree. Rafaella glanced back at the parlor door. What could be so private and important that Lawton would shut the door? He never shut doors.

She walked down the steps and snapped off an oleander leaf. The sharp smell reminded her that the leaf's poison could sicken a man and kill an infant. A smile creased the corners of her lips as she remembered the arrogant Roman family that had refused to let their daughter attend a ball with her father.

Her smile deepened as she recalled setting fire to an oleander garden in the family's yard. Smoke from the leaves had made the entire family sick. Rafaella discarded the leaf. She hesitated, then walked over to the driver. He climbed to his feet.

"You look very warm," she said.

"Doin' tolerably well in this heat, Miss."

"Yes, the heat is dreadful," she said. "I find it difficult to adjust to such heat and such dampness. I've only recently arrived in Adams County."

"That a fact, Miss," he said. "Same thing with the man I drove out here from Natchez. He done come from up to New York, he say. And he say, never seen nothin' like this weather for September."

"I wonder who the man is," Rafaella said. "We weren't expecting guests today."

"Oh, Mr. Anson, I don't reckon he's what you'd call a guest, Miss. He's one of them lawyer fellas, from what I gather. Done come all this way on business."

"What kind of business?"

"Wouldn't know, Miss. Mr. Anson, he didn't tell me nothin'."

Rafaella returned to the house. The parlor door was still closed.

Rafaella found her father in his room, staring from the window. His face was so white it frightened her.

"Daddy, what's wrong?" she asked.

"I've been taken ill, Raffles," he said. "Nothing serious. Only a headache."

"I know only too well why you have a headache," she said. "It's that New York lawyer who's talking to Lawton. That Mr. Anson. Oh, Daddy, why haven't you been honest with me? Legal technicalities, indeed! What's really wrong? Tell me, please!"

"There's nothing to tell," he said. "I've been honest

with you, Raffles. Lawton told me there would be a slight delay because of technicalities with the court. Perhaps I should have pressed him for more information, but what he said seemed reasonable. And we don't know that this lawyer has anything to do with us."

"Do you expect me to believe a lawyer would travel all the way from New York to discuss some technicality?" she asked. "There's something very wrong to bring that lawyer down here. Something *quite* wrong. And since you wouldn't let me attend that talk when Lawton told you about the delay, I have to believe you're deceiving me."

"See here, Raffles!" he said. "I won't have you talk to me this way."

"And I won't have you lying about something so important, Daddy! It's my estate, too, Daddy! When Mr. Anson leaves, please let me go with you when you talk to Lawton."

"Raffles, you're very mature in most ways," he said. "And I often depend on you as though you were . . . a much older person. But in many ways you're still a child, my dear. Despite your involvement in this matter, you tend to become too emotionally involved . . . An unfortunate temper tantrum, the wrong thing said, could cause more delay . . . antagonize Lawton."

"I'm not a child!" she screamed. "Don't ever call me that! You should surely know that, damn it! You don't love me anymore! Please, Daddy, I'll only believe you if you say I can go with you when you talk to Lawton."

"No, Raffles, I'm sorry but—"

Rafaella ran out, tears streaming down her cheeks. She locked herself in her room and hurled a heavy crystal glass at a mirror.

Lawton poured another glass of whiskey and turned back to the elderly lawyer.

"You're certain you won't have a glass, Mr. Anson?"

"Not in this heat, Mr. Deavors," Anson said.

"Heat or not, I'm afraid the information you've

brought forces me to take comfort in whiskey, sir," Lawton said. He took a swallow. "If only you had sufficient proof from your agent on the Continent, Mr. Anson. I don't want to make an important decision on the basis of hearsay. How can I believe this agent of yours?"

"I'd stake my professional reputation on the man, Mr. Deavors," Anson said. "In fact, I often have. His letter was sent in some haste to warn me—warn us—that his investigation of Blaine had raised serious questions, both about the man's documents and his past. He wrote that he would soon know the truth and, if his suspicions proved correct, that he would immediately forward the evidence to you."

"Very well, Mr. Anson," Lawton said. "I'll accept your confidence in the agent. But I'm determined to withhold any judgment about Blaine until I have the documents in hand. And if the agent's suspicions prove unfounded—the allegations must never leave this room. Why, forged documents . . . that's a serious enough accusation. But this other charge is monstrous. Why, the mere hint of such an atrocious thing would ruin Blaine and his daughter in Mississippi forever."

"I quite understand, sir," Anson said. "You can depend on my discretion. I only wish to emphasize that the estate should not be given to Roger Blaine until the matter is resolved."

"Of course," Lawton said. "There's no question of the estate goin' to them at the present time. It's just that we've accepted the Blaines as family, even planned a party in their honor."

"I appreciate your dilemma, Mr. Deavors," Anson said. "If Price Deavors had investigated his suspicions about Blaine before he reached his deathbed, all this could have been avoided."

"It's just that—"

Lawton didn't finish the sentence. He saw LeBeau riding toward the barn and wondered where Lucinda was. Then he saw her on the horizon. He wanted her nearby at a time like this. Not that he could tell her.

He'd keep this distasteful information to himself. He shuddered as he touched the papers that Anson had brought. Bad enough that there was some question about Blaine's documents. But to suspect that Roger Blaine was really an Egyptian! A Moslem!

And that he had once been a *slave* in Egypt!

Book
II

14.

Joleen and Rafaella had visited a dozen Natchez cloth merchants in three hours, and Joleen felt she would scream if Rafaella asked her opinion about one more piece of silk or satin.

". . . think yellow is really my color, Joleen," Rafaella was saying as they walked along a crowded street. "But others insist that blue goes better with my dark hair and eyes. What do you think? Yellow or blue?"

"What?" Joleen asked. "Oh, you look fine in either color, Rafaella." Joleen refused to call her Raffles, as the others at The Columns had taken to doing.

"I'm accustomed to far more of a choice, coming from a city such as Rome," Rafaella said. "Though I suppose I must accustom myself to what Natchez has to offer."

"Yes, that would seem like a clever idea, Rafaella," Joleen said. "Well, here's Santini Brothers. I have other errands to run. You really must make a choice in here."

Rafaella frowned. "Well, if I must, then I will."

The frown changed to a smile, the calculated, taunting smile around Rafaella's lips that always annoyed Joleen, because she reserved it for certain men, notably Lawton and her father. Now Rafaella was smiling at a slim, black-and-grey-haired man who was walking toward them.

"Good day, Miss Blaine," the man said. He bowed. Joleen was held for a moment by his vivid grey eyes.

"Why, good day, Mr. Ridgeway," Rafaella said. "Joleen, this is Mr. Wyman Ridgeway. Mr. Ridgeway, this is my cousin, Mrs. Aaron Clauson."

"How do you like Natchez, Mr. Ridgeway?" Rafaella

asked. "Have you found occasion to take up your dueling sword here?"

"Only once, Miss Blaine," Ridgeway said.

"And how did you end that duel?" she asked.

"I was the victor," he said. "The gods favored me. Perhaps you ladies will also favor me by being so kind as to take tea with me."

"Thank you, Mr. Ridgeway," Joleen said, "but we must decline your offer. We have several errands to run."

"Joleen, we have ample time for those stupid errands," Rafaella said. "It's impolite to decline Mr. Ridgeway's invitation. I'm quite thirsty, as a matter of fact. So I insist—"

"And I insist that we continue with our errands," Joleen said. "You have to select some dry goods. And I have to place an order for food and wine."

"Then go on and do your errands by yourself, Joleen," Rafaella said. "I'm perfectly capable of selecting the material alone, after I have tea with Mr. Ridgeway. In fact, if he wishes, Mr. Ridgeway could help me in choosing between yellow and blue."

"That's out of the question, Rafaella," Joleen said. "A girl of seventeen can't take tea alone with a man."

"I can do what I please!" Rafaella said. "Don't you dare lecture me. You're only twenty-two yourself. So there!"

"Now, enough of this!" Joleen said. "I won't hear another word. You give me any more trouble and you'll attend that party in a gunnysack!"

Ridgeway laughed. "Another time, then, ladies," he said.

Rafaella gave Joleen a look that could cut glass, but when she turned back to Ridgeway, she flattered him with her smile.

"Yes, another time," Rafaella said. "And I hope . . . oh, I know! Joleen, let's invite Mr. Ridgeway to the party. Wouldn't that be all right?"

"Oh," Ridgeway said, "I really couldn't intrude . . ."

"You wouldn't be intrudin', Mr. Ridgeway," Joleen

said. "We're givin' the party to introduce Rafaella and her father to Adams County. She can invite whoever she pleases."

"Then I'm most pleased to accept, ma'am," Ridgeway said.

They exchanged good-byes, and Joleen and Rafaella went into the Santini Brothers store.

After half an hour in the store, Joleen urged Rafaella to buy both yellow and blue material, enough for five dresses, and now they sat in the Blue Bird Tea Room.

Joleen sipped her tea and endured Rafaella's chatter about Wyman Ridgeway, but she heard little of what was being said.

She caught herself worrying again, brooding about the past and the future, slipping into gloom that was alien to her nature. She almost never brooded. She acted on impulses and seldom regretted what she did. Lawton was the one always plagued with doubt, indecision, and guilt. Perhaps his condition was contagious and she had been infected.

Aaron hadn't fully understood when she insisted that she stay at The Columns and let him go ahead to Ohio alone. Despite his sympathy, he didn't understand how much Lawton needed her. She had wanted to lessen the hurt that her brother felt at learning she had been living a lie with him, that she had been active in the Underground Railroad he hated and feared, that she had come to detest slavery and the way of life that he could not imagine even questioning.

She knew that, despite Lawton's feelings and his desperation that she stay at The Columns, he did not really trust her, even though she had been quite faithful to their truce. She knew that she could not remain faithful much longer. She found it impossible to live in a slave society. She missed Aaron, and he had written half a dozen letters begging her to join him. She had changed her mind day by day.

But she had not been able to leave. If she did, she feared she would never see her home again. And she had not been able to abandon her brother. With all Lawton's concerns, now he was saddled with these Blaines and the problems of probate court. And something was wrong. But Lawton refused to discuss the matter.

". . . meet your husband, Joleen."

Joleen looked up at Rafaella. "What? Meet my husband?"

"I *said* I'm looking forward to meeting him soon," Rafaella said. "Though I don't really understand. Is he in Ohio on business? He is an attorney, isn't he?"

"Yes, Rafaella, Aaron is a lawyer," Joleen said. "We're movin' to Ohio, and Aaron has gone on ahead to get us settled. I'll be goin' upriver shortly. So I don't know when you'll have the chance to meet Aaron."

"It must be lovely, growing up on a place such as The Columns," Rafaella said. "We had a pleasant house in Rome. And servants, of course. But to be mistress of a plantation, with hundreds of niggers at your beck and call. I can't wait until Daddy and I are settled on our own place. Joleen, surely it won't be much longer, will it?"

"Finish your tea, Rafaella," Joleen said. "We still have to order the food and wine."

Rafaella seemed to take a deliberately long time with her tea.

15.

Joleen remembered quieter Saturdays, when they had been able to drive at a leisurely pace from the Blue Bird Tea Room to the river in little more than five minutes. But on this Saturday the trip had already taken a quarter hour, and they were little more than halfway. The rutted dirt streets were crowded with people, horses, and wagons trying to pass through a maze of stalls and carts displaying everything from bloody pelts to smoked herring, braying mules, and tropical fruits and spices.

The sun was hot and glared in Joleen's eyes, even through her brown silk parasol. The open carriage had become so hopelessly tangled in traffic that she was tempted to get out and walk. But Rafaella was sufficiently fascinated and absorbed in the scene that she was being quiet for a change, and Joleen settled back to enjoy that blessing.

She had been so concerned lately with her own and the family's troubles that she had paid little attention to the constant talk about how Natchez was being invaded from the Carolinas and Virginia and was changing for the worse.

"Bustin' at the seams with the worst sort of men," Lawton's friend Theron Sumrall had said two evenings earlier at dinner at The Columns.

Joleen glanced about the crowd. There seemed a thousand faces in sight, and she did not recognize a single one. Only a few years ago, when she visited Natchez with her family, they had seldom encountered anyone they did not know.

Driving into town from the plantation this morning, Joleen had been startled by changes. Vast amounts of land were being cleared, new homes and stores and inns were being built as Natchez expanded in all directions. And many of the new buildings seemed to be taverns.

She was discouraged, too, to see the number of Negroes on the Natchez streets. There were far more slaves here than three months ago, despite the state law which forbade the sale of slaves by professional traders. Well, she told herself, Lavon Deavors had been clever enough to find ways around the law, and it was obvious that many other traders were equally clever.

The grate of iron-rimmed wheels and the shouts of angry men caught Joleen's attention. At the same time, Rafaella broke her silence.

"Oh, look, Joleen," she said. She pointed to a poster advertising a play that was being performed that evening. "It's starring Mr. Tyrone Power, the Irish actor! Oh, I'd love to see him! I haven't been to the theatre in so long, Joleen. And didn't you say he's coming to our party? In all common courtesy we should see his play so we can discuss it with him."

"I'm afraid that's impossible, Rafaella," Joleen said. "The Delsanos are expectin' us to be their guests at the fair and then at a social evening."

"Oh, all right," Rafaella said. "I suppose I'll have to content myself with talking about the theatre with Mr. Power, when I haven't even seen him act. By the way, how is it that someone like Mr. Power is invited to the party?"

"Apparently he's known Aunt Delma for years," Joleen said. "She wrote that he would be in Natchez and asked if we would extend our hospitality."

But she realized that Rafaella was no longer listening. Joleen welcomed the silence. And Rafaella remained quiet as they drove down the steep hill to the riverside wine and victuals merchants.

The fairgrounds were as crowded and noisy as the Natchez streets, but Joleen heard no curses or angry shouts, only the sounds of people enjoying themselves on a sunny Saturday afternoon.

Joleen, Rafaella, and the Delsanos—Juan, the aristocratic Spanish Creole planter, his wife, Consuela, and their twenty-year-old son Carlos—picked their way among booths selling food, stalls selling whiskey, ale, and patent medicines, gambling stands, and carousels filled with squealing children. Amid this tableau of pleasure was a black-draped platform, and on the platform stood the most famous of the circuit-riding preachers, Lorenzo Dow, promising hell and brimstone if people didn't mend their evil ways.

Joleen and the others listened to Dow a minute. They walked away smiling and joking about his sermon. They passed another platform, draped with red and

blue bunting. It was crowded with people dancing to
the music of three drunken fiddlers, totally oblivious
to Dow's sermon a few yards away. The group stopped
to watch a Negro man in tie and tails with four muzzled
brown bears who wore blue ribbons around their necks.
People laughed and clapped and tossed coins when the
man made the bears get up on their hind legs and dance
with each other.

As they left the dancing bears and headed toward the
racetrack, Joleen was jostled by one of many drunks in
the crowd. Two men fought each other with broken
whiskey jugs. She turned away from a bloody fight
between two pit dogs only to be even more appalled by
a brutal struggle between four dogs and a chained
bear.

Joleen was glad when Consuela Delsano said it was
time for the horse race. The race was their main
reason for attending the fair. Joleen had always loved
horses. As a girl, she was never happier than when she
was out riding. She recalled her eighteenth birthday
party, when her father had given her a chestnut mare.
How long ago that seemed. She had not been riding in
some time now, and she hadn't attended a race in
several years.

They reached the racetrack. Carlos took Rafaella
off for a lemon ice. Joleen and the Delsanos stood in
the paddock beneath sycamore trees and sipped champagne served by Negroes in frock coats.

"The favorite today seems to be Colonel Fredericks'
chestnut mare," Delsano said to a lawyer named Her-
bert Hedricks, whom he had just introduced to Joleen.

"Yes, I've wagered handsomely on Somerset,"
Hedricks said. "Finest horse I've seen in years. And
you, sir, will you go with the popular sentiment?"

"No, I've wagered on Lady Trafalgar," Delsano
said. "Have you seen her run, sir?"

"No, though I have heard talk from her partisans,"
Hedricks said. "That mare belongs to the owner of the
padwheeler *Mimosa*, doesn't she?"

"Yes, she does," Delsano said. "And I believe the

man's horse is as fast as his steamboat. Though I must concede there's no better jockey in the entire state than Sugar. I assume he'll be atop Colonel Fredericks' mare this afternoon."

Hedricks said that Sugar would be Somerset's jockey. "In fact, there they are now," he said.

"Isn't Somerset a handsome animal?" Hedricks asked.

"Yes, she's beautiful," Joleen said, though she was more attracted to a chestnut mare wearing scarlet ensigns.

Hedricks told them that Somerset had been brought by ship from England in a specially built padded stall said to be more luxurious than many of the passengers' cabins. Hedricks's wife joined the group and was introduced to Joleen. She started talking the second the introduction was completed.

"Have you heard the dreadful news?" she asked with the delighted tone of one who knows her listeners have not.

"What news, dear?" Hedricks asked.

"Why, it's simply frightful," she said. "A nigger escaped from the madhouse and was sighted larkin' around the fairgrounds not ten minutes ago."

"That is frightful!" Consuela Delsano said. "But what was a nigger doin' in the madhouse, if I may ask?"

"Well, I suppose he was crazy as a bedbug," Mrs. Hedricks said.

"No, dear," Hedricks said. "I think Mrs. Delsano is asking why any nigger would be placed in the madhouse. Why wouldn't his master see to his treatment or his confinement. I can answer that, Mrs. Delsano. It's become the highly questionable practice to put free niggers in poorhouses and asylums in some of the states, and I heard only yesterday they've picked up the practice here in Mississippi. I say it's a scandal!"

"What on earth is to be done with these free niggers?" Delsano asked. "I'm willin' to grant them their freedom, but surely they must be made to leave the state. Putting a nigger in a madhouse with white men? That I strongly oppose!"

Joleen was saved from a conversation she dreaded by the arrival of a man she did not know.

"And here's Lady Trafalgar's owner," Hedricks said. "Good afternoon, Captain. I've wagered on Somerset, to be honest, sir. Mr. Delsano has wagered on your horse. Is it true, as Mr. Delsano says, that your horse is as fast as your boat *Mimosa*?"

"Sir, I believe she is," the man said. "But not on the water, I would have to concede."

Everyone laughed. Joleen stared at the man. He was tall and rather handsome, and his red hair and beard were turning grey.

"You do know Mrs. Clauson, don't you, Captain?" Hedricks said. "I assumed you knew everybody here."

The man replied no, he had not had the honor.

"Then I'm embarrassed not to have introduced you at once," Hedricks said. "Captain Carter Ramsey, Mrs. Aaron Clauson. Mrs. Clauson, Captain Ramsey, late of His British Majesty's Mediterranean Fleet."

16.

Carter Ramsey fell into step with Joleen as the group walked to their boxes in the grandstand. She found Ramsey charming and she was diverted by his British accent and mannerisms. They talked as though they had known each other a long time as black men in red and blue livery served ices, champagne, sherry, and port on silver trays. Joleen and Ramsey drank champagne.

There was an overflow of racing talk, of wagers being made—over one hundred thousand dollars had already been bet—but everyone's high spirits were restrained by the thought of the mad Negro running wild. Half a dozen people coming into the grandstand said they had seen the Negro skulking nearby. The men swore vigilance, and brute force, if necessary.

The women grew pale and moved closer to the men.

Joleen noticed Ramsey didn't join in the mutterings and bravado.

"And who is your favorite today, Mrs. Clauson?" he asked.

"I suppose I have no favorite, Mr. Ramsey," she said. "Talk about your horse, Lady Trafalgar, has interested me. And during the parade, I was taken with the chestnut mare in the scarlet colors."

"Then perhaps I can persuade you to support her," Ramsey said. "Lady Trafalgar is wearing my scarlet ensigns."

Joleen was pleased. "Then I shall certainly support your mare," she said. "It makes a race much more interestin' when one cares about a particular horse."

Ramsey asked about Joleen's family. When she told him she was a Deavors, he said that he had heard a great deal about her family and The Columns, though he had only been in Natchez a few months.

Joleen sipped a second glass of champagne and found that she liked the attention Ramsey lavished on her, liked his harmless flirtations and compliments. She decided he was really quite handsome, and his grey green eyes intrigued her. She considered their time together an innocent thing and decided to let herself enjoy it.

"You were a British naval officer before comin' to Natchez, Mr. Ramsey?" she asked.

"A few years prior to my arrival here, actually, Mrs. Clauson," he said. "After leaving His Majesty's Navy, I became involved in export and import in the Mediterranean."

"What kind of goods did you export and import?" she asked. "And where? My, the Mediterranean seems so far from here and so vast."

As they spoke, a shout went up and the crowd rose. The first race, in which Somerset and Lady Trafalgar were the favorites, was beginning.

Somerset took the lead, took then held the inside rail. Ramsey's mare fell far back in the pack of twenty.

Joleen was disappointed. But when she looked around at Ramsey, he was smiling slightly. Behind them, Hedricks was extolling Somerset's virtues to a grim-faced Juan Delsano.

Lady Trafalgar was running well in spite of her position. As they watched, she began to move up in the pack. Joleen feared she was making her effort too late, but she gained third place on the backturn. In the stretch she took second place, but Somerset still led by three lengths. Then Lady Trafalgar put on a burst of speed, and in a blur of scarlet she caught Somerset and beat him by half a head.

There was a cheer. Men looked at Ramsey and called out congratulations. Ramsey went down to accept the silver cup, then returned to the box.

Joleen enjoyed sharing Ramsey's victory. People crowded around the box. Wagers were settled.

There was a ripple in the crowd. Carlos led Rafaella through.

"We saw the mad nigger!" Carlos said. "I'm sure it's the man. He was foamin' at the mouth. Word is, he attacked a white woman!"

"He disappeared under the grandstand!" Rafaella said.

Everyone glanced down at the floor as though the Negro might burst through at that moment. The men cursed and promised protection. The ladies whispered and grew pale.

But Joleen paid no attention to this. She was completely distracted by the look that passed between Ramsey and Rafaella.

Ramsey's mouth fell open. His eyes did not seem to believe what they saw. Rafaella looked startled. Her lips were drawn taut. Anger tightened her beautiful face into a cold mask, and tiny lines showed under her narrowed eyes.

"Pardon me a moment, Mrs. Clauson," Ramsey said.

Ramsey stepped to Rafaella, his back to the others. No one could hear their conversation, except Joleen.

"Miss Blaine," he said. His words came slowly, as

though he wasn't certain what to say. "Miss Blaine, may I apologize for my abominable behavior on the boat? Only a dire emergency prevented me from meeting you for tea."

"Do I know you, sir?" Rafaella asked. She was once again a young, beautiful, and confident girl.

"Carter Ramsey, Miss Blaine," he said. "We met on the *Yazoo Queen*, when the boat nearly exploded."

"Oh, Mr. Ramsey, of course," she said. "Now I remember. But I don't understand your apology, sir."

"I had asked you to tea," he said. "I trust you received my note of apology, and now I wish to add my personal expression."

"Oh, yes, your invitation," she said. "Now I remember. But, sir, I found it impossible to meet you. I received no note, but then, none was necessary, was it? Nor is any apology due now."

She smiled with the corners of her mouth and dismissed him by turning her attention back to Carlos, who looked at her with helpless longing, as if he had found his great love but already knew his situation was hopeless.

When Ramsey turned back to Joleen, she was curious about the rendezvous he had failed to keep with Rafaella, but refrained from asking. As Ramsey discussed a proposed trip to the Continent to buy racehorses, he glanced at Rafaella. There were a dozen men clustered around her young cousin, Joleen realized. More than her fine dresses and even her beautiful face, Joleen could see that Rafaella had a special magnetic quality. Joleen wasn't certain what it was; perhaps her unshakable self-confidence and the subtle mobility of her delicate face, the soft invitation of her lips, and the fragile shadings of her dark eyes. Rafaella seemed at the same time very young and innocent, yet older and boldly sexual.

Joleen listened as Ramsey explained that he not only owned several padwheelers but that he designed and built his own boats. She tried to seem interested, but she was aware that both she and Ramsey were more involved in Rafaella's conversation with her suitors than with their own.

The last race began as Joleen finished another glass of champagne. Carter Ramsey had left abruptly during the previous race, and Joleen had been absorbed in her own thoughts until the random realignment of the crowd thrust her next to Rafaella. Joleen was surprised at the strength of her emotional reaction to her cousin. She felt weary and short of patience with Rafaella, who was in a petulant mood.

Though Joleen thought the last race would never end, finally it was over—Rafaella's horse had won and her glee was charming if childish—and people had begun to leave the grandstand. The sun was down. The sky was darkening. Joleen noticed how the crowd in the fairgrounds was changing. The planters and lawyers and merchants and other "people of quality" were streaming out. They had come principally for the races. The fairgrounds would be left to working people who would stay late and become even drunker, who would gamble away their earnings. Some of them would even fight among themselves almost as savagely as the chained bears and the pit dogs.

A tide of men, torches, and shouts surged toward Joleen's party.

"The mad nigger was headed this way!" a tall man shouted. He held a torch in one hand, a rifle in the other. "Word is, he done attacked a white woman!"

"Anybody seen the nigger?" another man asked. He carried a pistol and a whiskey jug. "He ain't far 'way. Hidin' 'round here somewhere close."

The men were drunk, and their frenzy quickly spread to the entire crowd. Everyone looked around so frantically that no one saw anything.

But Joleen caught a glimpse of movement behind an empty stall. She tensed, and realized Rafaella had also seen the fleeing shadow.

"Joleen, didn't you see—?" Rafaella started to ask.

Joleen stepped close to Rafaella and spoke softly.

"Yes, I saw that stray dog over there," she said. She looked into Rafaella's eyes. "Don't let your imagination get the better of you, Rafaella."

"But it wasn't . . . are you sure? Well, we ought to tell them, just in case."

"Rafaella, the last thing we want is to get involved with this drunken mob," Joleen said firmly. "Let's just think about gettin' ourselves out of here safely."

Joleen and Rafaella stared at each other. Rafaella's look was suspicious and as cold as the one she had given Carter Ramsey. The confused mob swirled around them, drinking and cursing and searching. Seconds passed, anxious seconds for Joleen. She was certain she and Rafaella had seen the Negro. And a black man accused of attacking a white woman would never be sent back to the madhouse or put on trial. He would be burned alive.

"Now, Joleen, I insist," Rafaella said. "I'm certain that was a man I saw!"

"Be quiet!" Joleen whispered. "We're gettin' out of here!"

She took Rafaella's arm and pulled her forward. At the same time a new crowd of ragged, tough-looking men burst out from under the grandstand. Joleen and Rafaella were separated from the Delsanos and the other members of their party, and then, when she looked around, Rafaella could no longer see Joleen.

Rafaella realized that she was alone and lost in this dangerous mob. A tall, red-faced man lurched against her and she was knocked to the ground.

"How dare you!" she shouted, but he paid no heed, and when she managed to get to her feet, she was surrounded by grinning, leering faces. One man reached out to touch her breasts, and she screamed.

She shoved his hand away. "Help! Help!" she shouted.

"I'll help you, dearie," a fat man promised.

He reached for her arm and she twisted away. Rafaella felt real fear for the first time. Being Rafaella

76

Blaine meant nothing in this crowd. This drunken mob was blood-hungry and ugly.

"Help!" Rafaella screamed again, this time with a high note of panic.

She lurched from another man's grasp and stumbled in a blind panic that somehow took her to the edge of the mob, somewhere near the gate to the fairgrounds. She saw the open door of a carriage pulled up a few feet away. Instinctively she ran for it, scrambled up the step and inside.

Rafaella was fighting for breath when she recognized the man in the carriage. It was Carter Ramsey.

17.

"Mr. Ramsey!" Rafaella exclaimed.

"Miss Blaine!" Ramsey, his long legs stretched out across the carriage, had loosened his tie and his collar and was smoking a cigar. "Well! I am delighted to see you!"

"That crowd!" Rafaella gasped. "What a horrible bunch of ruffians!"

"Whatever were you doing out there alone?"

"I wasn't alone, Mr. Ramsey. I was just separated from my cousin by the crush. Perhaps you would be so kind as to drive me to rejoin her."

Ramsey's driver had maneuvered the carriage clear of the crowd at the gate, and they were already moving slowly down the road to Natchez. Rafaella glanced out the window but she didn't recognize the route. Her head was still reeling from the closeness of her escape, and she was more rattled by this sudden confrontation with Ramsey than she dared to reveal.

"Miss Blaine, I am delighted to see you. I am pleased to be called into service, perhaps by Fate itself, to be your escort for as long as you will permit me that fortunate role."

Rafaella was taking rapid stock of the situation. Perhaps it *was* Fate who had sent her into his carriage. At any rate, the situation intrigued her. It was just the sort of dramatic, unexpected event that she liked. It was like being back in Rome, where men had followed her in their carriages and in the streets, all hoping for a word or a glance of encouragement. She despised Carter Ramsey, but she would not let him know it yet. Just now she intended to play out this scenario to its conclusion. She had wanted an opportunity for revenge and this was it. She had intended to make Ramsey regret that he had insulted her on the *Yazoo Queen*, and now she had the opportunity.

Smiling with her best flirtatious smile, she grabbed at the fan she carried in her beaded reticule and opened it in front of her face.

"Thank Heaven!" she said. "I was quite frightened."

Ramsey was evidently not sure how much she knew about what had happened on the *Yazoo Queen*, but he was anxious to make amends. "I must again apologize, Miss Blaine," he said, "this time on behalf of my tempestuous fellow countrymen. They go wild when aroused. A young lady requires protection in such public places. Please reassure me that you are feeling quite well now."

"Oh, I'm really fine, thank you, sir. But may I trouble you to drive me to the Delsanos?"

"Better yet, Miss Blaine, please let me invite you to take some light refreshment in one of our better hotels. Custom prevents me from inviting you to my own home, but I can only believe that you really forgive me—and my rough countrymen—if you accept my hospitality."

"I couldn't trouble you, Mr. Ramsey," Rafaella protested. She had already decided that she would go. All she needed was a little time with this man. Actually, he looked quite handsome in his grey suit and striped waistcoat. His breeches were cut in the French style and his tie was a decent scarlet foulard. A little time and he would fall in love with her, she was sure. Then, she would do with him whatever she wanted . . .

"Please, Miss Blaine," Ramsey said, "look, here we are at the Mississippi Hotel. I'm sure you would benefit from a rest and some refreshments."

Rafaella smiled behind her fan at his earnestness. "Oh, I don't know," she murmured. "If this were Europe . . . but here . . . I hardly know you . . ."

"But under the circumstances, Miss Blaine, extreme as they were . . . I must insist. It's too late to refuse me, for here we are."

Sighing prettily, Rafaella accepted Ramsey's arm and allowed him to lead her up the steps of the hotel. Ramsey was well known there and immediately made arrangements with the hotel keeper and led her past the main reception room to a doorway at the rear which opened into a small private sitting room.

The room was simply furnished, but tasteful, Rafaella thought, for Natchez. The furniture was oak and included a round table with two chairs, a sofa, and three side chairs padded with green striped velvet, a chaise longue in striped satin of a similar hue, and even a spinet.

Ramsey settled Rafaella on the chaise longue and gave a black waiter an order for oysters and champagne.

"Are you quite comfortable, Miss Blaine?" Ramsey asked.

"Oh, yes, thank you," Rafaella said. She was aware that this interview wasn't going quite the way she wanted. Ramsey was so damn sure of himself, so confident as almost to seem pompous. What she wanted was to see the man on his knees, begging for her attention. Perhaps she had been wrong to allow him to bring her here. Perhaps it had given him the tactical advantage she wanted for herself.

"I can't resist telling you that you are quite the loveliest woman in Natchez," Ramsey said, pacing the room before he stopped at the foot of the chaise longue to speak.

"Why, Mr. Ramsey! We hardly know each other," Rafaella said. "And I expect you just finished telling my cousin Joleen the same thing."

"Not at all. In fact, I longed to ask Mrs. Clauson for details about you, Miss Blaine. I was astounded by my luck at meeting you on the *Yazoo Queen,* and quite devastated to have lost touch with you after that."

The liar, Rafaella thought, but she only smiled. "Indeed, Mr. Ramsey?" she said.

"I had to curb myself strictly, in fact. Only the knowledge that you are so very young compelled me to treat you with the appropriate paternal distance."

"So young?" Rafaella snapped. She couldn't help it. She hated being thought of as a child. "Indeed, Mr. Ramsey, I am young, but I am not unsophisticated. I have traveled . . . And what do you mean, then, by bringing me here today? Just what are your intentions?"

Ramsey was a bit taken aback by Rafaella's bluntness, but he was also amused. Boldly, he bent over Rafaella's reclining form and whispered, "I intend to persuade you . . . to like me . . . at least a little . . ."

Just then the door opened, and the waiter carried in a tray of bottles, glasses, and a platter of oysters embedded in shaved ice. Rafaella's eyes met those of the waiter, and she read curiosity and surprise in them before they blanked into an expression of habitual servility.

"Damn it, man, knock before you enter," Ramsey said angrily.

"So sorry, sir. I did, sir, I did knock," the black man mumbled.

"All right, then. Leave us, please," Ramsey said.

Nothing could ever persuade me to like you, Rafaella thought, watching as Ramsey poured her a glass of champagne and brought it to her. He pulled up one of the side chairs and took a glass for himself. Men are so foolish and vain, she thought. Or at least most men. Of course not my father, but most men . . .

"Delicious," Rafaella judged the champagne.

"Thank God it is now possible to get the best French wines," Ramsey said. "I, too, have traveled, Miss Blaine, and I find it hard to compromise myself to local standards."

"One should never compromise," Rafaella said.

"I quite agree. I, myself, have pledged my energies to living the best possible life, living it as well as I can," Ramsey said.

"Oh, really?" Rafaella said. "But what does a pledge such as that mean in an out-of-the-way place such as Mississippi? How can you even aspire to the best, in this state?" She took a draught of the champagne and immediately felt its stimulating effect in her head.

Ramsey laughed. "I admire your frankness, my dear," he said. "But as you are part of my plan, you must be careful how you malign our fair state."

"I? I am part of some plan? Hardly, Mr. Ramsey!"

"What I mean, Miss Blaine, is that I would judge you, too, to be the finest in your class . . . that class being beautiful and sophisticated young women. And as I am here today, surrounded by the best Natchez has to offer in physical comforts, passing time with the loveliest young woman in town, perhaps in the state, or even in all America, I feel privileged, and furthermore, I feel successful."

Rafaella's head was spinning with the champagne, but it was a pleasant feeling. She felt relaxed and much more amused with Carter Ramsey than she had expected to be. His compliments were a bit convoluted, it was true, but there was no mistaking the admiring, appreciative looks he was giving her as she reclined on the chaise.

"Really, Mr. Ramsey?" she asked, succumbing to a sudden reckless whim. "You feel successful? When you haven't even managed to kiss me?"

"That, too," he said, "is part of my plan."

"Every woman, Mr. Ramsey, is looking for a man who has a master plan . . ." Rafaella started to say, but she was interrupted by the touch of his lips on hers.

They were warm and soft and firm and very masterful. She was surprised at how masterful, and it gave her a tremor of anxiety.

"Delicious," Ramsey said, pulling back before Rafaella could protest. "Delicious and very inviting."

"Mr. Ramsey!" Rafaella gasped, but she was surprised to see that he was occupied with some odd pursuit. He had taken a small silver box from the pocket of his waistcoat, and as she watched, he slid open the lid.

"What is that?" she asked.

"This is also part of the plan," he said. She could see that the box contained nothing but some powder, white as snow and finer than dust. "This, my dear, is also the best thing in its class."

Rafaella felt overlooked and uninitiated. What peculiar American habit was this? She hated being ignored for even a minute. What a strange man this Carter Ramsey was . . . yet he would be like all the others when she was finished with him, she was sure of that.

"Ahhhh . . ." Ramsey sighed. He smiled and his blue eyes seemed brighter.

Rafaella squirmed a bit on the chaise longue and adjusted her long silk skirt. As she moved, she was aware that her full breasts were molded invitingly in the tight bodice of her dress. Why didn't he try to kiss her again? She longed for him to try, so that she could manipulate him.

Ramsey was studying the length of Rafaella's body outlined in the fine silk. "You are astonishingly beautiful . . . Rafaella," he said, "And your name suits you exactly." His hand reached out for her bare arm, slowly, then began to stroke the firm, round flesh.

Rafaella felt a flush of pleasure and a sense of power. The champagne had made her quite light-headed, and she was looking forward to whatever was to come.

"More than anything in the world," Ramsey murmured, bending over to kiss her again, "I would like to make love to you."

"Mr. Ramsey! I can't . . . I never . . . but if your words are sweet enough, I may let you kiss me again."

Sweat beaded Ramsey's forehead, and his hands trembled as he stroked and caressed Rafaella's arms and shoulders. His eyes were fastened on her pale, soft breasts as they spilled over the top of her dress. "My darling beauty," he whispered, "please, please . . ."

Rafaella sighed. She was amused and pleased to see Ramsey begging her, and she began to sense the desire he was feeling. Deliberately, she kicked off her slippers and turned onto her side, still reclining.

"I swear, Mr. Ramsey, you were right. I feel much revived by the champagne." She stretched, taunting him with the fleshy sensuality of her supple body. His hands followed her move, unable to resist sliding along her shoulders to her breasts. As he touched them, he groaned.

"I can make you feel so wonderful," Ramsey promised. His fingers probed under the top of her dress and found her nipples. Rafaella felt her nipples hardening, tingling, but she twisted away.

"Mmmmmmmm . . ." she whispered, "you mustn't . . ."

Ramsey had freed her breasts. They were large and perfectly formed—round and pale with reddish nipples. "Your skin . . . so beautiful," he said softly, burying his face in her breasts. "I must . . . kiss you all over."

Rafaella sighed, writhing against him. He had pulled her dress open to her waist and as he covered her chest and torso with kisses, he opened and slid off his own boots and breeches. She lay nearly naked now, her silk dress draped over her thighs and pelvis in a band.

"Please . . ." Rafaella whispered. "You must stop." She was amazed at her own daring, yet she knew that she was in control. He was becoming frantic and desperate, and she felt absolutely cool. How foolish men were about sex, she thought. All men . . . except, of course, her father . . .

Thinking of her father, she felt a flicker of sensuality. Ramsey looked nothing like her father, but seeing him, and enduring his excited probing fingers, reminded her of the night on the padwheeler when he had snubbed her and when she had watched her father making love to that woman who had called her a child. Rafaella's cheeks grew warm with her sudden anger.

"Lovely . . ." Ramsey murmured. He had hooked his fingers under the waistband of her under-petticoat and panties and was dragging them down. His mouth followed his fingers. "Let me see," he said. "Aaaaah . . . oh, my darling!"

Just a bit farther, Rafaella thought. She'd let him go just a bit farther and then she would leave him. He seemed so desperate, so intense. His lips were sucking, licking, wetting her stomach, her thighs. She wasn't sure what he was trying to do, but it was making him groan, and she could see that his entire body was broken out in sweat.

Through half-shut eyes she looked down at him. He had thrown his shirt off and was worshipping her as if she were an idol on an altar. His skin was flushed, she saw, and his penis was rigid.

"No . . ." she said softly, with surprise. "No . . . surely you wouldn't degrade yourself to do that!"

"I'd do anything for you, my darling," he gasped and then his mouth was fastened on her vagina, his tongue was probing, palpitating her soft flesh.

She felt invaded, and yet she felt herself opening further, felt new dampness. She idly stroked the top of Ramsey's head. His hair was thick and coarse, and his head was bobbing frantically and he was making gurgling sounds.

"Oh, my God!" he gasped. "Darling! Darling! You are a miracle, a goddess!"

Rafaella heard the agony and passion in his voice and felt a deep loathing. She was not aroused, really. Not at all. She opened her eyes and watched him dispassionately. How disgusting, she thought. How pitiful he is. Stretching out her arm, she selected a chocolate from the silver bonbon dish on the small side table. She sucked the chocolate as Ramsey raised his head.

"Don't I . . . can't I . . . arouse you . . . give you pleasure?" he asked.

"You don't excite me at all, sir," she said coldly. "Perhaps you are not manly enough."

Ramsey's eyes widened and his jaw dropped open. Rafaella smiled, and without speaking she pushed his head down until she could feel the hairs of his beard tickling her. After a moment's pause, Ramsey began to lick her again, more vigorously, running his tongue around the entire area, sucking and kissing, burying his nose in her moistness.

Triumphant that she had avenged herself and proved her superiority, Rafaella let herself relax and experience the sensations his mouth was producing between her legs. She felt a new pulsing, felt a tremor of excitement. Her hands fastened on his ears and she squeezed his head between her thighs.

"Mmmmmmmmmm . . ." she said.

Ramsey sucked harder, matching his efforts to the pulsing of her body. All at once, Rafaella forgot where she was, who she was, what was happening. She forgot to think, forgot to care; no longer standing back from sensation, she was forcibly dragged into orgasm, responding despite herself, agonized but absolutely open to his tongue and lips, helpless before their onslaught.

"Oh!" she cried. "Oh . . . No! Yes . . ."

Her thighs threatened to crush his head, and her fingers, entwined in his hair, pulled at it cruelly. She was achieving orgasm for the first time in her life, without being conscious of what the feeling was, yet experiencing it in every bone, every muscle, every drop of blood on fire.

"Oh!" she wailed helplessly. "Oh, Daddy! I love you!"

Ramsey, his ears crushed, hardly heard or heeded, but he felt her tremors subside and lifted his head, panting. "Now, now . . . my darling," he begged. "Let me . . ." Moving over her body, he tried to fit his penis between her legs, but she shoved him away.

"Stop!" she said in a voice that was flat and dead serious. "You are filthy and disgusting to do such a thing! How dare you touch me like that with your mouth!"

"But, Rafaella!"

Moving stiffly, she fastened her dress and stepped into her slippers. He was still on his knees beside the chaise, his face streaming moisture, his eyes blank with unconsummated lust.

"Please," he begged. "Please, I'll do anything for you . . ."

"You misunderstand, Mr. Ramsey, if you think me a woman to be toyed with," Rafaella said. "I never want to see you again. If you ever speak of this . . . of your disgusting attack on me . . . I shall have you called to the field of honor by my father."

Ramsey looked stunned.

"I'm leaving now," Rafaella said. "I need a long, hot bath. And though I trust I'll never see you again . . . I'm sure you will never forget me."

She opened the door quickly and nearly bumped into the black waiter, standing so close to the door that she suspected he must have been watching through the keyhole. Without a glance, she swept past him and went out to the lobby to order a carriage.

"Come here, you idiot!" Ramsey screamed at the black man, now framed in the open doorway. "Bring me a woman at once . . . that mulatto from the gambling salon. And forget what you have seen here this afternoon. I warn you, nigger. If you ever speak of this, I'll have your tongue ripped out."

"Yessir," the man said. "Yessir." And he hurried down the hall.

18.

The party was more elaborate than originally intended, but Lawton felt that both his family and his people needed a celebration.

The long gallery was cleared out and an orchestra from Elijah Bell's Mansion House Hotel sat on a platform at the rear and played for dancing. The gallery's walls were decorated with garlands of bougainvillea and honeysuckle arranged among clusters of brightly colored candles.

On the front lawn, lanterns were strung above the azalea and oleander bushes, and more than a hundred guests mingled amid tables spread with food and drinks, with the twelve massive white columns of the house as a shadow-washed backdrop.

In addition to the local fare—green and cured hams, roasts, pheasant and quail and duck, turkey and chicken and guinea hen, catfish and trout and bream—there were ice-filled bowls of fresh oysters and shrimp sent up from New Orleans, as well as imported smoked fish, pâté, and caviar. Big cut-glass bowls held rich, sweet ice cream flavored with lemon and berries.

Slaves in suits of dark blue and gold—and this was new, at Lucinda's urging, the first time The Columns' slaves had ever been dressed in uniform—kept the guests' glasses filled with port, sherry, cognac, Madeira, whiskey, gin, and punch.

But most of the guests drank mint juleps.

Juleps had always been popular in the county, but new interest in them had been aroused a month earlier when two men nearly fought a duel over the best julep recipe. Alston Nash had insisted that as the final touch a julep should float a pink rose petal. But Jean-Claude Marchand mocked Nash's recipe and contended that any fool knew that tiny strawberries were the only proper way to top off a julep.

Nash actually challenged Marchand to a duel, but their seconds settled the affair and no duel was fought.

There was no argument about the quality of the juleps served at The Columns that October night. Everyone agreed they were superb. Lucinda had sent Ambrose, one of the house Negroes, to learn how to make them from a bartender on the *Mimosa*, which was considered to have the finest drinks on the Mississippi. Ambrose had then trained two other house Negroes. But making each julep was so time consuming that eventually two more slaves had to help.

Four kinds of ice had to be chipped and grated and carefully piled into each tall glass, ice ranging from huge lumps to a snowlike fineness. Then mint leaves of an exact size, with no part of the stem remaining, had to be embedded in the ice. Then came a very fine grained sugar and wisps of fresh lemon.

To this were added cognac, port, and rum, and the mixture was poured back and forth between two glasses several times. The crowning touch was to insert a sprig of mint and rub the rim of the glass with lemon so that the mint's fragrant leaves would brush the drinker's nose while his lips savoured the tang of lemon on the glass.

The slaves could not keep up with the demand for juleps, and two women from the kitchen were drafted to help. A guest who arrived late at The Columns and had his first julep after the drafted help started making them might have said the quality was far below *Mimosa* standards. But by then the guests had drunk too many to notice any deterioration in the quality.

Talk of that near duel over juleps lead to discussion of a man who was a guest at The Columns, a man with a reputation for dueling, Wyman Ridgeway. Ridgeway's slim, handsome elegance, his wit, impudence, and unorthodox views, and his withered hand, along with the tales of his bizarre dueling habits that had drifted upriver from New Orleans, made him a figure of uneasy attention to both men and women.

So far Ridgeway had fought only one duel in Natchez, and in that affair he had been content merely to draw blood from his adversary and leave the man with little more than a flesh wound on his arm. But everyone said it was only a matter of time until Ridgeway called someone out and left him minus an ear, an eye, or part of a hand.

Drinking with a man capable of such behavior and finding him charming, cultured, and witty—Ridgeway had not advocated any of his more audacious ideas at the party—set off contrasting emotions that disturbed the men and intrigued the women.

Rafaella was having a marvelous time. She was wearing an elegant, rich cream-colored silk evening dress that was by far the most fashionable gown at the party. The dress had been made for her in Rome—the style and fabric chosen, as usual, by her father. It was cut low to display her fine throat and bosom, laced tight to a well-fitted bodice, and cinched with a wide sash of deep rose satin.

Her dress had exacted, Rafaella felt, the attention and admiration it warranted. Why, there wasn't another woman in the entire assembly who was wearing the new fitted sleeves, or even the fashionable draped, pleated front. Rafaella knew she was an object of envy and fascination in her new dress. All the women had stared, and already two men had told her they were falling in love. It was almost too easy. And yet . . . it wasn't everything she really wanted. There was a spirit of excitement—and even danger—lacking. Perhaps somehow . . .

Just before midnight, Rafaella was able to maneuver Lawton and Ridgeway behind a trellis of scuppernong grapes that isolated them from the other people.

"You look remarkably pretty in that fine gown," Lawton told her.

"I do agree," Ridgeway said.

"Thank you, sirs," Rafaella said.

She quickly turned the talk to the near duel over

the mint julep recipes. Ridgeway commented that it was a fairly diverting subject for crossing swords but ultimately lacked the imagination to forestall boredom.

"I'm afraid I don't hold much with the practice of duelin', sir, no matter what the cause," Lawton said.

"Why, Lawton, you mean you've never had to defend your honor or the honor of someone else?" Rafaella asked.

"Raffles, when you're managin' a plantation the size of The Columns, you don't have time to take up city customs such as sword fightin'," Lawton said.

"But surely you've never backed down from a challenge," Rafaella said.

"I've never backed down from anything that was important to me," Lawton said. "But there are other ways to settle personal differences. As for the boredom you spoke of, Mr. Ridgeway, I find that my family and my people provide me with all the diversion I need."

"Then I should envy you, Mr. Deavors," Ridgeway said. "But I think you and I . . . we simply have different interests and different values, it would seem."

"But Lawton, would you back down from a duel?" Rafaella asked. "Don't you even know how to use a rapier?"

Rafaella detested cowards, and to think Lawton might be a coward intrigued her. She was already angry with Lawton and hurt and bewildered by his refusal to discuss the Price Deavors estate. She had been provocative and flattering, she had begged and nearly threatened, but he was adamant in his refusal. He treated her like a child.

"I haven't had a rapier in my hand in years, Raffles," Lawton said evenly. "But we were taught fencing in school, and I was about as good as anybody. As for my courage, I don't think that's something a man talks about."

"Pardon me for seeming to scold you, Miss Blaine," Ridgeway said. "But, in all fairness, he is right. That is not a question one may ask a gentleman."

Rafaella was stung by the reprimand and she held Lawton responsible. She glared at him, her cheeks warm, her breath quickening. The recurring thought that neither Lawton nor her own father would tell her why Anson had come down or why the inheritance was being delayed had almost brought her fury to the bursting point. The men's unfair and hateful criticism added to that fury and nearly overcame her last vestige of self-control.

She had so wanted Lawton to love and admire her and be her very special friend. Now on top of rejecting her, he had insulted her. She told herself she would make him pay dearly, just as men had paid dearly in Rome. She calculated her next words. She would not let him know her true feelings. No, she wouldn't let either of the men know how angry she was, nor would she let them correct or ignore her.

Abruptly, she decided to be audacious in her talk, even if it made Ridgeway uncomfortable. She was certain he would rather be uncomfortable than bored.

"Do you remember Plutarch's account of the battle between the armies of Pompey and Julius Caesar?" she asked Lawton.

"No, Raffles, I don't," Lawton said.

"And you, Mr. Ridgeway?" she asked.

"I'm afraid it's been many years since I read any Latin, Miss Blaine," he said.

"Caesar represented the popular faction and Pompey the aristocrats," Rafaella said. "As Caesar led his cavalry into battle—and remember, his troops were common citizens, not aristocratic horsemen—he said, 'When you charge the enemy's cavalry, do not try to kill your adversaries but strike to scar their faces. They're brave men and not afraid to die, but they had rather die than be scarred.' "

Rafaella looked from Lawton to Ridgeway. Neither man spoke for a moment.

Ridgeway nodded slightly. "A curious little item, Miss Blaine," he said.

"I'm afraid it all seems remote from our life here in Adams County, Raffles," Lawton said.

"But Caesar's troops won the battle, and he became the emperor of Rome," she said and smiled.

"Yes, and a few short years later some of those same men mutilated his own body," Ridgeway said. "Did you know, Miss Blaine, that in our own day, young German aristocrats consider it a vital mark of honor and manhood to receive a facial scar while dueling?"

"If you two'll excuse me, I have to get back to my other guests," Lawton said abruptly and left them alone.

Ridgeway's grey eyes had narrowed, and there was something disturbing about his face. Rafaella wondered if her story had been too direct. She had succeeded in interesting him, but had she revealed too much of her own strong curiosity? She wanted to say more, wanted to know about his hand and his disturbing reputation, but she forced herself to wait. She sighed and fingered the ivory softness of her pleated skirt. She had to look down, away from his eyes. The silence between them had gone on too long, but she waited, taking her time. Despite her increasing uneasiness, she felt it was not her place to speak first.

"May I get you something to drink, Miss Blaine?" Ridgeway said finally. "Perhaps a julep. Or does your father allow you to drink them?"

"Of course I can have a julep, Mr. Ridgeway!" she said. "I've already had several and I daresay I can drink as many juleps as any lady present. And more than many of the men!"

Ridgeway smiled, and it was a smile he had not bestowed on her before, one quite like her own, a smile that hovered around the corners of his lips and could have meant anything or nothing at all. When Rafaella saw him smile, she was a bit shaken, and she feared Ridgeway was far less under her control than she had assumed. Now she dared not mention his hand.

"I didn't mean to impugn your ability to drink juleps, Miss Blaine," he said. "Nor to do anything else, for that matter. I'm certain you're quite formidable in any-think you undertake, including the consumption of dazzling quantities of wines and whiskeys."

Rafaella was quite uneasy now. Ridgeway's tone was mocking, his eyes were frightening. She hated him for making her feel uncomfortable, but she told herself she had to stand fast. Rafaella had hoped he would go on to speak of her beauty, but she settled for the ironic compliment.

"Thank you, sir," she said. She felt rather young and vulnerable. She was angry, yet she was . . . excited, puzzled, intrigued, uneasy. She wondered if he would try to kiss her. Of course she would not let him, not this first time alone, but she would welcome such an advance.

"Shall we go and get our juleps?" Ridgeway asked.

"I suppose so," she mumbled. She forced a smile. "Yes, Mr. Ridgeway, I am quite thirsty."

Ridgeway escorted her back to the crowd. They talked of the music and other harmless subjects while their juleps were being mixed. Her cheeks were warm. She hoped they weren't red. Their talk grew less personal as they sipped the juleps. Rafaella realized she was nearly gulping hers.

She wished he would ask her to dance. But it was Theron Sumrall, Lawton's friend, who approached with that request. Ridgeway made no protest. He only bowed and said, "I've enjoyed talking to you and hope to see you again, Miss Blaine."

Rafaella let herself be led across the crowded lawn to the gallery, far from pleased but somewhat relieved to be parted from Ridgeway.

Damn him, anyway, she told herself as she moved gracefully in the familiar step of a waltz. And damn Lawton! And damn this clumsy fool who was telling some story about a 'possum hunt!

She felt too warm. She had sipped her julep too quickly. She shouldn't be dancing so soon after the julep. She caught a glimpse of Lawton. He was talking to Joleen. This did nothing to improve Rafaella's spirits. Her anger at Lawton flared up again. He and his sister were staring at her. Rafaella suspected they were talking about her. Her anger spread to Joleen. She remembered Joleen's strange behavior the day of the race, and she was tempted to let herself think Joleen had deliberately let the Negro escape, that she had pro-abolitionist sentiments.

Theron was telling another dull story. Rafaella smiled automatically and asked herself if this dance would never end.

She couldn't understand these people, these Deavorses. They were so clannish, and all of them seemed to be keeping secrets from her. Even her own father. For the first time in her life, she suspected he was holding something back from her; for the first time she could not get what she wanted from him. She had tried everything, and still he insisted that he was telling her the truth about the inheritance, insisted that Anson's visit concerned only some legal technicalities.

The dance finally ended. As Theron escorted Rafaella out of the house, she saw her father on the lawn. He was talking to that cheap, silly Frannie Deavors. The thought that he might find that stupid woman attractive was almost more than Rafaella could endure.

19.

The other guests had been surprised to see Frannie Deavors at the party. She had always been shunned by Natchez society, even at the height of the power and influence attained by her husband, Lavon Deavors. Not only had Lavon been considered an outcast and a traitor to his class, but Frannie's father was a "nigger doctor," a man of no education who made a fortune by treating sick slaves with a bizarre assortment of remedies that killed more slaves than they cured.

Yet here she was, in a lavishly beribboned and obviously expensive blue satin dress, fluttering about the lawn of The Columns as though being invited to a Deavorses' party were the most ordinary of occurrences. Frannie was there because Lawton had seen her in Natchez a few days earlier. Both he and Lucinda agreed that Frannie should not suffer from her husband's conduct. It was a time for forgiving and healing wounds. And, after all, Frannie was a Deavors, if only by marriage.

So they sent Frannie an invitation. She was delighted to achieve by her husband's death what her marriage to him had never brought her, the one thing she most wanted, wanted even more than all her wealth: to be invited to The Columns and therefore be accepted into Natchez society.

Inevitably, Frannie had felt bitterness toward the Deavorses over the years, more because they snubbed her than because of her husband's vendetta against his family. And by the time of Lavon's death, he and Frannie were so estranged—he had hinted broadly that he intended to divorce her—that she felt little grief. Now she was being flattered and courted on the Deavorses' lawn. It was a great moment for her. It seemed her whole life had been aiming her toward this perfect, soft evening. And what made it even more perfect was the attention of this handsome, charming, and cultured gentleman from the Continent!

Joleen walked out onto the porch and watched Theron escort Rafaella to a table. Joleen was beginning to think of Rafaella as less of a spoiled child and more of a menace. She'd been nagging Lawton like a horsefly with her persistent flirtations and her questions about the Price Deavors estate. Joleen wished Lawton would confide in her. But Lawton refused to discuss the matter.

Joleen greeted friends and neighbors as she walked down the steps. Suddenly Rafaella looked around, and their eyes met for a moment. Then Rafaella looked away. Joleen had been waiting for Rafaella to say something about the incident with the Negro fugitive the day of the race. She knew Rafaella had not forgotten and was surprised she had stayed silent so long. She was certain that Rafaella had been suspicious about her behavior.

The incident had helped to convince her that she must leave Mississippi very soon. Of course she missed Aaron. But aside from that, she could not live in this slave society and stay aloof. She would be forced to act according to her principles, and the next time Rafaella or someone else might realize what she was doing and not stay quiet.

She took another julep, though she had not finished her last one. The party bored her and reminded her of how alienated she was from these friends and this sort of life, a sort of life that was rapidly changing. This party was far more lavish than any her parents had given. She was surprised at Lucinda's dressing up the house workers in fancy serving outfits. Lucinda had also taken additional field slaves, men and women, and she was training them as house servants, so they could be used for the increasingly frequent entertaining.

In addition, she had talked Lawton into bringing Ambrose in from the stables to become Cellus's assistant. Poor Ambrose, she thought, as she watched the former hostler tug at the tight neck of his stiff shirt. He had always been outside, had been Lawton's riding and hunting companion. He loved the out-of-doors, and now he was all dressed up and bowing and serving half-drunk planters and their wives.

Everyone was reading the novels of Sir Walter Scott. The way some people talked about manners and customs and honor and chivalry, one would think they were living in the medieval world of knights and ladies instead of the swamps and forests of America. Joleen reminded herself that she was still a Deavors and a hostess and that it was her duty to circulate among the guests.

She joined a group of women who were clustered around Tyrone Power.

"And have you found our poor theatre adequate for your needs?" a woman was asking.

"Yes, your theatre is quite adequate," Power said. "Though it is odd to find it situated in a graveyard. But what has most impressed me about your charming city is the quality of the horses and the passion for horse racing. In all my travels here in America, I've found nothing to equal it. And I'm told some of your men even visit the Continent each year to purchase the finest racehorses."

Joleen walked away. She stood alone a moment, sipping her julep, then reluctantly moved to another group of women.

"And let me tell you, if the truth be known, that Conway woman has more than a little bit of Greek blood in her," a woman was saying.

"Why, she's so cultured and educated and well-spoken," someone else said. "But . . . oh, it just doesn't seem possible. Greek . . . is that even Christian? Isn't that more like . . . like a Moslem?"

"Well, it's not really white," the first woman said. "And to think I nearly spoke to her in public just last week."

"One can't be too careful."

Joleen left the group before she lost her temper or some fool mentioned Jews—and they all suddenly realized she was present and that her husband, Aaron, was Jewish. They would blush and apologize, and it would be an impossible situation.

She sipped the julep and wandered among the guests. Many people were intoxicated. Talk was loud and inane. She made polite conversation, but there was little connection between her words and her thoughts, because mention of horse racing had reminded her of Carter Ramsey. She had tried not to think of Ramsey. But from time to time her thoughts betrayed her, and before she realized it, she was recalling some part of their afternoon, was remembering the excitement of his horse winning, and was seeing his face once more.

She admitted to herself that Ramsey was not only

handsome but rather intriguing. But what did it matter, really? She would soon leave Mississippi and join Aaron in Ohio, and in all probability she would never see Carter Ramsey again.

Joleen excused herself from a group of guests. She could no longer endure these drunken, pompous, inane people. She wandered aimlessly across the lawn and around the house, where she heard music and laughter from the direction of the quarters.

The sound of a fiddle and a banjo drew Joleen past the vegetable garden and through the quarters to a place where planks had been put down to form a dance floor. A huge crowd of slaves was drinking whiskey and dancing, not only slaves from The Columns but dozens of others who had accompanied their owners to the party.

Joleen stopped in the shadows of a water oak, watching the slaves obviously enjoying themselves. To be allowed this kind of party, and with whiskey, at the height of the harvest was most unusual. And Joleen had heard muted criticism of Lawton's leniency from a few of the guests.

Joleen again recalled her eighteenth birthday, when she had left her own party to come back to the quarters. The slaves' celebration had stopped abruptly when she appeared, and she knew that the same thing would happen now if she—or any white—intruded. So she stood in the shadows and watched the dancing and drinking of slaves who would be roused and sent into the fields at first light. She felt so awkward around slaves now, even the ones she had known all her life. She hated their condition and she wanted them to be free.

She also knew—and this contributed to her feeling of awkwardness—that some of the slaves would not understand her desire to free them, would not leave The Columns if they were given the opportunity. And some of them would soon have that opportunity, because she intended to free the slaves who belonged to her personally, the ones she had been given by her parents when she married Aaron. She dreaded the confrontation with Lawton when she came to the point of insisting on the slaves' freedom. He would be particularly upset about Filch, who was acting as the plantation's senior driver.

Joleen took a last look at the party, and as she was turning to leave, a man walked from the far shadows into the light of the tree-hung lanterns. She had to stare at him a full minute before she could believe what she saw. She knew the man. His name was Tolver, and she had known him in Ohio. He was a free Negro and a leader in the Underground Railroad!

Joleen was deep in the shadows, and the man could not possibly see her. She turned to go, then glanced back over her shoulder. Yes, there was no doubt the man was Tolver. He was passing himself off as a slave. And he would have no purpose in coming to Mississippi and subjecting himself to danger unless he were involved in some secret plot to free slaves. As Joleen crept away, she wondered what Tolver had planned and why she had not been informed of the plot. She also knew that now she certainly had to leave for Ohio as soon as possible.

"Well, if I was clearin' out those swamps, I wouldn't risk my niggers," Theron Sumrall said. "Swamp drainin's the most dangerous work you can put a man to, Lawton."

"Theron's right, Lawton," Juan Delsano said. "You could lose a fortune in niggers."

"Yes, that's my problem," Lawton said. "I'm willin' to take the chance, as far as buyin' all that land and plantin' the new acreage once it's cleared. But I don't want to risk my people."

Sumrall said. "Planter up above Natchez did just that. Hired him a gang of Irish laborers. Paid 'em by the day. That way there's no risk to your property. You lose a good nigger, could cost you a thousand dollars. Lose an Irishman, won't cost you a cent."

"Why don't you think of hirin' some day laborers?"

Lawton nodded. "That's an idea worth considerin'," he said. "How do I go about gettin' in touch with these Irishmen?"

"I was up to Rodney last week," Sumrall said. "And they'd been hired to clear some land up there. You probably know the place, few miles east of Rodney, 'bout half a mile off the Trace. The Hernandez place."

"I know the place," Lawton said. "I'll go up there and talk to the Irishmen. By the way, speakin' of Rodney—"

He was interrupted by the sound of a galloping horse. The men turned and watched a black man riding off the road, right through the groups of startled guests. The rider reined up and dismounted in front of Juan Delsano. Lawton recognized him as Macy, one of the drivers. Macy's head was gashed and bleeding.

"Beggin' your pardon," Macy gasped. "But they big trouble over to the place."

"What kind of trouble, Macy?" Delsano asked. "What in hell happened?"

"Overseer and me, we was checkin' up for the curfew in the quarters," Macy said. "We done come on three of our niggers sneakin' off, with a nigger we don't know. We chased 'em and they was some fightin'. One of our boys, he dead already. Others done been hurt or run off, 'long with the strange nigger. Mr. Bronkley, he cut in the arm . . ."

A posse was quickly formed. Men were given guns from the house. Riders were sent for the sheriff and doctor. Macy was taken back to Aunt Fronie to be treated.

Five minutes later, some forty riders left The Columns, cursing the abolitionists and the Underground Railroad.

20.

Word of the trouble at the Delsano plantation had reached The Columns at half past midnight, and exactly twelve hours later Joleen and Lucinda made uneasy conversation while seated beside each other in the Deavorses' best carriage headed for Natchez. Joleen's journey was in reaction to the previous night's trouble, Lucinda's the result of a summons from Alain LeBeau.

Both women had dressed carefully in figured cotton morning dresses, Joleen's with a black background and a trailing floral print, Lucinda's pale pink sprigged with roses. Each of them had told a lie to justify her trip into town. And each one, unknown to the other, carried a small pistol in her drawstring reticule. Joleen knew how to use the pistol. Lucinda had never put her hand on a gun. Neither had sought company, but since they were leaving at the same time, it was impossible to refuse Lawton's suggestion that they go together.

The carriage bumped over the corduroy road, only minutes from Natchez. Filch, who was driving, glanced over his shoulder at Joleen, who avoided his eyes and stared out at the thick growth dripping from a morning shower. The air was sweet and musky. It would be a hot day.

Both women were lost in thought and fell silent as they passed through the ramshackle quarters on the outskirts of the city. Some free Negroes and poor whites had rough shanties here. Chickens scratched at the roadside; a mule brayed, a pig squealed, and they saw without noticing that they were passing a field full of women picking corn. Joleen was startled when Filch pulled up in front of the Blue Bird Tea Room and Lucinda climbed from the carriage.

"Then we'll pick you up here at four," Joleen said.

"Yes, that will be fine," Lucinda mumbled.

They said good-bye and the carriage drove off.

Lucinda trembled as she rang the bell of Alain LeBeau's house. Oh, why was she here? Her last meeting with LeBeau had been the most devastating, most humiliating encounter of her life, and now she was meeting him again. She panicked in the fraction of a minute that lapsed before a liveried black man answered her ring. She turned to flee, but it was too late.

"Miz Deavors?" the huge black butler inquired. "Mister LeBeau waitin' for you upstairs. He says you to go right on up."

Icy with resignation, Lucinda followed the man to the foot of the stairs and mounted them alone. Halfway up, she heard LeBeau's laugh ring out. She would have no trouble finding him.

The hallway of the house was high ceilinged and dim. It was cool, and she shivered. Upstairs, the corridor branched to the left and to the right. LeBeau's laughter had come from the left. She turned and walked toward an open doorway.

The sight and sound and smell of it hit her all at once. She could smell whiskey and a gamey, nasty smell—like sweat and old bed linen. She heard a woman's squeals and gasping breathing. She heard LeBeau laugh again, and then, when she reached the open doorway of his bedroom, she saw LeBeau, naked, kneeling over the prone body of a young naked Negro girl.

The girl, her ebony flesh glistening with sweat, lay on her stomach, and Lucinda could see that LeBeau had entered her in the same brutal fashion that he had used on her in the forest. The girl's buttocks were heaving, she squirmed and cried out, and whatever she said made LeBeau laugh all the harder.

Lucinda was transfixed. She watched in horror, her own breath catching in her throat, stopping somewhere inside her, forgotten. The girl's flesh was lush, opulent. Her breasts were huge and soft, and he fingered them as he thrust into her again and again and pulled out with evident satisfaction.

"Dear Lord," Lucinda gasped. She felt her stomach

flip, choked on bile. The girl had risen to a half-kneeling position and her breasts swung free. LeBeau's penis was dark red and still swollen to a size that seemed inhuman.

At the sound of her voice, both LeBeau and the black girl looked up at Lucinda. She felt herself flush, she felt feverish, almost faint. She wanted to turn and run, but she was rooted to the spot. She felt her heartbeat throughout her whole body, felt a pulsing in her vital organs that was a mixture of revulsion and excitement.

"Well, well," LeBeau said. The black girl gasped.

"I . . . I . . ." Lucinda stammered. She was overwhelmed by the sight of both of them naked, by the sight and smell of all that sweating flesh. She turned as if to run, but LeBeau stepped over to her and took her wrist in a painful grip. She pulled back, but she could not pull free.

"Get out, Rosey," he said. "I'm finished with you now. I have some business to do with this lady."

"Let me go!" Lucinda begged. The teenage girl grabbed up a crumpled pink dress and ran out of the room.

"Let you go, Lucinda?" Alain asked. "Why, I've been waiting for you. I had to get Rosey, you were so late. But I knew that you wouldn't dare stay away."

"I don't know why I did come," Lucinda said. "But it was wrong. Please let me go, Alain!"

"You'll stay of your own will, Lucinda. Because this is a matter of honor. You owed me a debt and you defaulted on it. Now you must make it good to me, any way I choose."

"You are a filthy, despicable man!"

"And what are you, my dear? A good wife? It was you who set in motion the events that brought us together here today. And do you deny that the last time we were together—you enjoyed it?"

"Yes! I do deny it! I hate you, Alain. And I only came here to warn you!"

He dropped her hand. "My God, I don't believe it!"

he snapped. "What a frigid, unwomanly woman you are. Warn me!" He laughed, and when he stumbled toward the whiskey bottle on a marble-topped side table, Lucinda realized that he was very drunk. She shivered again, terrified, and yet excited to a pitch of utter sensitivity that was unlike ordinary awareness. Every detail of the scene was strong and clear to her: LeBeau's naked body with his penis half-hard and swinging free, the smell in the room, the sense she had of being on the edge of complete degradation.

"Yes, warn you," she said.

He reached out suddenly and caught her arm. She dropped her small purse, and he was on her before she could retrieve it. She struggled but he held her, and then the force of their struggle thrust them against a footstool and they crashed to the floor.

Despite her efforts, LeBeau held her down and began to stroke her breasts through her dress. Lucinda cursed him and beat at him with her fists and bit his arm, but nothing would stop him. He was wheezing and gasping, and the smell of whiskey was putrid on his breath.

Then he turned her over suddenly and began to pull up her dress in the back.

"Oh, no, God . . ." she groaned. Would he do it to her . . . again? The thought crazed her.

His grip loosened. She glanced around frantically. He was fumbling at her clothes. She froze for a moment, and he reached down with both hands. Then she scrambled away, crawling awkwardly, desperately across the floor.

Lucinda reached her reticule and tore it open. LeBeau was up on his knees, coming after her. She scrambled to her feet and pulled out the pistol.

He had gotten to his feet when he saw the pistol. His face went white. His mouth fell open.

"Put that damn thing down, you little bitch!" he cried. "What in hell's wrong with you?"

"Don't move!" she said. Her hand began to tremble. A terrible look came over Alain's face, a gruesome scowl.

"When I take that gun away, you'll pay for this, Lucinda," he said.

He sprang for the gun. But she had anticipated his move and she stepped aside. She almost stopped, but as he turned again to seize her, his twisted mouth and hateful face panicked her.

She lowered the gun and pulled the trigger.

The report made her gasp. She trembled and her knees buckled. She had to lean against the wall for support.

Alain stood against a chair, looking in disbelief at his right thigh, where blood seeped through a hole in the skin of his leg. The bullet had gone through the fleshy part of his thigh. He touched the bloody spot and groaned. His face was ashen. When he tried to speak, his mouth formed words, but the only sounds were guttural sounds of fear and pain.

"I didn't . . ." Lucinda gasped. "I . . . I only wanted to show you the gun, to warn you to leave me alone. But you . . you attacked me . . . I couldn't stand to feel that . . . way again."

"My God!" he said. "You nearly . . . you could have killed me! A doctor . . . get a doctor . . ."

"I'll have one sent," she said. She started for the door.

"Don't leave me," he groaned. "Dammit, don't leave me. If you do, so help me . . ."

Lucinda turned with her hand on the door. Her face was white and grim. She still held the pistol. "If you ever bother me again, if you fail to leave Natchez at once, Alain, as God is my witness, I'll shoot you . . . enough higher . . . so that you'll never be able to bother another woman!"

She left the room, left him calling out to her, and she trailed her hand along the wall for support as she hurried down the hall on her way out.

21.

Joleen waited impatiently for the banker to complete his paperwork and give her the money. She caught herself glancing nervously around the bank. She was out of practice at this kind of intrigue.

"And here we are, Mrs. Clauson," the banker finally said. He counted out two hundred dollars.

Joleen thanked him and left the bank. Filch was waiting in the carriage. He drove off slowly and was silent for the first block. Joleen suspected his silence would not last long. She was right.

"Mist' Aaron, he done made you promise not to get 'volved in none of this abolitionist business with him not here, Miss Joleen," Filch said. "Here you nearly ready to go upriver yourself and takin' this kind of chance . . ."

"I'm only goin' to give them some money, Filch," she said.

"Never could talk sense to you," Filch muttered. The big man hunched over the reins and Joleen heard him mumbling to himself.

She settled back into the seat and tried to stop worrying. She was hopelessly caught up in the mood of fear and hatred that had swept the county with last night's incident. There was talk of nothing else. Angry businessmen stood on street corners and talked of the hated abolitionists stirring up more trouble. Other men, not so well dressed, drank in the taverns and cursed "the goddam niggers and nigger lovers." They were hungry for the chance to vent their reawakened fear and hatred of slaves. Many of these men rode the streets of Natchez, as well as the roads and trails of the county, as members of slave patrols who sought fugitive slaves and abolitionists.

As grim-faced horsemen galloped back and forth past her carriage, Joleen knew that it was at times like this that white men went berserk and many Negroes were lynched. It was not unusual for slaves to run away. At any given time there might be dozens of fugitives hiding in the forests and swamps. Most of them would be caught routinely and returned to their masters. But when a white man was hurt and there was evidence of Yankee involvement, it was another matter.

If a slave patrol caught the fugitive slaves, it was difficult to say what would happen. Although they were Juan Delsano's property, they might be killed on the spot. If they were returned to him or taken to the sheriff, they would be severely punished perhaps hanged.

And what if Joleen herself were caught? She could imagine what a drunken slave patrol might do before turning her over to the law. In Ohio she had heard the story of a young woman who was captured in the Alabama forests with a fugitive slave who had shot a white man. The drunken men had raped her again and again, in the vilest ways, and the woman had ended up in a madhouse.

Joleen and Filch had left the city limits far behind. For some miles outside of town, new land was being cleared and new houses and taverns and inns were being built. But here, the Natchez Trace was nearly devoured by the choking growth that grabbed at the sides of the carriage and formed, with leaf-tangled limbs and grey moss, a dense canopy above the road.

Shadows were deep, despite the hot sun, and insects chirped relentlessly from the trees and undergrowth. A feeling of something secret and ominous exuded from the wilderness as surely as the smell of putrid water and the damp heat. The Trace had first been used by the Indians and later by the Spanish conquistadors. It had been the main trail south and west to Texas and Mexico. Settlers traveled it, coffles of slaves were driven over it. Robbers and rustlers had lurked in the shadows. Hundreds of men, red, black, and white, had died hideous deaths on this road.

The Trace was open territory for slave rustlers and bandits, such as the legendary John Murrell, the so-called Land Pirate, and even more unsavory men such as Harpe and Mason, who robbed and killed travelers and disposed of the bodies by filling their bellies with stones and sinking them in streams.

Thoughts of these stories and others she had heard all her life tightened Joleen's nerves as Filch drove on. Then he rounded a slow curve in the Trace, and she gasped at the most awful sight she had seen in her life.

Mounted on a pole at the side of the road was the mutilated corpse of Billy, a black man she had seen for years working at the Delsanos' plantation. Billy had been hacked to pieces; his hands and feet were severed from his body and nailed to the bottom of the pole. His head, still dripping with blood, was mounted on the top of the pole, and when Joleen saw his mouth set in a hideous grin and his eyes open as if they could still see, she could not hold back a scream.

Flies buzzed around the body, but it was evident from the color of the blood that it was fresh. Joleen gagged and fought a wave of nausea. She felt new, crippling fear, for herself and also for Filch. Was she crazy to be undertaking this dangerous trip?

With tears in her eyes, she looked away from Billy, just in time to see a long cottonmouth moccasin trying to crawl out of range of the carriage wheels. The left front wheel sliced the snake in two with a squishing sound that made the wheel skid for a few yards.

Thank God they only had a few more miles to travel, for it looked more and more as if Filch had been right. Joleen dabbed at her forehead with a lace handkerchief. So far Tolver and his friends had not managed things very well, to say the least. They had been discovered at what should have been a relatively simple act, helping slaves to slip away at night. They had left one dead Negro and a badly wounded white man, and as a result the county was up in arms.

Tolver had been reckless to drive out to The Columns

this morning and ask for her help. True enough, since he was posing as Frannie Deavors's slave, he could move about the county somewhat, and he had set up a logical excuse for calling at the plantation, saying he was picking up something Frannie had left. Joleen had covered that lie easily enough and had managed to speak to Tolver privately.

Tolver had told her that the steamboat captain who had originally agreed to take the fugitives upriver now refused. He was frightened because of the violence and increased chance of discovery. Their only hope was to bribe a captain they knew in Rodney. But the man demanded two hundred dollars, and they had to pay him in advance.

Joleen had decided that there was nothing to do but go into Natchez for the money and to take it to the fugitives herself.

There was the clatter of hooves behind the carriage. Joleen snapped her head to look. Her temples throbbed. She sucked in her breath. Six riders were closing in on the carriage.

She forced herself to look straight ahead. After all, she was a Deavors, she had done nothing yet, and even if they stopped her, even if they were suspicious that she was traveling alone, they could prove nothing.

The riders were slowing up as they approached the carriage. Her heart pounded. The leader was now beside the carriage. Joleen's head was high, her back ramrod stiff. She looked around and nodded hello.

The man was roughly dressed in a green coat with high leather leggings, cavalry boots, and heavy spurs. He looked at Joleen with surprise, then nodded back. He seemed about to speak but motioned with his hand and the patrol galloped on and disappeared around a curve. Joleen sighed. Filch glanced around, but he said nothing.

She wondered what Filch was thinking. He would be punished severely if he were caught with her on one of her missions. Despite his age and high status with the family, he would surely be tortured and killed, perhaps as painfully as had Billy.

Should they turn back? Joleen wondered, but she could not dwell on the thought any longer; it was too late. Another slave patrol was riding up. These men carried rifles and whiskey jugs. They slowed a moment, as Joleen's heart stopped, then they, too, nodded and stared, then galloped on.

Joleen sighed with relief, but a minute after they disappeared she heard a shot in the distance. She sat up and strained forward, but she saw nothing and heard only the clop-clop of her own horses.

Besides, they were nearing the place where they were to meet the fugitives. The shot could well have come from there.

The burned-out shell of the tavern lay in shadows to the right of the road. Filch halted the horses. He and Joleen looked around for any sign of the slave patrol. They saw nothing suspicious, only the charred building and the wild vines and bushes that were devouring it.

"Drive around the building, Filch," Joleen said. "They're supposed to be back down a little trail about five hundred yards—"

She bit off the sentence. She heard horses coming up on the road.

"Quick, get out of sight!" she said.

Filch drove around the building as the horses drew nearer. Loblolly limbs and greedy Virginia creepers slapped at the carriage, and a laurel branch stung Joleen's neck. She felt they were well enough concealed from the road now, particularly with the added cover of the heavy shadows. Her heart thumped.

There were five of them, and they slowed their pace as they reached the building. They stopped. They were staring in the direction of the carriage. Surely they had seen it.

Then one of the men took out a jug. He drank and

passed it around. Joleen froze. They had only stopped to take a drink. The last man drank, wiped his mouth with the back of his hand, and returned the jug. The men rode off.

Joleen waited several minutes, then told Filch to drive ahead. After two hundred yards they had to abandon the carriage because the trail was too narrow and the growth too thick. Already, Joleen was cut and bruised by thorns, vines, and limbs. She was bathed in perspiration, bitten by mosquitoes. A woodpecker tapped on a nearby tree. Every new sound from the deepening shadows made her more tense. She kept her hand inside her purse, curled around the pistol.

Suddenly she heard a new sound and pulled out the pistol as she jerked around. A black man loomed behind her. She nearly screamed.

"Lordy! Don't shoot *me*, Miss!" the man gasped.

Other men came from the shadows. One of them was white. He introduced himself as Jackson Gaddis. He introduced the black men. There was hurried talk. Joleen gave Gaddis the money. She warned him that the Trace was full of patrols.

"Yes, we know," Gaddis said. "We'll wait till night before we head for Rodney."

He thanked her profusely for the money and for the chances she had taken.

"We better get goin' Miss Joleen," Filch said.

"Yes, we . . ."

But then another black man came running up. "Patrol turnin' off the Trace at the buildin'," he whispered.

"We're lost," Gaddis mumbled. "We got two wounded men back there that can't run away."

"No, wait," Joleen said. "There must be . . . yes, if they only find the two of us, two white people . . ."

"But what excuse . . . ?"

"We won't tell them anything," Joleen said. "We'll let them find us . . . in a compromising situation. The rest of you, run hide. Filch, you go over there and sit behind that canebrake with your back to us."

No one moved. Gaddis shook his head. He looked at the Negroes.

"I don't know if . . ."

Then they heard the horses.

"This way, Luke," someone called. "Limbs broken . . . somebody's passed this way recently . . ."

"There's a carriage!" someone else called. "See, I told you I seen a carriage pull off the road. Keep your guns handy, boys!"

The Negroes fled back into the undergrowth. Filch dove into the canebrake. Joleen and Gaddis stared at each other.

He was a young man, she realized. Not much older than she was. His hair was a sandy color and he had a blonde moustache. She could not make out the color of his eyes.

"Hey, I see somebody . . ." a man called.

"Well, come on, kiss me and . . ." Joleen whispered. "Dammit, do you want to get us all killed?"

She put her arms around his neck and kissed his lips. He embraced her. There was a steady rustling behind them. The patrol was only a few yards away, she calculated. But they were moving in fast. She told herself that if the patrol were to be totally diverted from its mission, she and Gaddis would have to do more than merely kiss.

"Let's lie down slowly," she whispered. "We must be . . . seem more intimate . . ." Frantically, she opened her dress and pulled it off until it exposed her bosom and arms.

They sank to the damp ground, holding a kiss. There was no sound at all now from the patrol. Gaddis slid his hand down and caressed her breasts. She wrapped her legs around him and squeezed. She pulled away from his lips and made groaning sounds and he imitated her.

Twigs stabbed Joleen's bare back and she squirmed. She was startled at how quickly she was becoming aroused—and by the touch of a stranger! His body was hard and heavy against hers, she could feel his penis distinctly, and when he fondled her nipples she did not fake the cry of pleasure that came from deep inside. It had been so long—weeks, months—since she had been sexually aroused.

She closed her eyes, aware that they were being watched and yet lost in feeling, swept away by the honest physical response of her healthy, hungry body. Gaddis's hands were strong and firm. He slid them up her legs, pushing aside the soft stuff of her dress and opening her legs. Joleen moaned. She was quivering all over and she felt herself break out in a sweat. Involuntarily, she opened her legs wider and her fingers groped at Gaddis's trousers.

My God, she thought, in one more second . . .

With enormous effort, she sat up, twisting from under Gaddis's body. She looked around. Five men with rifles and jugs stood several yards away, staring at them with open mouths.

Joleen jumped to her feet. She held one hand over her breasts and brushed at her dress with the other.

"How dare you!" she shouted. "What in . . . Get out of here! Leave us alone! I'll have the law on you!"

Gaddis got up quickly. He looked stunned. "Yes, get the hell away and leave us alone or you'll answer for this . . ."

One of the men laughed. "Well, now, actual fact is that we are the law," he said. "Duly sworn patrol out huntin' down abolitionists and nigger fugitives. Seen the carriage goin' off the road. Had to follow up on our duty . . ."

"Well, obviously we're neither abolitionists nor niggers," Joleen said. "We have nothin' to do with anyone like that!"

"Well, now, ma'am, it's pretty obvious what you two are involved in," another man said.

The other men laughed and the jug was passed around.

"Will you please go away!" Joleen said.

"Yes'm, all right," the leader said. "But if I was you two, I'd find me some safer place'n this to . . . get together . . ."

The men laughed again and took another swallow. Then they turned and disappeared.

Ten minutes later Filch and Joleen were headed back to Natchez. She could barely quiet her frantic body. Never had she been more sexually stimulated.

She longed to be in Aaron's arms. She had missed him in so many ways, and now she desperately needed to make love to him. The admission calmed her mind, and she knew that her body would grow quieter during the long ride to The Columns. What she could not accept was the fact that all the symptoms of her fear and anxiety had fused into her sudden sexual arousement, for the presence of danger itself had been as arousing as a lover's kiss or the touch of a hand on her breasts.

22.

Ridgeway left his carriage to walk from the Parker House Hotel to the mulatto ballroom on a crisp October evening. He planned to make an arrangement with a woman in the ballroom, and he hoped to find one that interested him enough to take her as his mistress.

He walked slowly, without feeling or energy, his boredom approaching proportions that he knew would trigger violence if he did not find some way to divert it. His walk took him under huge oaks laced with grey moss, past stucco houses with iron balconies set on vast, well-clipped lawns full of palmetto and broad-leafed dagger plants, as Spanish as the town's heritage.

In truth, Natchez had a Mediterranean flavor, he realized as he passed into the business section. It was not only the slow, almost indolent pace of both whites and slaves, the climate, and the lush foliage, but also the thronged feeling of the market quarter, the way small merchants, following Creole custom, displayed their wares in open-air stalls.

Still, it was dull. And provincial.

An unexpectedly good glass of port at the bar of the mulatto dance hall reminded Ridgeway, as he had so often remarked, that only in the small details of life was there any importance.

He was also pleased with the beauty and elegance of the tall, copper-colored women dancing or sitting regally on burnt orange velvet sofas and chairs around the room. The women were dressed stylishly in elaborate evening costumes that displayed not only their bodies but tokens of affection their wealthy patrons had given them. He saw one woman in a silver-trimmed gown, the hem of her full petticoats tipped with silver filigree, her shawl ending in a tassled silver fringe. Her shoes were embroidered with silver roses and she showed stockings spun with silver thread.

Another pretty woman wore white satin, as pure and romantic as a wedding dress. Most of the women wore light shawls, draped to display their dusky satin skin. A few wore the new short sleeves, and many wore their dark hair high and twisted with jewels and ropes of silver and pearls.

One girl in her late teens caught Ridgeway's eyes. Her skin was the lightest in the room. She danced gracefully and wore a bright red silk dress. It was full-sleeved and trimmed with fresh flowers that accentuated her youthful freshness. In every detail of her being, from her dark, silky hair and jet black eyes to her slim, full-breasted body, the girl met his standard of womanly perfection.

When the dance ended, the girl returned to her mother's side. Ridgeway decided to walk over and let the girl's mother start a conversation with him. Ridgeway found this custom quaint and amusing, but he knew that in both New Orleans and Natchez ballrooms the ritual was rigidly observed. Well-bred mulatto girls never left home without a female escort, either their mother or some other relative. And it was the mother or the relative who initiated the talk, who did the bargaining, and who agreed to the terms. Typically, the girl received a small monthly allowance and gifts from her patron, and in return he had exclusive rights to her and to her house, where she was always ready to receive him with coffee, wine, or whiskey—and herself.

And the girl always remained faithful to her patron, so long as his commitment remained in effect. It was an odd twist of the social code that these "women of color" were considered quite honorable, even virtuous, so long as they were faithful. If a girl violated this code, however, even once, she would immediately be barred from the ballroom and classed as a common prostitute.

Ridgeway approached the girl's mother and questioned her.

"Yes, sir, Mr. Ridgeway, Eugenie has just turned seventeen," the woman told him. "Now, please, sir, may I entreat you to tell us about your exploits with the rapier?"

"Oh, please do!" Eugenie squealed. The outburst brought a look of reproach from her mother, but it was too late. Her squeaky, high-pitched voice broke the illusion of her perfection.

Ridgeway excused himself almost immediately and left the ballroom. After all, she would not do, and he was surprised at himself, for he had suddenly realized that Eugenie had attracted him because of her resemblance to Rafaella Blaine.

A bit later, Ridgeway sipped a somewhat less decent port and watched two giants, stripped to the waist, slice at each other with broadswords. He was sitting in the dueling salon of Pepe Bordeaux, the most popular of the dueling masters who had drifted upriver from New Orleans to open salons and dueling schools in Natchez. As he drank, Ridgeway rubbed a finger along the thin cut on his wrist, a cut he had suffered when boredom led to carelessness during his recent half-hour match with Bordeaux.

The two men with broadswords had been dueling too long. Neither had the strength left to inflict much damage on the other, but both men had deep gashes on their flanks and both had lost considerable amounts of blood.

They were fighting to settle a bitter argument over the best steel to use in a blade. Finally, the men's seconds conferred, and by mutual consent the duel ended. Ridgeway knew both men to be stupid, foul tempered, and arrogant. In a few days they would fight again and one of them would be dismembered.

Ridgeway drained his glass. He was wasting his time. These establishments were jaded, hopeless places where dandies and spoiled and wealthy planters' sons came to be taught dueling by an odd assortment of foreign soldiers of fortune. They were men who lived by blood and whiskey and sex and who were shunned outside their circles and their schools, men whose twisted pride and brute arrogance led them to fight duels with one another over the pettiest insults. Several dozen of these men now taught in Natchez.

But Pepe Bordeaux was an exception, Ridgeway realized. He was not only a fine fencing master but he was so popular and respected that, though he was a mulatto and no gentleman would meet him on the field of honor or accept him socially, it was considered a privilege to cross swords with Bordeaux.

Bordeaux joined Ridgeway.

"More port, Mister Ridgeway?" he asked.

"No, I must leave," Ridgeway said. He stood up.

"And your wound? Are you certain you don't want my surgeon to treat it?"

"Thank you, Pepe, but the wound is clean and the bleeding has stopped," Ridgeway said.

Bordeaux bowed from the waist. "Then I look forward to your next visit."

23.

Natchez was not a large city, and when Ridgeway left Pepe Bordeaux's, he encountered nearly everyone he knew in an hour's stroll. Not that he wanted to see any of them, except perhaps Rafaella Blaine. He found that he was very strongly attracted to the dark-haired girl—surprisingly strongly, considering how briefly he had known her.

Rafaella seemed to him physically perfect, yet she was absurdly young and absurdly proud. He knew women well enough to judge that she was arrogant and mocking, reckless and teasing, devious and manipulative. Some of this he attributed to her youth and her motherless upbringing. Some of her boldness was naivete, youth, and insecurity. After all, she, too, had just been transplanted into this strange frontier town.

He was both intrigued and wary. Beyond her own beauty and her contradictory nature, he was aware that she reminded him strongly, even painfully, of a woman he thought he had forgotten. Dammit! He *had* forgotten her, and vowed never again to lose his control in a matter of the heart. He would only take what he needed from women such as Eugenie, would have nothing to do with the likes of Rafaella Blaine, unless . . . unless it turned out that he could have her on his own terms. For she was damnably pretty and spirited. The thought of her did not bore him, and that was a lot.

Enough, he told himself, resolving to amuse himself. He entered a tavern near the courthouse, crowded with local men in tight-fitting green and brown waistcoats and high, muddy leather boots. They were drinking whiskey. Ridgeway ordered a brandy, but it brought him no relief from the tedium of his surroundings and his drinking companions. They were simple country men; still, they were no more tedious than Virginia aristocrats, or Baltimore merchants, or even congressmen. In fact, the two fat, quarrelsome men at the next table reminded him of the time he had fallen asleep during a crucial but hopelessly boring and futile session of the Congress.

It had been in his first term, when he still made some effort to conceal his contempt and to conduct himself as though he believed their political poppycock had any significance, when he still tried to show interest in the preenings and long-winded cacklings of the shallow and inane men who ran the country.

They all played the game very well. All but Ridgeway. Deliberately, he had alienated his congressional colleagues and ignored his electorate. Not that it mattered. He was protected by an election system that favored men of wealth, breeding, and property.

He ordered another brandy, recalling his encounter with Alain LeBeau just outside the courthouse tavern. LeBeau had been rushing toward the river with his luggage and his slaves in tow, and he had looked frantic.

"I can't stop to talk, Wyman," LeBeau had muttered. He was limping and admitted to a slight thigh wound. "I'm off to New Orleans, then probably the Continent . . . urgent business . . . I'll be in touch . . ."

And off he had limped, glancing over his shoulder. Ridgeway had seen little of LeBeau lately, and he was glad to be rid of the man. LeBeau had grown too familiar—and far worse, too boring—to be of any further use. Ridgeway sipped his brandy and wondered what LeBeau's flight had to do with his little affair with Lucinda Deavors. LeBeau's conduct with Lucinda Deavors had surprised him, when LeBeau bragged of it. It wasn't quite gentlemanly to humiliate a well-bred woman. To seduce her, no matter if she were married; to become her lover, yes. But to humiliate her was bad form. And furthermore, in the case of an intelligent, sensitive woman like Lucinda Deavors, it was to invite revenge. Lucinda seemed shy and delicate, but Ridgeway sensed depth and strength behind her pale fragility.

Perhaps that was it. Perhaps Lucinda had involved

LeBeau in a duel with her husband. But he had heard nothing of it. A duel involving a Deavors would be the talk of Natchez.

How, then, had LeBeau been wounded?

Ridgeway had a sudden delicious thought: was it possible that Lucinda herself had wounded LeBeau? Would she have dared? Could she have armed herself and defended her own honor? Had she frightened him so much that he ran for his life?

Ridgeway savored the amusing notion, along with another brandy. He was enjoying his mellow high when he glanced out the window and saw Roger Blaine and Frannie Deavors drive past in a carriage. Blaine's wooing of Frannie was the biggest scandal of the week, replacing speculation about the New York lawyer who had visited The Columns. How provincial these people were! Any visitor from out of town excited their curiosity. Yankees were suspect. Roger Blaine and his daughter were as exotic as Chinese peacocks. Ridgeway had to laugh.

"What's so funny, sir?" demanded a portly drunk seated near him.

"That happens to be none of your business," Ridgeway said and stalked out.

Ridgeway's restlessness and irritation increased as he stepped out of the way of a ramshackle farm wagon careening down the muddy street outside the tavern. If it weren't for Pepe Bordeaux . . . and the possibility of Rafaella Blaine, he would leave Natchez at once, he vowed. The place was almost insufferable.

He rounded a corner of Seville Street and confronted the very woman he had on his mind. Rafaella was walking with Lawton Deavors, swinging a red silk parasol and dressed very fashionably in a bright green silk dress with a filmy white tucker at the neckline. She looked extremely pretty and was chattering away to Lawton so vivaciously that Ridgeway decided he had a rival. Rafaella clung to Lawton's arm, he saw, and

Lawton stared at her as if he had never seen a woman before.

"How very splendid it was! Why, even Principessa Calderini . . ." Her voice was high and excited, and her neck and bosom, covered by the thinnest of lacy fabric, were flushed.

Ridgeway looked his fill. He found her quite lovely and provocative.

Then they saw him. Rafaella turned and smiled on the corners of her lips and tilted her head slightly to the right. Lawton turned also. His cheeks were red.

"Why, Mr. Ridgeway!" Rafaella said. "How pleasant to see you again."

"Miss Blaine, Mr. Deavors," Ridgeway said. He shook hands with Lawton.

"Your wrist, sir!" Rafaella said. "What happened to your wrist?"

"The result of carelessness on my part," Ridgeway said. "I was crossing blades with a fencing master in a friendly duel, but I let my mind wander."

"I trust the wound isn't serious," Lawton said. "I've been told more men are bled and killed in those dueling salons than on the field."

"My wound is quite minor," Ridgeway said. "But you're quite right, sir."

"I'm most curious about those salons," Rafaella said. "Why, that friend of Lawton's, Theron Sumrall, he told us he's actually studying fencing with some nigger . . . Pepe something."

"Pepe Bordeaux, Miss Blaine," Ridgeway said. "But the man's mulatto. In fact, by coincidence, it was he who gave me this wound."

"But . . . if he's mulatto . . ." Rafaella said. "I don't understand, sir. Why would any gentleman go to the salon of a man with colored blood? Surely you wouldn't meet him on the field of honor?"

"Of course, Miss Blaine, no white man would meet Pepe on the field of honor," Ridgeway said. "But despite his antecedents, he has the bearings of a gentleman, and he happens to be the finest fencing master in the city."

"If you'll excuse us, Mr. Ridgeway, we must be gettin' along," Lawton said.

"Oh, Lawton, that's not being polite to Mr. Ridgeway," Rafaella said. "Surely we can take a few more minutes . . ."

"I'm afraid not, Raffles," Lawton said. "My wife and sister are waitin' for us at the docks, Mr. Ridgeway. We must return to The Columns before nightfall."

"Please convey to your sister and wife my best wishes," Ridgeway said.

Ridgeway saw Rafaella glare at Lawton as they walked away. He was amused. Obviously she was a young lady who was accustomed to having her way. She had been spoiled by her father and was utterly willful. What would she be like when she had a husband instead of an indulgent father?

The thought excited and disturbed him. He pivoted and headed back to the mulatto ballroom. If he were going to court Rafaella, then he would definitely have to set up some girl such as Eugenie.

24.

Roger Blaine jumped his horse over the last hedge and trotted the horse up to the wooden fence where Frannie Deavors was waiting.

"I'll swear, Roger, I've never seen anybody could ride a horse like you can," Frannie said. "But, you know, I feel so . . . peculiar. Callin' you by your Christian name and here we've only been friends for less than two weeks."

"Now, Frannie, we agreed that this private intimacy would be our secret," Blaine said. The woman was so unsophisticated, so untutored . . . so naive.

"I got to confess, Roger, that I really like havin' secrets with you," Frannie said.

"I'll tell you something that isn't a secret, Frannie," he said. "You're quite beautiful with the sunlight shining on your brown hair. Yes, it brings out the little points of brown in your green eyes."

Frannie blushed and tilted her head up. Blaine knew she expected a kiss. It wasn't the first time she had looked up toward him in such a way. And he knew her reputation with men, had heard talk in Natchez. He also found her physically attractive. If all else about her was a disaster, at least there was this blessing.

But he was determined to court her in his own style, a kind of courtship Frannie had obviously never known. He kissed her lips softly and pulled away as she opened her mouth.

"Please forgive my boldness, but I couldn't resist the urge to kiss you," Blaine said.

"I . . . I forgive you, Roger," she said. Her cheeks were flushed deep red and her breathing was heavy.

"I've just been riding the bounds of your plantation," Blaine said.

"What . . . oh, the plantation." Again she tilted her head up and opened her mouth.

"I saw more of it today than I had before," Blaine said. "You must be very proud of your ability to manage such a large estate."

"Oh, but I can hardly manage it at all, Roger," she said. "There's a fortune to be made in cotton this year, and we're way behind in the pickin' and all. I just can't seem to keep a decent overseer. And I'll swear, I got the laziest bunch of niggers in Mississippi. I just wasn't raised to look after a place this size, Roger. My folks, they sent me to learn dancin' and singin' and all those cultured things, not about things that a man ought to take care of."

"Poor, dear little Frannie," Blaine forced himself to say. He put his arm around her shoulder and stroked her hair. She began to purr deep in her throat.

They walked slowly toward the house, a slightly larger replica of The Columns. On the south lawn Blaine could see Frannie's small son, Lige, with his nurse. The boy was crippled and stumbled about on the grass, his bad leg visibly thinner than the other.

"Poor Lige," Frannie murmured, following Blaine's glance. "Poor fatherless child."

Blaine knew exactly whom Frannie pitied, and what she wanted. Her ill-concealed appetite was enough to terrify a tired man. He frowned.

Frannie was known to be the wealthiest woman in Adams County. She owned this large plantation and several smaller ones, as well as having large interests in banks and other commercial investments. In addition, Blaine had heard that she had been involved in the illegal but still flourishing slave trade. Blaine knew she had turned down at least a dozen marriage proposals since her husband's death, although all of the men were quite respectable middle-class merchants or lawyers.

And she didn't turn them down because she was observing a period of mourning. Frannie was determined to use her vast wealth to win a husband who could give her a place in Natchez society. Social acceptance was her overriding goal. She was bound to marry a man who could give her social status. From what Blaine had heard and what Frannie had said, she had married Lavon Deavors for precisely that reason, although it hadn't turned out quite as she expected. Her father, Slidell Runnels, who had made a small fortune doctoring sick slaves, was a man of no education or breeding.

These "slave doctors" were common in Mississippi. They believed that Negro anatomy was different from that of white men, and they left a wake of suffering and death among the slaves they treated. Runnels and his family had led a comfortable life, and Frannie had been sent to study "cultured things," though Blaine knew they had been at the very bottom of the social ladder.

And then one Christmas, at a party, Frannie had

met Lavon Deavors. He had been disowned by his family. He was penniless and reduced to working with an unsavory man named Purvis Swan, who owned "nigger dogs" to track down runaway slaves. But Lavon was still a Deavors. Surely in a short time his family would take him back . . .

Every girl at the party threw herself at Lavon. But Slidell Runnels offered a sizable dowry for his daughter Frannie. Lavon had married Frannie, and with her dowry he and Swan became slave traders. They were as successful as they were unscrupulous. They grew rich, then richer. Lavon became powerful and feared throughout Adams County.

But Frannie had failed to enter Natchez society through Lavon. Despite his wealth and influence, the Deavorses and their planter friends despised Lavon for importing and trading slaves. Frannie was shunned and openly insulted when she tried to frequent the tea rooms that catered to the Deavorses and other "proper" ladies. Then Lavon's crazed, ruthless schemes to drive his family from The Columns further alienated him from Natchez society.

Frannie was far from devastated when Lavon was killed. She found herself a wealthy and available widow, the target of every fortune hunter in the county and disinclined to resist their sexual advances. She was flattered by the attention, but her goals still seemed hopelessly remote. Blaine knew he was the one man who could assure her a place in Natchez society.

They were walking through an arbor of scuppernong grapes when Frannie took his hand. He squeezed it. She tightened her grip and looked up with a blushing smile and damp, open lips. But Blaine only smiled and squeezed her hand and kept walking.

It would be absurdly easy. He had always disliked fortune hunters. But within minutes of learning about Frannie, he'd accepted the necessity of what he had to do. Frannie bored him. She had the worst reputation in the county, and she had that small son who was crippled in one leg.

He would do it, but on his own carefully calculated terms. He would not hedge or hesitate or lie to himself. He would try to be a decent husband and a good father to the boy. But he would marry Frannie Deavors and secure her vast wealth—only for Rafaella. When he had done it, he would somehow extricate himself.

And God help anyone who got in his way.

25.

Blaine knew that a confrontation with Rafaella was inevitable when he returned to The Columns a few days later, so he suggested they take a walk together before supper. He didn't want to be overheard.

The late afternoon heat was intense, still stifling. They walked slowly through the quarters and found some relief in the mottled shade of huge fig trees, shade they shared with birds that knocked rotting figs on the ground.

Rafaella had been silent since leaving the house. Blaine didn't know whether to begin to talk or wait for her. It was a talk he dreaded and had avoided as long as possible. Lately, Rafaella had been nearly impossible to live with. Blaine particularly feared her mood of the past few days. She had been very quiet and subdued. In the past, when she lapsed into these dangerous moods, she had broken them by doing something drastic.

Blaine hated to see his daughter unhappy. He knew how upset she was about his relationship with Frannie Deavors. It was a delicate situation. Blaine was now certain that Frannie would marry him, and on his terms. They would wed secretly, and she would sign a marriage contract that would give Rafaella half of her wealth when he died. Blaine was satisfied with the arrangement, but he knew Rafaella would hate it.

In her present mood, Rafaella might well confront

Frannie and ruin everything. He couldn't have that, not now. On the other hand, he couldn't bear to imagine Rafaella's fury when she learned that Frannie was to be her stepmother. He wouldn't think of it, not now. For now he wanted only to placate his daughter, to postpone the inevitable. He would tell any lie that would serve.

The marriage was just one of his worries. It was a minor one compared to his concern about what that Yankee lawyer Anson had revealed to Lawton. Blaine had not been able to bring himself to confront Lawton. It had been left between them that probate was being delayed a short time because of some technicalities.

Blaine knew that was not the truth. Rafaella suspected it, too, insisting that Anson would not have traveled all that distance to discuss legal technicalities. Blaine now guessed that the man who had been investigating him when he left Rome was Anson's agent. He was also certain that Lawton was delaying the probate proceedings because of some information Anson had brought.

Damn it, *what* information? Blaine had asked himself a hundred times. It could be merely hearsay. Perhaps Anson had spoken only in general terms. Perhaps they were waiting for some kind of documentary proof about Blaine's background. Or, Lawton might already have solid proof. Lawton might know the truth that he had hidden so carefully all these years: that he was really Salhan Rahdi, a Muslim, a former Egyptian slave.

And that all his documents were forgeries.

The uncertainty was driving him mad. Yet if he confronted Lawton and Lawton knew nothing specific, and if no proof ever came from the Continent, it could be a fatal blunder. He had to wait.

Blaine cursed the day he ever decided to leave Rome and take over the plantation. He should have known old Price Deavors would not let a son-in-law he mistrusted, one he resented for having taken away his only daughter, inherit an estate so easily.

If his secret came out, both he and Rafaella would be ruined in this slave-holding society. They would be shunned, dishonored, banished, or worse. Even if no hint of this came out, Rafaella would be devastated. She was incapable of understanding it, and he knew she would hate and revile him. She was so proud, so haughty, so fanatically committed to her own superiority. Even the suspicion of a slave background would be the end of her. He had to protect her in any way he could.

The last thing Blaine wanted now was the damned Price Deavors estate. He wanted to avoid all cause for investigation. Anyway, he didn't need it. He had Frannie's property nearly in his grasp. But how could he suddenly renounce the inheritance without raising suspicion? And if Lawton already had some hideous proof, renouncing it would do no good. Rafaella would never understand that, either. He was confused, tired. He had considered a score of schemes, but he was still uncertain about what to do.

"She's so common . . . so cheap, Daddy," Rafaella said suddenly. "I know that a man has to have the . . . the company of a woman sometimes. Why, everybody in Rome had a mistress. And she's pretty enough in her own crude way. If you'd only seen her once or twice as you usually do with a woman. But you're . . . you actually seem to be, well, courting her!"

"Please don't get so upset," he said hopelessly. "Remember, I am your father, and no matter how much we share, well, it's hardly necessary for me to ask your permission every time I see a woman."

"Daddy, of course it's not," she said. "But you haven't been confiding in me—not about the estate or what the lawyer told Lawton. So I have to suspect something else about the attention you're lavishing on that woman, who happens to be very wealthy, and a widow."

"Raffles, I won't have you speak like that!" he said. He couldn't look at her. She was far too clever. She could easily ruin his plans.

"Raffles, if you'll calm down a moment, I can relieve your anxiety," he said. "I was going to tell you that

I'm going to stop seeing the widow. But I must confess that my flesh is weak."

Rafaella looked up at him searchingly. She seemed on the verge of tears. Blaine wanted to hold her, comfort her, reassure her as he so often had. Now he dared not touch her.

"Daddy, until recently I thought I knew you very well," she said. Her voice was soft, almost breaking. "And I trust you and love you so much. All right. I'm ... I'm glad you won't see that woman anymore. But why have you been treating me this way? Don't you love me, Daddy? What's happened? I'm so bored here that I could die. I don't want to live."

"Raffles," he said. "Darling, you're right! I *have* treated you unfairly, though all I've done has been for you. It hurts me that you think I could ever stop loving you. That's why I wanted us to take this walk. So we could be close again."

She looked up at him and brushed tears from the corners of her eyes. He was hurt by her obvious pain, and he was chilled by the way her face had altered from youthful vulnerability to a surprising maturity with thin-drawn, bloodless lips and narrowed eyes.

"You'll tell me everything, Daddy?" she asked.

"I swear I'll tell you everything Lawton has told me. In rather blunt terms, I'm afraid I . . . overestimated Lawton. I trusted him too fully."

"I don't understand," she said. "Do you mean Lawton's been lying to you about the reasons for the delay? Why would he do that?"

"I admire Lawton and I'm in his debt," Blaine said. He hesitated. He was determined to cover himself with Rafaella in case his secrets were ever revealed by Lawton. "I . . . don't want to accuse him of lying. Let me say that I don't think he has yet told me everything . . . about Anson's visit."

"But that's not like Lawton, Daddy," she said.

"What did he tell you?" Blaine asked, and hoped his fear wasn't betrayed by either his voice or his face.

"He hasn't told me anything at all," she said. "And

I've asked and asked! But just the last week he's been much nicer to me. Daddy, I've come to know Lawton quite well. And honestly, I don't believe that he would delay probate for some underhanded reason. It's not like him. Besides, the way things are, I don't think that Lawton would ever do . . . anything at all to hurt me."

"Raffles," Blaine said, still trying to decide what to say, "Raffles . . . what do you mean, the way things are?"

"Oh, Daddy, that look of yours is silly," she said. "Nothing wrong has happened between Lawton and me! And, of course, nothing will. He's a married man. It's just that we're becoming very special friends, and I suspect we . . . well, we could be falling in love . . . in a purely harmless, Platonic way, of course. That's why I've been so . . . well, so upset, to be perfectly honest."

Blaine dared not let Rafaella and Lawton become allies. He knew only too well her ability to manipulate men, and if Lawton hadn't yet fallen under her spell, he would soon, in all likelihood.

"Raffles, calm down, dear," Blaine said. He shook his head. "I won't even attempt to . . . tell you how deeply you've hurt me by . . . trusting Lawton . . . over me. No, no, wait a minute! You've done quite enough talking, young lady, which is one of our difficulties. You don't give me the opportunity to tell you everything I wanted to."

"I'm sorry, Daddy," she said. "Please tell me everything."

He told her that, on his last trip into Natchez, a banker had told him of talk that the Deavorses were planning to acquire a great deal of new land. They had too many slaves now, with Aunt Delma's, for the existing acreage. The banker, Blaine said, hinted that Lawton and his family had enough influence in the county and in the courts to get what they wanted and make it look legal.

"I've hired an attorney to look after our interests, darling," Blaine said. "A local man named Grady Weston." He didn't say that Weston was ill and going downriver to a New Orleans hospital as soon as the marriage contract was signed. "I'm also planning to hire an agent to . . . to investigate the Deavorses' plans. No, wait, Raffles. Please give me a little time, just a week or so, to substantiate these things. You must stay calm . . . and don't try to pry information out of Lawton. If I find out the rumors are without foundation, then I promise that we will confront Lawton together and resolve this whole situation."

She continued to look at him with the same waiting, listening expression.

"I won't say a word to Lawton, I promise. I . . . I really feel much better, now that we've talked. I love you, Daddy."

She stretched up and kissed his cheek. He was pleased, then trembled as her breasts in the thin, clinging silk dress pressed against his chest and her damp lips lingered on his face. She pulled away slowly and started walking. He followed, consumed by anxiety and a nearly sickening sexual excitement.

"We should be getting back for supper," he said as they crossed a narrow stretch planted in cotton and entered a grove of white oaks near the swamp.

"Oh, there's time yet," she said. "Don't forget, supper is late tonight because the Sumralls are coming over to eat and say good-bye to Joleen. And we've had so little time alone lately, Daddy."

"A short walk, I suppose," he said. His head was spinning.

Rafaella turned to him and took his hand. "I do love you very much, even when I say terrible things or act cross," she said.

She ran away then, disappeared around a curve that led into the swamp. He hurried on and found her beside a stream. She was taking off her boots.

"It's such a hot day and the water looks cool," she said. "I think I'll go wading."

"No, Raffles . . ." he started, but he did not finish the sentence.

She had looked back at him sharply, but now she

smiled, not just with her lips but a full, happy smile he saw only rarely. The smile made her look even younger, reminded him that in the not-too-distant past she had been simply a beautiful little girl, a daughter he loved very much, only a child . . . not a girl grown up too fast, a girl on whom he had become too dependent in too many grown-up ways, a girl who was far too dependent on him . . . in other ways.

He was both sad and proud as he watched Rafaella wade into the stream, her silk dress bunched up in both hands, innocent pleasure on her face. Sadness and pride mixed with tenderness and an almost unbearable excitement. Rafaella waded deeper into the dappled shade of overhanging branches, her dress pulled higher to bare her knees, her face still innocent and touchingly young. She was simply a girl who didn't want to get her dress wet. And yet when she reached the middle of the stream and glanced back, the innocence was gone, and it had been replaced by a calculating self-consciousness.

She had been standing with her back to her father, and now she turned slowly in the thigh-deep water, turned very deliberately, her face still half-shadowed. As he watched, she squeezed her pale thighs together, then spread them, splashing water on her own pale skin. The water ran off her legs like rivulets over ivory. She pulled her skirt higher. Blaine's breath came in a rush. His heart pounded.

Usually she stopped when her skirt was this high, and splashed water on herself; perhaps this time she would bare more of her breast, almost to the nipple . . . He could not speak. He expected her to stop, but she raised her skirt even higher over her wet thighs. With a boldly sexual rhythm, she squeezed her thighs tight, then spread them, bent down into the water and rose up. Her skirt lifted an inch higher, and in the deepening twilight Blaine was not sure any more what he actually saw and what he only imagined. Did he see clearly between her thighs? Or wasn't her skirt raised quite that high?

She posed for him, swaying slightly, bending slightly,

squeezing, spreading, dripping, all pale wet skin and dark shadows. He could not see her face. She dropped her skirt on one side. With her free hand she teased at her bosom, traced the yellow bodice that bound her breasts. Then she slowly, tantalizingly loosened the bodice and bared her breasts. It had been a long time since Blaine had seen them bared, and they were the breasts of a woman, too large for her slim body, too full, too beautiful.

His loins ached until he nearly doubled up from the pain and excitement. Finally he turned and stumbled away, along the path. He was sweating and gasping, and he mumbled to himself that this was the last time, that he must end this madness, must never again be tempted to watch. He must discipline Rafaella, must take a woman or go mad . . .

26.

Blaine forced his mount to a gallop, though he knew the danger of pushing a good horse in rain and mud. He was in a hurry and a reckless mood. He savored the danger and ignored the rain. His rendezvous with Frannie had gone even better than he had hoped. She had accepted his marriage proposal and his terms. She had agreed to a secret marriage—"secret until the Price Deavors estate is settled," he had told her. She had signed Grady Weston's marriage contract and made Rafaella heiress to a vast estate.

Their wedding was to take place in two days.

Blaine lashed his reins across the horse. Despite his success with Frannie, he was not content. Rafaella would be furious when she learned of the marriage. And he could not forget that scene at the creek.

He was considering a plan to take Rafaella away on a long trip as soon as he was married. It would placate her, and they would be able to work out whatever was

. . . unhealthy in their relationship. He was determined to do so. She was nearly eighteen, he reasoned, and now she had an enormous dowry. Though he would be heartbroken, she must marry soon.

Now the marriage contract was signed, and after the wedding Weston would leave for New Orleans. There would be no way Rafaella could contact him.

She could get to Simon Gregor, the agent Blaine had hired, ostensibly to investigate Lawton Deavors. But even Rafaella's manipulations couldn't overcome Gregor's greed. Gregor would do anything for the money Blaine was paying him, including forging documents proving that Lawton wanted the Price Deavors estate, as well as spreading rumors that would be certain to reach Rafaella.

Blaine's immediate plan was to precipitate some crisis at The Columns and take Rafaella away before she realized what was happening. They would move into a Natchez hotel for a short time. He wanted to get her away from Lawton. Then slowly, logically, with his "proof" and the rumors, he would convince her that Lawton was scheming against them and intended to deny them the estate. He would complain to her of innocuous rumors about his past, ones she knew for certain couldn't be true.

The wet wind stung his cheeks. He leaned forward into the wind. All that mattered to him was Rafaella. He would do anything necessary to protect her, to prevent her learning the truth.

The truth! Blaine laughed bitterly. Although he thought himself an atheist, many years of living as a Moslem had marked him with a fatalism he could never totally shake. What did the truth matter? All that mattered was that he should protect and provide for the reputation and happiness of his daughter.

It was all so absurd! Nearly all of his life lived like this—lying and scheming and plotting and running. He hated it, but he did it now without hesitation. How far he had come . . .

He, Salhan Rahdi, who had killed more than a dozen men one day when he was only sixteen. He had ridden to battle with the Mamelukes, resplendent in fine garments, mounted on spirited, pure-bred Arabians, ridden to a glorious victory. And now he was racing down a muddy road by the edge of a weed-choked swamp, thousands of miles from Egypt, thousands of miles from the unknown Balkan town where he had been born, from which he had been kidnapped in another absurd twist of his fate.

He had been a prince, a warrior, the Select of Allah. And then he had been driven from Egypt, lucky to escape with his life. Other Mamelukes had fled to the Sudan after the massacre in Cairo. They had regrouped and returned to fight Muhammed Ali, but they had been defeated and their survivors had been hunted and killed by Ali's agents.

Salhan Rahdi had fled to India, helped at first by the British colonel who had taken him in and treated his wounds. No one looked for the Mamelukes in India. Rahdi was intelligent and ambitious. He had learned the silk business and perfected his English. In time he had returned to the Mediterranean and established himself in Italy as a silk importer and dealer. He posed as an English gentleman and he prospered. He was very alert, very wary, but as time passed, he had begun to live without constant fear of the agents of Muhammed Ali. Without constant fear, but never without wariness or the haunting dread that someday . . .

Nevertheless he had married the American Sarah Deavors, despite the bitter objection of her family. They had married for love and lived in Rome. There Rafaella had been born, to their delight. She was a beautiful, brilliant child. When Sarah died, she had become the center of his life.

It was for her that he had entered into this further unlikely exile, surely the last of his life. He had fled Rome abruptly when he learned that someone there was making inquiries about him. It was a time, too, when he had tired of his business, which was doing less well. But the inquiries had upset and worried him. The legacy of the Price Deavors estate had seemed a godsend, another gesture of his fate.

For wasn't it all, ultimately, in the hands of fate? He laughed again and settled back into his saddle as he rode onto the approach road to The Columns. *Insh' Allah*, Allah willing . . . he would survive this hazard, too, would manage to avoid investigation, would secure Frannie Deavors's wealth for Rafaella. They would endure.

Having come so far, survived so much, so long, why did he doubt that he could bring off this last scheme?

With fresh hope, he rode straight across the wide green lawn, up to the twelve massive white columns that distinguished the mansion where his wife's cousins lived. His confidence faded when he saw Lawton Deavors standing on the wide porch, talking to the red-bearded English naval officer he had last seen aboard the *Yazoo Queen*.

27.

By the first week in November, Lawton was certain the cotton harvest would be the best ever. The weather held fair and hot, and every able-bodied slave was in the fields from daybreak to sunset in a rush to finish the cotton picking. Confident of a good harvest, Lawton had commissioned his agents to purchase the vast tract of uncultivated swampland that lay between The Columns and the Mississippi River.

He rode up to Rodney and made a deal with the Irish workers to begin clearing his land in January. But the harvest and the new acreage were the only projects that gave Lawton any satisfaction or sense of fulfillment that fall.

One mild, humid evening Lawton wandered down to

the rose garden and tried to put his thoughts in some kind of order, tried to understand what was disturbing him. For one thing, Cellus, who had never fully recovered from the brutal beatings and branding last July, was ill again.

"Nothing to worry about, he just got up too soon," the doctor said, and ordered Cellus back to bed.

And then there were Joleen's plans to leave. He dreaded seeing her go. It would depress him for weeks, he knew. He loved Joleen and wanted to take care of her, wanted to protect her. He did not want her to return to Ohio and to Aaron and the Lord only knew what new dangers, new crimes.

Besides, he realized how much he needed Joleen, how much he depended on her. He didn't see how he could get along without her strength and her intuitive understanding of things. If she would only stay, if she would change her dangerous thinking, if she could only become the sister she once was . . .

Then Lawton thought of his suspicions of her in the past few weeks, thought of their arguments over her plans to free her own slaves, and he tried not to think of her any longer. Lawton picked a late yellow rose and smelled it, then dropped it to the ground. As he wandered toward the wooden gazebo, he thought of Lucinda. For the past few weeks she had been agitated and restless—was it since the day she'd gone into town with Joleen? She insisted nothing was wrong, but he sensed a change.

Lawton valued and needed the support of these two women, and yet he tried to spare them as many of his worries as possible. For instance, he wouldn't share his concern about the Price Deavors estate. They were both curious about the delay. As was Rafaella Blaine.

"There's nothin' to discuss, really." He had said it so many times it had become a kind of ritual speech.

The ritual went on: "It's just that I'm not used to this kind of dealin's with the court, and right here at harvest time. Of course, that lawyer's visit was purely routine.

It's just that there are some technicalities with the will, and probate takes an eternity in the best of circumstances . . ."

Lawton climbed the creaking steps and stood in the gazebo watching the slaves coming in from the fields. He looked back at the quarters, at the big white house and its columns. His great-grandfather had built this house, had floated the huge wooden columns, six Doric, six Corinthian, down the Mississippi from Cincinnati.

Lawton looked away from the house, staring at the tangle of late-blooming roses. Dammit, perhaps he should discuss all his problems with Lucinda and Joleen. He wanted and needed their advice, particularly since he felt Cellus was still too sick to be troubled. Lawton didn't know what to do. It seemed the most explosive dilemma of his life.

The Yankee lawyer Anson had alleged that Roger Blaine was a former Moslem slave and wanted for murder in Egypt. Though Egypt was far away, it was a serious charge to make against a man, as was the charge that all Blaine's documents might be forgeries. Even if the allegations proved untrue, and Lawton hoped with all his heart they would, Lawton dared not let the information pass on to anyone else, not even to Joleen or Lucinda. Just the hint of such a taint would ruin the Blaines in Mississippi.

Lawton paced the gazebo, and his mind raced with contradictory thoughts. He wished he'd never met Anson, never heard the scandalous charges. He wished he'd never gotten involved, never taken on the responsibility of administering the Price Deavors estate.

"Dammit, dammit," Lawton muttered. It couldn't be true. If only it were settled. If only more damned information would arrive from Anson's agent; if only he had some proof that the charges were groundless.

Time and again as he had talked to Blaine, dined with him, drunk whiskey with him, he had stared at the man and told himself that it was preposterous. The man was so English he couldn't be a Moslem, an Arab, an Egyptian slave. And as for Rafaella, why, he was proud to claim the beautiful girl as a member of the family.

There was a flash of pink at the edge of the rose garden, and Lawton recognized Rafaella. She wore a low-cut pink silk dress with a full, pleated skirt. She was so lovely, so young, there was such naivete and vulnerability in her face, that Lawton's throat tightened as he glanced at her. He wondered if she knew anything at all about her father's true background . . . if she had ever faced such allegations.

Lawton doubted it. Rafaella had tried several times to get him to discuss the inheritance, and she seemed genuinely curious and innocent about the whole matter. Of course, Lawton told himself, she could be working on her father's behalf, trying to get information. But he couldn't believe it.

Rafaella was looking away from the gazebo. Lawton wondered whom she was expecting . . . and if she had seen him. He didn't want to talk to her now . . . and yet he did, he realized.

Her constantly shifting moods had made him uneasy. She was so different from any other woman he'd known. There was no doubt that she was extremely beautiful, but she was so mercurial. She could seem the little girl, and then in the next instant the flirtatious woman of the world. She could be spoiled, demanding, and outrageous, or soft, gentle, and very sweet. She could be very willful and almost maddeningly provocative.

And yet she seemed so . . . lonely, Lawton told himself. He realized that, except for her father, she had no close friend. She seemed eager to have Lawton as a friend, "a very special friend," she had once said.

So he had spent increasingly more time with her, and there was no doubt that they were becoming very special friends. Of course it was only friendship, he told himself. She was family. It was totally innocent, he felt, and it was partially because he felt sorry for her, felt obliged to her, since he couldn't give the Blaines the estate they had come to claim.

It wasn't wrong, it wasn't really even flirting, Lawton told himself. They were practically cousins.

But, as he hesitated, his heart began to pound. Rafaella turned slowly and looked in his direction, as though she had known all the time that he was there. She stared. Was it at him? He thought he saw the little smile on the edges of her lips, but he wasn't certain.

Then she headed for the gazebo. He watched her walk through the English-style rose garden. She was carrying a basket. He realized he was staring at her rosy yet delicate skin, at her bosom, nearly spilling from the tight bodice of her gown.

He turned and hastened down the steps to meet her.

"Havin' a walk before supper, too, I see," he said, and he felt both excited and awkward as he spoke. He realized that he often felt awkward when he talked with her.

"I was goin' to pick some roses for Daddy's room," she said. "Come walk with me, Lawton, and I'll pick some for you, too."

"That's very kind of you, Raffles," he said, "but you don't have to pick flowers for me. The house niggers—"

"Oh, Lawton, let me, please," she said. "They're so lovely now. And I enjoy doing things for . . . you and Daddy."

"Of course, I'd like for you to," he said.

They walked to the garden. She took out a small pair of silver scissors and started cutting roses. He took them from her and laid them in her basket.

"I've been wanting to discuss something with you, Lawton," she said.

"Of course, Raffles," he said. He hoped she wouldn't bring up the probate proceedings.

"Lawton, you wouldn't . . . oh, I feel rather silly even asking," she said. Her face seemed older and yet more vulnerable. He stared into her dark eyes a moment before looking away. "We have become rather special friends, haven't we?"

"Of course we have," he said.

"And I can . . . trust you, rely on you?" she asked. "You wouldn't ever do anything to . . . hurt me, would you?"

"Raffles, what do you mean?" he asked. "Of course I wouldn't. Never!"

She was shaking her head. "No, no, please, I shouldn't even have asked," she said. "It's only that you've become . . . oh, really, I've let myself get . . . carried away, I suppose. But let me ask you something else, if I may."

"What is it?"

"I always pick out Daddy's clothes and I want to get him something special for Christmas," she said. "I wondered if you could recommend a really good tailor in— Oh, look, I caught you with the thorn when I handed you that rose! Oh, I'm sorry, Lawton. I wouldn't hurt you for anything."

Lawton looked at his wrist. Blood was seeping from the scratch, and there was a sharp throbbing of pain.

"It's nothin'," he mumbled and stood and inhaled her perfume while she took out a fragile handkerchief edged in deep French lace and very slowly, very softly, soaked up the blood in the cobwebby silk.

28.

Joleen looked out from her bedroom window and saw Rafaella walking toward the rose garden. She told herself it was hardly a coincidence that Lawton had headed that way a few minutes earlier.

She turned away and went back to her desk. She had determined to finish the letter she was writing to Aunt Delma. It was just one of the last-minute tasks she had to complete before beginning her journey north to Aaron. Norvina, her maid, had been in her room packing all afternoon, but Norvina's chatter about leaving had made Joleen nervous and she had just sent her away.

The packing wasn't yet finished, and her room had a disturbed, cluttered feeling that matched Joleen's own. Surely Lawton wasn't attracted to that little nuisance, Rafaella, she told herself. Surely he didn't fancy her. Yet he seemed to spend a great deal of time with her.

She sat down at her elegant French rosewood desk, shipped upriver from New Orleans many years ago, and she cursed the day the Blaines had ever come to The Columns, cursed the day poor Lawton was ever burdened with administering the Price Deavors inheritance. She knew there was something about the situation that Lawton was keeping to himself. He was brooding and he wouldn't discuss the matter, not with her and not with Lucinda. Joleen wondered what could be causing the delay, what that lawyer could have told Lawton, but she didn't have the slightest idea. Well, the affair would be settled soon enough, she supposed, and the Blaines would be long gone from The Columns when she next came home.

She put down her pen, in no mood to write letters. When she came back . . . When *would* she ever come back? And even if she did return, there would be only trouble. Even now, things were uncomfortable here . . . between her hatred of living among slaves and her arguments with Lawton over manumission. She had decided to postpone freeing her own slaves, because it was a lengthy and involved process that required court action. She would now be leaving so soon, and Lawton had seemed adamant, almost bitter, about the matter. She'd just wait and discuss everything with Aaron, and then she could take the necessary steps from Ohio.

Joleen was determined and she would not change her mind, but she could not bear any more ill feeling and misunderstanding between Lawton and her. Enough existed already, and it made her so sad. She had to go; it was time; but she had little enthusiasm for leaving. She rose and wandered over to the window, but turned before she reached it. She went to the door and put her hand on the knob. She paused, then started pacing the room.

Once again, she thought of Carter Ramsey's last visit to the plantation. She was sorry that she had missed him. She wondered about his coming out to the plantation. He told Lawton it had to do with arranging her accommodations on his steamboat. Perhaps he had other reasons. He had told Lawton he was going to the Caribbean for a time and had sent her his most sincere regards. Very likely she would never see him again.

She was surprisingly sorry. She had spent far more time thinking about Ramsey than she liked to admit. Few men had interested her as much as he did. Of course, she loved Aaron. The thought of him gave her a good, solid, warm feeling. She had missed him so very much. How could she have stayed away from him so long? His letters showed that he missed her, too. He was busy and anxiously awaiting her return. He wrote of the exhilaration of his work, of the new home he had found for them.

Slowly Joleen's sadness at leaving the plantation gave way to a yearning for Aaron and an excitement about living in a free society.

Lucinda walked from the nursery in the quarters and paused in the door to watch the weary slaves coming from the fields. She nodded and spoke as the people passed, walking slowly, the exhaustion showing on their faces.

Filch came up. He limped slightly. He had a bad foot where a rattler had bitten him years before. "How's the sucker doin', Miss 'Cinda?" he asked.

"Aunt Fronie says the baby will be all right now," Lucinda said. "She had a touch of the croup, but the coughing has died down."

"Glad to hear that," Filch said.

"How's the pickin' comin', Filch?" Lucinda asked. "The people seem very tired . . . more than usual . . ."

"It's been a hard week, tell the truth," he said. "And this here bein' Saturday, after six days work, it's only natural they all tired out. I'm glad Mist' Lawton's not sendin' 'em out tomorrow."

"Yes, they need a day's rest, for sure," Lucinda said.

"Goin' to be a record year," Filch said. "If the rain holds off. We 'bout caught up now, after that last hot spell. Won't have to work so hard next week."

"When you get a chance, Filch, I'd like to talk to you," Lucinda said. "With Cellus still down, we're going to have to start thinking about winter clothes and all for the people."

"Yes'm, we sure will," Filch said. "But maybe we could wait a few days. Cellus, he might could be up on his feet and, well, Miss 'Cinda, he's always taken charge of that before, him and Miss 'Stell . . ."

"All right, let's wait a few days, Filch," she said. "There's enough time left. But, as you know, we'll be going into town Monday. Do the people need anything?"

"Can't think of nothin' offhand," Filch said. "Well, I wouldn't want to spoil the people, but since they workin' hard and still a few weeks 'til the harvest finished, well, some little treat might be good. Just somethin' simple. 'Course, I know you'd have to discuss it with Mist' Lawton and Cellus."

"Not necessarily," Lucinda said, an edge on her voice. "I think I'm capable of deciding on my own, Filch."

" 'Course you are," he said quickly. "Didn't mean nothin'. Just that, Miss 'Stell, when she was mistress . . ."

"But now *I'm* the mistress," Lucinda said. "And despite my respect for Mrs. Deavors, I can't do everything just as she did. I agree with you. Some little treat will be good for the people. I'll see to it while I'm in town."

"Yes'm, they'll sure appreciate that," Filch said. "Well, if you'll 'scuse me, I'll be getting 'long to my cabin. Evenin', Miss 'Cinda."

"Good evening, Filch," she said.

She walked slowly from the quarters. Smoke curled grey from the chimneys as suppers were cooked. Men chopped wood for the cook fires and tended to small gardens and scrawny chickens. Young girls were lined up at the pump, and small children played running games.

Lucinda was on her way back to the house but she detoured through the vegetable garden. The scene with Filch had shaken her confidence. And just when she felt she had overcome her anxiety and depression from her violent confrontation with Alain LeBeau. Those few minutes in Alain's house had been the worst of her life, worse even than the time in the forest when he'd so humiliated her.

She still found it difficult to believe she had actually shot him! Afterwards, she had fled his house and nearly collapsed in the street. She had gotten through the ride home somehow. When she returned to The Columns, she'd gone straight to bed. Everyone thought she was ill, and she let them think so. For days, she had lived in anxious dread. What if someone guessed? What if Alain told someone what she'd done? What if he sought revenge? If he didn't leave Natchez, how would she find the courage to follow through with her threat?

Then word came from town that Alain had left with all his possessions and his slaves. And slowly, Lucinda began to feel better. She knew she had done the right thing, no matter how dangerous and reckless it had been. If she hadn't acted boldly, Alain would have plagued and threatened and humiliated her for an eternity, she knew. Her marriage would have been in jeopardy. She would have felt constant anxiety and fear.

But more important, she felt her whole character would have been undermined if she had let Alain intimidate her. All her life she had been shy, had lacked confidence, had deferred to people, had been unsure of herself. Confronting Alain was the most active, the most independent, the most important step she had ever taken. For the first time, in an odd way, it had made her feel a real woman, truly mistress of The Columns, truly Mrs. Lawton Deavors.

She loved Lawton and the plantation and the people, and though she respected Lawton and depended on him, she could also see his weaknesses and see that he needed her support, just as he had always needed Cellus and Joleen. Without great personal strength and self-confidence, she knew she could not succeed as Lawton's wife or be truly the mistress of The Columns. Lawton needed someone strong, especially with Joleen returning to Cincinnati now.

And Lucinda was determined to succeed. That was why the talk with Filch had upset her. She resented his references to Cellus and to Lawton's mother. Lucinda knew she had to move out of Miss 'Stella's shadow, even Joleen's. She loved Joleen, but she wasn't altogether sorry to see her go to Ohio. When Joleen was gone, it would be easier to assert herself as the plantation's mistress.

There was a rustling sound in the cabbage patch a few feet away. Lucinda froze. Was it a snake? She began to tremble, forgetting her firm resolves, remembering only the night the coral snake had crawled on her foot. Then she saw a field mouse scurry across the red earth.

She exhaled and steadied herself. She had to learn about snakes and conquer her fear of them. Normally, poisonous snakes never came near the house. After all, she was no longer a city girl. Her New Orleans life was past. She was the mistress of a plantation at the edge of a vast swamp. She must stop cowering at every sound, stop avoiding important decisions. She must take on more managerial tasks.

Lucinda suddenly headed for the kitchen. She was going to confront Beatrice, the cook. Earlier they had disagreed about trying a new dish for dinner, and Lucinda had deferred to Beatrice's experience. Now she regretted it.

But from now on things would be different!

For the third time a black steward lavishly appointed in red and gold livery walked through the salon of the boat, ringing a bell.

"Last call . . . all guests ashore, ladies and gent'men," he called. "Boat's fixin' to sail. Captain says, last call, all guests ashore . . ."

At the last minute, Joleen was terribly sad to be parting with her family, though she had controlled her tears. Her sadness had been tempered by a final argument with Lawton over manumission and by the excitement she felt at the prospect of being with Aaron again. She hugged Lawton one final time. When he pulled away, there were tears in the corners of his eyes. He walked from the salon with an arm on Joleen's shoulder; then they parted. He went along the deck and started down the gangway without speaking again.

At the bottom, when he joined Lucinda and the others, Lawton looked up at his sister.

"You send us a letter the minute you get to Ohio," he called. "Let us know you got there all right, Joleen."

"I will," she called down. "I'll write first thing. Good-bye!"

The gangway was pulled up. Smoke rose white and choking from the enormous funnel. Steam hissed. The two huge sidewheels began to churn. The boat pulled from the dock. Lawton and the others watched until they could no longer see Joleen on the deck.

Lawton was leading his family to their carriage when a familiar figure caught his eye. He curled his hands into fists and took two hesitant steps toward the figure, but it disappeared into the crowd.

"Lawton, what's wrong?" Rafaella asked. "Your face is gone white! Are you ill?"

"No, no," he mumbled as he moved toward the carriage again. "Just upset 'bout Joleen's leavin'."

He stumbled and cursed under his breath. Repeatedly, he caught himself glancing over his shoulder at the crowd. Had he really seen her? Would she dare to come back to Natchez, after being given her freedom and money and promising never to return? And that child whose hand she held, the boy whose face Lawton had not quite seen. He went cold thinking what the boy might look like.

Nettie had belonged to The Columns. Though a slave, she had looked white in every way. She had been Lawton's first woman, and when his father learned of this, when he realized that the child of a slave so white might bear a striking likeness to Lawton, he had broken one of the Deavorses' cardinal rules: never to let a slave go out of the family. Nettie had been given her freedom and a sum of money, and she had promised to leave Natchez and never to return.

But what if that *were* Nettie? What if there were a boy walking the Natchez streets who was his son, who looked like him, like a Deavors, looked white, but who was legally a Negro?

Lawton rarely drank so early in the day, but he decided to leave the others at the bluffs and have some whiskey.

29.

On a warm, humid morning early in November, Roger Blaine and Frannie Deavors were married in the presence of Grady Weston. It was a simple, private ceremony in the home of a black-coated Baptist preacher.

After the wedding, Blaine and Frannie drove back to her plantation. Frannie had worn a white silk gown sent upriver from New Orleans. It was trimmed with swansdown. She wore a white bonnet with orange flowers, her reddish hair shone, her face glowed with happiness. Blaine had long been in need of a woman, and after a quick drink together on her verandah, he took his bride upstairs to bed. Frannie was willing, eager, and appreciative. It was a fine sexual union, and Blaine quickly satisfied his lust. Afterwards, he bathed, left his wife in bed, and set out for The Columns, promising to return the next day. Riding through the lush fields he now owned, he calculated how long Frannie would keep the marriage secret. Despite her promises, he did not trust her. He had convinced her that his remarriage might complicate the proceedings with the Price Deavors estate. But even that probably would not keep her quiet for long.

"Why, honey, we don't even need that other place," she had told him recklessly. She was rich, richer even than he had hoped, and not just in land, but in business investments and in the continuing contraband trade in slaves.

The thought made Blaine feel slightly ill, but he reminded himself that it was all for Rafaella. Half of all Frannie's holdings would be hers when he died.

The ride seemed endless. He was in a state of anxiety, in spite of the success thus far of the secret marriage; he felt smothered by what he faced as much as by the damp, oppressive heat. Not only must he tell Rafaella about his marriage and deal with her reaction, but he must try to isolate her from Lawton and get her away from The Columns, while putting into effect his scheme to discredit Lawton in her eyes.

It was all so complicated, so desperately important, so ironic that the secrets of his life should be pursuing him here to this godforsaken wilderness, threatening his happiness. Adding to his anxiety was his fear of Carter Ramsey.

On the padwheeler, he had thought of the English gentleman only as someone attracted to Rafaella. It was damnably unfortunate that Ramsey had seen his shoulder at the time of the explosion. However, Blaine had never expected to see Ramsey again. And then the damn Englishman had turned up at The Columns!

The sight of him had triggered all of Blaine's instincts for caution, self-defense, flight. If Ramsey had come to threaten him, had come with blackmail in mind, he would kill the man without hesitation.

Even though the reason behind Ramsey's visit to The Columns had proven to be a logical one that the Captain lived in Natchez and might at any time mention the brand.

Blaine met Lawton in the study. Lawton was smoking a cheroot.

"I've heard some rumors in Natchez, Lawton," Blaine said. "I must speak to you candidly about this, sir. The rumors, quite frankly, are that you want the Price Deavors estate for your own, and that is why you're delaying probate."

"Why, Roger, that's scandalous talk!" Lawton said. "I won't hear of—"

"Sir, allow *me* to speak of slander!" Blaine said. "For the rumors say that slander is your instrument for undoing me and taking away my inheritance! And may I say, sir, that these are not the rumors one finds in taverns, but the talk of bankers and lawyers."

"But, Roger, what slander? I haven't spoken a word against you. I swear it!"

"Save your oaths, sir! I know what lies your man Anson spread around Natchez. Lies about the legality of my marriage, murderous lies about the legitimacy of my daughter!"

"But, Roger, Anson's not my man. I never met him before. And he said nothin' to me about your marriage or your daughter. For God's sake . . ."

"I'm sorry, I don't believe you, sir," Blaine said. "How can I, after this excruciating delay . . . while you speak only of technicalities in the will? No, I've suspected that Anson had some dark motive for coming out here to see you, and now I begin to understand your scheme."

"Roger, please. This is all preposterous. Let me . . . explain. I wasn't . . . I didn't tell you the true reason for Anson's visit because I thought there would only be a short delay, until . . . well, Roger, he did indicate some . . . some questions about your past, though certainly nothing about Raffles' legitimacy. But his suspicions were so . . . so monstrous that I could hardly accept them without proof. So I . . . How can I even repeat what he told me?"

"I don't care to hear any more slanders, sir!" Blaine said. "And I give you fair warning not to repeat them . . . not to me in this room and not in town. If I hear of one more rumor against me, sir, despite my gratitude for your hospitality, I'll feel myself honor-bound to call you out!"

"Call me out?" Lawton said. "Roger, this is a terrible misunderstanding . . . And, sir, I deeply resent your unfounded charges against me, when I've been saddled with a task I didn't want and have tried to act only in your best interests. Do not speak of calling me out!"

"As for the Price Deavors estate, sir," Blaine said, "if you wish it so strongly that you must resort to slander and deceit, then you may have it! I hereby renounce any and all claims to the estate."

"You can't be serious. The property is worth a small fortune."

"My reputation and that of my daughter are worth far more. I'm having my lawyer draw up the necessary papers to file with the court."

"But . . . there are no other heirs."

"Only you, sir!"

"But I don't . . . Dammit, sir, give me some proof of these slanders of which I'm accused. Let me explain about Anson's . . . charges. Dammit, I demand a further explanation."

"I would suggest you demand nothing from me at all," Blaine said. "And, sir, stay away from my daughter! I'm taking Raffles and we're leaving The Columns this very day. I forbid you to so much as speak to her again. And I warn you, as God is my witness, if I hear any new rumors in the Natchez streets, I shall hold you accountable!"

"Dammit, Roger . . . I won't have you—"

But Blaine had left the room.

30.

Rafaella paced the parlor of a suite in the Parker House Hotel in Natchez, angry and anxious for her father to return. His absences had become increasingly lengthy in the three days since they had left the plantation. Rafaella didn't believe that he could have this much business with lawyers.

She stared miserably at the rain flooding the street outside her window, and thought about their hasty and ill-explained departure from The Columns. She had been out riding; when she returned, she discovered all their trunks packed and waiting in a carriage and her father pacing the front porch. Before she knew what was happening, she was in the carriage, being driven to Natchez. She didn't even get to say good-bye to Lucinda, and Lawton had barely spoken to her. She had never seen him so distraught, or in so grim, silent, and distant a mood.

By the time they reached the end of the house road, she regretted that she hadn't insisted on a talk with Lawton. After all, they had become very special friends. And she was disturbed by her father's brief account of their scene. It didn't seem logical to her, and it all made her feel unhappy.

And insecure. Her father had showed her a letter, written by Lawton, which spoke of his ambition to own the Price Deavors estate. She had talked to her father's agent, Simon Gregor, and she had overheard a conversation about Lawton downstairs in the restaurant. It was shocking; and yet, even after all this, she wasn't ready to condemn Lawton.

Instead, Rafaella had sent two urgent notes to The Columns, begging Lawton to get in touch with her. So far she had received no reply.

It was intolerable. She hated the feeling of betrayal and loss of control. She also had deep suspicions about her father's hiring lawyers and fighting for the estate. Why hadn't he succeeded yet? Was he still keeping her in the dark, not telling her what was really happening?

She asked herself why Lawton would possibly want to disinherit them. He already owned thousands of acres, hundred of slaves. And he had such fine family feeling. It wasn't his nature to cheat them. Though her father had pointed out that Lawton obviously wasn't content with his holdings, since he had bought up a vast tract of new land and was having it cleared for spring planting.

She turned from the window and thought of the slanders Lawton was supposed to be using against them. Her parents' marriage, her own illegitimacy . . . She stamped her foot. She grew angry thinking of such slanders. If Lawton was doing this she would never forgive him, and he would pay dearly.

Rafaella paused and looked at herself in an ornate mirror. She was flushed. Her dark eyes were wide. She remembered Lawton's blue eyes and his boyish, handsome face with the dimples that so rarely showed. She smiled at the memory and returned to the window.

Surely Lawton would never do anything to hurt her. He wouldn't spread hateful rumors about her and her parents. She just knew he wouldn't. She and Lawton had grown so . . . so fond of each other the past few weeks. She could tell when a man was interested in her, and she had no doubt that Lawton felt deeply about her, considered her far more than just a special friend. Far more. If he weren't married to that insipid little Lucinda, she was quite sure that he would eventually ask for her hand in marriage. And she would certainly accept.

Yet there seemed to be so much proof to substantiate her father's charges. And why hadn't Lawton responded to her notes? Dammit, she thought. Where was her damn father? She was sick of being left alone, of knowing that once again he was excluding her from his plans.

She swore that she would find out the truth from him when he returned.

Rafaella had another hour to wait while her anxiety and anger deepened. She watched the rain grow heavier, swept along the street by a high wind that rattled the hotel windows.

With great relief, she heard a key in the door. When her father entered, he was sneezing and dripping water. She ran over to him.

"Oh, Daddy! You'll catch your death of sickness. What happened? Why didn't you take a carriage?"

"I was late and I couldn't find a carriage, Raffles," he said. "I didn't want to upset you."

Blaine sneezed again.

"You'll come down with the grippe!" she said. "It's just the time of the year when everyone gets it. You simply must get out of those wet clothes and get warm."

"Yes, I'm both wet and chilled. I'll go into my room for a minute. I won't be long."

"By all means, change your wet clothes," Rafaella said. "And I'll call the porter to start a fire. It isn't enough to get dry. You must get warm."

She turned to ring for the porter, then hesitated. She had just realized that her father had arrived with a new cane—one with a silver handle. And yesterday he had come in wearing a new suit. He seldom bought clothes for himself; she almost always bought his things. This new suit looked provincial, badly tailored. Why had he purchased it?

Rafaella decided she would start the fire herself. She did not call the porter. Her father was out of sight behind a gilded screen in the corner.

"Is that you, boy?" he called. "Make it a big fire. And pour me a brandy. A double one."

Rafaella smiled as she prepared the fire. Then she poured a double brandy and stood waiting for her father, the glass cupped in her hands.

"Here, boy, come rub me down with a towel," her father called. "And hurry with that brandy."

Rafaella crossed the room. Through a crack in the screen, she saw that her father was naked. Though he didn't know it, she had seen him naked many times, but she had never been so bold about it.

"Here's the brandy, Daddy!" she called, and held the glass over the screen. "And if you want to be rubbed down, I'll be glad to—"

"Raffles! I thought you were the porter. Get the hell out of here, dammit!"

"I started the fire," she said. "And here, I warmed the brandy in my hands."

"I said leave the room, young lady," he said. "I'm . . . I have no clothes on, dammit!"

"Daddy, I can't see through the screen," she said. "Your modesty is preserved."

He reached up and took the glass. Their fingers touched. His fingers were cold. They lingered an instant, then he pulled them away.

"I'll wait on the couch," Rafaella said. "And you should get to the fire. Why, your hands are like ice."

She poured herself a brandy and sat down on the couch. The rain was falling harder. There were thunder and flashes of lightning.

"This is a beautiful suite," she called. She sipped the brandy.

"It's comfortable," he said.

"But how can we possibly afford such luxury?" she asked. She drank more brandy. The alcohol warmed her inside, and the leaping flames in the fireplace made her skin glow.

"It's just a provincial hotel, dear," he said.

She drained her glass and poured more brandy. She took a sip before speaking.

"When did you get the new cane?" she asked. Her voice was lower, her throat almost raw. She felt the different kinds of warmth, in her mouth, on the tip of her tongue, in her stomach. She was flame-warmed along her cheeks and neck and arms. And her feelings of anxiety, suspicion, and excitement added another kind of warmth.

Blaine came from behind the screen. He was wearing his dressing gown. His glass was empty. Without speaking, he walked over and refilled it. He took a swallow, not a sip, then another swallow. He still had not looked directly at her. But finally, he turned slowly. They stared at each other and sipped brandy, and all the warmth made Rafaella's skin tingle and made her feel her blood rush.

"What did you say?" he asked finally.

"I asked where you got the silver-headed cane," she said. And then she exploded. "Daddy, you're lying to me! We can't afford a suite such as this. I know it. You're treating me like a child again and excluding me from your plans. And to think I trusted you after our talk that day in the fig grove. Dammit, tell me the truth!"

Rafaella stood up. Her legs were weak. She was shocked at her own daring.

But to her surprise, her father seemed cowed by her. He sighed. "Yes, Raffles, I will tell you the truth," he said. He drank more brandy, and she poured herself another glass. "Raffles, I wish you wouldn't drink so much brandy. You know it's the one drink you simply can't handle."

She said nothing. She merely continued to sip.

"We're not going to inherit the estate, Raffles," he said. "I've known that for some time now, but I couldn't bring myself to tell you. I was determined to try everything possible, but nothing has worked. Lawton wants the place for himself and he's too influential in the county for me to fight."

"We're . . . not getting the estate!" she gasped. "I can't believe it! And I don't . . . Daddy, I still find it difficult to accept. What you say about Lawton. I want more proof! And I . . . Why should I believe you now? You've been so secretive! And what have you done about . . . about our financial situation?" He wouldn't look into her eyes. She gulped her brandy and nearly choked as she waited for the next terrible blow.

"I had to do something drastic. We have to live in

style, Raffles. You must attract the most eligible men in the state as suitors, must have a sizable dowry."

"Tell me what you've done!" she cried. "I'm beginning to imagine you've sold us both for gold and silver!"

He drained his brandy.

"I've married Frannie Deavors," he said.

"Married!" Rafaella said. All the heat tightened in her throat and her stomach. She felt nauseous. Dizziness flooded her body and drained her strength.

"Raffles, are you all right?" Blaine asked. He had never seen a look like the one on her face. "I know you don't like her, Raffles, but it has to be. Don't look so! Between us, we'll . . . things will still be the same . . . we'll live in style, we'll be together, and we'll go away on long trips, just the two of us, just like before, without Frannie. And soon you'll probably marry, too."

"You married that . . . that stupid woman . . . that common floozy . . . that whore!" Rafaella shrieked. "Yes, that whore! That cheap whore is your wife and my . . . my stepmother! Why? Why, Daddy? You said you'd never get married, Daddy! You said it again and again. You promised me!" The words choked her. Tears swam in her eyes. She felt she might faint.

"Raffles, please," he pleaded. "Please calm down. It has to do with money. Let's talk about this rationally."

"It's a little damned late for talk, Daddy!" she said. "You've saddled yourself with a whore, made us dependent on a whore's money. And every night I'll lie awake and know you and that whore are in bed together! Or will there be nights when she's not home, when she's out with one of her other men?"

"That's enough of that talk, Raffles!" he said. "I'll have no more!"

"I won't live with her!" Rafaella shouted. "I swear to God I won't live under the same roof with her. Or you. Oh, God, I hate you! How could you be so disgusting? And because of my dowry. Well, I won't have it. The money *or* the dowry! I'd as soon sell myself under the hill. Why not? Isn't that what you've done, Daddy? Sold yourself, become a whore, a gigolo?"

"I've had all of this I'll hear," he said. "Now, go to your room, and we'll discuss this another time."

"Go to my room." She mocked his words. "Send the little girl away, Daddy, because you can't face what she has to say. All these years I've been a grown-up lady for you. Haven't I? Haven't I been like your wife, Daddy? In every way except . . . And now I'm going to become the little daughter, and Frannie Deavors is going to take my place."

Rafaella hurled her brandy glass aside without looking to see where it fell. She brushed hot tears out of her eyes. Her eyes were black with rage.

Blaine winced at the sound of shattering crystal.

"It's the brandy making you talk this way," he said. His face was crimson. His breath came in gasps.

"I hate you!" she shouted. "How could I have ever loved you so . . . respected you so?" She looked at him full face and slapped his cheek with all her strength.

"Wasn't I enough of a wife, Daddy?" she said. "I suppose just watching me wasn't enough. Oh, no, I wasn't the whore your little Frannie is. I never bought you a silver-handled cane. And I never . . ."

Her eyes snapped. She brushed away a flood of tears with the back of her hand. Her father still stood without moving, his hands in loose fists at his sides. Blood trickled from his nose.

"You're bleeding," she mumbled. "Oh, Daddy, I didn't mean to hurt you. I wouldn't hurt you for anything." She stumbled toward him, but he stiffened.

"I won't . . . hurt you any more, Daddy. Here, let me wipe away the blood." She took out her yellow lace handkerchief and patted at his face. He flinched uncontrollably, then stood rigid. "I'm sorry for saying all those things, Daddy. I was so . . . so surprised. But nothing's done that can't be fixed, Daddy. You made a mistake, but we can fix it. You can divorce that woman. You will, won't you, Daddy?"

"No, I'm afraid I can't," he mumbled. "Perhaps I've made a grave mistake, Raffles, but divorcing Frannie now is out of the question."

"I said—*you will divorce that whore*!" Rafaella screamed. I'll *make* you divorce her! I'll find some way, dammit!"

Without a word, Blaine turned and left the room.

Rafaella stood alone, her eyes blank, her shoulders shaking, her stomach knotted.

"You *will* divorce that whore!" she whispered.

She picked up her father's brandy glass and smashed it against the fireplace, then threw the half-full bottle through the window.

31.

"I do enjoy seein' my family all together," Frannie said. She sat proudly in a red plush armchair in the front parlor of her town house. "How 'bout 'nother currant tea cake, Raffles, honey? They go so good with buttermilk, I always say. Don't you always say that, too, Mama?"

Blaine watched his wife, daughter, and mother-in-law from the corner of his eye. He'd passed up tea in favor of whiskey and had already drunk more than usual, trying to endure the occasion, which he found tedious as well as vulgar. At his right sat his father-in-law, Slidell Runnels, blathering about the problems of doctoring slaves. Though Runnels had never finished the first grade, he had made a small fortune by styling himself a "slave doctor."

Most of Blaine's attention was trained, apprehensively, on Rafaella. She was seated demurely between two women he knew she detested. Only the day before she had lost her temper and called Frannie a whore in four languages. Fortunately, Frannie understood none of them. It had not been her first tantrum in the week since they'd moved into Frannie's Natchez house.

Blaine was deeply worried about his daughter. Between violent outbursts of temper, Rafaella had locked herself in her room and taken long walks alone. At first she had refused to speak to him at all, and he found this far more ominous than her outbursts. He feared she was planning some desperate move, and so after her tirade the previous day, he had resorted to yet another round of lies. He had promised Rafaella that he would divorce Frannie as quickly as it could be arranged.

"You know, I don't really believe you," she said. "I don't think I'll ever believe you again. Or respect you."

"Please give me a little time . . . give me just one week, Raffles," he said. "Surely you can endure the situation that long. I made a terrible mistake. I'll admit that. And now I must extricate us with some kind of financial settlement. You know Frannie. It will be simple enough to catch her in a situation of adultery. Then we'll take the settlement and go away, just the two of us."

Rafaella had smiled at that, had kissed his cheek. But the smile had been fleeting.

"I still don't trust you, Daddy," she had said. "But I'm so miserable, I don't see that I have much choice. I swear, if you're lying to me again, you'll be sorry. I'll make you sorry, Daddy. Oh, I love you so much."

Now he watched her suffering Frannie's talk about culture in Natchez and about the way she had been redecorating this town house. It was in abominable taste, though her plantation house was decorated acceptably. Frannie had said that her husband Lavon, the slave trader, had imported items from all over the Continent to make his plantation grander than The Columns.

"Real elegant and real pretty." Frannie was boasting to Rafaella about a carved swan. Apparently, Frannie had heard that sculpture was a sign of culture, so she had found a local man who called himself a sculptor and had become his most enthusiastic patron. The wood-paneled parlor in which they sat was now crammed with some two dozen ill-carved fauns, nymphs, and muscular figures in heroic poses.

"Treatin' your nigger for cancer's lots different than treatin' your white man," Runnels was saying. "You follow me, Mr. Blaine? Their insides is different from those of a white man."

Blaine nodded. "Yes, I follow you, Mr. Runnels," he said.

"Now, say your nigger's got cancer in the stomach," Runnels said. "Way to cure him is to wrap a rabbit pelt around his middle. And dropsy in your nigger, sir, why, best thing is a mixture of ground-up grape vines, some mustard seed, some juniper berries in a couple of gallons of hard cider. And then for good measure you throw in a half a pound of rusty nails."

"Indeed, Mr. Runnels," Blaine said, and drank more whiskey.

Runnels was drinking whiskey also, and his red-veined cheeks glowed redder beside his red whiskers. His small, sharp blue eyes darted about as he talked, but not once had they met Blaine's. Now he was discoursing about the deficiency of red blood cells in the black man and the necessity for an annual spring bleeding as well as the advisability of frequent emetics.

"For fall complaints," Runnels confided, "I give 'em red pepper. Pops 'em right up. Good for sore throats, too." Blaine looked miserably over at Rafaella and Frannie while he nodded at Runnels's talk. With small provocation, he would have set down his glass and strangled Runnels to silence him. He was as stupid and common a man as Blaine had ever met, and he was matched by his son, Frannie's brother, Charlie, who ran nigger dogs and chewed tobacco. He detested both men, along with Runnels's skinny, fast-talking wife. He detested Frannie and her whining, crippled son. And in the past week he had come to detest himself—and not without good reason, he told himself. Rafaella had more character and spunk in her little finger than he had in his whole head.

Blaine was in an increasingly hopeless dilemma, he knew, and he had made many mistakes. The worst mistake was marrying Frannie. How could he have thought he and Rafaella could live with people like this? They were worse than common—they were trash, the lowest sort of people. All of Frannie's great wealth was built on her husband's slave trading—a practice that, though now illegal and openly despised by Natchez society, was still being carried on by her agents and overseer. Frannie's first husband, Lavon Deavors, had started out penniless in partnership with a man named Purvis Swan, dead now, but whose own dubious "profession"—tracking runaways—was being carried on with great pride and pleasure by Frannie's brother.

Whenever he thought of it, Blaine was swamped by despair. And why hadn't he realized how violently, bitterly Rafaella would react? She was out of control with rage and resentment. He still winced at the memory of the scene at the hotel when he had told her he was married. He had been truly frightened by her that night and had fled the hotel for a tavern.

That had been the first time she had thrown the sexual situation at him, had blamed and taunted him. Why had he ever let it develop, let it continue? How had he allowed himself to become obsessed with desire for his own daughter's body?

For a long while he thought she did not know or understand it. Then he came to realize that she understood quite well and that she posed for him deliberately. She had been right when she'd said she had become his wife in every way but one. He had become far too dependent on her and had allowed her to become too dependent on him. They were too close, dangerously close, unnaturally close . . .

Yet he could not deny that he loved his daughter above all else and that he was physically sick when she was angry with him. In truth, he was afraid of her, repelled by her power over him almost as powerfully as he was attracted to her. How had this come to be, he asked himself.

What kind of a daughter had he raised? But he knew he didn't really care about her morals. He loved Rafaella, worshipped her as she was. And most of all, he knew that he could never bear to lose her. He would die first. No, he would control his love, change it; he would get them both out of this mess, somehow.

Staying here was impossible. No amount of money was worth it. The most important thing in his life was Rafaella, and he would pay any price, commit any act, to keep her love and her respect.

He knew now that he must extricate himself from this situation and do so quickly. Rafaella was not patient. She was as reckless and ruthless as he was, and she too was capable of swift, devastating action. He had seen it before. He remembered once in Rome, when she was only fifteen. She had been angry, and the man who had crossed her had died.

He had little time. He glanced at the clock. Rafaella was watching him, affecting cool interest in Frannie's bric-a-brac. Out of the corner of his eye, he saw her deliberately knock her glass of buttermilk onto the ugly green carpet.

"Oh, no!" Frannie shrieked. "Bessie! Bessie, come at once!"

A matronly slave appeared in the doorway. Directly behind her was Charlie Runnels, Frannie's brother, smelling of his own slave dogs.

"Chewing a particular kind of yellow clay'll cure a nigger's malaria 'most every time," Slidell Runnels was saying. "Why . . . why, what's wrong?"

"Excuse me, Mr. Runnels; excuse me, ladies; but I must attend to some business," Blaine said abruptly.

He rose and hurried past Charlie Runnels, out of the house.

32.

A week later, Roger Blaine spurred his horse up the tree-edged road to Frannie's plantation. He had nearly given up hope. Relations between Frannie and Rafaella were worse than ever, and he was half-mad with anxiety over the situation.

He had tried. Deliberately, he had stirred up Rafaella's mind against the Deavorses, convinced her that they were still scheming to get hold of the Price Deavors estate. Bribing witnesses had cost him the last of the money Frannie had given him for a wedding present. But Rafaella was still in a murderous mood. His only hope was to take Rafaella and flee. But where? With what money? He had no way to get a good sum from Frannie without taking her along.

The house came into view. It was huge and grand and well proportioned. Yet the sight of it gave Blaine no pleasure. From the end of the rose-walled lawn, he could see that both Frannie and Rafaella were standing on the front verandah. He had no doubt that they were both waiting for him. He groaned, but he dug his spurs into the horse's flanks and trotted up to the mansion. A groom appeared and Blaine tossed him the reins as he slid off.

"Roger!" Frannie wailed.

"Oh, Daddy!" Rafaella called impatiently.

"You've just got to do somethin' with the child, Roger, honey," Frannie said. "Why, she used the dirtiest language in insultin' me, and she just won't ever obey me."

"I'm no child, you cow," Raffles said. "And I'm not about to obey you. Daddy, this is hopeless. Just look at her! And listen to the way she talks! Daddy, she's *ridiculous*!"

"Oh, Roger, she's just impossible!" Frannie said, as she clutched at Blaine's arm. "And she's got the rudest manners. Why, when Mrs. Emmeline Eyar was visitin' and we got to talkin' 'bout art and culture and all, why she actually said we was ignorant as pigs."

"I have no manners, you bitch?" Rafaella said. "*You've* got the manners of a field nigger, and less wit."

"Listen to that talk, Roger," Frannie said. "I won't stand for it. Do somethin', honey." And Frannie leaned up and kissed his cheek.

The color drained from Rafaella's face.

"My God, how cheap!" Rafaella said. "Would you make love to him right here on the porch, to get your way? I'm sure it wouldn't be the first time."

"Your dirty mouth!" Frannie screamed. She clung to Blaine's arm and hugged him tighter. He felt the pressure of her breasts against him. "Roger, I demand she be punished. She needs a good whippin'! Nobody talks to me like that. I'm a Deavors! I got more money than anybody in the county! I been educated at the Miss Forlone's School for Ladies! Oh, honey, do somethin' to her, and I'll make it real nice for you, like I done last night in bed . . ."

"Be quiet, Frannie," Blaine said. "And please let go of my arm."

"My God, Daddy!" Rafaella shouted. "How have we come to this?"

"You be quiet, too, young lady," Blaine said. He tugged at Frannie's fingers, but she held on. Brazenly, she was rubbing her breasts against him. Rafaella's face was flushed again, with that strange smile curling her lips. She was capable of anything in this mood, and Blaine saw disaster only a moment away.

"I can tell how well you've been educated," Rafaella said. "Where was Miss Forlone's School located? Under the hill? On one of those barges?"

"Goddammit, be still, Raffles!" Blaine said. "And you, Frannie, goddammit, let go of my arm!"

"But, Daddy, Frannie'll make it real nice for you, like last night in bed," Rafaella said. Her little smile was deadly, half-crazed.

"Roger, honey, you swore to me you'd make her behave!" Frannie cried. "Just two nights ago you promised anything on earth to make me happy, and I said I just couldn't take no more of Raffles' bein' snotty."

"Did you really promise her that, Daddy?" Rafaella asked. "How obliging you've become! And how about what you swore to me? You promised you'd leave this bitch in a week's time! But perhaps your vows to her mean more to you. After all, I haven't made it real nice for you, have I, Daddy? At least not yet."

With a brutal gesture, Blaine tore free of Frannie's hands. He had to end this disastrous scene at all costs.

"What did you say about leavin' me?" Frannie squealed.

"Be quiet, Frannie!" Blaine said. "I'll talk to you later. Raffles, come with me. Come on, dammit!"

Blaine was prepared to carry Rafaella away, even kicking and screaming. He could bear no more. But she accompanied him without protest. They walked inside, up the great front staircase to her bedroom. He opened the door and she walked in. He followed and closed the door.

"Raffles, I cannot tolerate—" he began.

Rafaella turned on him. "*You* can't tolerate!" she snapped. "I can't tolerate it! Your wife! It's outrageous! Lying to me and lying to her. Talking about me! I just hate you for that."

"Raffles, I am trying to do what's best," Blaine said. He felt utterly helpless. "I had to tell the woman something. The important thing is that . . ."

"The important thing is that Frannie's real nice to you," Rafaella said. "She's using her sex—and, God, she must have enough experience at it—to separate us."

"No, Raffles!" Blaine said.

"And you don't even realize what she's doing! We've always been together, just us, since Mama died, and we've never needed anyone else. But now you've married that woman and she's becoming more important to you than I am. Why? Why did you do it, Daddy? Don't tell me it was simply for her money. There's something more, a lot more."

"Raffles, please listen," Blaine said. "Let me explain."

"I wouldn't believe anything you said, Daddy!" she said. Tears swelled in her eyes and rolled down her cheeks. "I don't care what your reason was—just marrying some slut like Frannie, just sleeping with her, kills my respect for you."

"Don't talk like that, Raffles, please," he said.

"Lying in bed with her while I'm alone here! *I'm* the one you love! You *know* it!"

"Goddammit, please stop, Raffles!" Blaine said. He was desperate, yet he had no idea what to say to her, no idea how to handle her. Her statement that she no longer respected him was a crushing blow.

"I won't stop!" she said. "I want all this ended now. I swear I won't spend another night in this house. I'm serious. Even if I have to . . . to go into Natchez and sell myself. Tell me, Daddy, would it have been different if I had been *real* nice to you? I did everything else for you, didn't I? If you had asked me, I'd have done that, too. I'd have done anything for you, Daddy. I let you watch me undress, let you watch me bathe. I posed for you. Though lately I haven't, have I? Is that it? Do you want me to undress for you, Daddy? Right now? I vow I can please you better than that woman!" she gasped. He couldn't stand to see her so upset.

"Please, Raffles, don't. It was all a mistake, my mistake. Watching you . . . I'm sorry. I shouldn't have. But it could never have gone any further. Oh, Raffles, I've failed you. If only I hadn't . . ."

"No, Daddy, I expect I've failed you," she said. Her words were high-pitched. He realized she was hysterical. "If you had to turn to someone like Frannie, I failed you miserably. If I'd . . . been bolder about . . . undressing and posing and all . . . I could have bound you to me. None of this would have happened. Lock the door, Daddy, and I'll make it up to you. I'll get undressed for you. And pose . . . in all kinds of ways. And you can . . . you can touch me . . . and everything."

"Oh, God, stop this!" Blaine cried. "Raffles, I love you. Please stop this or I'll go mad!"

There was a knock. Blaine ignored it. Another knock.

"Roger! Come out! Open up!" Frannie's shrill voice called.

"Goddammit, Frannie, leave me alone!" Blaine said.

"Why, Roger!"

"Why, Roger!" Rafaella mimicked. She ran to the door, locked it, seized the key from the lock, and tucked it into her bodice.

"Raffles, give me that key! What are you doing?"

Her eyes snapping with excitement and anger, Rafaella ran across the room from her father and lifted her skirt to unfasten her stockings. "I love you, Daddy," she said. "And I want to do everything for you."

"Stop! You mustn't . . ." he protested.

"Oh, yes, I will! I can't stand to have you . . . prefer her." Rafaella kicked off pink satin slippers and unrolled her long white silk stockings. "Let's just pretend we're back at the fig grove, Daddy. Look, wasn't it like this?" As he stared, she lifted her full pleated silk skirt and bared her knees. Her face was flushed, but the skin of her legs was pale, unblemished, delicate.

His mouth was dry, but sweat had broken out on his forehead. "Stop, Raffles!" he begged. He put out his hand to grab the key from her, to stop her from turning round and round in a flashing, spinning display of legs and silk petticoats. When she saw him reaching for her, she stopped suddenly and tugged open her bodice. The key fell out and jangled to the floor, and his hands were full of the soft, sensuous weight of her full breasts.

"Oh! Yes, please, Daddy, touch me . . . kiss me . . . oh, tell me I'm beautiful, Daddy. Tell me I'm prettier than she is." Before he could speak, she pulled away again and fumbled at the hooks that held her petticoats to the cinched waist of her corsets. Her breasts swung free and Blaine stared at them. He could not look away. He was fascinated, fevered, sick with guilt and horror.

Her breasts were large for the slightness of her back and shoulders. They were topped with round, dark-red nipples, as rosy as berries against the snow white globes. Lacy, filmy silken sashes and slips dangled for a moment on her round, white hips, then slid to the floor.

She was naked. "See, Daddy? . . . all for you . . . do I please you? You'll have to show me how . . . you'll have to teach me what you want me to do . . . what I need to do to make you happy. I'll do anything you want . . . anything, Daddy."

Her voice was a whisper. Blaine groaned. He was reeling with desire and guilt. He wanted to die and he wanted to touch her. He knew, finally and terribly, how far his obsession with his daughter had gone. It was out of control. She was out of control. His fingers ached to touch her skin. His arms tingled with longing to hold her. He was sexually excited in a way that he had never been before.

"What are you waiting for, Daddy? Isn't this what you wanted? Isn't this what you raised me for? Don't I please you anymore? I always used to please you. You brought me up to please you, didn't you? What's the matter? You look funny. Why are you turning away from me?"

"Raffles! I can't . . . you mustn't . . . I mustn't . . . I wouldn't. I never meant to . . ."

Blaine scrambled on the floor for the key. He felt waves of dizziness, felt he might lose consciousness.

"Daddy! You can't mean to leave me! You can't leave me now. I love you . . . you love me . . . I can't live without you." Rafaella ran over to her kneeling father, spread her naked body over his clothed one, her legs on either side of his back, her arms and hands clinging to him, her breasts and belly pressed against his back.

He felt her soft weight with a sickening pleasure. She squirmed. "Rafaella! Stop that! Get off at once!" He tried to turn, tried to rise, and she fell alongside him, grabbing at him with astonishing strength. Her mouth was open and her eyes were black with excitement.

He could not help but see the soft, sleek planes of her body, the curves, the silken mound of her stomach, and the perfect triangle beneath, where her legs joined the core of her sex. Her skin shone with a fine, transparent beauty. He had to touch it. He could not help himself. His fingers trembled, reached out, stroked her from shoulder across her torso to the swell of her hip.

Rafaella whimpered. "Yes! Yes, Daddy . . . I want you to . . . I always knew you would . . . be the first man to make love to me. And I want it. . . now . . . oh, please, please kiss me, too." She wriggled under him, and his fingers felt the satiny resiliency of her belly, then felt the softness below.

"No! I can't! Oh, God, Raffles," he gasped helplessly.

"Kiss me, Daddy! And look into my face! Know it's me . . . your beloved . . . who always loved you best."

His eyes were shut against the horror of what he felt himself about to do. Her fingers were scratching at the buttons of his trousers. Desperately, he forced himself to open his eyes, to look into her face.

"After this, Daddy, you'll always be mine, won't you? We'll stay together, always, just us, we'll belong together, won't we? No one will ever be able to come between us, Daddy."

Blaine looked into Rafaella's face, and what he saw stopped his heart. She wore her tiny smile, the one that affected only the very corners of her beautiful mouth. And her eyes were wide open, glazed, but not with passion. The look on her face was one of sheer triumph. She was ecstatic with victory, with the joy of triumph.

"No! No, Raffles, No, no, no, no . . ." he gasped. He fought to get out of her grasp, away from her fingers, her clinging flesh. He was profoundly frightened by the intensity of the look on her face.

Somehow his fingers closed over the key, and he scrambled to the door. "Get dressed!" he called to his daughter. There was more pounding on the door, but the voice that called to him wasn't Frannie's.

"Mist' Roger! Mist' Roger!" a woman called, a house slave by the sound of her voice.

"Just a minute!" Blaine said. He quickly adjusted his clothing, stalked to the door, and opened it just wide enough to step outside. In the hallway, Blaine confronted Fennel, one of Frannie's house slaves, and behind her, a male slave Blaine had seen at The Columns.

"What in hell is it, Fennel?" Blaine asked.

"Awful sorry, Mist' Roger," the woman said, "but Mr. Lawton Deavors, he done sent this nigger over from The Columns. He say it mighty 'portant you go over and see him."

"Yes, yes, all right, I'll attend to it," Blaine said.

The Deavors slave stepped forward. "Mist' Lawton, he say it awful urgent you come right 'way," the man said. "Mist' Lawton, he say to tell you—"

"All right, all right, goddammit!" Blaine said. "I understand. I'll get over there. Now both of you, get the hell out of here. And Fennel, I don't want to be disturbed again."

"Yessir, Mist' Roger," Fennel said. "But Miss Frannie, she done asked me to tell you she 'spects . . ."

Frannie had crept up the stairs during this conversation. Blaine saw her hesitating near the top of the balustrade. The sight of her infuriated him.

"I said get the hell out of here and leave me alone!" he shouted. "So help me God, if you come near me or bother me again . . ."

Frannie and the slaves fled down the hall. Blaine stood there a long moment, his hands opening and closing at his sides. His breath came in great rushes. So it had finally happened, he told himself. Proof had reached Lawton. And now there would be the confrontation, and his past, hidden for all these years, would be thrown into his face. And everyone would know. He would be ruined, and Rafaella would find out. *That* on top of everything else!

Blaine turned toward his bedroom. He had never been in so desperate, so murderous a mood. He told himself that surely there was still time to reach Lawton before the boy showed the evidence to anyone else, time to silence Lawton one way or another. One way or another, he repeated to himself. He would do anything to keep the worst secret of all from Rafaella.

In his room, Blaine grabbed his pistol. He would go at once. It must be settled immediately. He would do whatever was necessary. He had already gone too far with Rafaella. After a certain point, life was not worth living. Now there was no turning back.

He left the house and mounted for his ride to The Columns.

33.

A mist fell on the burying ground as the Reverend Dawkins prayed over Roger Blaine's coffin. A small half-circle of white mourners stood in the damp, pungent red dirt. Behind them were assembled hundreds of blacks—all the slaves from The Columns and from Frannie's plantation.

Earlier, Reverend Dawkins had delivered a lengthy funeral service at the Benton Presbyterian Church. Now, instead of simply reciting the usual prayer of ashes to ashes, he was launching into a second eulogy for a man who had not attended his church, a man he had never met, and his audience was getting wet and restless.

Rafaella stood apart from the others. She was a small, pale figure in a black silk dress and a black hat with a black veil. She stood with her head down, her feet together, her hands clasped in front of her. She was so still she didn't seem to be breathing.

Rafaella had been in a frightening, nearly catatonic state of silent grief for the past two days. When Lawton had discovered Roger Blaine's body on the house road and come to tell Rafaella that her father had killed himself, she had gone into terrifying hysterics. She had cried until her face was swollen. She had screamed her throat raw. She had begged Lawton to say he was lying. Her body had been racked with convulsions. She had smashed two mirrors and scratched ugly gashes into the arm of a house slave who had tried to lead her to a chair. Lawton had watched in horror.

Frannie's entry into the room had intensified Rafaella's hysteria. The sight of Frannie triggered new energies. Rafaella had attacked her, scratching and biting, and it had taken all Lawton's strength to tear her fingers from Frannie's hair.

"He wouldn't be dead if he hadn't married a slut like you!" Rafaella had shouted. "I hate you . . . you whore . . . you bitch! He died because of you. I hate you!"

Rafaella had calmed down somewhat when Frannie fled. She stood swaying, her eyes red; little mewing, hacking sounds came from her throat.

"Please help me, Lawton," she whispered. "I don't think I can stand any more." She swayed. The house slaves hung back, afraid to approach her.

Lawton rushed to help her. He put his hands on her shoulders to hold her up, but Rafaella had pressed her body against his and clung to him, her nails digging into his back. Her tears had wet his chest through his linen.

Rafaella had cried and raved almost incoherently. "He couldn't be dead. Not my father. Why would he kill himself? Why? He loved me too much to kill himself. He wouldn't leave me alone like this. I've never been alone. I want to die, too. It wasn't supposed to be. I loved him so much. It's not my fault. It wasn't! Not my fault . . . I loved him . . ."

Later, when Lawton recalled the scene, everyone was touched. Neighborhood women had cried and called Rafaella "a poor, lonely little girl, left penniless and an orphan in a strange land."

But Lawton told no one how Rafaella had rubbed her body against him, how her hips had ground against his groin, how her nails had crept up his back and raked his neck.

He told no one how he had become sexually aroused, how his loins had ached, with what difficulty he had fought back desire as she cried and rubbed against him. Not even to himself did he admit that she had stirred a sexual excitement more intense than any he had ever before experienced.

Nor had Lawton told anyone how, after he had held Rafaella in his arms, her sobs had become angry accusations. "It's your fault, too, Lawton. You're to blame, too. You made him kill himself. You and all the Deavorses. He told me how you wouldn't let us have our estate and how you were spreading slander about him. I won't ever forget, Lawton . . . I hate you. I do. I hate you and your whole family. You made him kill himself and I loved him so much and now I'm alone. It's not *my* fault. I didn't do anything wrong. It's your fault, Lawton. I hate you."

Then she had gone still, and so limp that Lawton had had difficulty holding her up. She's just upset, he'd told himself. Don't pay any heed. When she spoke again her voice had changed, become softer, supplicating. "I didn't mean that, Lawton. I don't hate you. You wouldn't do that to him, to me. I'm so scared, Lawton. I need you, Lawton . . . I love you. I really do. Please help me, Lawton. I'll do anything for you . . . I'll be nice to you, just like I was to Daddy, Lawton. I don't have a father now. All I have is you, Lawton."

He stayed with her as long as he could, then saw that she was given a sedative and put to bed.

As Lawton rode home he was so consumed by guilt, sorrow, anxiety, and desire that he'd had to dismount and vomit at the side of the road.

Reverend Dawkins had finally spoken the words "ashes to ashes," and Blaine's coffin was being lowered into the grave. Rafaella had not moved, had not shown

174

the slightest sign of life. Several men were ready to rush to her side if she seemed about to faint. Lawton, too, tensed himself to move quickly to Rafaella—and realized that the tensing stirred memories of her body pressed against him.

With the rush of sexual excitement that tightened his loins and made his cheeks burn came a rush of guilt. If he had handled things differently, he told himself, perhaps Blaine wouldn't have killed himself.

For the hundredth time he asked himself why Blaine had done it. Was he responsible? He'd sent a message to the man, intending to beg him to reconsider his renunciation of the property. Blaine had come and had shot himself—in full view of The Columns. Why? Was it fear of the report from Price Deavors's agent? Dread of those rumors coming out? Or despair at his hopeless marriage to Frannie? What else could it have been? How pitifully desperate he must have been.

And what now was he to believe about Blaine, about the agent's only half-substantiated evidence that the man had once been an Egyptian slave? It mattered little now, he told himself. He must see, above all else, that the rumor went no further, never tarnished Blaine's memory, and far more important, that Rafaella was never tainted by it. The very whiff of such a scandal would ruin her, of course. To be thought the daughter of any slave would make her a hopeless outcast. He would never repeat that allegation. That was the most important thing. That, and to see that she was well taken care of.

The coffin struck ground and the ropes were pulled up. Reverend Dawkins picked up a small scoop of mud and offered it to Rafaella. She paid no heed. Seconds passed, half a minute, and she did not look up. The mist was heavier. Dried rust and salmon-colored leaves swirled down from the overhanging sweet gum trees.

Finally Rafaella lifted her head. Someone gasped. Lawton felt a chill travel along his spine. He had never seen such a young, beautiful face show such agony. In her black eyes was a haunted, pained look of great loss. Beneath her deep-set eyes were strange patches of dark misery that looked like bruises. Her lips were clenched together, her mouth a thin dark line in flesh as pale as that of the corpse.

"Do you wish to . . .?" Reverend Dawkins started to ask, but Rafaella shuddered and blinked, as though waking from a trance, and he bit off the sentence.

Rafaella looked slowly from the minister to the scoop of mud. Her lips fell open. She shuddered again. She reached for the scoop. She took it in her trembling fingers but she could not hold it, and the scoop fell to the ground.

Lawton was the first to reach her. He hesitated an instant before putting an arm around her shoulders. She stiffened and glanced up, frightened. Then she smiled. It was a sweet, vulnerable smile, one Lawton had never seen before.

"I knew you'd come to me first," she whispered.

Lucinda joined them. Neighbors and cousins clustered around, then fell behind as Lawton and Lucinda led Rafaella toward the assembled carriages. Frannie had been standing on the other side of the grave. Now she sloshed through the deepening mud and joined them. She babbled about tragedy and how, even though she was suffering terribly, poor little Raffles's tragedy was much worse; how they were all Deavorses and had to stick together during this time of sorrow.

"Well, here's the carriage, Raffles," Frannie said. "Tolver, you get down and help Miss Raffles inside, you hear me! That Tolver! He run away and I swore I'd have him whipped when he was caught. But he come back of his own free will, so I just had him locked up for a couple of days. Usually, he's such a good nigger."

Rafaella shrank back from Frannie and Tolver. She glanced miserably from Lucinda to Lawton.

"Please, may I speak to you . . . alone?" she whispered.

The three of them walked away from the carriages and stood under a sweet gum tree a few yards away.

"Please, I can't go home with Frannie!" Rafaella said. "Please, Lawton . . . Lucinda . . . I just *detest* that woman. You know what she's like. I just can't. Could I come stay at The Columns with you? Just for a day or two. Then I'll leave, I promise."

"Of course you can, Raffles," Lucinda said.

Lawton mumbled, "Of course."

They returned to the carriages. Lawton told Frannie. She protested, but not very strongly.

"Only for a couple of days, though," Frannie insisted. "Then you got to come back home, Raffles. We Deavorses got to help each other out in this time of sorrow."

Rafaella turned and walked away while Frannie was still speaking. Lawton and Lucinda followed her to their carriage.

All the white people but one had left the cemetery. The slaves were being loaded into wooden wagons that rolled slowly down the muddy road. Finally there remained only one horse and one wagonful of slaves.

The rain was falling harder, and the slaves tried to shield themselves as they looked back at the fresh grave. Two men stood on opposite sides of it.

Wyman Ridgeway was one. He stayed only a couple of minutes after watching Rafaella ride away with the Deavorses. He scratched his withered left hand with his right, brushed rain from his face, then hurried to mount his horse and trot away.

Cellus was left alone at the earth-heaped grave. Though the slaves in the wagon were soaking wet now, no one dared call out to him to hurry. For many years, Cellus had been an ageless and awe-inspiring figure to most of the Deavorses and all their slaves. No one questioned his authority. Lawton had been raised to respect and rely on the rigidly moral grey-headed man, and he depended on him now more than ever. Cellus seemed more than a slave, somehow above most men, black or white, especially since the awful night when

Lavon Deavors and his slave patrol had tied him up and beaten him and branded both his palms.

"No ordinary man could survive such a beating," Dr. Stacey had said at the time. Cellus was no ordinary man, but even so his recovery had been slow. Only in the past two weeks had he regained enough strength to resume all his duties. His duties were considerable, as everyone knew: he ran the house, supervised the buying and bookkeeping and accounts, and he had as much say in important decisions as Mist' Lawton, and far more than Miss 'Cinda.

Now Cellus stood at the graveside in the rain, a tall, solitary, ramrod-straight figure. No one knew what he might be thinking as he looked off into a distance of his own.

Five minutes had passed, and still Cellus stood beside the grave. Rain soaked him and the waiting slaves. Finally, he began to walk slowly toward the wagon.

34.

Lucinda was alone in her bedroom when she saw a man on horseback in the distance, halfway up the road to the house. The rider stopped as though watching the slaves move in from the fields to the quarters. It was deep dusk, the time when the picking stopped because it was too dark to distinguish the white pods from the rest of the cotton plant.

She could see that the people moved very slowly. Many were bowed, stooped with weariness. Some seemed to be dragging themselves along, barely able to put one foot in front of the other. Lawton was worried that the people were working too hard, and Lucinda thought he might be right. Although some pods were already rotting, and although the picking could be finished in a few days if everyone worked full time, Lawton insisted that the people be given half of Sunday off. Lawton and Lucinda had discussed this plan and decided it was necessary. Some of the people were worn out.

"We'll have to see what Cellus has to say, of course," Lawton had added.

"Of course," Lucinda had agreed, without thinking. But now she found herself resenting that Lawton relied so much on Cellus, that he felt he couldn't make a decision without Cellus's advice, though he had run the plantation perfectly well during Cellus's convalescence and had recently bought up all the land to the river entirely on his own. Lucinda loved and admired Cellus, and she appreciated his importance to The Columns, but Cellus was getting old, she told herself. She was determined to take over more of Cellus's duties and to become mistress of the plantation in fact as well as in name.

Only a few weeks earlier, she had marched into the big, open kitchen and confronted Beatrice, the cook, about what to serve for supper that night. Lucinda wanted to have more French food, the sort she'd eaten at home in New Orleans. It was a trivial dispute, on the surface, but she had always before bowed to Beatrice's authority and had actually been afraid to invade her kitchen. But this time Lucinda had insisted, Beatrice had deferred, and Lucinda felt elated as a result. Beatrice had tried her hand at *boeuf à la daube*, and everyone had praised it, especially Lawton, and Lucinda had basked in reflected glory. She was willing, of course, to leave day-to-day management of the kitchen and larder to Beatrice, as long as the cook knew who was mistress of The Columns.

Lucinda saw that the rider was moving toward the house again, approaching very slowly. He sat slumped forward in the saddle as though the slaves' weariness were contagious. Lucinda still didn't recognize him.

Her thoughts drifted to the Harvest Ball. It was her main concern these days. The Deavorses' famous Harvest Ball had been held annually for decades, and an invitation to the affair was considered a necessary proof of a family's social standing in Adams County. Invitations had already been sent out, and acceptances were arriving. After much hesitation, she and Lawton had sent an invitation to Frannie Deavors. It was an awkward situation, and they certainly didn't want her to come. But she was a Deavors, by marriage. Actually, by two marriages. And with her stepdaughter staying at The Columns, how could they not invite her?

Not that Rafaella wanted to see Frannie. Indeed, when Frannie had come calling a few days earlier, Rafaella had refused to leave her room. Rafaella could not stand to hear the woman's name. It had been accepted, without any discussion, that she could not return to Frannie's just yet, and her stay at The Columns had stretched on to a week, ten days, now two weeks.

Lucinda's feelings toward Rafaella were mixed. She could see that the girl was still in a very vulnerable and disturbed state. At times she seemed almost unbalanced. But Lucinda no longer thought of her as a "poor, helpless little orphan." Despite her natural sympathy for bereavement, Lucinda could not consider Rafaella helpless. Actually, she was a tyrannical house guest. She made no effort to adjust to the life of the family, demanded special foods at odd hours, ordered the slaves around as if she were their mistress, and rejected Lucinda's offers of sympathy.

Lucinda resented particularly that Rafaella had smashed the crystal teardrop lamp that had been the gift of her French aunt, Amie, a lamp that had come upriver with her in her bridal trunks and had always rested prominently on the parlor mantelpiece. Rested there, that is, until Rafaella brushed against it and it shattered in a thousand glinting shards on the marble hearth. Lucinda wasn't at all sure Rafaella's gesture had been accidental.

Even more strongly, she resented Lawton's attitude toward Rafaella. She loved Lawton and she respected his judgment, but he seemed positively daffy about the girl. He would hear no complaints about her behavior and had gone too far, in Lucinda's estimation, in catering to her—sending trays to Rafaella's room when she refused to come out, sitting for hours beside her bed to comfort her. Unlike Lucinda, Lawton considered Rafaella a frail, delicate creature, on the verge of total breakdown.

But perhaps Lawton himself was feeling guilty about something. It made no sense, but neither had Roger Blaine's suicide. There was something odd about the whole thing, and Lawton steadfastly refused to discuss it. Sometimes Lucinda wished Joleen were still here. Joleen had always been good at understanding and communicating with her brother, and in this particular situation, Lucinda felt increasingly helpless.

She felt helpless, she resented Rafaella, and she was more than a bit upset with Lawton. And it was such a busy time of year! She hoped that as soon as the cotton picking was over, things would be cleared up. Something such as this could not stand between husband and wife without having an adverse effect on their marriage. And she was certain the strain of secrets and suspicions between them was the main reason why their lovemaking in the past couple of weeks had been infrequent and unsatisfying.

Lucinda looked from the window again. The rider was nearing the house now and she recognized him. It was Wyman Ridgeway.

On the same afternoon, Rafaella stood at her bedroom window and watched Wyman Ridgeway ride toward the house. She knew he was coming to call on her.

She turned away from the window. She had mixed feelings about Ridgeway's visit. She found him intriguing, despite his crippled hand. Fascinating, in a way. Repulsive, in another. At least he was not a bumpkin. He was certainly the most sophisticated man she had met in Mississippi, and despite his cynicism and abrupt manner, she felt confident that he was strongly attracted to her.

Of course, she was still in mourning. She was still

sick and miserable, yet she had already realized that misery was boring. So was trying to get along with Lucinda, so was isolation, so was life at The Columns. She was absolutely alone in the world now, and she knew, deep down, that she would have to stir herself soon, take some steps to get what she wanted.

Yes, she decided, she welcomed Ridgeway's visit. It would be a diversion. She was so restless. So unhappy! And so hot! She snatched up a black satin folding fan and began to fan herself rapidly. She was covered with moisture. At times she felt her lungs would stick together or she would smother in her sleep! The Mississippi climate was ghastly, doubtless terribly unhealthy. It was far hotter than a Roman summer, and it was already late November. The pernicious damp heat crept from the swamp as though it were the middle of July.

A minute of furious fanning exhausted her, and she sank down in a silk damask slipper chair. She really had no strength at all, and Dr. Stacey had warned her not to exert herself in any way. At times she felt her father's death had drained off all her strength forever, and she really didn't care if she slowly wasted away. She had not cried for four whole days now, for just as her strength had deserted her, she felt she had used up all her tears.

In the first few days after her father's suicide, she had considered taking her own life, and might have, if only she'd had the strength or the will. She had been more than half-dead, anyway. The shock of Lawton's news had been violent, deranging. During those first few days, there were other strong feelings that competed with her grief. Disbelief. Guilt. And, very powerfully, hatred. She hated Frannie. She hated Lawton. She hated all the Deavorses. She even hated her father, hated him for leaving her alone, hated him with a sickening intensity.

And, then, for brief periods, she hated herself as she lay sedated and semiconscious in the damp bed and thought of her father's suicide, tried to understand why he had killed himself and left her alone. She thought of their last time together, thought of how she had undressed and posed and teased to taunt him with her sex. Guilt washed over her at the memory, and she sucked in her breath trying to stop the pain of remembering. Her stomach felt hollow. She slid to the floor and started for the door, but stopped and returned meekly to the bed and sat down again.

She had been so very wrong even to consider hating her father, she told herself. How awful of her! He had always loved her best, and he had realized his mistake in marrying that loathsome woman. But still, *why* did he have to kill himself? Oh, damn it, it was unbearable!

It wasn't his fault . . . wasn't hers . . . so it must be . . . oh, it made no sense, no sense at all! No matter how badly that last scene had gone, he had loved her too much to kill himself because of it. It just had to be . . . oh, it was so awful, so wrong. They could have left the slut, could have done something . . . anything.

She groaned. She could stand no more speculation just now. Somehow, she must bear it, must take care of herself. As her Daddy had always done, as her dear cousin Lawton had been doing these last days.

Sweet Lawton. He had been so thoughtful, so kind during her stay at The Columns. He was so handsome, so competent. Really, she liked him better than ever. And he liked her, she knew. He promised he would take care of her in any way she needed, and he had proved his willingness.

When she couldn't bear to go down to dinner, it was Lawton who brought a slave with food to her room. Lawton himself stayed by her and encouraged her to eat. In fact, many times when Lucinda wasn't around, he'd come to her room, just to talk, and twice he'd brought her flowers.

She wished . . . she wished . . . sometimes during these awful days and nights she had lain awake thinking of what it would be like if her father had died differently—in some battle, or some duel, as a hero, of course, not by his own hand—and if Lawton weren't married, and he were calling on her and courting her, and when she had recovered from her grief, he begged her to marry him.

Rafaella forced herself to stand up again. Blood pounded at her temples. She was short of breath. Again, she felt she was smothering. She walked over and leaned from the window. A slave was leading Ridgeway's horse around the house, cooling it off.

Rafaella turned from the window. She decided she would go down and receive Ridgeway at once. Surely, he would distract her for a few minutes from her grief. Not that she cared for Ridgeway, romantically. The only man she really wanted was Lawton, and he was married . . . married to Lucinda, who didn't really like her, she was sure. And Lawton, amusingly, didn't like Ridgeway. So much the better. She would enjoy making Lawton a little jealous.

For the first time in two weeks, she began to feel mild enthusiasm for something. She would dress and go down. She went over and opened the door and called to her maid, Florncey, who was waiting just down the hall.

35.

"Is it true that you fought two duels this week already, Mr. Ridgeway?" Lucinda asked.

Lucinda, Lawton, Rafaella, and Ridgeway were sitting on the porch after dinner. As was the custom in isolated areas, Ridgeway had not only been asked to supper but invited to spend the night at The Columns.

"Yes, I believe it's been two, Mrs. Deavors," Ridgeway said. He sat slumped in his chair, as though so weary he could not manage to sit straight.

"And what were the causes, sir?" Lawton asked.

"Ah, it's always difficult to remember after a few days," Ridgeway said. "I believe one fellow became insulted and called me out when I suggested that his dancing was nearly as atrocious as his manners. The other had been going around Natchez denouncing me. I can't imagine why. I had never done him a favor. In any case, he denounced me to my face, and what can one do on such occasions, on these endless, damp fall days?"

"The days are getting much shorter, sir," Lawton said.

"Ah, yes, Mr. Deavors, but then the nights are longer," Ridgeway said.

"Oh, here's Florine with some refreshments," Lucinda said.

Brandy was served to the men, sherry to the women.

"And how did these duels end, sir?" Rafaella asked.

"I was the victor, Miss Blaine," Ridgeway said.

"Yes, of course you were, sir," Rafaella said. "What I meant was, in what way did you . . . disable your adversaries?"

"I fear that's no fit topic when ladies are present," Ridgeway said. He turned to Lawton. "Tell me, sir. How is your harvest coming?"

"We've been fortunate," Lawton said. "With any further luck, this cotton crop will be the best in years."

Rafaella sipped the sweet, smoky sherry. Her cheeks had flushed with anger. She had asked Ridgeway a perfectly logical question and he had dismissed it! He had turned to Lawton and ignored her! Damn the man, she told herself. Damn him and his hideous crippled hand. And yet with the next sip of sherry, she found herself once again speculating about his hand, pondering why he only crippled, but never killed, his adversaries. Surely it was because of his own hand. Or was that too simple an explanation?

Actually, he was quite handsome, she thought, evaluating his profile. Nearly as handsome as Lawton, but more delicate, not quite so ruggedly handsome.

Talk turned from the harvest to conditions at the county madhouse.

"I find it hard to believe that, despite lack of adequate funds, niggers would be allowed to become the wardens of white people," Lucinda said.

"But that is what has happened, Mrs. Deavors, from what I hear in Natchez," Ridgeway said. "It's quite the scandal of the autumn season. Which gives one some idea of just how dull autumn has been so far."

"Has the chief warden been dismissed for his conduct?" Lawton asked.

"I've heard nothing to that effect," Ridgeway said. "It's my understanding that he intends to stand for Congress, where he believes his time at the madhouse will stand him in good stead."

Rafaella smiled at Ridgeway's remark. Neither Lucinda nor Lawton seemed amused at all. They were both so serious, Rafaella told herself.

Ridgeway's visit brought welcome news of outside events. More drinks were poured. There was talk of runaway slaves fighting for independence in Texas, of Martin Van Buren standing for the presidency against Daniel Webster and William Henry Harrison, of the work of the Underground Railroad, of a terrible steamboat explosion downriver. Rafaella was interested in all of it, but Lawton and Lucinda looked very tired.

"Well, why don't we go inside, Lucinda?" Lawton said finally.

They said good night and left Ridgeway with Rafaella. She had told Lucinda flatly that she wasn't fatigued and would go upstairs when she wanted to.

Ridgeway took more brandy. "May I ask how you're getting along, Miss Blaine?" he said. "Is there anything I can do to help you through your time of mourning?"

"Thank you for your consideration, Mr. Ridgeway," she said. "No, no, I lack for nothing. The Deavorses have been kind to me."

"If I can be of any service, Miss Blaine, please do not hesitate to call on me," Ridgeway said. His grey eyes looked at her, held her. His voice was low, deliberate. This was the first time she had heard him speak without a mocking, cynical tone.

"Yes, I . . . yes, I will, Mr. Ridgeway," she said.

"I sincerely hope so, Miss Blaine," he said. "I wish

you would do me the honor of thinking of me as your . . . friend . . . a very special friend."

"Yes, a friend," she said. "A special friend." She looked at him through lowered lashes, not sure what to say. She wasn't sure, after all, he wasn't teasing her. He was so ironic. Rafaella became anxious, and her anxiety fused with her present emotional insecurity and caused her to gulp too much sherry and nearly choke. She suddenly wished Ridgeway would go away, would leave her alone; wished it were dear, sweet, safe Lawton sitting here talking to her instead.

"And how is your charming stepmother?" Ridgeway said abruptly.

"What . . . my . . . Frannie?"

"Yes, the bereaved widow Blaine," Ridgeway said. His words were mocking, and Rafaella was pleased, yet annoyed to think of Frannie at all. Ridgeway knew full well what Rafaella thought of her stepmother.

"I haven't seen her since the funeral," Rafaella said. "She called here one day, but I . . . didn't come down to see her. From what I know of Frannie, I'm sure she's surviving quite well, Mr. Ridgeway."

"Yes, Miss Blaine, she is a sort who always survives," Ridgeway said. "Ah, I nearly forgot." He called to a slave who was waiting some distance down the porch. "Go up to my room and bring me the saddlebags on my dresser," he said.

"Did you have a pleasant ride out from Natchez, Mr. Ridgeway?" Rafaella asked.

"Yes, it was pleasant enough," Ridgeway said. "Though quite frankly, I'm forever amazed that people live so far out here in this . . . well, wilderness, Miss Blaine. How else can one describe the area? Of course, once here, The Columns is a magnificent place."

"Yes, it is a fine plantation," Rafaella said. "But there is such tremendous isolation. I suspect I'll never be content in any place but a city such as Rome."

"Sometime soon, perhaps you would consent to travel into Natchez and be my guest for the theatre and dinner," Ridgeway said.

"Why, thank you, sir," she said. "Yes, I think I need such diversion. Tell me, have you visited Rome?"

"I was there twice," Ridgeway said. "On my first journey I visited the famous sights, and on my second I found myself sitting for hours in the Caffe Greco. Do you know the place?"

"Oh, yes, of course, right off the Piazza di Spagna," she said. "Many interesting men . . . artists . . . of letters . . . go there."

"Yes, quite true," Ridgeway said. "The conversation was among the most civilized and witty I've encountered."

The young slave came silently onto the porch and handed Ridgeway his saddlebag. Ridgeway unfastened the flaps and took out two handsome leather-bound books.

"I hope these help you to pass the time," he said. He handed the books to Rafaella.

"Why, thank you, sir," she said as she took the books. "How very kind, but I don't know if I can accept them."

"Of course you can," Ridgeway said. "Aren't we becoming friends? And I can imagine how long your days must seem."

Rafaella stroked the fine morocco leather as she examined the books. They were beautifully embossed editions of the English poets John Keats and Percy Bysshe Shelley.

"Oh, they're lovely, Mr. Ridgeway," she said as she looked up at him. She smiled. "And I so love poetry. Especially the great English poets."

They agreed that American writers were provincial and ultimately boring, which Rafaella knew by now was Ridgeway's most damning judgment on things.

Rafaella thoroughly enjoyed the talk, and especially enjoyed Ridgeway's subtle compliments. Several times she found herself staring openly into his grey eyes, studying his lean, aristocratic, and wearily handsome face.

They talked easily, with increasing rapport, as though

they had known each other for years. The only times the conversation faltered were when Rafaella tried to steer the subject to Ridgeway himself in an attempt to discover more about his past or his dueling. Finally, she stopped trying.

Their talk lasted until half past midnight. By then Rafaella realized she was totally exhausted, so tired she could barely stand. Ridgeway offered to help her up the stairs to her room, but she asked him to call Florncey. She wasn't at all sure she wanted Ridgeway to put his arms around her.

At the staircase, he looked curiously at her, and for one moment Rafaella thought he would try to kiss her. She stiffened at the thought, but she thanked him for the books and said she had enjoyed their conversation.

"Then I'll say good night, Miss Blaine," he said. "I believe I'll take a walk before retiring. The hour is so early for me that my poor body, creature of habit that it is, would not know what to do if it felt a mattress at this hour."

Florncey helped Rafaella up the stairs. Each step was slow, difficult. Her chest seemed constricted. Breathing was difficult.

As she mounted, Rafaella saw a tall shadow moving down the hall. By the time she reached the top, the shadow had disappeared. She flushed with excitement. She knew without a doubt that the shadow was Lawton's, that he had been keeping watch over her while she sat up with Ridgeway. Despite her exhaustion, she was pleased.

When she had been undressed and helped into bed and had taken her nightly sedative, Rafaella still tossed about. She dreamed of Lawton and of Ridgeway . . . and of both men fighting duels for her love, for her honor, of both men willing to die for her, just as her father had died for her.

36.

During the harvest, Lawton went to the fields with his slaves each morning at first light. Like the slaves, he carried a snack for his noon meal and stayed in the fields until the increasingly early dusk made it impossible to distinguish the white cotton pods from the leaves.

Early morning was cool with heavy dew. Lawton wore a waistcoat and the slaves wrapped themselves in blankets. But as the sun burned off the dew, they tossed aside their wraps, and by late morning many of the men were sweating so much they stripped to their waists. Women worked with the men, wearing handkerchiefs and bandanas tied around their heads. Everyone dragged long bags into which they stuffed the cotton.

Lawton rode the endless rows, shouting encouragement at the slaves, promising, scolding, talking to his drivers, and reminding his weary people that only a few more days of picking remained. Then there would be several days of rest, followed by the slaves' own harvest party.

The pickers moved mechanically. Their exhaustion expressed itself with each gesture. They shuffled from plant to plant, weighed down by the two huge bags of cotton pods suspended around their shoulders. Many of the pickers' fingers trembled as they squeezed off the pods. As the day's heat bore down and the swamp's dampness crept out, the slaves moved even more slowly and mechanically, like old machinery that was rusting and grinding to a stop.

Each day the total amount picked was less than the previous day. At the height of the harvest, the hands would average some two hundred pounds each, and several of the pickers proudly reached three hundred pounds. Some of the best pickers were women. But now

Lawton was satisfied if the day's average reached a hundred pounds.

Now, as he stood at the scales and watched his people drag their baskets along to be weighed, he felt his own weariness, bringing him near exhaustion, and he longed for the harvest to end. The cotton picking had seemed more all-consuming than ever this year. All normal life had been suspended. He was especially concerned about his life with Lucinda. It was not only that he seldom saw her during the day. When he dragged himself in for supper, he was so tired that he could barely speak, and he ate with the same mechanical weariness with which his people picked cotton. His brain was numb, blanched by some twelve hours in the saddle. At times he realized he was nearly mumbling. Real communication was beyond him.

He knew Lucinda was tired herself, busy with her preparations for the Harvest Ball and the holiday season. Lawton tried, without much success, to show some interest in what she was doing. He'd also tried to show some enthusiasm for making love to her, but he was too tired. Their lovemaking went from awkward and stiff to bad. For the past ten days, they had not made love at all. He knew Lucinda was worried about it.

Despite his exhaustion, Lawton found it increasingly difficult to sleep each night. He tossed and turned and tried not to wake Lucinda. He thought of the harvest, of the pounds picked, of the wagons rolling to the cotton gin, of the new land that must be cleared all the way down to the river. He reviewed his daily talks with Cellus. Cellus had taken over all his old duties, including those of keeping the plantation's books, and Lawton wondered how he had ever gotten along without Cellus's help.

Sleepless hours brought him other thoughts, other worries. He was concerned about Joleen in Ohio. He missed her and hoped she was safe. He was worried about that woman and little boy he had seen at the river. Could it really have been Nettie and her son . . . *his* son? How could he find out if she had returned to Natchez? And what could he do about it? How could he endure having a child who was white and resembled him but who was legally a Negro?

And increasingly, his restless thoughts led to Rafaella Blaine. The arrival of Roger Blaine and his daughter had permanently altered his life, bringing him first the responsibility of the Price Deavors estate, then far heavier concerns and responsibilities. He'd never wanted to investigate Blaine, hadn't wanted to know the secrets of his past.

Now Roger Blaine was dead by his own hand, a death Lawton could not help but feel some guilt about, and Rafaella was left alone, penniless, grief-stricken, afraid, her only other relative a brainless and loose woman she despised.

Lawton couldn't help but feel responsibility for Rafaella. Great responsibility, great pity, and great affection. She was such a lovely girl, so physically perfect and so innocent of the unsavory allegations against her father. He couldn't bear to think that they were true or that she would ever be hurt by them.

Especially that. Rafaella had been so overwhelmed by grief, so broken down with mourning that he had feared she would die. Dr. Stacey had warned him, "All this grief could cause permanent damage to her, Lawton. She might never fully recover." And so Lawton had done all in his power to help her, stealing time from the harvest, from his wife, to coax her to eat, to listen to her half-conscious ravings, and to give her the prescribed medicine.

During their hours together in her dark, warm bedroom, as she lay somewhere between consciousness and death, he had vowed that he would, that he must, make it up to her. She had begged him to help her, to take care of her, to protect her as her father had done. And he intended to do so.

His feeling for her had grown, stirred by her beauty and by his guilt and pity. She was so lovely, so vulnerable. He remembered one particular night. She had cried herself to sleep with one round white arm loose above the covers and her lacy white sleeping gown a mass of wrinkles. Lawton had sat for hours, staring at her half-exposed body, at a flash of knee, at a bared shoulder, once even at the most intimate part of her thigh.

Whenever she was lucid, they talked, and he enjoyed these discussions. With Rafaella, he did not seem so tired. He did not ask himself why, if he was too exhausted to respond to Lucinda's talk, he could respond to Rafaella.

It disturbed him, and he determined to extricate himself from Rafaella's increasing, if flattering, dependence on him. And to remove himself from a situation that he felt was getting beyond his control. Abruptly, he stopped spending time in her room. He was rigid about this and he used the harvest as an excuse. He feared the consequences, but Rafaella seemed to be sufficiently recovered. She began to dress, to function, to read, to eat. She had even come downstairs when Wyman Ridgeway called, and she was much like her old self, though she still wouldn't get out of the house as the doctor had recommended.

Lawton told himself it had merely been her grief and loneliness and the drugs that had caused her to act as she had, only weariness and concern for her health that had caused him to respond as he had. It was not too late. Nothing had happened between them that he need regret.

That night the temperature dropped drastically, and there was almost a frost. Lawton slept soundly for a few hours, but when he saw the first light, his waking thought was of Rafaella. He lay there and resolved that when he came back in the evening, he and Lucinda would discuss Rafaella's situation. They must decide what to do. It was a decision that was Lucinda's, also. Though she had said nothing so far, Lawton knew he could no longer exclude his wife from his dealings with Rafaella.

37.

Aaron Clauson drove his carriage toward the river from his fine red brick house in the fashionable Cincinnati suburb of Mt. Auburn. On his own block he maintained a façade of serenity, but at the first intersection he glanced apprehensively over his shoulder. He saw no sign of the men who had followed him the previous day.

Cincinnati lay in a beautiful natural amphitheatre formed by rolling hills. But he could feel little relief or pleasure as he drove down into the city. He wished now he had confronted the men rather than have to worry about them while on his way to meet Joleen.

Aaron was certain the men had been hired by a Kentucky planter named Carey Hawkins. Recently, Aaron and his associates in the Underground Railroad had helped two slaves escape from Hawkins's plantation just across the Ohio River, and now the fugitives were hiding in Aaron's own cellar until they could be transported across the border to safety in Canada.

Aaron didn't know how Hawkins had learned of his involvement in the Railroad. He had been careful to disguise his work and conceal his true feelings about slavery. He posed as a foppish and cynical lawyer. But evidently he had somehow been found out. As soon as Joleen was home and settled, he would have to discover how his security had broken down.

Aaron cursed his luck at the development of such a dangerous situation just when Joleen was arriving. Thugs such as those that Hawkins had hired were capable of anything, and blatant acts of violence to recover fugitive slaves were common in Ohio. Aaron swore that he would let no harm come to Joleen. He would confront Hawkins and call the man out rather than endanger Joleen, even if it destroyed his effectiveness with the Railroad. He had missed Joleen sorely, more than he had thought possible. Now that she was finally coming home, he was determined that nothing should spoil their life together.

Aaron's carriage had reached the bottoms, called the Basin, on the Ohio River. The low land was a maze of small factories. It was strident with a general bedlam of crowds and horses and wagons and it was heaped with mounds of cartons and crates. Above the din was a steady chorus of pigs grunting and squealing, for Cincinnati had become a center of hog packing ever since the Miami Canal had been completed in 1827, connecting the city with towns north of it.

Aaron left his carriage and picked his way through the crowds and the cargo on the docks. He saw that Joleen's boat, the *Mill Creek*—named after a stream that flowed through Cincinnati—was being tied up at the dock.

Excitement consumed his apprehension and he forgot the men who might be following him. He rushed to the dock. The gangway was being secured as Aaron reached the dock.

"How long before I can go on board?" he asked a black roustabout.

"Not long, sir," the man replied. "But you'll please have to wait till the purser comes down and he says it's all right."

Aaron walked up the dock a few yards, then returned to the gangway. People were scurrying about the decks and peering from the portholes. He did not see Joleen. What if she weren't on the boat? The thought hit him like a physical blow.

His steps described a circle in front of the gangway. Again and again he glanced up, hoping to see Joleen or at least the purser. But he was disappointed at each glance. He began to look around for the thugs. He worried whether he should tell Joleen of this new threat. He even dredged up worries about the often-discussed plan of some of the more radical abolitionists to organize a filibustering expedition and establish Cuba as an antislavery base. He was interested but he knew how strongly Joleen would oppose the idea.

Aaron could not wait any longer. He returned to the gangway.

"I must go aboard," he told the roustabout. "It's an urgent matter."

"Well, sir, like I said, the purser got to come down first—"

"Here," Aaron said. He thrust a coin into the man's hand. "I'll take full responsibility."

The man shrugged. "Can't see as it'll do no harm," he said. He unfastened the rope gate and let Aaron through.

Aaron rushed up the gangway and stopped a steward on the deck.

"I'm looking for Mrs. Clauson," he said. "Could you tell me her cabin number?"

"Mrs. Clauson? That'd be . . . let's see, she got the blonde hair? Young, pretty lady? Come up from Natchez?"

"That's right."

"That'd be Cabin 2-C. Promenade deck, sir. That's down the corridor here, last door on your left."

"Thank you," Aaron said as he hurried off.

Joleen scurried about her cabin, scolding both herself and Norvina for putting off packing until the last minute. She picked up a dress. She began to fold it carefully. Then she threw it onto the bed.

"Damn the packin'!" she said. "You finish on up. I'm goin' out to see if I can find Aaron."

Joleen ran to the door, but paused to look at herself in the mirror. "Do you think Aaron will like my new dress?"

"Lord, Miss Joleen, I done told you he would," Norvina said. "Told you 'bout two dozen times this mornin' alone. What you frettin' 'bout? Mist' Aaron, he always find you a pretty lady. You ought to know that by now."

"But he hasn't seen me in so long," Joleen said. Again and again, she had remembered how handsome and dashing Aaron was. She was certain that many beautiful women must have been throwing themselves at him. She knew this was a childish speculation but she could not stop worrying.

"You ought to stop your fussin' and get on out and lay your eyes on him," Norvina said. "I can finish up the packin' easy enough by myself, for all the help you been."

"I *am* actin' like a child, Norvina," Joleen said. "Like I was sixteen."

"No, ma'am," Norvina said. "You never did act this way, even when you was lots younger than sixteen."

Joleen smiled at Norvina. In a few days Joleen would go into the Ohio courts and free Norvina, the first of her slaves to be freed in Ohio, as she and Lawton had agreed. Joleen felt strangely sad about it, in a way that disturbed her. She was glad that Norvina had decided to continue to work for her and Aaron when she was free.

"Go on, you get out of here," Norvina said fondly.

Joleen glanced in the mirror once more, then opened the cabin door and ran out. She ran right into Aaron.

She was stunned, both physically and emotionally. Apparently, so was Aaron. They stared at each other. Joleen tried to catch her breath.

Almost timidly, as if she had not really expected to see him, Joleen looked into Aaron's eyes. She had forgotten how dark his eyes were. Someone had described them as too shrewd, too disturbing. She felt that she alone understood the softness behind the shrewdness. His eyes had first attracted Joleen. And now they held her, as they had so often in the past, while she sucked in her breath.

"Joleen," he began. He was so handsome, Joleen thought. She was thrilled to hear his deep, confident voice. "I . . . are you all right? Did I hurt you?"

"No, you didn't. Oh, Aaron!"

Joleen threw her arms around Aaron's neck. He hugged her to his body.

"You're so beautiful, Joleen," he said. "I'm so glad you're home. I've missed you so much."

"I've missed you, too, Aaron," she said. "So much."

She leaned up and kissed his lips. They kissed for half a minute, and warm excitement flowed through Joleen's body. She pressed harder against Aaron and felt something hard and metallic at his waist. She stiffened, then pulled back. She saw a pistol in the fob of his trousers.

"It's nothing, Joleen," he said. "Just a precaution."

"But why, Aaron?" she asked. "Here in Cincinnati? You stopped carrying a gun in Mississippi. And you promised."

"It's just that the city is so near the Kentucky slave owners. One can never tell."

"Aaron, please," she said. "We lived through too many lies in Mississippi. They almost destroyed us."

"Yes, yes, I know," he said. "All right. Perhaps I'm being an alarmist, but two men have been following me."

And Aaron told her very calmly about the fugitive slaves hidden in their house.

"I see," she said. "And what do you plan to do? Surely you don't plan to shoot the men."

"Joleen, I honestly don't know what to do," he said. "I'm damn sick of posing and hiding and subterfuge. I swear I'd rather be open in my antislavery work and let others have their turns at being secretive and living lies."

"We'll have to . . . to talk about this at length," Joleen said. "But please, Aaron, can't we have our own time together first? Just a few hours for ourselves?"

"More than a few hours, Joleen," he said. His rare smile flashed. It excited her. She ran her fingers through his dark hair and kissed his cheek.

"Now tell me . . . oh, Aaron, tell me how you've been," she said. "What all you've been doin'. I just hate letters. They're such a poor substitute for talkin' and all."

He kissed her lips. "Yes, a hopeless substitute for telling you how very much I love you. Now, what about your luggage?"

"Well, Norvina is finishin' up the packin'," Joleen said. "Can't we make arrangements to have the luggage sent on later? Oh, Aaron, I love you so much."

"Of course," Aaron said. "We'll send the luggage on later. I'll just tell Norvina."

Aaron spoke to Norvina briefly. He made arrangements for her and the luggage to be taken to the house when she finished packing. Then he left the boat with his wife, hand in hand, smiling, laughing. Joleen was glowing with happiness. Nothing could touch her spirits, not even when she noticed Aaron glancing around the docks and looking over his shoulder as they headed home.

38.

That afternoon Lawton sat slumped in the saddle on a stretch of cotton land adjacent to the swamp. As he stared, only half seeing, at the panorama of bent-backed slaves tugging along sacks of cotton, he heard a horse behind him. Slowly he twisted around in the saddle.

It was Rafaella. She looked cool and beautiful in a trim-fitting brown and white riding habit, made with a nearly transparent white muslin tucker that could not hide the bounce of her full breasts. A few strands of her long black hair had come loose and curled in the humidity.

Lawton smiled as she reined up beside him. He was glad to see her. It had seemed an endless afternoon.

"What brings you out here, Raffles?"

"Oh, it's so close in the house," she said, "and I'm so lonely. Everyone else has things to do. Wouldn't you like to come for a ride with me? It must be cooler somewhere."

"I'd love to, Raffles," he said. "But it's impossible today. The pickin' will be finished shortly. Then I'll have more time."

She frowned. "By the way," she said, "I've been meaning to thank you for watching over me that night Wyman Ridgeway called."

Lawton wasn't sure what to say. He felt embarrassed.

"Oh, well . . . it's not exactly that I thought you needed chaperonin'," he mumbled. "But with Wyman Ridgeway . . . I'm not at all sure of the man, Raffles."

"Be honest, Lawton," she said. The little smile on her lips added to his uneasiness. "You simply don't like Mr. Ridgeway in the least, do you?"

"I'm not sure I . . . I don't so much dislike Mr. Ridgeway. But I find little to recommend the man. At least in his present way of life. To give up what seemed to be a promising career in the Congress and live simply to fight duels, to cripple and maim opponents." He hesitated, but could not resist adding, "Are you interested in Mr. Ridgeway?"

"Oh, I don't know, Lawton. I really haven't given it much thought at all."

Lawton was relieved at her reply. He reasoned with himself that, after all, he was responsible for Rafaella now and he had to take some interest in her suitors.

"There are other things I'd much rather talk about with you, Lawton," she said.

"I'd like that," he said. "But I'm afraid the cotton won't wait. Some time soon, though, I'd like to talk to you, very much."

There was just the hint of a frown on her pale face. She tossed her head. Her nostrils flared a bit with a sharp intake of breath.

"If I had a dollar for every time you've put off our conversation, Lawton," she said, "I wouldn't be a supplicant at your doorstep."

"Raffles, please, I . . ."

"Perhaps I've come too far in this heat," she said. "Isn't there a creek down that trail? I must get cool. I think I'll go wading."

"The current's too swift for wadin' in that creek, Raffles."

"I believe I'm quite capable of taking care of myself, no matter what you may think, Lawton."

"I can't let you—"

She rode off, leaving him with the sentence unfinished. He cursed under his breath. Only a month ago, a girl had nearly drowned in the creek. He glanced around for one of the drivers to send after Rafaella. But no one on horseback was nearby. He cursed again and turned his horse onto the swamp trail.

"Raffles!" he called. There was no response, only the throbbing of insects from the thick undergrowth. It was so hot he was drenched in sweat.

There was no sign of her, but he found her horse tied to a bush in a sandy clearing beside the stream. He dismounted and ran to the water. For a moment he didn't see anything and he called out.

Then he saw a blur of white moving behind a tangle of thorn bushes that grew under a dead oak all the way up to the overhanging creek bank.

"Raffles!" he called again. "Damn you, answer me!"

The only sounds were the insects and the rushing water. Lawton bent over, fighting to get off his boots. When he raised his head, he saw her brown and white riding habit much closer, only half-concealed behind the feathery limbs of a weeping willow. As he stared, his heart pounding, he saw her brown skirt was pulled up. Her petticoats were moving up her legs. He saw her bare calves, her knees.

His penis tightened. His loins ached. He gasped for breath.

The last layer of petticoat went high, above her knees. Through the willow he saw her pale thighs. She bent down slowly in the water, then stood up. Water dripped from her sleek, pale thighs. As he watched, they squeezed together, then spread in an unbearably provocative way.

The time without making love had taken its toll on Lawton, and he had to take a half step to relieve the pressure of his tight pants against his rigid penis. He was racked with an excitement that brought back a shock of forbidden memory—memory of the day when he'd stood in nearly the same spot and watched Joleen, then the same age as Rafaella, wade out and slowly undress.

He groaned with desire and guilt and turned around to go. The sound of a shout and of splashing water stopped him.

"Lawton! The current!"

"I'm here . . . I'm comin'," he called. He crashed through the underbrush on the creek bank. "Grab hold of the trees, Raffles! I'm comin'."

When he burst through the willows, he could see her full-length in the water, clinging to a tree stump while the swift current tugged at her thighs. Her face was beyond white. It was ashen.

"Oh, God, help me, Lawton!" she gasped.

He had difficulty keeping his own balance on the slippery bank as he worked his way to Rafaella. The instant he reached her, she let go of the tree stump and grabbed desperately at him. Her weight and the stream's force dragged him several feet into the water, but just in time, he managed to brace his foot on a stone. With Rafaella clinging to his neck, he pulled free of the current. They stood wrapped around each other for nearly a minute, fighting to catch their breath.

"You saved me, you saved my life," she whispered hoarsely. The wet silk of her underclothes was plastered to her skin, and he could feel her body heat under his hands.

"Dammit, you could have been drowned!" he said.

He had difficulty breathing, much less speaking. Her body was completely pressed against his, her breasts slowly rubbing against his chest, her loins tantalizing his loins, her fingers on his neck, her breath hot and wet in his ear. He was so aroused that he felt an almost total helplessness.

"Here, let go, you're safe now, dammit!" he snapped.

But she did not let go. "Please let me hold on to you, Lawton," she whispered. "Please, darling. I love you.

I need you so much. I've never been alone before. I'm afraid. I'll do anything for you, Lawton. I have to be a woman, to be loved the way Daddy loved me. I want you. Please."

"Raffles, calm down," he muttered, trying to pry her loose. The action only further excited his flesh. "Dammit, let me go! Damn you."

"Please don't fuss at me," she begged as he began to break away. "Please, Lawton, be my special friend. No one need know but us, darling. I'll be good to you like I was to Daddy, Lawton. I'll do anything for you. I've seen the ways you look at me, know the way you feel now."

"No!" he shouted and flung her to the bank with a strength and desperation that surprised him and stunned Rafaella.

"Lawton, don't reject me, please," she whimpered, making no effort to get up. "I'm so alone. I can't take charity. No one has ever had me, Lawton. No one."

She had fallen against the bank. Her muslin tucker split. Her breasts had spilled out. They were flushed and lovely, the fullest breasts he had ever seen. She saw his glance and pulled up her wet petticoats.

"You do want me, Lawton," she said. The little smile played around the corners of her mouth. "I know how much you do. All you have to do is . . . tell me you want me . . . tell me you'll . . . like me more than anyone, as much as I like and need you. And for you only, darling, I'll be the kind of woman you hoped for."

Lawton stared at her damp breasts, at her luscious nipples, at the flesh bared below the dress. He wanted her more than he had ever wanted any woman, felt a desire so strong he could barely move, a desire so strong that his loins ached. But something blocked him.

"No! Stop, please, Raffles," he gasped. "We'll talk later, when we're both calmer."

He turned to go, but she reached for him and her voice was cracked as she scrambled to her feet.

"No, don't go!" she cried. "I swear I'll kill myself if you do!"

She clung to him again. Her grip was powerful.

"Dammit, let me go!" he shouted. "And dammit, cover your breasts, Joleen!"

Speaking that name stunned Lawton and brought a curious look to Rafaella's face.

"Did you do this with Joleen, Lawton?" she asked. "Do you want me to be Joleen? I can be Joleen for you, if that's what you want. I can be just like Joleen or anybody else you want. But don't humiliate me this way!"

Lawton stumbled as if wounded, hiding his expression from her.

"I'm sorry, Raffles," he mumbled as he pulled on his boots. He didn't know what to say. He was overwhelmed by shame, by guilt. And he was terrified about having slipped and called her by his sister's name.

"No, you're not sorry, Lawton," she said.

He stared at her. Her eyes were tight with anger. He might have been gazing at the hate-filled face of a wrinkled old woman. The effect chilled him.

"You're not sorry! You don't care! You let me beg and humiliate and offer myself, and then you brush me off as though I was some field hand. Damn you! I'll never forget this! Nobody ever humiliated me this way, Lawton. No one ever turned me down."

"Raffles, stop! Don't look that way!" Lawton said. "This is no . . . we can't . . . we'll . . . when we're both calmer."

"I'll never forget this!" Rafaella raged. "I'll never forgive you, any of you, ever! Oh, God!"

"Please, Raffles, stop!" Lawton begged. "You're just overwrought—the heat, the fright you had. You're not well yet. You know what Dr. Stacey said. Later, this evenin' or tomorrow, we'll talk. You and Lucinda and I. We'll discuss your future, Raffles. You don't have to go back to Frannie, if you don't want to. You know, I've already been thinkin' it would be a good idea if you went off to school. Lucinda knows some fine schools for girls in New Orleans."

The rock she picked up and hurled barely missed his head. He ran away and left her kneeling in the sand, her head down, tears streaming down her face and running in rivulets over her bare white breasts.

39.

Joleen was oblivious to the sights of Cincinnati during their drive up to Mt. Auburn. She sat with her body pressed boldly against Aaron and repeatedly touched him and kissed his cheek.

She loved the red brick house he had bought for her, but paid it little attention. She was polite but impatient with the two Negro servants who welcomed her. And she studiously ignored the existence of the two fugitive slaves hidden in the cellar. Her boldness increased as they went upstairs, and she was pleased and flattered at Aaron's enthusiastic response.

In their bedroom, a bottle of champagne stood in an ice-filled bucket beside their four-posted canopied bed. Joleen drank two glasses quickly, her hands and lips never far from Aaron's face. Already her nipples were growing firm beneath the touch of his hands.

Joleen had been a virgin when she married Aaron and she had never had another lover. The incident on the Trace with the young abolitionist had almost been her undoing. Her deprived and highly responsive body had been awakened and demanded love. She had realized that she could not be happy without Aaron, without the release of her passions.

She put aside her third glass of champagne and slipped into Aaron's arms. He lowered her to the bed. Their kisses became urgent. Joleen searched Aaron's mouth with her tongue and savored the gentle strength of his fumbling hands and the feel of his rigid penis.

Then she lost all track of time and shut her eyes, giving up all thought to pure feeling. His skin was warm and she took delight in rubbing herself against him, first with her hands and face, then, as he removed her new silk dress and tore off her petticoats and underbodice, with the length of her sensuous body.

She gasped as he ran his finger over the long white scar on her thigh. Aaron was a skillful lover, made more skillful by the depth of his feeling for Joleen and the period of deprivation that he, too, had gone through. Finally, he could wait no longer and he entered her. She cried out at once in orgasm, and his own climax was quick to follow hers.

"Oh, Aaron," she whispered, "I could never love anyone but you."

The next evening, Joleen stood alone at a velvet-draped window in her front parlor and watched the rain fall. She was waiting for Aaron to return from a rendezvous with the man who would guide the fugitive slaves to Canada. Joleen tensed at every sound or sight of a horse or carriage on the quiet street, hoping that it would be Aaron, yet worried that it might be Carey Hawkins or some of his men. Aaron had not wanted to leave her alone, but she had insisted that he go at once to make the arrangements that would take the slaves from their basement, and they dared not leave the house unguarded again.

But even if everything went well, tomorrow there would be a new scheme. Joleen's distaste for all the subterfuge had brought her to question her commitment to the abolitionist cause. Aaron had been the instrument of her change in feelings about slavery, and she wondered if she weren't wed more to his strong beliefs than to the cause itself.

She hated slavery and wanted all slaves freed. But she wanted to work against slavery in the open and not have to hide her beliefs. Yet Levi Coffin and other abolitionist leaders insisted Aaron was most useful working under cover and pretending not to care about slavery. So once again she was caught up in intrigue, posing, lies.

A knock on the front door startled her. The knock became a pounding. She glanced from the window. She had heard no horses and she saw no carriage.

Norvina was hurrying down the hall from the kitchen. She paused and looked over at Joleen. Joleen nodded, and as Norvina walked to the front door, Joleen ran to the desk in Aaron's office and opened a drawer. She reached for Aaron's pistol. She hesitated, then replaced it and slammed the drawer. Slowly, with an appearance of calm she did not feel, she went into the hall.

When Norvina opened the door, she was nearly knocked down. Two men burst in. Joleen knew the fat man in expensive clothes was Hawkins. A tall brutish man who lurked behind him was obviously one of his thugs.

"I didn't invite you to my home, Mr. Hawkins," Joleen said. "And my husband and I are taking steps to end your unforgivable behavior in following us about the public streets."

"How did you know . . . well, I guess you might. And I guess you know what I've come for."

"It would appear you've come to show me your bad manners," Joleen said.

"Mrs. Clauson, my manners are good as any man's in Kentucky or Ohio," Hawkins said. "But not when I'm dealin' with thieves who steal my niggers."

"Where I come from in Mississippi, Mr. Hawkins, our niggers send men of your bearing around to the back door."

"Now see here!" Hawkins said. His face was red. His voice was high. Joleen smelled whiskey on his breath. "Who are you to stand there and insult me?"

"A woman whose home you've invaded. You've interrupted dinner preparations. Please leave before your drunken behavior causes you to make a spectacle of yourself. And I warn you again, sir, to end your harassment of my husband or you'll answer to the law."

"*Me* answer to the law! I've come for my niggers!

And I intend to have them. And you or nobody else is goin' to stop me. I know they're in this house. I got a man out back so they're not goin' to get away. Now step aside!"

"You mean you honestly think I'd admit you to my house and allow you to search it?" Joleen asked.

"You ain't got much choice."

Joleen felt that no matter how drunk or angry, Hawkins wouldn't use force against a woman. But his man was probably capable of anything. And having hired the man and brought him here, Hawkins might not back down. Joleen's knees were weak. Her heart pounded. She fought to remain calm. If she showed her fear, she was lost.

"I have no choice?" she said. "I promise you that if you step one foot further into my home, sir, you'll be arrested for assault, because you'll have to assault me to get inside."

There was a crash from the back of the house. Hawkins and the tall man glanced at each other. Then Joleen understood the noise. A third man was coming in through the back door. And the door to the cellar was in the kitchen!

"Norvina, show these men out," Joleen said bravely. "If they refuse to leave, go find a constable."

Joleen turned and ran down the hall. In the kitchen stood a red-headed man even more brutish looking than the others. The back door hung by one hinge. The two kitchen servants huddled in a corner.

"Get out of my house!" Joleen said.

"I'm goin' find those niggers, lady. You'd do well to stay clear of me, 'cause I'm a man who likes to earn his money."

"Damn you, get out!" Joleen shouted. She heard the other two men coming through the house. She raised an arm to the red-haired thug, but he shoved her aside and she was slammed against the stove. A steaming teakettle sloshed over and burned her arm.

The red-headed man was reaching for the cellar door. Joleen picked up the teakettle and hurled it at his head.

He screamed as the pot struck the back of his head and boiling water poured down his neck.

Hawkins and his man had stopped in the hall door. Joleen was crying now. Her arm ached. She didn't think her legs could hold her up.

The burned man was screaming. He had dropped to his knees and was trying to claw open his clothes to get at the burned skin. His agony froze everyone's movements. Then Hawkins's man took a step toward Joleen. She reached around and grabbed a kitchen knife. The man pulled out a pistol.

They stared at each other, and Joleen tried to stop her trembling. Her strength was failing her. The knife shook in her grasp. The man had taken a tentative step toward her when a sound in the hall stopped him. He glanced over his shoulder as Aaron burst into the room. Hawkins shrank back. The thug turned his gun on Aaron.

"Get out of my way, mister!" he shouted. "There's nothin' I'd like better'n to shoot a nigger lover."

Aaron advanced on the man.

"Stay back or I'll blow your guts out, I swear it!" he shouted.

Aaron did not stop. He closed in on the disbelieving man and grabbed for his gun. The man outweighed Aaron by fifty pounds and stood a good five inches taller. Joleen sank back against the stove as the two men fought. Aaron finally knocked the gun from the man's hand, but the man hit Aaron in the face and Aaron's head snapped back. Blood spurted from his nose and lip.

"I'll kill you!" the thug roared as he lurched toward Aaron.

Aaron stood in a crouch, as though ready to wrestle with a giant. But in his blind anger the man blundered in too close, trying to choke Aaron and caring about nothing else.

Aaron had made himself look vulnerable, and the huge hands were already closing around his neck when he snatched up a bottle and smashed it into the man's temple. The man bellowed in pain and his hands fell away for a moment. Aaron hit him in the face. The man screamed and touched his lacerated face. Aaron kicked him in the groin. He doubled over and Aaron smashed a chair across his back.

Then Aaron stumbled over to Joleen and put his arms around her.

Two hours later Joleen lay in bed, snuggled against Aaron, who held her in his arms. From time to time she trembled, and Aaron kissed her cheek and held her more tightly. Her arm still hurt from the burn, and she wondered if she would ever forget the agony on the thug's face as he felt the scalding water. She feared the whole terrible ordeal was permanently etched in her memory.

Aaron had retrieved the pistol and forced the three men to the front of the house, two of the thugs immobilized by pain, Hawkins sweating and shaking and moaning. Joleen had had enough presence of mind to send the fugitives out of the cellar and away from the house before the two constables had arrived. Since Aaron was a respectable lawyer in a prominent neighborhood, since Hawkins had no proof of guilt and Aaron insisted that the constables search the house, Hawkins and his men were arrested for trespassing and assault.

Joleen's burn had been treated by a doctor, and she had let Aaron carry her up to bed. She was still in pain then, and tears stung her eyes. She felt too weak to move. Yet the tension had excited her, and when she lay beside Aaron, safe and relieved, the excitement led her to initiate a long and passionate bout of lovemaking.

Now Aaron was sleeping, but Joleen could not fall asleep. She was content to lie beside Aaron and remember how brave and angry he had been. Whatever he must do, she would stand by him.

40.

Rafaella had just wakened from a bad dream when the knocking started again. She lay curled on the wrinkled satin cover, dressed in only a light wrapper, her knees drawn up against her. She sat up to stare out the window at the heavy rain. A mosquito whined at her ear. Her head was hot and pounding with a miserable splitting ache. She had refused to unlock the door since returning from the creek the previous afternoon. Both Lawton and Lucinda had pleaded with her, but she had turned them away. She thought they'd given up, but now it had started again.

"Go away!" she screamed. Her voice was high-pitched, her throat so raw from crying that even the two words made it tighten with pain.

The knocking was louder and more persistent than before. She remembered her dream. She had been back at the creek with Lawton, saw herself offering herself, begging him for love. And he had rejected her!

It was unbearable! He had rejected her and humiliated her and said she was to be sent away to boarding school, like some unwanted little orphan the family had found itself saddled with.

"I *hate* you," she mumbled into the damp pillow. "And I hate you, too, Daddy, for abandoning me this way. I'm glad you're dead. You rejected me."

The knocking was louder.

Rafaella scrambled up and sat on the edge of the bed. "Damn you! Go away and leave me alone!" she shrieked.

"Miss Raffles?" Florncey called. "Miss Raffles, honey, they say this nigger done come all the way over from Miss Frannie Deavors, say it urgent he talk to you, say Miss Frannie got urgent business with you."

"Florncey!" Rafaella shouted and stumbled toward the door. The thought that it wasn't even Lawton or Lucinda pounding but only some slave infuriated her even more. She wrenched the lock open with trembling fingers.

"Miss Raffles . . ." Florncey started.

"You damn nigger!" Rafaella shouted. "I'll have you whipped for this! I told you to go away a dozen times. How *dare* you disobey! How dare you try to beat my door down!"

"It was me doin' the knockin'," a man said.

Rafaella wiped at her eyes as the man stepped around Florncey. The man was Tolver, Frannie's driver.

"Do you want to take the whipping, Tolver?" Rafaella asked. "I told you to stop knocking! Somebody's going to pay for this!"

"I'm Miss Frannie's slave, not yours," Tolver said quietly.

Rafaella glared at him and wiped at her eyes again. She had never liked Tolver. He was not humble enough, had too much pride and independence for any two slaves.

"You'll find out soon enough whose nigger you are," Rafaella said.

Tolver sighed and shook his head. "Miss Raffles, Miss Frannie, she done sent me to say it's real important you come back to the place with me."

Rafaella couldn't believe that after being rejected by Lawton, she was being patronized by the slaves. She was too depressed to flare up again, too hurt and humiliated. Word must have spread all over the place; even the slaves had been given license to treat her as a mendicant. She felt so miserable she wanted to die. At that instant, unable even to look at the faces of the two slaves, she resolved that she would do as her father had done and take her own life.

"No, go away, Tolver," she said wearily. "I'm not going anywhere with you."

"Miss Frannie, she say for me not to come back without you," Tolver said.

"Couldn't Frannie have come here herself?" Rafaella asked.

"Miss Frannie, her mama done take bad sick and she can't leave the place," Tolver said.

"I don't care," Rafaella said. "I'm not going."

"Miss Raffles . . ."

It was another man's voice. A deep, confident voice. Once again, and even more slowly this time, Rafaella turned back from her room, and saw that the man coming down the hall was Cellus.

"What's all this commotion up here?" Cellus asked. "I done come in from the quarters and it sounds like the upstairs is bein' knocked down. And you, you Miss Frannie's nigger, aren't you? What you want to The Columns?"

"Miss Frannie, she done sent me to fetch Miss Raffles; say it's real urgent, somethin' to do with legal matters," Tolver said.

"You shouldn't have come up here on your own, boy," Cellus said. "You should have wait outside for me or one of the white folks."

"This nigger here, she say the white folks not here."

"But I'm here," Cellus said. "And Mist' Lawton, he leave strict orders this child here feelin' poley and not to be disturbed."

"I'm no goddamn child!" Rafaella said. "And if Lawton and Lucinda are gone, I ought to be in charge, not you!"

"But you not exactly family," Cellus said.

"I am . . ." She could not finish the sentence. "I'm nothing, I guess," she whispered, to herself. She felt shockingly low and weak. Perhaps she would kill herself. Yes, she was less than nothing after being humiliated and abandoned by both her father and Lawton, less even than these annoying, patronizing slaves.

Hopelessly, she turned back to her room, but she was halted by Cellus's firm voice.

"Just a minute, Miss Raffles. And you, Tolver, you go with Florncey here. Florncey, take him to the nigger kitchen, see he get some supper. Make him comfitable while he wait for Miss 'Cinda to come back from the Sumralls' or Mist' Lawton to come in from the swamps."

"What's Lawton doing in the swamps?" Rafaella heard herself asking in a whisper.

" 'Gator done killed two pigs," Cellus said.

"I hope it kills him," Rafaella said bitterly. "Now, are you finished with me, Cellus? May I return to my room?"

"Miss Raffles, don't talk that way," Cellus said. "I don't mean to upset you. I know how poley you been feelin'. If you want to rest some more, you go right ahead. I'll take Tolver to the quarters and Florncey, she can stay with you. It's just that this gentleman, he done come all the way out from Natchez and he waitin' downstairs to see you."

Rafaella shook her head. "I just can't. Cellus, please tell Mr. Ridgeway that I . . . I'm indisposed . . . for the rest of the evening. But that I appreciate his calling on me. Would you see that he has supper and . . . if you will, please, offer him the hospitality of The Columns for the night. Is that all right, Cellus?" She sniffled and the words nearly choked in her throat. "Am I allowed to do that? Offer the plantation's hospitality to a friend? Why, I don't know if I'm even allowed to . . ."

"Miss Raffles, you talkin' nonsense," Cellus said. "Course you can. What I said 'bout family . . . shouldn't have put it that way. I meant, you still young and all. Anyway, the gentleman ain't Mr. Ridgeway. He say his name is Grady Weston. He's an attorney. He say he was your daddy's attorney and he been sick in New Orleans and just now he come back to Natchez."

Rafaella turned. "Daddy's attorney?" she asked. "New Orleans? I didn't . . . What does he want with me, Cellus?"

"I don't rightly know, Miss Raffles. But he done come out in some haste, and my guess is it's mighty important. If you want, I can give him the plantation's hospitality 'til you feelin' like receivin' him."

"No, no, Cellus," she said. "I guess . . . I'll try to . . . Daddy did say something about an attorney, now that I think about it. Please tell Mr. Weston that I'll be down shortly. Florncey, come in and help me get ready."

Rafaella was both tired and anxious as she walked back into her room. She had a sudden hope, which lasted only an instant and then was replaced by a new dread that her father had sent her some final, terrible news from beyond the grave. Yet, she thought, how could things possibly get worse?

41.

Half an hour later, Rafaella sat in the parlor at The Columns and tried to comprehend what the fat, bald lawyer was telling her.

Grady Weston had started by apologizing for letting his personal life interfere with his profession. In New Orleans, he had contracted a nearly fatal fever that had completely robbed him of his faculties for a brief time. He had been unconscious for days and had responded very slowly to treatment. Only this morning, when he returned to Natchez, had he learned of Roger Blaine's unfortunate death.

"My very deepest sympathies, Miss Blaine," he murmured. Rafaella, dressed primly in black silk, nodded.

Then he told Rafaella that before her father married Frannie Deavors, they had signed a contract that provided for half of all Frannie's wealth and property to go to Rafaella when Roger Blaine died.

Rafaella asked the lawyer to repeat this astonishing news. Her shocked, fearful mind seemed unable to absorb it. She had never suspected this; it was too much to believe. Why, it gave a whole new meaning to her father's death. Her eyes glazed.

"Are you all right, Miss Blaine?" Weston asked.

"What?" she asked, and looked up blankly. "Oh, yes, I'm all right, Mr. Weston. Please go on."

"Well, as I was saying, Miss Blaine, you are now one of the wealthiest young ladies in the county, if not the entire state. As I mentioned, I'm to administer your estate until you reach maturity or until you marry. Though I must warn you that your stepmother is already tryin' to break the contract. But I can assure you that in my professional judgment there is no way on earth she can do it."

"She just sent a nigger with a message that I was to return with him. Said it was urgent, some legal matter."

"My advice, my legal advice, Miss Blaine, is to avoid your stepmother in every way for the time being," Weston said. "Now, there's one further matter. Your father also left a letter for you in my care. I was to hand it to you personally in the event of his death."

"A letter from Daddy?" She held the white envelope in front of her and stared at it. "And I thought he just forgot all about me. How *could* I have?"

Her throat tightened. She felt almost faint.

Weston stood up. "If you're all right, I'll leave you alone to read the letter, Miss Blaine," he said.

She nodded. "Thank you."

Weston went out and closed the door. Rafaella's fingers trembled as she slowly tore open the envelope.

Rafaella read the letter a second time and then a third, her lips moving with each syllable. Each reading had strengthened her, had augmented her restored self-confidence, and had focused her anger.

My dearest Raffles,

First of all, and for the last time, I must tell you how very much I love you. You have been my only love since the death of your mother, the mainstay and focal point of my life, my sole reason for existence. You have brought me so much happiness, so much pride, have been a perfect daughter, and now you are a beautiful young woman.

I must leave you now, as you well know, by the only circumstances under which you will receive this letter. I am not a coward, dearest Raffles. Nor am I afraid of death, except in the sense that it will grieve you and separate us. This is not a rash act, but something I have thought out carefully.

It is very important to me that you understand my reasons for taking my life and leaving you alone, and that you understand that my only reason for marrying Frannie was to provide for your support by means of the marriage contract. Mr. Grady Weston, an attorney I trust completely, will act as your guardian and executor until you come of age or marry.

I found, dear Raffles, that I had no will to continue a life that—despite my love for you—had become unbearable for me, and was in all certainty going to get worse for both of us.

I warned you of the slanders that the Deavorses were perpetuating to secure the Price Deavors estate for their own. They were prepared to slander us and delay the probate proceedings, as they already have. I had a futile confrontation with Lawton. I thought of calling him out, but it would do no good. Once launched, rumors will persist, and Lawton spoke not just of rumors about my marriage and your legitimacy, but of rumors even more shocking. I have just learned of the existence of further slanders about my past, about my being a fugitive criminal, an infidel.

I know the suggestion is painful, but my death will stop the pain. They have driven me to it, but I can no longer refuse. They have won, so that you may win, my darling. I have renounced the Price Deavors estate. As it goes to the Deavorses, they will cease slandering me. And now that you have wealth and property, there is no need for you either to depend on them or to continue your claim for the estate. I strongly advise you not to fight Lawton on this matter. And above all, dear Raffles, please believe nothing you hear about me from the Deavorses. I can go to my grave willingly only if I can believe this of you.

Remember now and for all time how very much I love you, dearest daughter, and remember that my last thoughts were of you. I do what I must to protect my name and your future. I suffer what I must in the hope and belief that you will have a long and happy life.

With all my love,
Your Father

Rafaella refolded the letter and tucked it inside her bodice. She sat huddled on the long sofa, her elbows pressing against her sides, her head bowed. The shivering started as chills up her back, but in a minute her whole body was shaking.

If she had known of this letter at the funeral, she would never have asked Lawton and Lucinda for help! If she had known of the letter, she would never have let herself love Lawton, would never have thrown herself at him! If only she had listened to her poor father's warnings about Lawton! Why hadn't she remembered her father's advice?

How she hated Lawton! How evil he was, how weak! She was so sorry for all the terrible things she'd thought about her poor father. She had blamed him so wrongly. Everything he had done was for her. He had submitted himself to an unbearable marriage. He had sacrificed his very life! He had done it to provide her with wealth and dowry, to protect her name against the worst sort of slanders.

And, horribly, he was dead! He was gone forever, and here she was, crying and begging and being humiliated in the home of the man responsible for his death!

Lucinda's voice in the hall snapped Rafaella's head up.

"I don't care how she feels, Lawton," Lucinda was saying. "We can't wait supper any longer." Someone knocked on the door. "Raffles," Lucinda called. "Do you want supper? If you do, you'll have to come and eat now. We can't wait any longer."

Rafaella got to her feet. She swayed, steadied herself. She could not yet speak.

"Raffles?" Lucinda called. She knocked again. "Really, Raffles, be reasonable for once, and answer me."

Rafaella walked to the door with determined and measured steps. She jerked the door open and startled Lucinda, who had just raised her fist to knock again.

"My Lord, are you all right, Raffles?" Lucinda asked. "You look as though . . . you look positively ill!"

"Where's Lawton?" Rafaella asked. "Where is he, Lucinda?"

"He's back in . . . What do you want Lawton for?" Lucinda asked. "I think he's had quite enough of your carryings-on, Raffles. I've tried to understand your grief and all, but your behavior has become quite burdensome, and Lawton has too much worry with the harvest to put up with you anymore, so just tell me what you—"

"Get out of my way, Lucinda!" Rafaella said.

"Not till you tell me what's wrong now. We might as well settle this here and now. Lawton and I just now had a long talk and we decided to send you away to boarding school as soon as possible."

"You're not sending me anywhere, Lucinda," Rafaella said. "And when I finish with you and your husband . . ."

"Oh there you are, Raffles," Lawton called from down the gallery.

Rafaella turned. Her cheeks blazed as she waited and stared at his handsome, sun-browned face. The shivering started again, and she had difficulty staying on her feet.

"Raffles! Mr. Weston tells me your father arranged a sizable inheritance," Lawton started. "That's just—"

Rafaella slapped Lawton's cheek with her right, then her left hand.

"I hate you!" she screamed. "You killed my father! He's dead because of you!"

She doubled her hands into fists and tried to pummel Lawton's face, but he ducked away and grabbed her wrists. Blood trickled from the corner of his mouth.

"Lucinda," he said, "you'd better go. I'll handle this better alone."

Lucinda left without a word, closing the parlor door behind her.

"Stop it, Raffles! Stop at once! Have you taken leave of your senses! Calm down. Dammit, calm down and talk sensibly!"

"You drove him to it!" Rafaella screamed. She

struggled, but she couldn't free her wrists and this made her even more furious. "You threatened him with slander . . . Daddy . . . us . . . he tried to warn me but I wouldn't believe him because I loved you and trusted you! Oh, God! It's your fault! It's your . . ." She had to pause for breath. She twisted her wrists, but he was too strong. His hands were hurting her.

"That's absurd, Raffles," Lawton said. "Absolutely absurd. You don't know what you're saying. Your father was badly mistaken if he—"

"He *wasn't* mistaken!" Rafaella screamed. "He wasn't! He was right, and now he's dead because of you and I hate you . . . hate you both . . . hate all of you!"

Lawton released her wrists. He wiped at his mouth with the back of his hand.

"Raffles, what was in that letter? Mr. Weston said he gave you a letter from your father. If he said anything about our spreading slanders, then he's badly mistaken."

"He's dead!" she said. "Don't you dare call him a liar! Of course, you'd say he's lying! But I saw proof of your slanders!"

"Raffles, I don't . . ." Lawton stammered. "I've only tried to . . . to protect you. I didn't think you knew, didn't think your father wanted you to know. I was waiting for proof from the Continent. I've kept it all to myself. I haven't even told Lucinda. I promise you, the information will never leave this house."

"Then you admit it!" Rafaella said. "Oh, God, I hate you! It's true. You have said those things about him, about us."

"I swear I've told no one," Lawton said. "Since no proof has arrived, I have to assume those things Mr. Anson insinuated were untrue. I never believed them, Raffles. And anyway, I would have protected you and your father. I would never have breathed a word about his being an Egyptian slave, a Moslem. It's too preposterous to—"

"A *slave!*" Rafaella snarled. She felt cold and sick. Her knees were trembling. "A Moslem? What do you mean? That wasn't . . . I can't believe . . . Why, Daddy warned me you'd try worse and you have. You seem capable of the vilest things."

"But I thought from what you said that you knew."

She shook her head slowly. Her rage was lost in shock. She felt her legs would buckle at any moment. Yes, her father had warned her there would be worse, more preposterous slanders, and Lawton had indeed borne out his prediction. A slave. If Lawton ever spread the rumor that her father had been a slave, she would be ruined, an outcast. A slave. A slave's daughter. Why, it took generations for a slave's character to change. A slave's mentality was inbred.

"Oh, Lawton, please," she gasped. She felt sick. "Not *that*. Don't tell people *that*. How vile can you be?"

"Raffles, please, I won't tell anybody anything. Please, let's sit down and talk about this in a rational way."

"No!" Rafaella said. "No, I won't talk to you any longer. Or ever again. I won't have my poor father slandered in his grave! I'm no longer a poor little orphan, no longer a mendicant at your beck and call. I'm leaving here. *Now*. I'll never forgive you. And I'll make you pay for killing my father. And you'll pay double, I promise you, if one word of those vile slanders gets out, Lawton."

"You can't go, just like that."

"I can do whatever I please," Rafaella said. "I can buy you or ruin you and your precious plantation. Now, where's Mr. Weston?"

"He's in the dining room," Lawton said. "But I can't let you—"

"You can't let me *what*?" Rafaella asked. "Mr. Weston is my guardian now. And I'm going to have him take me away from here right now. Right now! And I'm going to make you sorry for killing my daddy and I'm going to make you pay for those slanders you spoke against him and I'm . . ." She staggered back and her hand flailed out and caught the wall for support. Her eyes wouldn't focus and her head was swimming. Chills racked her body.

"I'll never forget, and I'll never ever forgive you . . ."
She heard her own voice as though from very far off,
and then she was floating . . . floating . . .

42.

Christmas Eve was bright and clear, and a festive
holiday mood prevailed at The Columns. Following
their tradition, the Deavorses were giving a small party
for some two dozen close friends and family, and the
slaves were having their own party in the quarters.

The house was decorated with greenery and candles.
Great bunches of holly, magnolia, pine, and mistletoe
were suspended from the ceilings of the halls, dining
room, and drawing room. A tall, spicy-smelling pine
tree had been set up in the parlor and decorated with
the family's antique ornaments, strings of popped corn
and red berries, and candles. A great china bowl stood
on a small table near the tree, ready to hold the
traditional eggnog. Oysters would be roasted on the
coals of the dining room hearth, in full view of the
guests. The kitchen, which stood down a covered but
open-sided passageway some twenty feet from the back
of the house, was a center of hectic activity as Lucinda
and Beatrice directed the kitchen staff in roasting,
baking, and cooking special treats for the occasion.

Lucinda had been assuming more and more responsibility in the day-to-day running of the house, and
Beatrice had continued to give ground. This would be
the first Christmas fully under Lucinda's authority, and
she was determined it would be a memorable one. By
mid-afternoon on Christmas Eve, she was nearly dizzy
with excitement and fatigue, but she was proud of her
efforts and gratified that the slaves were accepting her
as the plantation's mistress in fact as well as in name.

To top it off, Lucinda was still riding high on the
praise she had received for the Harvest Ball some four

weeks earlier. Everyone said it was the finest party ever given at The Columns, and Lawton had praised her so highly it had become embarrassing. It was nearly enough to make her forget she had any worries.

But not quite. Lucinda had been very busy with party and holiday preparations and buying winter clothes for the slaves, too busy to give full rein to her underlying anxiety. But as she moved about the kitchen that Christmas Eve afternoon, her mind whirled with accumulated fears and worries.

They all concerned Lawton. Lawton didn't seem happy. True, he was very pleased that the record harvest had been brought in on time and that the cotton was on its way to the New Orleans markets. He was satisfied with the land he'd bought up and with the Irish laborers he had hired for its clearing.

Despite this, Lucinda knew that he was brooding about many things—about Joleen's absence at Christmastime, about Roger Blaine's suicide, about the scandal of Rafaella's stormy departure from their home.

Lucinda had never been sure she understood everything that had happened with Rafaella. She had sensed a passionate depth to the girl's feelings, an intensity to her hatred and bitterness that only made sense if something had happened between her and Lawton. Not that Lucinda thought for a minute that Lawton had been . . . unfaithful with Rafaella. But any girl who had such a high opinion of herself, any girl who flirted so openly and outrageously, any girl who was so desperate might well . . . offer herself.

No, no, Lucinda told herself, as she watched Beatrice take a brandied peach pie from the open. Lawton had said nothing had happened, and she must certainly believe him. Still, it did seem strange that their once ideal sexual life had not returned to normal. They seldom made love now, and when they did it was as though they were awkward strangers. During the harvest she had attributed the problem to Lawton's weariness each evening when he came in from the fields. But even since the harvest . . .

"No, no, Phoebe!" Lucinda scolded a young slave girl. She shook her head. "That fire is getting *much* too hot. You'll burn the corn puddings for sure. Here!"

Lucinda supervised the banking down of the fire. As two slaves shoveled coals and ashes, she resolved to stop speculating on Lawton and Rafaella and simply give things time to return to normal. Surely, after the holidays, everything would settle down, and then she and Lawton would recapture the sexual pleasures of their love.

"Let's make an extra sweet potato pie, Beatrice," she said. "Aunt Delma loves sweet potato pie. You know, in her last letter she complained that she hasn't tasted a good one in all of New . . ."

Out of the corner of her eye, Lucinda saw Lawton and Filch riding in along the rear of the house. They dismounted. Ed came running from the barn. The three men talked and gestured excitedly toward the quarters. Lucinda realized something was wrong. She ran from the kitchen and stopped in the corridor that led to the dining room. She saw Ambrose and Cellus in the dining room, looking toward the barn. They were talking in grave voices.

"What's wrong?" she asked. "What's happening?"

"I'm not certain, Miss 'Cinda," Cellus said. "But I'm afraid we got a problem with some of the people. Seems like four of 'em done run away, and the sheriff caught one of 'em, halfway to Natchez."

Lucinda brooded about the runaways as she continued with the preparations for the Christmas festivities. There was something unusually strange about it.

Except for the long-ago trouble with the mechanic named Essie, no one at The Columns could remember any other slaves running away from the plantation. Essie had been tied up in Lavon Deavors's schemes and had eventually paid with his life. No one knew what would happen with these four. Everyone wondered. Lawton never liked to whip his slaves, they knew that. The news of the captured runaways raced over the plantation and dampened everyone's spirits. After the rigors of cotton picking, the Deavors slaves had been given three days off. They had held their own harvest party. Instead of the usual fiddler or two, Lawton hired Dackney's Colored Orchestra from Natchez to provide music. The seven musicians played until nearly dawn. There were roast pig and turkey, and Lawton made sure his people had sufficient whiskey and rum. As a bonus for their hard work and the record harvest, Lawton had given each of his people a gallon of molasses and each adult half a hand of tobacco.

Things settled back to normal after the three-day holiday. Field hands still worked from "sun to sun," but now the pace was slower as they performed more leisurely winter tasks. They were given half a day off each Saturday and one whole Saturday free each month. Those who wanted them were given passes to visit friends or relatives on neighboring plantations.

The slaves' morale had been helped by the rumors that filtered out from the house; Miss 'Cinda was buying fine winter clothes and shoes, and there would be special Christmas gifts this year, as well as an elaborate feast on Christmas Day.

The feast was long anticipated by the slaves. Lawton fed his people better than most masters did, making sure they had root vegetables and eggs and occasional meat or chicken. He encouraged them to raise their own greens and keep chickens for eggs. But their staple diet was fatback and cornmeal, bland and monotonous fare, so the talk about a Christmas feast, with some special foods cooked in the house, had everyone excited.

Then the four slaves had run away. And now one of them had been caught, and word was that Mist' Lawton was beside himself, and so was Cellus, and there might be no treats, no gifts, no party, no feast. And the runaway, who was being brought back by the sheriff, would certainly be severely punished.

225

The captured slave, a carpenter named Flobert, was returned to The Columns in the late afternoon. He was tired and scared and sullen. He offered no good reason for running away, just that he was "tired of bein' a slave." Lawton ordered him locked in the slave jail for a week and said he was to be denied any Christmas gifts.

The rest of the people were relieved. Lawton did not plan to take out his displeasure with the runaways on them. In fact, deeply disturbed by the fact that four of his people had run away at the happiest time of the year, Lawton was determined to combat any feelings of restlessness by providing his people with a festive and memorable Christmas.

So he told the fiddlers to strike up the music in the late afternoon. Field hands made dozens of small outdoor fires, and around each fire there was a merry group. He had the drivers open the drums of whiskey and persimmon beer earlier than ever before. And he had the food sent down to the quarters at dusk. Two small calves and four whole pigs were being barbecued for the slaves, as well as chickens and turkeys. Over the campfires, they fried great pans of liver and baked hoecake after ashcake, ashcake after hoecake, gobbling them up, drenched with sorghum, as soon as they came off the fire.

When the music was gay and the fires were snapping, Lawton and Lucinda went down to the quarters to supervise the passing out of Christmas gifts and treats. The women were given bright cotton handkerchiefs and the men felt hats. The men received two pipes each, the women enough calico for a good dress. The children were given molasses cakes, wooden toys, dolls, and tricks. And everyone was given a gallon of molasses, a hand of tobacco, and half a pound of coffee.

As they walked back to the house, Lawton and Lucinda reached for each other's hand at the same moment, as though they shared a common desire. They did not speak as they walked together slowly, the sound of the fiddles and banjos and the steady rhythm of dancing feet growing louder behind them. It was a very special moment, and their eyes met in one special glance.

It was just about half past five, and their guests would begin arriving in less than an hour. Lucinda still had things to do in the house. But their hands, their shared glance, clearly communicated a mutual need, and for the first time in their married life they went upstairs and shut the door to their bedroom and made love in the afternoon.

The lovemaking began slowly, gently, as Lawton kissed and fondled Lucinda's body. He whispered to her how beautiful she was, then undressed her. He kissed her small, firm, freckled breasts and buried his face in them while she moaned softly and scratched her nails down his neck.

Their urgency increased as they kissed and stroked each other. The weeks of overwork and abstention had left them both tense and needing. Lawton took Lucinda more roughly than usual, and they thrust urgently, almost desperately, to reach their climaxes. Then they lay wrapped around each other, gasping out their breath and whispering their love and contentment.

As they began to get aroused a second time, Lucinda took the lead, though in a gentle, subtle, almost unnoticeable way. This time they moved very slowly together. But when their release came, it was with even more ecstasy than the first time.

Three days later, their happiest and most successful Christmas party now only a pleasant memory, they sat together in a carriage riding back from Natchez to The Columns. They had fallen silent following a brief exchange of news just after leaving the city. Lawton had left Lucinda in town while he rode the quarter mile to make final arrangements for the Irish laborers who would begin the swamp-clearing work in January. He was enthusiastic about the project and his thoughts were of it.

Lucinda had spent the afternoon shopping and visiting the Adams County Music Society. She now planned to join the group and take part in their activities. After leaving the music society, a strange, somewhat disturbing thing had happened to her. She had been walking along the crowded street when a drunken man staggered out from behind a wagon and knocked into her, nearly driving her to the ground. She gasped and struggled, but he clung to her, begging for a kiss. Suddenly, just as Lucinda had begun to panic, a man had appeared at her side and grabbed the drunk by the arm.

It was Wyman Ridgeway. The drunken man had pulled a dagger from his belt, but Ridgeway had immediately produced a pistol and waved it at the man, who was shouting obscenities now in a manner that Lucinda hated to recollect. He was no match for Ridgeway, though, none at all, and Lucinda was thankful to see him skulk away as soon as it was clear that Ridgeway meant business.

Lucinda had thanked Ridgeway profusely, and they had exchanged greetings and inquiries about the health of her family. She felt slightly strange talking to him right in the streets of Natchez, for she knew vaguely that Lawton didn't like the man, but in all honesty she had to admit that he had been most chivalrous to her.

Lawton had seemed only slightly concerned at hearing about Ridgeway when she had reported the incident to him in the carriage. Well, that was reasonable enough, Lucinda thought. Lawton had enough worries of his own without being concerned about her safety on the streets of the city, and she didn't blame him for disapproving of Ridgeway's caustic style and bizarre dueling habits. Still, though it wasn't at all like her, she felt strange and almost a bit guilty as she sat with her hand in Lawton's and recollected Ridgeway's compelling, mysterious grey eyes and his poor withered hand.

She'd heard plenty of gossip about Wyman Ridgeway and Rafaella Blaine in Natchez. It was the first thing her old friend Selma DeRivers had wanted to talk about. The gossip was that, though half the eligible men in the county were trying to call on Rafaella, Ridgeway was the only one she would see. In fact, word was that Ridgeway was calling on Rafaella every night.

Lucinda was vastly relieved that Rafaella was no longer part of their life. She didn't want to disturb Lawton with what she had heard, but Blaine's suicide and Rafaella's huge inheritance were the talk of all Natchez. There were a dozen theories about why the man had killed himself, most of them farfetched. And she'd heard that Frannie Deavors had hired a smart lawyer to try to break the marriage contract. Everyone said it was ironclad, especially Grady Weston, who had drawn it up in the first place, and at whose Natchez home Rafaella was now staying.

"You know, I think I'll try to put up the laborers in those empty houses on the edge of the quarters," Lawton said. "Seems a shame to have to go and build new quarters for them for just a few weeks."

Lucinda looked up at Lawton. They began to discuss the laborers, the clearing work, the feeding of the men and other aspects of their stay on the plantation. Lucinda was thankful to have something "real" to talk about, and she squeezed Lawton's hand tighter as they conversed.

43.

The sixth of January was wet and cold in Natchez. Rafaella stood at the window and remembered that a year ago, last Epiphany, she had been in Rome. The day had been sunny and mild, and she and her father had driven out along the Pincio.

Now she heard the sound of children's feet running above her head. A baby screamed. Another screamed louder. There were five Weston children, all badly behaved, all spoiled, to Rafaella's mind. For days it had been too cold and wet for her to walk outside, and the confinement had driven her nearly to despair.

Rafaella was alone in the parlor of Grady Weston's house. She paced from one window to another, from a window to the hall door, back to stare absently at horses and carriages grinding through the mud of the Natchez street. A carriage stopped in front of the house. A man climbed out.

Rafaella recognized the man. He was a doctor named Scott LeSeur, coming to pay her court. He had called before, but Rafaella had refused to see him. Now she turned and fled the parlor, up the stairs and past the squealing, playing children and into her room. She slammed the door and walked over and sat down on the edge of the bed.

She heard the front-door bell and then a slave coming down the hall. Soon there was a knock on her bedroom door. Rafaella dismissed the slave abruptly with her usual answer to the endless parade of men who called on her: she was sorry, but she was indisposed and she could not receive any visitors.

By now most of the men had stopped coming, but the doctor was doggedly persistent. Rafaella jumped up and walked over to the window to see him go. She told herself that if LeSeur didn't stop pestering her, she would have the dogs turned on him.

Another carriage was pulling up in front of the house. To her relief, Rafaella saw that Grady Weston and his wife, Martha Anne, were getting out. She went back downstairs and met them in the hallway.

"Hello, dear, did you have your rest, like a good girl?" Mrs. Weston asked. She was as fat as her husband, a motherly, rotund busybody who meant well but who drove Rafaella half crazy with her hovering ways.

"I know you're anxious to hear what I learned at the courthouse," Weston said. "But I'm afraid that it's nothing at all, my dear. Oh, don't worry. As I've said before, there's no way your stepmother can break that marriage contract. I should know. I drew it up myself."

"But why can't the matter be resolved?" Rafaella asked. "I've had my fill of waiting for courts to take action, I can tell you that."

"Yes, I'm sure you have," Weston said. "You know, the mills of justice and how slowly they grind. I can assure you, though, that within the next few days, all in good time, the judge will throw Frannie Deavors's suit out of court."

"Would you like some tea, Raffles, dear?" Mrs. Weston asked. "We were just going to take some tea. Oh, listen, the children are up, aren't they?"

"Yes, the children are up," Rafaella said. "As for the tea, Mrs. Weston, I believe I'll decline your offer. I . . . I have some things to do in my room . . . some important correspondence." She told herself she could not endure another dull tea party with the six fat Westons. Her patience was being stretched to the limit by this situation. "So, if you'll excuse me . . ."

"Oh, we encountered Wyman Ridgeway in town," Weston said. "And he mentioned that he hoped to call on you again this evening. You're seeing quite a lot of Mr. Ridgeway, aren't you?"

Rafaella resented his question but she tried to remain calm. "Yes, Mr. Weston, I am seeing Mr. Ridgeway," she said. "I hope he meets with your approval."

"Oh, Mr. Ridgeway is every inch a gentleman of breeding and intelligence," Weston said. "It's simply that his rather peculiar habits are . . . they cause quite a bit of talk around town."

"Do you wish to discuss Mr. Ridgeway's dueling habits with him this evening, Mr. Weston?" Rafaella asked. "I'm sure he would find—"

"No, no, you misunderstand me, my dear," Weston said quickly. "I was merely commenting on the style of his dueling. We both—my wife and I—find him quite acceptable."

Rafaella was glad she had taken the offensive concerning Ridgeway. Grady Weston might be the best lawyer in town, but he was also one of the town's biggest cowards. The very mention of cross-examining Wyman Ridgeway about his dueling habits had drained the color from his plump cheeks.

"Please excuse me," Rafaella said. "I'll go up to my room now."

She gave the children a cold, hostile look as she passed them on the stairs, not sparing their nursemaid the same treatment while she was at it.

So far during her time at the Weston house, Rafaella and Ridgeway had met only in the parlor or, in fine weather, on the spacious grounds. But on the evening of Epiphany, Rafaella decided to accept his invitation to attend a concert. The Westons were unsure of the protocol of allowing Rafaella to go out with Ridgeway unchaperoned, so it was decided that Delcimer, an ancient slave woman, would go along with them.

Surprisingly, Ridgeway found the idea of the ancient chaperone amusing. Rafaella was annoyed enough for two, but his good humor finally reached her and she had to smile at his banter with the woman about the severity of her duties and the importance, not only of Rafaella's honor, but of his own.

"After all, Delcimer," he said in the carriage, "Miss Blaine is foreign-born, while I'm a humble American by birth. We can't know what these foreigners have in mind, can we? Have you ever had to chaperone an unsophisticated American gentleman in the company of a foreign woman of the world before this evening, may I ask?"

"No, sir, can't say I has," Delcimer mumbled, obviously bewildered by his conversation. Finally Ridgeway lost interest in her and left her to sit silently in her corner and stare out at the rain.

Ridgeway plied Rafaella with some Natchez gossip about a Baptist preacher and a woman who owned a tavern under the hill. But Rafaella wasn't really listening to Ridgeway's story. Her mind was full of recurring thoughts about Lawton, about her father and his letter, about her predicament.

The thought of Lawton made her furious. She had needed him and offered herself to him . . . and he had not only rejected her, but humiliated her. And all that time, he had been scheming to ruin her and her father; had actually driven her father to take his own life!

She swore again that Lawton and his family would pay for her father's death! Last week she had gone out to the cemetery and sworn an oath on his grave that they would pay and pay!

But revenge was one thing. She was faced with another urgent and desperate task. She had to make certain that the slanders about her father never got out. She had to be sure of Lawton's silence. If a word were ever breathed that her father was a Moslem . . . a former slave . . .

As always, she could not physically bear the thought. Just the edge of it on her consciousness caused her to shudder. And as always, it triggered treacherous, poisonous doubts: all the questions she'd always had about her father's past, the mystery of the strange scar on his shoulder.

". . . What?" she asked. "Oh, please forgive me, Mr. Ridgeway. My mind wandered for a moment. What did you ask me?"

"I asked your opinion of present-day techniques of potato farming, Miss Blaine."

"Potato farming, Mr. Ridgeway? Oh, you're mocking me, sir! And I deserve it. For not paying attention." She always got upset when he mocked her, and he did it often, but she was determined not to show her discomfort.

They began to talk of the concert. But Ridgeway soon redirected the conversation.

"May I tell you how beautiful you look tonight, Miss Blaine," he said. "I can assure you no one will be looking at the poor musicians once you enter the hall."

"Thank you, sir," she said. His compliments were

always graceful, if not as frequent as she would like. But she had dressed carefully tonight. She wore a dress her father had especially liked. It was pink flocked silk, full-sleeved and low-necked with a fashionable deep rose sash. She had arranged her dark hair in an Apollo knot and added two fresh gardenias.

"Perhaps it's fortunate we have Delcimer with us," he said. "I might not be able to control my . . . desire if I were alone with so lovely a lady."

Rafaella smiled. "But, sir, I thought Delcimer was here to protect *you*," she said.

"Am I in some danger then?" he asked, and returned the smile. "I sincerely hope so!"

"Perhaps you should indeed live in some apprehension, sir," she said. They stared at each other for a moment in the dim light. So far she had been very strict with him and had not even let him kiss her good night. Perhaps, she decided, tonight she would grant him a rather more passionate kiss than he expected.

But the thought of the kiss brought back the memory of Lawton. She suddenly felt she was smothering, felt close to hysteria. Would she never be able to kiss a man without thinking of Lawton? She hated him more than she had ever hated anyone!

By the concert's intermission, Rafaella's spirits had improved considerably. She was pleased and flattered to see heads turned when she entered the box with Ridgeway. The music was quite good. Ridgeway was courteous and attentive. Now they stood in the lounge and sipped champagne, and as Ridgeway talked, Rafaella looked into his grey eyes and realized that very soon, in all probability, Ridgeway would ask her to become his wife.

The realization excited her, though she wasn't sure at all how she would answer. She caught herself stealing a glance at his crippled hand. It was surely horrible, but somehow it didn't seem to disgust her as much as it had at first. Wyman Ridgeway was such a superior man, anyone would forget he was . . . mutilated.

Should she actually marry him? She surely would marry someone—and soon. Until she married she was trapped in the Weston house. Until she married she could not claim the money her father provided for her. Until she married . . . But Ridgeway? A cripple? A man whose greatest passion was maiming other men in duels? But then, who else could she choose, she asked herself. The rest of them were provincial bumpkins.

"Why, yes, I will take more champagne, thank you," she said.

"Here, boy," Ridgeway called to a black man in silver and blue livery. The man carefully poured champagne into their glasses. Ridgeway lifted his glass and looked at Rafaella. "To you, Miss Blaine. The most beautiful lady in the hall tonight. In all of Natchez, I'm certain."

"I accept your compliment, sir, since I'm sure no one is in a position to be more certain than you."

Ridgeway almost laughed out loud at this, but they both smiled, gazing into each other's eyes, and took a deep sip of champagne.

Another couple drifted over to join them. Rafaella had to make conversation with a silly woman while her husband discussed dueling and hung on Ridgeway's every word. Finally Rafaella could endure no more of the woman's talk. She excused herself and walked to the back of the hall for a breath of air.

It was there she encountered Lawton. The sight of him jarred her more than she would have dreamed. He was smoking a cigar and was dressed elegantly in a green waistcoat over dark brown trousers. His blonde hair shone, and his face was smooth and clearly marked by confidence and happiness.

Rafaella was stunned. Damn him, how content he was without her! How smug and confident in his family's power and reputation!

She couldn't control her jealousy and resentment.

"Lawton," she whispered, her huge dark eyes narrowing. He leaned forward expectantly.

"Hello, Raffles," he said unsuspectingly.

"Lawton, I hate you! I *hate* you!" she hissed at him.

His mouth opened in astonishment. He looked confused and hurt. She turned away and headed back to Ridgeway. Before she was halfway across the crowded vestibule, she saw that he was now talking to a slim, redheaded woman. She was annoyed even before she realized that the woman was Lucinda Deavors.

Lucinda looked pretty and animated. She was obviously completely at ease, and Ridgeway looked as if her chatter was amusing him. The sight plunged Rafaella into despair. Damn those Deavorses! She flushed with anger.

Her feelings were out of control. She turned and ran back toward the cloakroom, cursing both of them, and Ridgeway, too. She refused to come back to her seat for the second part of the concert.

44.

Wyman Ridgeway got no kiss that night, and hardly a civil word from Rafaella during their ride home. Rafaella was tense and silent, leaving Ridgeway at her door with a cursory good-night.

But when Ridgeway called the next night, she received him readily enough. She was still angry, but she felt even more desperate than usual—reckless and stirred up with contradictory emotions and thoughts. A few moments before, a bad scene with the Weston children had sent her into a temper tantrum that was embarrassing even to her.

It was a pleasant evening, and Rafaella and Ridgeway went out into the garden at the side of the Weston house. Ridgeway had been witty and amusing. But when they were alone near the rose arbor, his expression grew serious.

"Obviously I offended you last evening, Miss Blaine," he said. "And I was hard put to understand what I had done. Then, just this evening, I realized that it must have to do with my conversation with Mrs. Deavors. Yes, I can tell by your reaction that I am right. I'm sorry, then. I didn't know. I don't know what passed between you and the Deavorses."

"It's not a matter I wish to discuss," she said.

"I wish you *would* discuss the matter with me," he said. "As you surely know, Miss Blaine, I've become fond of you, if I may speak so boldly. I wish to be your special friend, to help you in any way I can. If you would only ask . . ."

"Why do you torment me by insisting I discuss a matter I find both insulting and unbearable?"

"I'm sorry," he said. "I won't mention the matter again."

"I hate them!" she said suddenly. "I hate Lawton! He's responsible for my father's death! And he . . . Lawton insulted me, sir! Took advantage of me! Humiliated me. I feel I have no honor left, no pride."

She burst into tears. Sobs racked her body. She laid her head against Ridgeway's chest and cried, and he put his arms around her.

"Miss Blaine . . . Raffles . . ." Ridgeway said. He held her tighter. "Tell me if you wish. I want to help you, to protect you."

"I hate him!" Rafaella muttered. "I was so alone, so helpless. My father was dead. I trusted Lawton and turned to him. And he . . . he humiliated me."

Rafaella found her lace-edged handkerchief and rubbed at her eyes. She drew her head back from Ridgeway's chest and looked up into his face.

"Lawton Deavors attacked you?" Ridgeway asked. His voice was low and his words cold as death. "Ravaged you?"

Rafaella swallowed hard. She couldn't look away from Ridgeway's grey eyes. "I . . . he . . . Lawton . . . No! Oh, don't think that of me, please, sir," she sobbed. She didn't know what to say. "I'm still . . . I'm still a virgin. Lawton didn't . . . I was able to . . . stop him. But he . . . oh . . . he did, dammit!"

"Then the man is despicable," Ridgeway said.

"Now that I've told you, you'll never respect me," she said, wondering if she hadn't gone too far. What if Ridgeway didn't believe her assertion that she was still a virgin? What if he, too, rejected her?

"Of course I respect you," Ridgeway said. "How could I not respect a woman I love so very much?"

"You what?" Rafaella asked. "Love me? Oh . . . I didn't expect . . ."

With every ounce of her spirit, Rafaella wanted this moment to continue. She wanted it all . . . and more, wanted him to hold her, to flatter her, to speak of his love. She looked into his eyes and saw that at this moment he would do anything for her, anything at all. Slowly, she put her arms around him and lifted her face. His kiss was soft for the first instant; then she opened her mouth, hesitated, then parted her lips wider. He responded with such intensity that it sent a jolt of excitement up her spine.

She would have continued the kiss, would have slipped her tongue boldly into his mouth, would have let him caress her body, even surrendered her breasts to his lips—but Ridgeway's withered hand reached up . . . up to the back of her neck, and when she felt its caress, she had to control a shudder that she knew would ruin everything.

Fighting panic, she pulled away from his mouth and eased herself away from his hands.

"Please, sir, don't you also take advantage of my plight," she said.

"Not on my life would I do such a thing," he said. "But please don't begrudge me that one kiss, our first kiss."

"No, Mr. Ridgeway," she said, "I do not for one moment regret our kiss. Only, we must go no further. I think it best that I return to the house."

"If you wish," he said. He retrieved her fallen handkerchief. The rain had stopped.

"And Mr. Ridgeway," she said as they reached the

house, "I implore you, please keep my secret to yourself. I'm so ashamed to have to confess it."

"Of course, I'll keep your secret. But you have nothing to be ashamed of. The fault lies entirely with Lawton Deavors."

"Perhaps, but I feel I shall never be the same person," she said. "And I fear that by telling you I have . . . lowered myself in your eyes."

Rafaella basked in the praise and flattery that followed. Ridgeway asked if he might call on her the next night. She said she hoped he would.

When she went up to her room, she had no doubt that Wyman Ridgeway would propose marriage to her very soon.

45.

Lawton watched the Irishman stagger from his shack. The man shook his head, then looked up at Lawton on horseback. The man's face was red and so were his eyes.

"I sent word I'm too sick to work today," the man mumbled.

"More likely, you're too drunk," Lawton said. "I can smell the whiskey from here. What's your name?"

"Name's Tad Reilly," he said. "And I been takin' whiskey on doctor's orders, to cure the gout I get when it's wet and cold like this. Tomorrow I'll be out for work. You can count on it, Mr. Deavors."

"I am countin' on it, Mr. Reilly. Don't forget, sir, that you get paid by the day."

"But if a man's sick . . ."

"Our agreement calls for a day's pay for a day's work, Mr. Reilly," Lawton said. "There's no provision for bein' sick. I'm not an unreasonable man, but you can't come out reekin' of whiskey and claim you're too sick to work."

Reilly muttered a curse, but he looked at the ground as he spoke it. Lawton saw another rider from the corner of his eye. He glanced around. It was Filch, coming in from the fields. Lawton was afraid it meant more trouble, and he had promised Lucinda they would go into Natchez tomorrow.

"You got a minute, Mist' Lawton?" Filch asked.

"Yes, I'm finished with Mr. Reilly," Lawton said. "Come. Ride a ways with me, Filch, and we can talk. I'm goin' down to see how the men are comin' along in the swamp."

Reilly was still staring at the ground and mumbling curses as Lawton and Filch rode away.

"What's on your mind, Filch? How's the ditchin' comin' along?"

"Ditchin's doin' okay," Filch said. "I put two of the women from the washhouse to ditchin'. They don't seem to mind too much. But the people doin' the hoein' and choppin' of the old cotton plants, they startin' to complain 'bout bein' worked too hard, 'bout the weather and all."

"The rain's stopped now, Filch," Lawton said. "And the people, they're just comin' off the Christmas holidays. They have no cause to complain. Or is somebody spreadin' discontent again? One of the niggers that ran away?"

All four runaways were now back on The Columns. Two had been captured by the sheriff, one by a slave patrol, and the fourth had come back himself. All had received the same punishment: a week in the slave jail adjacent to the barn and no Christmas treats or gifts.

"Hard to tell, Mist' Lawton," Filch said. "Not like the people to complain so soon after a holiday. I been tryin' to seek out the trouble. I'll tell you this, though. They no little bit of unease 'mong the people 'count of those white men comin' here to work."

"Filch, the white men are here to do a job I wouldn't want to set my people to doin'," Lawton said. "Don't they understand that?"

"I reckon they do," Filch said. "But they some unease, all the same, some concern you might be plannin' to hire more white men and sell off some of the people to a sugar cane plantation."

"That's absurd, Filch. You know we never sell our people. *Never*, dammit! I'm beginnin' to think the problem is that the people are gettin' spoiled, gettin' lazy. They should see what kind of holidays they'd get on most other places, see what kind of work they'd do. I won't hear of their complainin' this way. Not unless someone has a special grievance. You understand?"

"Yessir, I understand," Filch said. "But I thought you ought to know how they feelin'."

Lawton rode on a minute without speaking. He had never been able to understand those slaves running away. He tried to do his best by his people, and felt he succeeded by and large. Yet he had heard mumbling of general discontent among the slaves. He was bewildered and did not know how to handle this new malaise.

He also wondered about Filch. There was no question of his competence. He had never seen a better driver than Filch, and no man worked harder or more honestly. Lawton felt sure Filch had the plantation's best interests at heart. But Filch had lived in Natchez with Joleen and Aaron, and he knew of their activities with the abolitionists. He also knew that Joleen planned to free him very soon. Lawton could not be sure how far to trust Filch now, beyond trusting him to keep Joleen's secret from the rest of the people. Perhaps Filch was the wrong man to deal with the slaves' discontent. But to think of replacing him as senior driver was a serious decision. He decided he would discuss the matter with Cellus.

They continued their ride in silence. They were passing through the last of the fields now, fields still soggy from the heavy rain, fields of withering, brown cotton stalks waiting to be chopped and hoed and cleared by the slaves.

Thinking of Filch turned Lawton's thoughts to Joleen.

She had written only one letter since she went upriver, saying that though she missed the family and the plantation, she was happy to be with Aaron again. Lawton and Lucinda had written Joleen three times. Though Lawton had enjoyed Christmas, he had particularly missed Joleen. And he was worried about her illegal activities in Ohio. He worried that she might act rashly, putting herself in danger. He hated to think of her so far away. In his heart he wished she were still his little sister.

The fields ended a few hundred feet ahead, and Lawton was glad to leave off that train of thought. He saw a dozen of the Irishmen swinging axes and shoveling out mud and sand at the swamp's edge. There were supposed to be fourteen working today.

"How's it coming, Mr. Murphy?" he called as he and Filch reined up in front of the dark-haired foreman.

Murphy dug his shovel into the ground and wiped his face with the back of his hand.

"It's coming along, Mr. Deavors. But it's slow, murderous, let me tell you. And in the name of the Lord, I think everything that bites, crawls, or stings must live in this swamp. Why, we killed a dozen poisonous snakes already."

"Anything I can get you?" Lawton asked.

"Yes, you could get us about a dozen niggers to do the nigger work," one of the men called.

Lawton glanced at the man. He realized that all the men were looking at Filch. He could see they resented seeing a Negro on horseback while they were doing such hard dirty work. He resolved to keep his drivers away from the Irishmen in the future.

"Where are your other two men, Mr. Murphy?" Lawton asked.

"They just took a short break, Mr. Deavors," Murphy said. "They're taking a rest back there a bit. Don't you worry. They're good workers. You'll be getting your money's worth, without a doubt."

"I hope so, Mr. Murphy," Lawton said. "Come on, Filch."

They turned their horses and rode back across the fields without talking.

That evening after supper, Lawton asked Cellus to have a glass of whiskey with him in the study. They sipped the whiskey slowly and talked about what had to be done while Lawton and Lucinda were going to be in Natchez. They had decided to stay over an extra day, and Cellus would be left in charge of the plantation.

At this time of year, there were all the seasonal tasks for the slaves to perform, in addition to cleaning up after the harvest—ditching and chopping and hoeing the old cotton stalks. In the winter, rails had to be cut, bush had to be burned, fences repaired, trees marked and pruned. The grounds around the house and barn had to be cleaned thoroughly. Bricks were made, charcoal was burned, the plantation equipment repaired. The wells and cisterns had to be cleaned out. In addition, potatoes were readied for early planting, corn was shucked and ground into hominy. Plans were already being made for the important work of hog killing.

Indoors, the slaves were busy with weaving and spinning and knitting, with mending clothes and making shoes, for Lawton was determined to make the plantation as self-sufficient as possible. He planned to increase to forty head the cows he kept in order to supply the family and the slaves with dairy products. He stall-fed oxen for a year before slaughtering them for beef.

As Lawton and Cellus talked, Lawton wondered if he shouldn't have asked Lucinda to join them. She was taking more and more responsibility in running the house, and she seemed to have extended her authority over Beatrice in the kitchen. Lawton had decided to let her handle the domestic situation herself, so long as things went smoothly and Cellus wasn't offended.

"Another whiskey, Cellus?" he asked as he drained his glass.

"Just a small one, Mist' Lawton," Cellus said.

This surprised Lawton, because although he always

offered Cellus a second drink, he could not remember Cellus's ever having accepted the offer. Lawton poured them both more whiskey and held his glass up in both hands. He looked through it toward the lamp, absorbed for a moment by the clear, amber liquid. Slowly, he lowered the glass and saw that Cellus was looking at him. Their eyes held for a moment, and Lawton studied the dignified, ageless man in front of him, studied his broad, angular face, his serious dark eyes, the proud set of his mouth. Cellus—born Marcellus—had been on the plantation all Lawton's life, and many, many years before that. He was an institution, indispensable to the operation of The Columns. But Lawton had no idea what Cellus thought of things, had no idea what Cellus really thought of slavery.

The realization made Lawton uneasy.

Lawton took a sip of whiskey. "Cellus, what do you think about the four niggers who ran away?" Lawton asked.

"I think what you done was the right thing," Cellus said. "Lockin' them up, takin' away their Christmas treats."

"No, no, that's not what I mean, Cellus," Lawton said. "I mean . . . what do you think about their running away? Except for Essie, we've never had trouble with runaways before. Why would they want to run off?"

Cellus shrugged. "Don't have no idea, Mist' Lawton," he said. "Guess it's human nature. Maybe we been more lucky than most places, far as runaways are concerned."

"Dammit, that's no answer!" Lawton said. He drank more whiskey. "Just today, Filch was tellin' me that the hands are complainin' about the work. And right after the Christmas holidays. What's goin' on, Cellus? What's happenin' to the people?"

"Mist' Lawton, I don't know what's goin' on," Cellus said. "And I haven't heard nothin' in particular. It upsets me, too, the people runnin' away like they did. But we got so many people on the place now, well, the more people, the more chance a few goin' to get it in their heads to run away."

"Cellus, how do you . . ." But Lawton couldn't bring himself to ask Cellus his feelings about slavery. He drained his glass and rephrased the question. "Cellus, what do you think about Filch?" he asked.

"What do you mean, what do I think about Filch?" Cellus asked.

"Well, he lived in town with Joleen and Aaron," Lawton said. "Joleen means to free him. He was livin' with them when they were involved with the abolitionists. I don't doubt his . . . his loyalty to the family and all, but . . ."

Cellus set his glass on the desk. He hadn't yet taken a sip of this second drink.

He shook his head. "It's somethin' I don't think about," Cellus said. "Leastways, I try not to. Miss Joleen . . . all her doin's. She's still young. As for Filch, well, I never had no reason to question him, Mist' Lawton. Things goin' to be gettin' bad here to The Columns if we go to doubtin' men like Filch."

"I guess you're right," Lawton said. "Yes, of course you're right, Cellus."

When Lawton left Cellus and went upstairs, Lucinda was waiting for him in bed, reading a novel by Sir Walter Scott.

Lucinda looked beautiful, her pale, freckled skin and red hair set off by a pale green silk wrapper tied over her nightgown, which revealed the shape of her small breasts and the fine white skin of her throat.

Lawton sat on the bed next to Lucinda, put his arm around her shoulders, and kissed her cheek. She snuggled against him and returned the kiss. But Lucinda wanted to talk. She had a new idea—to take two of the slave boys and train them as footmen for the carriage. She also wanted the house slaves to dress better. Lawton thought it all pretentious, but it seemed so important to Lucinda that he agreed.

She smiled happily and kissed him. Then she read him a description of a jousting tournament in medieval England. Lucinda took great delight in this kind of pageantry. And she loved historical novels. She often read to Lawton, hoping to interest him in books. He enjoyed her pleasure in books but found her selections both unrealistic and dull.

As dull, he reminded himself, as he would probably find the concert tomorrow night in Natchez. But again, he would take pleasure in Lucinda's pleasure, and she would be leaving the next day to visit her aunt in New Orleans. And it was with that in mind, knowing they would soon be parted for a while, that he gently took the book from her hands and put it aside. He looked into her eyes for a half minute before kissing her or touching her. Then he made love to her softly, whispering how much he loved her, telling her how beautiful she was.

He kissed down to her breasts, to her firm, upstanding nipples, to the freckles on her flat, white stomach, while his fingers stroked her thighs and slid through the curly red hair to the lips of her vagina. He even let his lips linger along her thighs before he slid them back up. They made love slowly, softly, for a long time.

Later, Lucinda slept with her body pressed against his, but Lawton lay awake. He couldn't find sleep, but he didn't mind. His insomnia was peaceful, almost welcome. He felt a great contentment. He loved Lucinda and he felt her love for him. Despite some problems, things were going well with the plantation, and he was pleased with his efforts to clear land and plant all the way down to the river.

How far behind him seemed his troubles over Roger Blaine . . . and Rafaella. He was pleased to think that Rafaella hadn't entered his mind tonight as he'd made love to his wife. Surely he had forgotten her by now. He must forget her, for he dearly loved Lucinda . . . sweet Lucinda. How he would miss her while she was downriver visiting her aunt.

Lawton turned carefully to face Lucinda. He kissed her loose auburn hair and delighted in her soft sigh. He had never been more content.

46.

The next night as Lawton drank whiskey in the Delsano parlor after the concert, he felt no contentment at all. He heard, without really listening, the talk of his friends about steamboats and cotton prices, cotton gins and markets. His anxiety mounted, and he drank more whiskey.

Both he and Lucinda had arrived in town in high spirits. Lucinda had joined Consuela Delsano for some shopping. Lawton headed for the courthouse for news and business, but not two blocks from the Delsanos' he saw a sight he had dreaded—a woman who reminded him strongly of Nettie, a white-seeming woman with a little boy. He was so stunned that he hesitated for a full moment as they disappeared into the crowd. When Lawton recovered enough to follow, he could not find them.

Lawton was upset and determined to know if Nettie had indeed returned to Natchez, if that child . . . were his son. He searched the market quarter frantically for an hour or so, pushing past farmers buying seeds and selling hogs, once seeing a young woman who looked like Nettie from a distance, but it was hopeless. She had disappeared.

About noon, Lawton gave up the search. He went to the nearest tavern, where he sat in a dark corner and brooded. Nettie looked as white as . . . as anybody, he thought. And her son would probably look totally white. The boy, his only son, might well be the image of Lawton, and he might be walking the Natchez streets. Anyone might see the resemblance and know of Lawton's indiscretion. Or was this a farfetched notion inspired by his guilt? Lawton was anxious to see the boy and know the truth, and yet he could not bear to know, for what could he do? The boy, his son, would look white, but he could never *really* be white. He would be . . . what?

Lawton drank a second whiskey and tried to remember all the complicated laws and rulings that covered such situations. He had heard of various cases, and none of them had ended well. It seemed that what it all boiled down to was that a person who wasn't totally white wasn't white at all.

Lawton gulped his whiskey. This train of reasoning had led him to thoughts of Roger Blaine and Rafaella. He left the tavern and went out to walk in the Natchez streets, but he wasn't thinking of Nettie. He was thinking of Rafaella, poor Rafaella, and the scandalous allegations against Blaine. Of course, only he knew of them; no further proof had arrived from the Continent, and Lawton swore he would never let the rumors about Roger Blaine get out. But he could not forget Rafaella or her sudden terrible expressions of hatred. What if Blaine *had* been a Moslem slave? Then Rafaella was a Moslem slave's daughter, and half her blood was Moslem blood, slave blood. Or worse, what if Roger Blaine also had Negro blood in his past? After all, Egypt was in Africa, wasn't it? He had dreamed of Rafaella during the night, dreamed of the fierce expression on her face as she cursed him at the concert, but he would not let himself think of it now.

The river was busy with houseboats and small craft, teeming with Negroes and low-life riffraff from Under-the-Hill. The spirit of excitement connected with Mississippi river boating was contagious, and Lawton felt his pulse quicken as the big craft with Lucinda aboard whistled and hooted and slipped away from the dock. Cheers rose up from the crowd on the dock, and everyone shouted farewells. Lucinda waved from her place at the railing on the top deck, and Lawton waved back until she was out of sight.

Somewhat sadly, he walked back into town and felt the weight of his emotional entanglements. Nettie was very much on his mind; so was Rafaella. It was almost a relief to have Lucinda out of town, much as he loved her. As he walked through the downtown of busy crowded Natchez, his spirits fell even lower. Every slight, hurrying young woman reminded him of Nettie, every dark head of Rafaella. His blood stirred, and he determined he had better finish up his business and return to The Columns.

When he headed back toward the Delsano house, he felt somewhat calmer.

As Lawton was crossing the street, someone called his name from behind.

Lawton turned.

"Mr. Deavors," Wyman Ridgeway said.

"Yes, Mr. Ridgeway?" Lawton said.

Ridgeway slid off his glove. With a sudden motion he stung Lawton's cheek with the glove.

"Sir, I demand satisfaction on the field of honor," Ridgeway said.

"What?" Lawton asked, touching his stinging cheek.

"For the honor of a lady you have insulted, a lady who by the code must remain unnamed, but whose identity we both know," Ridgeway said.

"Dammit, sir . . ." Lawton said.

"My second will call on your second-designate to make the arrangements," Ridgeway said.

Lawton looked into his death-grey eyes, did not look down at his withered hand. Ridgeway bowed.

"Good day, sir," he said and left.

A crowd had gathered. Lawton felt fear on his spine like ice. His cheek was burning. Without thinking, his hand slid up and touched his ear, his eye, his nose.

47.

As the rapier flashed through the air, Lawton stumbled and parried the blade with an awkward gesture. He thrust his own blade forward, but Theron Sumrall easily rejected the thrust and came forward with a quick cut through Lawton's defense.

"Wait a minute, Theron," Lawton said. He stepped back and wiped sweat from his face with the back of his hand.

"Lawton, you got to stop bending your elbow like that," Theron said. "I was doin' the same thing wrong till Pepe Bordeaux corrected it."

"Theron, what difference does it make?" Lawton asked. His head drooped toward his chest. Slowly, he tapped his rapier against his boot. He sighed and looked up.

"Lawton, when you were in school you were damn good with a sword," Theron said. "We got all day to practice."

"I could practice all day for a month and it wouldn't make much difference against a man like Ridgeway. No, dammit, let's forget all this. I've got . . . got a dozen things to do today."

Lawton hurled the sword to the soft, black earth.

"Listen," Theron started. "I'll come with you."

"No, please, Theron. Some things I have to do alone."

Theron nodded. "All right," he said. "When shall I . . ."

"What time are we due at Vidalia?"

"At eight. Eight sharp, I reckon," Theron said.

"Then I'll meet you at the Benton crossroad at . . . say at half past three. That should give us enough time to get across the river."

Theron nodded again. "Lawton," he said tentatively.

"We can do our talkin' then, Theron."

They shook hands, and Lawton turned and walked away.

Lawton had given in to his longing to ride around the entire plantation. As he rode, he sensed the uneasiness among the people. They gathered in little groups and whispered. Mothers held their children close to their bodies. Word of the duel had spread among the slaves, and they were terrified of what might happen as a result. Their fears and tension increased Lawton's own, and he abandoned the project of riding the bounds. He turned his horse back toward the house, then dismounted and led the horse.

Memories had haunted him during his ride, and now as he led his horse across a field of frost-blackened cotton plants, he recalled another January afternoon, years ago, when he had come home for a weekend visit from the Natchez Institute. He had gone hunting with Ambrose. They had bagged several quail and partridge, and Lawton had been elated. After their shooting, they had walked their horses back, and Lawton had savored the feeling of being home, where he belonged.

His father . . . his mother . . . in his mind he saw them as they had been then. Now they were dead. And poor Tillman, his brother, dead. Just himself and Joleen left of the family, and Joleen was so far away. Well, he was glad that she wasn't here for the duel, and that Lucinda was gone, also.

Lawton stumbled and shook his head. He looked around at the familiar fields and meadows, at the gardens, the house, the barn and sheds, the corral, the slaves' quarters, the sun bright and low in the sky behind a lone, red-tinged cloud. He took the reins and walked slowly toward the house again. As he passed the edge of the quarters, Aunt Fronie came out of the nursery. Lawton looked into her wrinkled face. She was the oldest of all the slaves; she had been midwife and nurse on The Columns longer than anyone could remember.

"Mist' Lawton," she said, straining her withered neck and twisting her head around slowly. "Word goin' 'round 'mong the people 'bout what you be doin' come mornin'. We all worried, Mist' Lawton. All your folks dyin' and all. Miss Joleen done gone 'way. Not no family hardly left."

"Don't you worry, Aunt Fronie," Lawton said. "Everything will be all right."

"I been here to the place all my life, Mist' Lawton," she said. " 'Fore Mist' Athel. Born here when his daddy was the master. Mist' Lawton, please don't go and leave us to strangers."

"Nothing like that's goin' to happen," he said.

She reached up and hugged him. Her body was frail and brittle, as though her bones would burst through the grey parchment skin.

"You come back to us," she said. "No matter . . . you get cut up with the knife . . . you come back here. Aunt Fronie, she cure you, make you well again."

Lawton pried her hands away. "Yes, I will," he said.

"Here, you need this," she whispered, as he leaned close. She pressed something into his hand.

"Thank you." He looked down. It was some kind of charm, some kind of bird's talon with tiny red ribbons and bits of grey and white hair attached. He put it in his pocket.

"It protect you, Mist' Lawton," she said. "Bring you back here to your people."

"Yes, thank you," Lawton said. "I'll be back. Don't you worry."

The horse neighed and stamped its hooves. Lawton tightened his grip on the reins. He felt the talon in his pocket. The claws were sharp. Aunt Fronie had talked about getting cut with the knife, as though she sensed that Lawton wouldn't die, that he would return to the plantation, but that he would be badly cut.

His hand moved up to touch his ear, but he stopped the motion. He clenched his fingers into a fist. To fight and be killed was one thing. That he was prepared to do, if necessary. But to be left maimed, a cripple. To have your ear sliced off, or your eyeball taken out. To have Lucinda return to find herself married to a deformed man.

Lawton sucked in his breath. He dropped the reins and started running toward the house.

48.

Lawton was sitting in his study and staring at an untouched glass of whiskey when Grady Weston arrived with the will. Lawton offered Weston a drink and forced himself to sip some whiskey while Weston had two quick glasses.

Weston talked rapidly about the will's provisions, and Lawton sensed that the lawyer was nervous. Weston wouldn't look Lawton in the eye.

Lawton took a long swallow of the whiskey. Weston's nervousness was contagious, and Lawton was already uneasy enough for half a dozen men. He asked himself if Weston were already seeing him a crippled, mutilated man, a one-eyed man, or one without fingers, someone to be pitied. Did he already seem a man set aside from normal men? Would people have to look away from him the way they did from Wyman Ridgeway's hand?

Lawton choked and poured more whiskey.

Later, he walked to the window of Joleen's room and stared out at the shadows on the front lawn, the trellises, the gardens, the house road. The moon was bright, the clouds misty and fast-moving in the rising wind. There was a hint of ground fog among the bushes.

He turned, holding the full glass of whiskey in both hands. He set the glass on the bedside table. It offered no solace.

He lowered himself to the bed. A memory came as he touched the soft mattress: wrestling with Joleen on the bed when they were both . . . oh, less than ten certainly, fighting over the last blackberry muffin that Beatrice had baked that day.

Lawton sprang up. That memory brought another: he and Joleen in the shed getting tobacco for their father, the pungent smell, the dark room. They had tripped over some gunnysacks, and he had fallen on top of her and had felt such a stab of desire for her that he was nearly nauseous. And later that summer, after he had followed her and watched her swim naked several times, there had been a night at the Sumralls when he and Joleen were alone in the dark, and they were very close. They did something very wrong . . . but he hadn't violated her, hadn't really . . .

He swallowed and nearly choked. That was years ago. Nothing had happened between them since those desire-blurred days, and he must never think of them again. It had happened. They were young. Now they were grown, and he loved her only as a brother should love a sister. He was married to Lucinda. And Joleen was married and she had changed. Joleen had become so different, so alien . . . a stranger . . . and she was so very far away this foggy night.

Lawton groaned. He needed her so much tonight. He walked to her closet. He opened the door, fingered the dresses she had left, old dresses she had worn as a young girl. He remembered the blue dress she had worn the night of a birthday party, but could not see it. He sighed. He closed the closet, took a step toward the door. He paused. He thought of the letters he had written. One to Joleen. He had written it half a dozen times, but when he was satisfied, he had suddenly torn it up. What good would it do to send her an urgent letter when he didn't know what would happen? She would be frantic with worry, and she would then have to wait for another letter. No, he had written her a short letter to be mailed if he were killed in the duel. If he lived, if he cared to live as a cripple, he would write still another letter and explain everything.

He had also written to Lucinda. It was horrible to think he might never see her again, might die with her away. Or that she might return, beautiful, loving, eager, to find him mutilated or crippled. When she next made love to him, would her soft, shy hands caress the stub of an ear, the empty socket of an eye?

He thought of Wyman Ridgeway, and wondered how much the man had manipulated Rafaella. In her misery, grief, loneliness, and hatred, she might be easy prey for a man such as Ridgeway. He might have initiated the duel without her knowledge.

Lawton sipped whiskey and thought again of blame and guilt. It was so much a part of his life, had always been. He shook his head, then put the glass down on his desk and started pacing the room again.

Once again he was in the study with Cellus. They sat soberly facing each other. Cellus declined a second glass of whiskey.

"You don't have to do this duel, Mist' Lawton," he said.

"Yes, I have to, Cellus," Lawton said. "I'm a Deavors."

"Mist' Lawton, what other Deavors ever fought a duel?"

"I don't know, Cellus. But I reckon no Deavors ever backed down from a challenge. My family has a place of honor and importance here in Adams County. Dammit, what would the Deavors name be worth if I acted a coward!"

"What's the name Deavors goin' to be worth if you dead and there's nobody to take care of the people and The Columns?" Cellus asked.

"Cellus, we went through all this before. And we're not goin' to get anywhere with this kind of arguin'. And like I said then, I'm not goin' to be . . . Ridgeway hasn't yet killed an adversary . . ."

Lawton broke off the sentence. He sipped whiskey and despised the taste. He shoved the glass away.

"I reckon I can understand how you feel, not bein' able to back down from a challenge," Cellus said. "And you right. Won't do any good to go on arguin' about things this way. But couldn't you tell me what that man wants to challenge you for?"

Lawton shook his head. "I'm afraid I can't," he said. "Maybe some other time, maybe later. But not now, Cellus."

Cellus nodded. "All right, Mist' Lawton," he said. "We better talk, then. They plans to be made, 'bout the place, the people, Miss Joleen, Miss 'Cinda. Lord, for both of them to be away at a time like this. Miss 'Cinda's goin' to be real upset, Mist' Lawton."

They talked about the plantation and the people. Lawton told Cellus about the will. He said that the Sumralls and the Delsanos would come to look after the place until Lucinda returned, though it would only be for appearance' sake, since Cellus could certainly handle things by himself. And Lawton told Cellus to assure all the people that no matter what happened, no one would be sold.

A strange, debilitating feeling came over Lawton as they talked. It wasn't fear, he didn't think. Or hatred. It was a kind of sadness, a loneliness, as he talked of his family and people and The Columns . . . and riding away from them all in a few hours. He cupped the whiskey glass and squeezed, then released the glass. How could he have ever put anything—a duel, honor, whatever people might think—above his responsibility to the plantation and its people and to his family?

He shifted in his chair and felt the sharp talons of Aunt Fronie's charm. Something caught in his throat. The sadness took a new form. He swallowed hard and realized that Cellus was staring at him.

"Well, guess there's nothin' more to say," Lawton mumbled. He barely got the words out.

Very slowly, he rose to his feet. Cellus stood up, also.

"Cellus, I . . ." Again, the words wouldn't come out.

Only once in his adult life had Lawton cried, and it had been in this same room, and also with Cellus there. Now Lawton gave way to all his fears and feelings and cried openly.

Four hours later, Lawton walked slowly downstairs from his bedroom. It was three in the morning. Cellus was waiting at the foot of the stairs. They walked silently down the gallery toward the back.

A group of house slaves was waiting at the back door. Beatrice stepped forward. There were tears in her eyes. She hugged Lawton and pulled back, looking into his eyes. She had been his nurse when he was young, had raised him nearly to manhood before she took charge of the kitchen.

Ambrose was there, and he and Lawton shook hands. He seemed about to speak but said nothing. Lawton merely nodded and walked down the steps, where he shook hands with Ed and Filch. Ed was holding the reins of his horse.

Lawton took them from Ed and mounted.

From the shadows came other figures, dozens of them. They were all the people, and they had been waiting there for him. Now they moved forward slowly and silently, some three hundred black people, all looking up at him.

Lawton sat there a moment, looking around, nodding without making a sound. Then he dug his heels into his horse's flanks and rode around the house. He looked back only once, to glance at the twelve white columns rising out of the ground fog. Then he urged the horse into a trot and rode hunched forward against himself.

49.

Rafaella woke suddenly, filled with anxiety and anger. She felt so miserable. It must be that the fault lay outside—with Lawton . . . with Ridgeway . . . with both men. It was the day of their duel. She looked at the clock. Another hour until the duel, she told herself. She dressed quickly and began to pace her room, wringing her hands. She went to the door, paused, turned, and walked to the window.

It was a brilliant winter morning. The sky was robin's egg blue and cloudless. Japonica bushes were bright red in the garden. Ridgeway had given her a single red japonica blossom last evening, she remembered, as they stood in the light fog in the garden and talked.

Rafaella stared at the wilted red blossom on her night table. She hated Wyman Ridgeway and cursed herself for all that she had let happen in the last two days. She had agreed to become Ridgeway's wife, and he had challenged Lawton to a duel to defend her honor.

"Damn him," she whispered. "Damn *both* of them, all of them!" She didn't know whom she hated more, Ridgeway or Lawton.

She wanted Lawton punished for the way he had treated her, for her humiliation and her father's death. Lawton should suffer some terrible punishment, and what could be worse than that of Wyman's sword?

And then Rafaella remembered Lawton's clear blue eyes, his strong handsome face, his deep, slow voice, and she nearly burst out crying. What if he were killed?

She turned from the window and ran to the door, but once again she paused. She sighed and leaned against the door, her breath heavy and labored. She was frantic to do something, but she felt totally helpless—and more than a little frightened by Ridgeway.

"You knew perfectly well I was going to challenge Lawton Deavors," he had said last night after giving her the japonica. "I made the challenge for you, Raffles. I once swore I'd never fight another duel in anyone's name, only for myself. I broke my oath because of you, and by God, don't dare even whisper about calling off the affair or, fiancé or no fiancé, you'll rue the goddamn day you met me!"

A minute later he was all tenderness and love and flattery. She again believed she had the power to manipulate him, but she couldn't bring herself to try. And she suspected that if she insisted he not hurt Lawton, he might hurt him even worse.

And now, this morning, Ridgeway was on his way out to the dueling field, and poor Lawton would be hurt. How could she bear to see the man she loved mutilated?

"But I hate him," she muttered and shoved herself away from the door. "And I hate Wyman Ridgeway even more."

The Weston children had awakened and were screaming at their nurses. Rafaella went to the open window, put her hands on the sill, and leaned out. It was cool but not cold. Yet she started shivering. She pulled back inside. She thought of her sleepless night and of her longing to break off the engagement with Ridgeway. But now, in the light of morning with the children screaming again, she knew she had to go through with the marriage and as quickly as possible.

Unless she married, she would be marooned with the Westons until she was twenty-one. Grady Weston would have control over all her property for those three years, unless she married. She couldn't endure another week in this house with the noisy children, with all the restrictions, with the Westons hovering over her. Mrs. Weston had even mentioned something about adopting her. Aside from not wanting to be adopted, least of all by the Westons, Rafaella was suspicious that they had some design on the estate her father had killed himself to provide her with.

Rafaella turned from the window. She wanted that legacy and she wanted it immediately! It was hers! And every day she was helpless, that whore Frannie might be setting up some new way to cheat her out of it. As soon as she married, she would be rich and independent. She could avenge the nasty things Lawton had said about her father. She could . . . she could protect his name—and her own—in the event that anyone ever . . .

She shut her eyes a moment. Blood throbbed at her temples. She couldn't bear to think of that accusation. Of course it was ludicrous even to think those things about her father. But as long as he lived, Lawton might spread the slander. She could never trust him completely. And yet the thought of seeing him hurt was too awful to bear.

Rafaella decided to go out. She had to move, to act. She opened the door and fled down the hall, Delcimer catching up with her as she reached the stairs.

Rafaella had never been out in the Natchez streets in early morning, and for a time the scene absorbed her. The markets were being set up; crates and boxes were being opened and fruits and vegetables arranged for sale. One woman was selling baskets, brooms, and wicker bird cages. Other merchants hung half-sewn clothing from hooks in front of their stores. Trappers strung up foul-smelling pelts, some of them still dripping blood. Rafaella hurried past, down a street lined with mules and donkeys and chickens, enduring Delcimer's grumbling that a lady shouldn't be out at this time of day, when she came on a sight that stopped her.

It was a slave auction. She stared at a dozen half-naked men on the wooden platform, then bolted to the cover of a magnolia tree. She had to see more. Through the thick, waxy leaves she watched a white man poke and prod the slaves as he extolled their merits to farmers and other men who wanted to buy. Rafaella's heart began to pound as she watched.

She had never seen a slave auction before, and though she knew that the Mississippi constitution of 1833 had outlawed the selling of slaves by professional traders, she also knew that the law wasn't often enforced and that clever traders circumvented it easily. Since the law did allow Mississippi residents to buy and sell slaves for personal use, it was simple enough for traders to claim local residence and sell Virginia or Carolina slaves to a farmer for a nominal fee, then buy them back and resell them the next morning.

"Not no place for a proper young lady," Delcimer said. "Miss Weston, she goin' to have a hissy fit she find out."

"Shut up!" Rafaella said.

She looked back at the auction. Some white men had climbed onto the platform. They were poking fingers into the Negroes' ribs and opening their mouths to examine their teeth.

Rafaella realized that her heart was pounding. She felt strange, flushed warm, yet a little chilled. She felt very excited, It wasn't guilt about spying, she knew. She did what she pleased, and she loved to spy on forbidden things.

She wondered if she felt this strange way because some of Frannie's wealth—and therefore her own—came from slave trading. Frannie had sold off most of her husband Lavon's trading connections. Natchez society disdained slave trading, and Frannie didn't want anything to impede her entry into society. Slave dealing had been the foundation of Lavon Deavors's estate, but now the wealth lay in rich cotton acreage and in hundreds of slaves, as well as sizable interests in several business ventures.

Still, for all Rafaella knew, some of those slaves being sold were her slaves; the money being exchanged was her money. It was a strange feeling to watch from behind the magnolia tree and to speculate. Though she had never thought much about the morality of slave trading, she realized that she felt an aversion to the auction. But even that didn't account for her odd feeling, she knew. It was something else.

Four full-grown Negro men had been sold. More white buyers had arrived. As she watched, a new coffle of slaves was brought up from what seemed to be some kind of pen behind the platform. Among the new arrivals was a girl of only sixteen or seventeen. The girl was very light-skinned. She was hesitant, obviously afraid, and had to be prodded along onto the platform.

When she reached the top of the steps, the slave girl suddenly lurched forward and had to be restrained by the white auctioneer. Tears rolled down her cheeks. Her breasts heaved with her gasping and crying. Her white dress was thin, her breasts quite full. Her nipples were outlined against the cloth, emphasized with each heaving sob. The men clustered below her. Rafaella saw the leers and the nasty gestures, and she could imagine what the men were saying.

A tall Negro man was being auctioned at the other end of the platform. The bidding for him was high. He was a massive man with muscular arms. He stood silently, his back straight, his head high. Only once did he show any emotion, when he glanced down toward the crying girl, and his lips twitched slightly.

Finally, the man was sold. A fat white man in a green suit heaved himself up onto the platform and counted out money to the auctioneer. He gestured for his new slave to leave the platform. The big man hesitated, glanced down the row of slaves.

"No, Daddy, please don't go!" the girl cried. She tried to run to her father but stumbled.

The Negro man rushed toward her, knocking his new owner to the ground. Several white men tried to grab him, but he fought furiously.

"Daddy, Daddy!" the girl was screaming.

Rafaella turned and ran blindly down the street away from the platform.

"Oh, Lord, I want to die, too," Rafaella mumbled into her damp pillow. She had been stretched out crying, half-hysterically, for nearly an hour. Her dead father's face appeared again and again in her obsessed, grief-torn mind.

Now she had few tears left, and her body was racked by painful dry sobs. She couldn't live without him. There was no life without him, she told herself. All her life she had been with her father; he was part of life itself; she could not endure one more day without him. What can I do? she moaned. Her grief was reborn, raw and agonizing. She bit her trembling lips.

A knock at the door invaded her thoughts. She started to call out "Go away and leave me alone," but she suddenly remembered the duel. She struggled up and stumbled across the room toward the door, but she caught a look at her disheveled hair and red eyes and tear-stained face in the mirror. She paused and brushed at the tears with the back of her hand.

"What do you want?" she called.

"Gent'man downstairs to see you," Delcimer called. "He say it important, Miss Raffles."

"Tell him I'll be down shortly," she said.

She crossed over to the dressing table and began to make herself presentable. She knew the man wouldn't be Ridgeway. It would be a violation of the code of honor for him to go to her directly after defending her honor. But it would be someone with news.

Her fingers trembled as she combed her tangled hair. Poor Lawton! What had Wyman done to him? Would he be disfigured, his handsome face slashed, missing an eye or an ear? She gasped. And then a terrible thought came to her. What if, for the first time, Wyman hadn't just crippled an opponent? What if he'd killed Lawton this morning?

"Oh, please, no," she whispered.

Rafaella dropped the comb. She ran from the room. Lawton couldn't be dead. Not Lawton, too! She couldn't endure it with Lawton gone, too. Oh, yes, she hated him but she didn't want him dead! She wanted him to suffer and to pay for her father's loss, and to . . . yes, to adore her. But then she couldn't look at him, couldn't touch him, if he were deformed. He would be as repugnant as Ridgeway.

The man was waiting in the parlor. Rafaella hardly heard his name when he introduced himself. She couldn't wait for him to finish with the formalities and tell her what she so dreaded to hear.

". . . affair of honor has been concluded, Miss Blaine," he was saying.

"Yes, yes. Who . . . What happened?"

"Mr. Ridgeway drew first blood, and he was declared the victor."

"Dammit, oh, please, what did he . . . what happened to Lawton Deavors?"

"Mr. Ridgeway inflicted a wound along his neck, a relatively minor wound, Miss Blaine."

263

50.

On a mild afternoon in late January, Frannie Deavors Blaine sat in the back of an elegant carriage driven by her man Tolver. She was trying to contain her accelerating excitement, trying to control her heavy breathing while she recollected her talk a few minutes earlier with her father and her lawyer, Mason Hoopes.

She just had no head at all for those lawyer talks, she admitted. Here she was, all alone, saddled with a huge plantation and hundreds of niggers. No man; just that damn marriage contract and that little bitch of a greedy stepdaughter.

But her daddy had told her that they had to put their minds to working things out so they could get that marriage contract broken and get back all her property. Her daddy and Mason Hoopes seemed to think it could be done.

Frannie squirmed in the carriage seat and arranged the fullness of her bottle green silk dress. When she looked up, Tolver was glancing around at her. Was he admiring her? She caught herself about to smile at him, but looked away. He turned back and cracked the whip over the washboard road.

It was sure smart of Mason Hoopes to figure out that something had been awfully wrong about Roger Blaine and that Price Deavors estate, Frannie told herself.

Her daddy had added that it had to be something pretty bad to make a man in the pink of health and married to a wealthy and beautiful girl like Frannie put a gun to his head and blow his brains out. And Mason Hoopes said he had poked around the courthouse and paid out some bribe money, and that though he hadn't been able to come up with much, there was a sure feeling that Roger Blaine was a man with something to hide.

Mason Hoopes had pointed out that it was stranger still for Roger to go and renounce the estate, which was worth a small fortune, after he had told her getting the estate was the reason for the secret marriage. Nothing made sense, and the least sense, as her daddy had said a hundred times, was her ever signing a marriage contract giving Roger's daughter half of her own estate. How she hated that smart-alecky little trollop! Why, the things that girl had said! The ways the child had insulted her, Frannie Deavors! She just knew that she and Roger could have been real happy if it hadn't been for Raffles. If it hadn't been for her, Roger wouldn't have killed himself, she bet! She hated that damn girl, and she would make damn sure Raffles didn't get any of her money!

But that fat old Grady Weston, why, everybody said he was the best lawyer in Adams County. Even Mason Hoopes said he had never seen a tighter contract than the one she had signed. Mason Hoopes said there might be no way to break that contract in court. If so, there was no way they could stop Raffles from inheriting half of everything. Already Grady Weston had assumed control of lots of the plantation and slave doings for Rafaella. And now if she was going to marry that Wyman Ridgeway, she'd soon do her own handling.

Frannie twisted around in the seat again and smiled. She couldn't wait until she had that spoiled, naughty girl penniless and helpless, till Raffles had to come begging and crawling and asking for help.

Tolver was slowing the carriage. It lurched to the left, along a trail so narrow that limbs and vines slapped at Frannie's shoulders and skirt, and one willow branch nearly knocked off her bonnet.

"Tolver, slow down!" she called, but he didn't seem to hear. A thorn vine grazed her wrist. She just hated Tolver when he acted all independent like this, just like he was a white man. But, she told herself, maybe he was only anxious to get there, like she was. Her heart was thumping wildly now, and her large breasts were heaving with her labored breathing, and her nipples were all tender . . .

He was a man, too, even if he was her slave, she reminded herself.

"Tolver, you hear me, nigger? Slow this buggy down, or I'll have your hide!"

Tolver reined in the horse, and the carriage came to a stop. They were at a completely isolated clearing, shielded by dense bushes and trees. He jumped down and helped Frannie out. She tensed at the touch of his huge, calloused black hand.

"I've warned you 'bout drivin' fast like that," she said. "What got into you, Tolver? I'll swear, sometimes I just don't know what I'm goin' to do with you. And believe me, people talk about your smart ways and how you go puttin' on airs."

"Sorry, Miss Frannie," Tolver said. "Guess I was just anxious to get here."

He squeezed her hand and her heart beat faster. She would not look at him yet.

"And what about those new runaways?" she asked. "You promised you'd try to find out what's goin' on in the quarters. And you yourself a runaway. You ought to know somethin'."

"Couldn't find out nothin' yet," Tolver said. "But I'll keep tryin', Miss Frannie."

"You better . . . Oh, Lord . . ." Frannie sucked in her breath as his rough hands boldly caressed her breasts and mashed the tender nipples under the green silk. She shuddered at herself. It was totally forbidden. She had to stop doing this with a nigger man. She'd be run out of the county if someone found out, and poor Tolver, why, they'd likely burn him alive.

"Oh, yes, honey . . ." He was lowering her to the ground, where he had spread out the carriage robe. His hands were dextrous, authoritative, searching. He caressed her breasts, stroked her tense shoulder muscles. She felt like a child in the care of a strong father. She shut her eyes as she lay back and enclosed his thigh with her silk-clad legs. She squeezed his thigh as he kissed her lips roughly.

51.

Without thinking, Lawton scratched the scar across the left side of his neck. The scar itched. As they often did, Lawton's fingers lingered on the alien ridge of flesh. Remembering, he again saw the thin sharp blade slicing toward his face—toward his eyes, his nose, his ear, his fingers. He went cold as he relived the instant when the blade had sliced into his flesh and pain engulfed his body and blood spurted onto his face, that one nauseous instant when he didn't know it was merely a flesh wound, when in his blind panic of blood and pain he thought he had lost an ear—or worse.

It had taken some time, after Theron led him from the Vidalia sandbar and the surgeon treated his wound, to fully understand that he had suffered only a relatively minor wound, that Ridgeway had ended the duel without leaving him disfigured.

Lawton slumped in the saddle. The quarters lay just ahead, noisy with the sound of hammering and sawing. Esau and four other carpenters were finishing up the new cabins for the Irishmen, who had first resented and then refused to live in the old slave cabins. Reluctantly, Lawton had agreed to have new cabins built for them, reasoning that the cabins could later be used for his own people. At the same time, he was having plank floors put into all of the existing cabins, as well as having them given their annual coat of whitewash.

Lawton tightened the reins. He was in no hurry to reach the house. His fingers moved toward his neck once more, but he stopped himself, taking the reins firmly with both hands. He had tried to forget the duel and its aftermath, but he could not. Not a night passed without dreams of it . . . and, dammit, of Rafaella.

He had encountered her recently. He thought of their encounter now. Lawton had been walking in the park high on the bluffs above the Mississippi. He was tired from a day of price setting and negotiations, and he had thought he was alone in the park.

Rafaella had appeared to him suddenly, like a vision standing under a magnolia tree, stunningly beautiful in a pale yellow silk dress. The sight was stirring and painful. She was a beautiful, desirable woman, but she was also the agent of his agony, his scar, and much of his anxiety.

Strong and contrasting feelings had flooded him as he stood there in the waning light and watched Rafaella approach. He was swept with desire, with anger, with pity for her solitary fragility, and with a fear that she would once again involve him in a dangerous predicament.

He had braced himself for more of her hatred, insults, threats. He had tensed as he looked into her dark eyes, aware in an overwhelming physical sense of her body —her glowing pale skin, her full, round breasts, half-exposed in the pale yellow silk décolletage. He had stood there helplessly and waited for her to speak first. Instead, she came so close he could smell only her perfume. Her small hand rose to his face.

She touched his scar, and he trembled.

"Poor Lawton," she said, nearly whispering. "I'm . . . I'm so sorry. *Really* I am. No matter what I said, I would never have wanted you hurt. I tried to stop Wyman. I did everything in my power, Lawton. But he was like a man possessed and . . . and all I could do was make him promise that he wouldn't hurt you badly."

Lawton could not speak. His throat was hot and raw. Moments passed. At last, he managed to whisper, "I suppose I should thank you, Raffles."

"I'll try to control Wyman in the future, Lawton,"

she said. "But I don't know if I can . . . if he feels he must challenge you again. No, I'm sure I can. I must . . . because last night he said that next time you'd leave the field of honor . . . without your manhood."

Lawton winced. "You're gettin' married," he had heard himself mumbling as he digested her ugly, soft words. Later, he wondered what in the world he had thanked her for.

"Yes," she said. "Yes, I am, Lawton. Oh, how did it all happen? I wish . . ."

"Wish . . . what, Raffles?"

"Oh, God, Lawton. I've been so alone . . ." Her fingers moved toward him again. "Lawton, I . . ."

"No, Raffles . . ." he said as steadily as he could.

A smile twisted her lips, and the little gesture aroused him and made him even more uneasy. His loins tightened, and he sucked in his breath as she touched his scar again. He wanted to pull her fingers away from his neck; she was responsible for this, she was dangerous, unpredictable, vengeful. And yet she was so alone, so young, so vulnerable, and so lovely. Perhaps if he had handled things differently, if things had been different that day at the creek when he called her Joleen . . .

"Lawton, after all that's happened . . ." She took her fingers from his neck. The smile was gone now. There was a subtle but disconcerting change in her expression. It was difficult to see clearly in the twilight, but something hard and bitter had taken control of her face. "I don't really hate you. I meant to hate you, Lawton, but I'm also quite fond of you, despite what happened—Daddy's death and all."

"Raffles, please . . ." he had started. He couldn't bear the blame for that, but he didn't know what to say. How could he be standing here in a public place, talking to this girl who had caused him to risk his life, who was responsible for his scar? How could he reconcile his feelings about Raffles with his love for Lucinda? Yet despite his fear and his principles, he couldn't walk away from the moment, from her dark eyes, from her powerful sexual presence, and from his own powerful feelings of guilt.

For a few moments, neither of them could speak. A woodpecker tapped at the trunk of a massive oak spreading its branches above them. The sound was as steady as a heartbeat, as persistent as desire. Then Lawton shook his head, and she smiled again, a deeper, more deliberate smile.

"I'm sorry, Lawton," she said. "Perhaps, I shouldn't harbor such bitterness. But I've been so alone and so sad, Lawton. And to have you as an enemy is hard because of the way I felt about you."

"Dammit, I'm not—"

"Please don't interrupt me, sir!" she said sharply. Then she smiled. "Lawton, I want to . . . to give you a chance to . . . oh, I don't know. Lawton, you were willing to slander me before the duel. You wouldn't seek revenge now, would you?"

"Of course I wouldn't, Raffles!" he said. "And I've *never* been your enemy, never would think of slanderin' you."

"I've slept very little lately," she said. "I've been simply sick with fear, Lawton . . . that those slanders might come out, and I might be disgraced."

"Now, dammit, Raffles, this is all in your head," he said. "I wouldn't ever . . . I haven't . . ."

"Oh, damn you, Lawton Deavors," she said. "Are you calling my poor father a liar? I *have* to believe him. Oh, Lawton, if only I could really trust you. Please, please, despite all that's happened . . . Lawton, I don't want anything from you. You can have the Price Deavors estate."

"Raffles, on my oath, your father was wrong. Or dammit, let's be plain about it. He lied, that's what. I've never had the slightest interest in the damn Price Deavors place. I'm part of no plot against you. And not a word of those . . . those rumors will ever get out, I promise you."

"They better not, Lawton," she said. "Not even a hint of them. Because if they do get out, I can't be responsible for what Wyman might do. I hope you understand that. Oh, Lawton, I'll try to trust you. I want to trust you. Then we could even . . . visit a little like this from time to time. I'd like that."

"No! We can't, Raffles!" he said, although there was nothing he wanted more.

Denying it, they leaned toward each other and touched for a moment. Then they pulled apart, and he walked away.

Lucinda had not yet returned from Natchez. Lawton, restless, went into the study and poured himself half a glass of whiskey. He sat down at his desk and stared out of the window at the budding trees and early flowers. It was nearly spring. He would have to go into town soon and complete arrangements for the planting and other expenses.

The thought of his business schemes and responsibilities invigorated him. If the good prices held through the year, he would make a lot of money on his cotton crop. There would be more cotton, and he would build a landing of his own on the river to save transporting the harvest to Natchez en route to New Orleans. Perhaps this was the year he would build his own gin. Perhaps . . . he was becoming increasingly in favor of the Liverpool project, a concept that had seemed over-risky to him when Theron Sumrall first proposed it.

Sumrall had suggested that a few of the planters get together and arrange to sell their cotton directly to Liverpool textile merchants. It was a bold idea; it required a good-sized investment in ships and a fair risk of failure for the chance of a huge profit. It would likely include travel to England to set up the venture.

His scar was itching, but he tried to resist the urge to scratch it. He sipped whiskey and watched slaves working on the horizon. The next thing he knew he was scratching his neck.

There was a sound in the hall. He hurried over and opened the door. It was Beatrice, dressed neatly in a clean white uniform with a neat white cap.

"Is Lucinda back yet?" he asked.

"No sir, not yet," Beatrice said.

Lawton closed the door and sat down at the desk again.

He hoped Lucinda didn't have to stay in Natchez overnight. He was worried about things between them. Everything was not as it should be, and they had not made love since her return from Louisiana.

Lawton drained his glass and stared into it as he thought of the catastrophe of Lucinda's return from New Orleans, of her hearing all the wild talk in Natchez before he'd been able to tell her about the duel. Not that it would have mattered much, he told himself. He had been stunned and hurt by her bitter reaction, though Cellus had warned him. After her first, obvious relief at seeing he was not badly hurt, after touching his neck and shuddering, she had gone into an uncharacteristic rage. Lawton had never seen her so angry.

Lucinda had shouted that he was damned irresponsible to fight a duel when he didn't even believe in dueling, to take a chance on leaving her a widow, on leaving three hundred slaves without a master. And especially to fight while she was away—that was the most unforgivable part of all. She wasn't at all moved by his argument that, according to the code, duels must be fought immediately.

"The rumors in town, Lawton!" she had said. "And the way people looked at me! Why, that hateful Mrs. Barceau just couldn't wait to imply that the duel was fought because of something to do with Rafaella Blaine!"

Eventually, Lawton had admitted that indeed Raffles was the cause, but he insisted that it was all a terrible misunderstanding, that Wyman Ridgeway was a madman, that he, Lawton, had not been involved with Raffles in any way, dammit! Guilty as he felt, he had never dealt with what had happened with Rafaella that day at the creek.

For a whole terrible day, Lucinda had refused to speak to him at all. Whenever he tried to explain further, when he decided to confront what happened at the creek, she refused to discuss the matter. For the first week, things had been nearly unbearable. Lucinda had been so cold, so quiet, and so distant.

Since then, their relationship had been slowly, steadily improving, but it still wasn't right. Lucinda had been spending far more time in town than in the past, and Lawton was very unhappy about it. He wanted to end their feud, wanted them to become husband and wife again, in every way.

52.

Lucinda strolled along alleys of bright, sweet-smelling orange blossoms in the park high above the river. She had dismissed Romulus, her driver, telling him to return in half an hour. She could not decide whether to return to The Columns or stay another night with the Delsanos. She was still very much upset with Lawton, but when she'd stayed over an extra night two weeks ago, he had been so mad she promised not to do it again. Now she regretted her promise.

She wanted more time to think, and anyway, she had not quite finished her shopping. An expected shipment of silver and rugs from England would not arrive until the next day. She had come into town to meet it and wanted to take the new shipment out to The Columns. And then, there would be another meeting of the music society tomorrow. It was a long ride from Natchez to the plantation. Normally, she wouldn't hesitate about staying over, but things were far from normal in her marriage.

Honestly, she didn't know if she could ever forgive Lawton for fighting the duel while she was away. And over the question of Rafaella's honor! The risk he had taken made her furious. It implied such irresponsibility. She might have returned to find herself a widow, in charge of the whole plantation and some three hundred slaves. Her life might have been utterly changed, ruined, and without a good-bye from Lawton. The whole thing was so unlike him, she thought, and it had all happened so quickly. Several of their male friends had tried to convince her that Lawton had no choice, but she dismissed their arguments impatiently.

Before her trip to New Orleans, Lucinda had become increasingly upset with Rafaella's behavior and several times had started to speak to Lawton about it. The girl was a cousin, after all, and her carryings-on and quarreling with Frannie Blaine had somehow reflected on the Deavorses. She'd been relieved, although distressed, when Rafaella had left The Columns, for she'd flirted outrageously with Lawton while she was there. Not that she suspected Lawton had responded to Raffles. She had too high an opinion of her husband's good sense for that. But to disembark in Natchez and find the town wild with gossip about Lawton's duel over Rafaella's honor!

The recollection was painful and embarrassing. She had determined to forgive Lawton, however, for she loved him. She understood some of the deep feelings of guilt and chivalry that could drive a man to such an act. But it was hard to forgive him, and just when she felt she could, and when things were returning to normal, he had tried to confess something about an incident at the creek when Rafaella had gotten half-naked and tried to seduce him. She'd cut off his confession. It was outrageous. That girl was outrageous. She wouldn't hear another word.

Now she didn't know what to believe. It was the first time she had ever had the slightest doubts about Lawton's honesty or his faithfulness. And the idea of his approaching her sexually disgusted her. She walked to the edge of the bluff and inhaled the sweet-smelling grey moss that hung from the towering oaks. The smell reminded her of pineapples, she realized. She stared down at a passing padwheeler, at the rafts and flatboats tied ten or a dozen deep along the banks, at the taverns and shanties of Natchez-Under-the-Hill. A din of muted noise came up from the crowded riverbank settlement. She turned away.

Despite her own unhappiness, she believed that in time the rift in their marriage would heal and be forgotten. Lawton was a man who felt things deeply, and she was deeply sympathetic, despite her anger, about his suffering over the duel. And she was even more disturbed, and frightened, by his continuing dread at being challenged to another duel by Wyman Ridgeway.

"I just couldn't fight another one," he had mumbled one night when he had brought a bottle of whiskey to bed. "I swear, I'd murder the man first if I had to."

She had come to understand his feeling. He wasn't afraid to face death as much as the possibility of being mutilated. His fear of mutilation was profound and was still gnawing away at him. Nothing she could do or say seemed to comfort him. It seemed to be beyond her ability.

Or perhaps it was because Lucinda had some doubts and fears, some secrets of her own. She knew a strange, unspoken, undeveloped feeling existed between herself and Wyman Ridgeway. It was not love, and could not, she was sure, lead to adultery, but it was there . . . it was there.

She had not been able to help wondering what part it played in all this. It was almost bizarre. Recently, she had seen Ridgeway in Natchez—again and again—always accidentally and always with an odd, powerful effect on them both. The encounters couldn't have been more innocent, she reassured herself, public encounters in the streets or shops or at the music society. Innocent they were, but were they all coincidental? And wasn't it true that she had begun to look forward to them, to what seemed inevitable?

Lucinda could not understand why she found Ridgeway so attractive and interesting. She despised his barbaric dueling habits and his brooding cynicism. Yet, instinctively, she sensed an elegant melancholy below the surface of his cynicism, and even suspected that she had the power to make him see the world in a different way. Her sympathy and curiosity were deeply stirred by his hand, and she longed to know how it had become deformed. At times she had thought, unwillingly, of that hand caressing her flesh. Her body had responded with reactions so strong, so forbidden, that she felt she might faint. But all of that had been a fantasy, unreal and unformed. She had put it out of her mind. Reality was Lawton and her life as mistress of The Columns.

She had nearly forgotten Ridgeway during her trip to Louisiana. Then she returned—returned to learn about the duel. It was agonizing and infuriating. She hated them both for doing it, hated them for doing it behind her back, and was both astounded and profoundly thankful that, for the first time ever, Ridgeway had not left his opponent mutilated or dismembered. As she rode home to The Columns, frightened and anxious and angry, she was stirred as well by her deep suspicion that Ridgeway had spared Lawton because of his regard for her.

Two weeks ago, Ridgeway had confirmed her suspicion. He'd had the audacity to confront her as she strolled here in this very park! It was unthinkable for her to talk to him, scandalous to be seen in public with a man who had fought a duel with her husband over a woman's honor. Lucinda had told Ridgeway so in blunt terms. But after her outburst, she had not walked away.

"Yes, Natchez decorum would be shocked to its roots by this, I suppose," Ridgeway had said in his low, deep voice, his grey eyes directed at her, disturbing her, as always. "Thank God, I will be leaving this town soon. But Mrs. Deavors, that sort of decorum is made for those who lack the spirit to ignore it."

"Yet, sir, with respect to the decorum of dueling, you seem to be a purist," she said. As she spoke, she had thought of Lawton's continuing fear of him and wondered why she didn't hate him for causing such suffering.

"Oh, not at all," he said. He scratched his bad hand with his good one as he spoke, and she glanced down from his eyes to his hand. "I refuse to act on principle. No man has to accept a challenge. Refusal would shock society, but I'm far from shocked by anything. A refusal would be a refreshing twist, a new amusement to help save one from a boring day."

"And your victims, sir! Do you find amusement in causing them a lifetime of suffering?"

"Ah, Mrs. Deavors, now that Lorenzo Dow has departed Natchez, are you to mount his pulpit and take his place with sermons on morality?" Before she could answer, he had said, "Do you wish to see me punished before God for wounding your husband?" He pulled out a short but deadly looking knife and offered it to her. She stared at it and found she could not speak.

"Here, take this knife and use it on me when you think I deserve to be punished," he insisted. "There are only two people in all of Natchez to whom I would make such an offer," he added. "And as long as I feel this way, your husband need have no fear of another encounter with my blade."

"Mr. Ridgeway," she said, avoiding his eyes, trying to hide her excitement and confusion, "I don't know what to think." Blood pounded at her temples. "Mr. Ridgeway, I am grateful that you . . . that you spared my husband, that you will spare him. But I will not be in your debt. Do not expect me . . ."

"Mrs. Deavors, I am a man who long ago learned to expect nothing. Except that night follows day in a tedious and unimaginative routine that our all-powerful, all-knowing Creator managed to devise. Merely allow me to speak to you from time to time. Only when no one can observe us, I may assure you. I hope we can speak as we have in the past, of gentler matters, speak with some humor. Your honor is quite safe with me. After all, I am soon to be married, and I would never think of dishonoring the marriage vows in the slightest way."

He had bowed and left her on the bluff, and at almost this very place, she realized as she inhaled the pineapple smell of the grey moss. Had she returned to the spot deliberately, without realizing it? Had she come here because it was almost the same hour she had encountered Ridgeway the last time?

Surely not, she told herself as she hurried away. It was merely coincidence! She had hardly thought of Ridgeway since, and she would not speak to him again. Yet she had to consider Lawton's debilitating fear. As long as her innocent friendship with Ridgeway lasted, Lawton was safe from another duel.

"I can't ever remember the azaleas blooming so early," Consuela Delsano said as she and Lucinda greeted other music club members in the side garden of the Delsanos' handsome Natchez home. It was a warm afternoon, splendidly sunny with brilliant blue sky accented by a few fast-moving clouds.

"Yes, there are still several days left in February," Lucinda said. "I remember last year the full flowering didn't come until the first week in March. I only hope a frost doesn't get them."

The talk about flowers was comfortable enough to allow her thoughts to roam as the women sipped tea. Almost defiantly, like a willful child, Lucinda had decided to stay over in Natchez. Then, like a good child, she had sent a slave hurrying out to The Columns with a rather lengthy and involved note of explanation for Lawton.

She forced a smile as Martha Anne Weston joined the group. She had never been fond of the fat lady's endless and inane talk, and since the trouble with Raffles and the duel, she felt rather uncomfortable in Mrs. Weston's presence. The other ladies had decorously avoided the slightest mention of the duel.

Now the women were discussing flowers and herbs that grew in medieval times, an enthusiasm of Consuela Delsano's. She was encouraging the group to plant a garden with only plants and herbs that grew "in that marvelous time Sir Walter Scott writes about."

Lucinda had never more powerfully realized the prestige and power of the Deavors family. Most women whose husbands had fought a duel over another woman —although that was just one of the scandalous rumors in circulation about the duel—would have been snubbed, mocked, driven to distraction. Instead, Lucinda had received everyone's support. No one wanted to cross a Deavors or fall into the family's disfavor. Lucinda had never felt more strongly that she was indeed a Deavors, and that it was comforting to be protected by the shield of the family name.

"Not merely plant such a garden," Mrs. Delsano was saying; "why don't we think of actually recreating a whole medieval tableau? With music and costumes. The gentlemen could dress as knights at arms and mount their finest horses, and they could have mock jousting contests and wear their ladies' colors."

The women clustered around. There was a chorus of enthusiastic approval. Lucinda joined in the talk. She found the idea exciting. She had always loved romantic novels set in courts and castles, and she loved to fantasize about living in such a glamorous, chivalrous time. People were even saying that their part of America resembled such an era, with its aristocratic citizenry, its elaborate manners, and its sophistication.

Lucinda was quite pleased, half an hour later, when she was chosen to be a member of a committee to plan the medieval spectacle for the autumn. Her pleasure was only slightly tempered by Mrs. Weston's inclusion on the committee.

A slave came up to Lucinda as she and Consuela Delsano were showing the last of the ladies out. Mrs. Weston was still babbling about how difficult it would be for her poor Grady to find a horse stout enough for his bulk.

"Lady name of Frannie Deavors here to see you, Miss 'Cinda," the slave said.

Mrs. Weston stopped in midsentence and looked around at Lucinda.

"Please tell Mrs. Deavors that I'm busy now and not receiving callers," Lucinda said. She and Lawton had decided that, family or not, they wanted no more of Frannie's social climbing. Not at their expense.

"Yes'm, I told her you busy," the slave said. "But she insist. Wouldn't leave, Miss 'Cinda. Say it mighty important and can't wait. Say to tell you it got to do with legal matters."

Lucinda shrugged her shoulders. "Oh, all right. Please excuse me, Consuela, ladies." It would be easier to deal with Frannie at once and dismiss her than have her interrupt again.

53.

Rafaella lay alone in bed, anxious and apprehensive. It was her wedding night, and she was waiting for Ridgeway to come from his dressing room. He would come at any minute, and she dreaded it. She had a throbbing headache.

They had been married at four that afternoon, the first day of April, and Rafaella hadn't been able to repress an appreciation of the coincidence that she should marry and surrender her virginity on April Fool's Day.

A noise startled her. Was there someone at the door? She sucked in her breath and turned away. She waited, looked back at the door. She had been mistaken. She tossed about miserably. Sweat stood in little drops on her forehead and ran in rivulets over her stomach and along the insides of her thighs. She cursed the damp heat that was adding to her misery. Why was it so hot at the beginning of April?

Rafaella closed her eyes. What could she tell Wyman? She had to think of some excuse, something to prevent him from taking her tonight. Once, in Italy, she had spied on her father violating a virgin—a maid in their hotel—and she had delighted in her father's triumphant pleasure and the girl's moans and thrashings. But to think that Wyman would now do that to her, invade her body for his pleasure and possibly leave her to bear his child, the child of a deformed man . . . The idea was outrageous, unbearable. It made her feel like screaming.

An old, forbidden fantasy came into her mind. She and her father were in her bedroom at Frannie's, and he lay between her thighs, aroused and wanting her more desperately than he had ever wanted any woman. She felt glorious, exalted. She wanted to surrender, let him violate her. Then she would claim and hold his love for all time.

The simple ceremony had taken place in the Westons' parlor. Grady and Martha Anne Weston were the only attendants. It was not the wedding of her dreams—far from it. All her life, she and her father had planned for an elaborate, romantic wedding, but she knew she did not want such a wedding with Wyman Ridgeway. In fact, she had convinced herself that this was not her real wedding, that some day in the future she would have another, with a man like her father, a man her father would approve.

She so resented her marriage to Ridgeway that she had not worn the exquisite wedding gown of handmade white lace that had been made for her in Rome. That gown still lay in a trunk. Instead, she had worn a plain white *peau de soie* dress, cut severely and modestly with a high collar and long sleeves.

The Westons were troubled that there were no wedding guests. But there was no one Rafaella wanted to invite. Ridgeway seemed to find it amusing. He joked that he thought he hadn't yet alienated everyone of quality in Natchez, but maintained that he was pleased to see that he apparently had. Rafaella was not amused. Ridgeway had left too many permanently disfigured victims on the dueling field not to be shunned with increasing frequency, and it was only a matter of time before all doors were closed to him. His duel with Lawton had hastened his rejection by Natchez society. Rafaella knew she was responsible, she admitted it; still, it only had added to her resentment.

This time there was an unmistakable sound at the door. Rafaella bit her lips and curled her knees up, hugging herself as the door opened. It was Ridgeway. He was wearing a blue velvet dressing gown. Rafaella forced herself to straighten out her legs. She stared at his strong, manly face, shadowed in the low, flickering light. He was handsome, she admitted to herself. She found herself staring at his hand as he approached the bed, imagining its withered flesh scraping along her thighs, those twisted fingers invading her body.

A low whimpering sound rose involuntarily from deep in her throat, and she realized that she was pressing her thighs together. She shut her eyes, fighting for control. Ridgeway hovered over her in bed. A moment passed, and she forced herself to look up, to relax, to smile, to conceal her anxiety. Ridgeway sat down beside her on the bed. His proximity intensified her panic. She checked the impulse to run from the room, then suddenly remembered the champagne in the silver bucket at the head of the bed.

"May I have a little champagne, darling?" she asked in a little-girl voice, and then everything happened slowly, as if in a dream that she seemed to be watching from far away.

As they drank champagne together, it seemed better. He spoke to her gently, in that manner that seemed so alien to his nature because it was reserved for very few people. He praised her beauty and even recited a few lines from a sonnet by Shakespeare. Carefully, he smoothed a long curl that had fallen from the top of her head, then leaned down and kissed her lips. She accepted the kiss without feeling and put her arms around his neck. They kissed again, and she forced herself to remain calm when he began to caress her breasts. She was perspiring even more, but felt nothing.

Then, as she watched with detachment, the lies she had to tell came smoothly and easily. She smothered him with small kisses, she stroked his neck.

"I want you, too, Wyman," she heard herself saying. "And I've very nearly let myself become . . . let myself become reckless. But I must tell you that Dr. Murdine told me yesterday . . . some silly woman's complaint . . . he forbade me . . . for a few days or so . . . nothing serious, if I'm careful . . . go back to see him next week . . . then we can have our wedding night . . . oh, a little pain, but not too much . . . nothing serious . . ."

It succeeded. He not only accepted her story but was quite solicitous, concerned for her health, apologetic for not asking earlier what the doctor had said.

They lay side by side, then, enduring the heat, her hand resting on his chest, and Rafaella thanked creation she had taken the trouble to visit the doctor the day before. She had deliberately allowed the doctor to watch her while she undressed, and had noticed his fascination with her body. She would return in a few days, be very artful while posing for him, and act the innocent, young, frightened virgin bride. She would make sure the doctor agreed to go to Wyman and tell him that her minor complaint forbade intimacy for at least a few weeks. And in return, she would pose for the doctor in any way he wanted.

54.

Joleen had never been happier than during the first few weeks after her return to Cincinnati. She and Aaron were constantly working and loving together. She enjoyed being able to speak openly of her feelings about slavery. She did not care whom she offended. She cared only for Aaron and their abolitionist work, which she considered right and important.

At first she thought Aaron was content and well settled also, and that their life together would never change. Then she began to notice a gradual alteration in him. He was increasingly serious, tense, grim. She saw he was still capable of killing for his principles, and the fire in his eyes frightened her.

The arguments among the abolitionists became more drastic. Aaron disagreed with moderate abolitionists and was often abusive with them. Joleen tried to discuss his behavior with him, but he was evasive. She knew his symptoms, and her worst fear was that he was becoming engrossed in the Cuban expedition. Like many abolitionists, he was determined to free the black slaves there from the cruel rule of Spain.

When their argument on the subject of Cuba started, it lasted half the night. There was never the slightest ground for compromise. Joleen was bitterly opposed to Aaron's going, and the more he talked the more determined he seemed. He talked in grand terms of historical importance, of its being criminal to pass up this opportunity. She began to despair.

His intensity was frightening. His arguments were eloquent. But no amount of passion could undercut her primary fear. She feared that Aaron would be killed and she would be left alone. Her love was her strongest argument in the end, not her objections that the plan was foolhardy and ill planned and had little chance of success.

They settled nothing that night. The next morning they woke up arguing. They argued for days, a week, two weeks. Nothing else was of equal interest or importance. Joleen came to hate the radical abolitionists. They were both anxious and edgy, and Aaron became angry at the slightest thing. Joleen wept and threatened to return to The Columns. Words became useless.

Joleen and Aaron fought through the long summer days, one by one, hour by hour, and came together only to take desperate pleasure in their love and love-making.

Gradually, Joleen began to accept the inevitable. Aaron would go to Cuba. She resented it. She hated to accept that it meant more to him than his love for her, but she knew that to do anything drastic to prevent his going might end that love.

55.

Rafaella steadied her horse. She was alone in an area of jungle-dense forest off the madhouse road just north of Natchez. She was waiting for Lawton Deavors, and increasingly apprehensive about it, as well as frightened at being alone in the tangle of thorn vines, grey moss, bougainvillea, and massive water oaks. Sudden sounds from the shadowed undergrowth made her tense. And she had seen loathsome, crawling things in the slime-covered bayou nearby.

She heard the whistle of a steamboat on the river that lay only a few yards away through the growth. Actually, she was less than a quarter mile from town. Yet she felt she was in the middle of nowhere. It was the only place Lawton had been willing to meet her.

Rafaella wiped perspiration from her face. The humidity was choking and it was insufferably hot. Her silk pongee dress was so damp and crumpled it would be ruined. It was only the second time she had worn this dress. Her father had had it made to order for the *carnevale* ball in Rome a year ago. Thinking of that ball, of her father that night, so handsome, so full of love for her, she wanted to cry, and she very nearly burst into tears. Instead, she swallowed and tossed her head.

She heard some rustling from the narrow trail. She

leaned forward and peered into the shadows. There was no one visible, only the sounds of birds and insects and splashing in the bayou behind her. Oh, it was all so frightening and hateful!

Dammit, why was she here? She would give Lawton two more minutes and then she would leave. And damm him, she would . . . Would what? What could she do? She knew now that it was Lawton she needed— desperately, as profoundly as she mistrusted him. Of course, Hiram Cranston, her new lawyer, told her that Lawton was her worst enemy. Cranston was a lawyer who was every bit as unprincipled and greedy as Mason Hoopes—exactly the kind of man she needed to deal with Frannie.

And Hiram Cranston assured her that he had proof that Lawton had schemed against her—with Frannie! Proof. She'd had to believe it, although something within her told her that Lawton wouldn't—couldn't— lie. But if he *would* do that, why wouldn't he spread the stories and allegations against her poor father that he had promised her never to reveal? She was distraught with worry, and that was why she had to meet him again.

Cranston was clever and ruthless. Already, he had suggested ways to destroy Lawton, and his whole family, if she decided she was still in danger of slander. But why? she asked herself. Why would he do it? It would bring such dishonor to the family name. And with Frannie? No one liked Frannie. It made no sense.

At last she saw Lawton riding slowly toward her through the deep shadows. Her horse whinnied nervously, and she patted his neck to steady him. Lawton reined up beside her. He looked stern. He shook his head. "Raffles, this is madness," he said. "To meet like this. I very nearly didn't come."

"But you did come, Lawton," she said. "And after all, we *did* meet before—in the Natchez park."

"That was by chance," he said.

It had not been at all, but she decided not to tell him that. "Lawton, we're quite alone here in these woods. And if you're worried about Wyman, well, he's gone downriver for a few days."

"Still, Raffles, I don't want anyone—"

She smiled. "Why, Lawton, what could be more innocent than two cousins happening to meet while out riding? Here, please. Please help me down."

He dismounted and courteously helped her to the ground. His hands lingered for a moment around her waist. She pretended to steady herself and deliberately brushed her breasts against his arm. He stiffened. His cheeks were burning.

"I wouldn't call meetin' here in this place innocent," Lawton said. "In fact, it's dangerous for you to be here alone. Now, what did you want to talk to me about, Raffles? Your message said it was urgent."

"What if I only wanted to see you, Lawton?" she asked. "Just to see you." He had stepped back, awkwardly, and she moved closer to him. Despite her uneasiness, she felt incredibly glad to be with him. He made her feel . . . well, happier. She had been so lonely and miserable with Wyman. Every day she'd been married, she feared him more.

"Then I wouldn't have come," he said.

"Very well," she said, stiffening inside. He would pay for that hateful remark. "I do have something important to say, Lawton." She hesitated, then took a package from her saddlebag and handed it to him. "But first, here, take this. Though you're being so unpleasant, I don't know why I went to the trouble."

She loved the helpless way he was looking at her. Through lowered lashes, she could see him staring at her breasts. His cheeks were flushed a deep red. He could not conceal his feelings.

He took the package and opened it.

"Do you like it, Lawton?" she asked. "I believe that shade of blue is just right for your eyes."

He held up the sleeve of a blue silk shirt. "It's . . . it's real nice, Raffles. But I can't have you buyin' clothes for me."

"Well, why not, if I want to?" she asked. "I chose

all of Daddy's clothes, and don't you think he was always elegantly dressed? And he chose all my clothes, too, Lawton."

"I appreciate this, Raffles," he said.

He was so handsome, she told herself. So noble-looking, so attractive, and so . . . so wary of her. She knew he hated to give in to his lust for her. She was certain he was desperate to adore her—to caress her body and kiss her. And she would let him if . . . if only he would explain away everything and if he . . . if he did not reject her when she needed him most.

To relieve the tension, she chattered. "I saw you on the street last week. And honestly, Lawton, for some-one as good-looking and tall as you, well, you should pay more attention to your clothes. At the tailor's, there was a simply beautiful new rust-colored merino. Why, I think you'd be the handsomest man in Natchez in that color."

"No, Raffles," he said. "I do appreciate your gen-erosity and good taste. But I can't have you buyin' me expensive clothes in the future."

"I don't see why not," she said. "I will if I want to. I can certainly afford it. And I want to. That is, if we remain friends. Though, I must say, there's some doubt we will after your most recent betrayal."

"Now, listen, dammit, Raffles," he said. His voice rose. "You're hardly the one to talk of friendship and betrayals. I bear this scar on account of you. I fought a duel over you. A duel that's become the scandal of Natchez. We're both married. We can't go carryin' on as though things were different. Can't you understand that? And I'm gettin' sick and tired of your damm threats and charges!"

"Please spare me your profanity, sir!" she said. She was dizzy, and her whole body was sticky wet. It was so damn hot, and she hated to be scolded or rejected. Lawton was just asking for trouble. She wondered if she should be giving him this last chance. Why was she giving him another chance? She'd almost forgotten why.

"I'm sorry about the profanity, Raffles," he said. "But can't you understand why this is all impossible? Can't you understand that I'm sick and tired of your groundless charges about slanders and attempts to cheat you and ruin you? Now, please, what do you want to talk to me about? I have business in town."

"You'll regret behaving in such a hateful manner," she said. "Just you wait and see! I'm no longer your mendicant cousin, sir! We'll conduct our business, then, and in a businesslike manner. And to think I nearly . . . why I wanted to . . . to speak personally with you before we discussed business."

"Well, as long as we're here, Raffles, you can if you want to."

"No!" she said. "Not now!" Her emotions, as always, took a wide swing. She just hated him! She wanted to cry. Why wouldn't he give in to her? He wanted to, she knew it. He had been staring at her breasts again. She felt like slapping him! "I was going to discuss a very . . . intimate matter, as I used to with my father. I have no one to talk to now, no one to advise me or take care of me. Certainly not my husband! And it's all your fault, Lawton Deavors, damn you! And I can't trust you. Last time I took your word because of my feelings for you, and now I've found out about your scheming with Frannie."

"Raffles, what on earth are you talkin' about?" he asked.

"How dare you interrupt me, sir!" she said. She realized she was nearly shouting and warned herself to stay calm. It was an important moment. She licked her lips and stared at him a moment. His face was deep red. He wouldn't look into her eyes. She moved a step closer. For an instant she didn't know if he would bolt backward or reach out to embrace her.

He only dug his nails into the palms of his hands. "This is hopeless, Raffles," he said. "You're talkin' in circles again. Now either tell me something definite—or I have to go."

"We're talking in realities, Lawton," she said. "And

since you seem to think me naive and stupid, I'll spell out the realities for you."

Rafaella told him that Martha Anne Weston had reported Frannie's visit to Lucinda. She said that she knew Anson had returned to Natchez and visited The Columns. She knew that Lawton had called on Frannie in her Natchez home, and that Lawton had received Mason Hoopes just yesterday at the Delsano house.

"So it's obvious you're up to something, Lawton," she said.

Lawton tried to explain that Lucinda had refused to deal with Frannie, that Anson's business brought him to Natchez every six months or so and he'd only paid a social call, that he had visited Frannie on a matter concerning her son Lige's education, and that he despised Mason Hoopes and had refused even to meet the man.

"And I resent the fact you've been havin' me followed around Natchez," he said.

"My having you followed could be the least of your worries, Lawton," she said. "I'm far from helpless now, and I don't mean just because of Wyman's blade. Well, are you going to explain yourself? Or are you taking time to think up some lies?"

"Raffles, calm down," he said. "You're gettin' hysterical. And you're talkin' absolute nonsense! Who puts these ridiculous ideas into your head? You talked about reality and you mentioned some visits and nothin' more. All right, the woman is out to ruin you, but I'm no part of her schemin', Raffles. Can you give me one shred of real evidence that I am, dammit? You're as wrong about this as you and your father were about my wantin' the Price Deavors place."

"Lawton, I won't have you—"

"Just listen a minute, dammit!" he said. "The court put the Price Deavors estate up for auction, and it was bought yesterday by a planter from North Carolina."

"I don't believe you."

"Then check the court records." Lawton was breathing rapidly. "Or the Natchez *Gazette*. The auction is mentioned in today's *Gazette*. So you're the one who should be explainin'. Oh, to hell with it!"

They stared at each other. Rafaella did not know what to say. He wouldn't lie when he could so easily be found out. What, then, was going on? What could Lawton possibly be up to?

In all this time, she had to admit, there was no indication of any slanders from Lawton. She was surely safe now that . . . But if Lawton didn't want the Price Deavors estate, then her father had blamed him wrongly. And if Lawton wouldn't slander her now, he wouldn't have at the time of her father's warning.

So her poor father had been badly mistaken. Or he had lied. No . . . no . . .

She sniffled. She was shivering despite the smothering heat, and her head felt light. She still didn't trust Lawton—she had too much at stake. One word from him could destroy her. Or save her soul.

Why couldn't he say one comforting word to her? Or just say she was beautiful? Why wouldn't he give in? He was so obviously obsessed with her. She had never been wrong about a man's feeling for her, never. She just knew she could make him beg for a kiss, beg her to let him touch her, or to watch her undress. Yet he had resisted her that day at the creek, too. Why didn't he give in to his feelings, as any other man would?

She had never been alone with a man who was so infatuated with her and given that man so much . . . encouragement . . . and had him resist her like this. She could not understand what was wrong.

"No good will come of this kind of talk," he said finally. His breathing was heavy and he had difficulty speaking. "Frannie is your enemy, not me. But the way you're actin', I can hardly be your friend."

She stepped closer. Her breasts brushed his arm. He stiffened. Sweat streamed down his forehead and cheeks. She put her hand on his neck. It was hot and moist. He shoved her hand away.

"Dammit, Raffles, enough of this," he gasped. He moved back a step.

"Lawton, I've been so frightened that awful, unspeakable rumor about my father will get out," she said. She was desperate to keep him from leaving, to gain his sympathy. "Please understand, Lawton. If you had too much to drink one night, just a word could ruin me. Or if you told Lucinda and . . ."

"Dammit, Raffles, I wouldn't ever . . . not *ever* . . . I . . . I can understand your fear, Raffles. But nothin' will ever get out. You have my promise. And I've told no one else, not even Lucinda."

"I have to trust you, Lawton," she said. "I'm so alone, so alone." She touched his neck again, and though he stiffened, he let her finger stroke his neck. But when she moved close enough to kiss him, he jerked his head back. There was a frantic look in his eyes. He was nearly gasping for breath.

In that instant of rejection, as though he dreaded her touch, a horrible thought came to Rafaella, so horrible her stomach tightened and she felt nauseous.

"Why . . . you believe those slanders, don't you?" she asked in a low, horrified voice. "That's why you reject me and act so mean and hateful, Lawton. You believe it! You think I'm the daughter of a Moslem . . . a slave . . . that I'm . . . untouchable . . . Oh, Lord in heaven!"

"Now, Raffles, that's ridiculous!"

She pressed against him and locked her hands behind his neck with a fierce strength. She felt hot flashes, chills. Why, this explained everything! Lawton was rejecting her as an untouchable, an infidel slave. Her lips began to quiver. She was an outcast in his eyes, a born slave, human chattel. When she closed her eyes she saw that light-skinned girl screaming on the auction block in Natchez, the men poking her body. It could have been her.

"I don't believe any of that . . ." Lawton was gasping. "Of course you're not . . ."

She rubbed against him, arousing him.

"Then prove it, Lawton," she whispered, leaning closer to his face. She dug her nails into his neck. "Prove you don't find me untouchable, a slave's daughter. Kiss me, Lawton. Prove you won't flinch to have your lips against mine, Lawton."

"No, I . . . that's not why . . . " He was trembling. "I . . . if it means that much . . . just a kiss."

He bent down to kiss her. Her doubts melted. She had him. She opened her mouth. When she touched his tongue with hers, he groaned and slipped his arms around her body and squeezed her. No man had ever kissed her with such urgency. She sucked his lips harder, tasted his mouth, nibbled his tongue.

But she was detached, physically unaffected by the kissing, and with her new fear that Lawton believed the slanders lingered another fear, vaguely defined, but awful. Her father had warned her Lawton would try to prove that she was illegitimate, to prove that Sarah Deavors wasn't her mother. If he did so, she would have no Deavors blood, and Lawton could exclude an impurity from his family and at the same time slander her without hurting his family's name.

She withdrew herself. Lawton's face was scarlet, his breathing labored. He made low hacking sounds deep in his throat.

"Raffles, please, don't back away now . . . let me kiss you again, Raffles . . ."

"Not now . . . another time, Lawton." She stepped away from him. She knew she could have him at this moment, any way at all, but she was too confused and uncertain to act. She must get away to think about this new horror, must decide what to do.

"Raffles," he mumbled. He reached for her.

"No . . . I can't . . . soon," she said. She ran to her horse and mounted without waiting for help. She moved the horse into a trot, then a gallop, ignoring the sting of the vines and limbs as she raced down the narrow trail.

56.

Lucinda sat in a white wicker armchair, under an arbor of pink roses, with Wyman Ridgeway. She found it hard to believe that she was doing it. She had actually postponed her return to Natchez to meet him for a second time.

"And how did you leave Miss Delma today?" Ridgeway asked. They were drinking rum punch on the terrace of the Hotel New Orleans.

"Oh, Aunt Delma is fine, as always," Lucinda said. She thought of the lies she had told Aunt Delma, lies about an earlier boat upriver.

"I wish I could have called on her," Ridgeway said. "But it would have greatly complicated things for you."

Lucinda looked away from his probing eyes and sipped her punch. Her cheeks were warm, and she knew they must be pink. Why had she come? To endure insinuations when she only meant to have a talk, to protect poor Lawton. And certainly she would never meet Wyman Ridgeway alone again.

She knew she should make herself clear, but she did not know what to say. She sipped more punch. He was staring at her. She knew if she looked up from her glass she would be intimidated. The silence stretched on until she could bear it no longer.

"Wasn't it a coincidence, though?" she asked. "Our meeting, I mean. I couldn't have been more surprised to see you in the street, Mr. Ridgeway."

"It was no coincidence," he said. "I knew of your plans, and I contrived to meet you."

"But, Mr. Ridgeway," she said. Her cheeks were feverish. She felt dizzy. His audacity excited her. "Mr. Ridgeway, if I had known, I certainly wouldn't have come."

"Oh, but I think you would have."

She looked up from her empty glass. "Sir, I must say

you seem very sure of yourself. And for a gentleman, you are very blunt."

He smiled. "I've never claimed to be a gentleman. Only an aristocrat. I'm merely being honest. I've found that, oddly enough, honesty has its uses."

"Then I shall be honest, also," she said, "when I tell you that I must go at once."

"Go where?" he asked. "Your boat doesn't leave for another three hours. Here, have another rum punch. Waiter!"

"No, I've had quite enough, sir," she protested, but he ignored her and ordered the punch.

"One never has enough of something that's enjoyable," he said.

"You assume I find this enjoyable," she said.

"Either that or you take pleasure in things which are not enjoyable," he said. "No, I think in our hearts we're both pleased to be here."

"I can endure no more of your audacity and vanity, sir."

"To be sure, by common standards, I'm an odd character," he said. He smiled again. "I possess both audacity and confidence in gross proportions. Even less kind descriptions have been hurled at me. Bizarre, grotesque, half-mad. I left your husband with a scar he will carry for the rest of his life, and still you are pleased to see me."

"Sir, you . . . you are trying to humiliate me," Lucinda mumbled.

She waited for his apology. He said nothing. The silence grew between them. The sound of birds singing in trees overhead suddenly seemed very loud. The punch arrived on a silver tray. She knew if she drank more she would become intoxicated. She sipped the punch.

Ridgeway spoke again, but in a gentler voice. They talked about poetry. Lucinda talked animatedly and finished the punch before she realized it. Her protests were feeble when another was ordered.

It was intensely hot and airless. The sky was nearly

covered with pale grey clouds. Ridgeway spoke of his travels in the Mediterranean, of the startling quality of the light in Greece, of how the changing, darkening light here in the garden shadowed Lucinda's face and brought out new aspects of her beauty.

Lucinda felt quite light-headed. She blushed, suddenly realizing that she must leave soon. His flattery was becoming embarrassing. She resolved to change the subject.

"And were you in Greece when the poor Greeks were fighting for their freedom against the Turks?" she asked.

Ridgeway laughed, a harsh laugh that startled her. "Soon afterward," he said. He lit a cigar and laughed again. "Freedom, indeed! There are probably not ten men in the whole of Greece who know what freedom is or have the courage to be free men. Freedom! For that rabble? Why, I'd as soon have freedom for our own rabble, our niggers or poor whites."

Lucinda shuddered.

His voice fell, and he laughed at his own fervor, then beckoned to a slave with a huge palmetto fan on a stick.

"Now I seem to be the one to climb into a pulpit," he said. "Enough of such talk. The air is very still, but with the wind coming up, the temperature will fall soon and most likely it will rain."

"I feel quite dizzy, sir," she said. "And . . . somewhat short of breath."

"Then we should move inside."

"It doesn't matter, really. I must be leaving soon."

Despite her protest, Lucinda felt shaky enough to let herself be led inside to a small private sitting room with a table, chairs, and a red velvet sofa. She felt a sudden chill as she sat down on the sofa, and then a sudden warmth. Sitting outside on the hotel terrace was innocent enough. But to be in this little room alone with Wyman Ridgeway was quite another matter. She was about to rise when he startled her by mentioning that he had seen Alain LeBeau earlier in the day.

"He asked about you," Ridgeway said.

Lucinda knew she was blushing again. A slave had set another silver cup of punch in front of her. She sipped at it absently, glancing away from Ridgeway's curious grey eyes.

"Alain . . . he . . . how is he?" She felt a tremor that reached all the way to her toes. Had Alain told Ridgeway what had happened between them? She would be mortified to have it known. The memory flooded her, and she felt she was smothering. The shiver that had crept down her legs seemed to have taken with it all her strength and will. Passively, she watched Ridgeway's withered hand move several inches along the sofa. It lay on the back now, just an inch from her shoulder. She was very aware of it, and she felt she would scream if the hand touched her, yet the thought was strangely fascinating.

"Are you all right?" Ridgeway asked very softly. His mouth was only inches from her ear, though she had not seen him move. She shuddered. She must leave, she knew, yet she was hot and cold and she did not think her legs would support her if she tried to stand up.

She nodded "I'm . . . I'm all right."

"You were asking about Alain. He's still the same, I fear. Headed for damnation fast as he can go. Now, that's fine, to seek damnation through pleasure, but poor Alain, he seems to have aged years since I last saw him. I wonder . . . is it debauchery alone . . . or are you part of his premature aging?"

"I think we've had enough intimacy, sir," she said. She had to leave, this instant. Would her legs support her?

His twisted fingers brushed her shoulder. She stiffened and jerked away. "No," she said. She swallowed hard. Her heart was pounding. She put her hand on the sofa to support herself as she stood up.

His fingers touched her again and lingered. She froze.

"No!" she cried out and moved her hand to stop

him, but she could not bring herself to touch his fingers. Nor could she stand up.

"Please stop," she whispered. "Please."

"Are you appalled by the touch of such flesh?" he whispered.

"You shouldn't touch me at all, Wyman. You shouldn't. You said my honor would be safe. Please stop."

Ridgeway moved in against her and talked softly into her ear. His breath and his lips were warm, and each small, nearly accidental touch of his lips against her ear heightened her unbearable excitement and anxiety.

Before she could resist or question it, he kissed her cheek, then her mouth. She returned his kiss helplessly. His hands cupped, freed her breasts. She felt her dress ease off her shoulders. Smooth fingers, withered fingers stroked her soft skin, gently squeezed her nipples until they grew hard and ached with excitement.

Without speaking a word, he eased her back on the velvet sofa. Her dress fell open; he deftly rolled off her stockings. His twisted fingers slid over her tight stomach. Her head was reeling. She whimpered and shivered when the fingers rubbed her smooth, damp thighs. Her mouth held his as she caressed his neck, his back. His fingers nearly drove her mad, made her moan and whimper, twist and shiver, and finally cry out when they slid against the lips of her vagina . . .

57.

On a May evening some weeks later, Lucinda traveled upriver on a padwheeler after another visit to New Orleans. She was alone on the unsheltered deck, leaning against the rail long after the other first-class passengers had gone to the salon or to dress for dinner. She stood stiffly. The wind was blowing warm spray into her face, and sparks from the boat's engine showered over her head, bringing curses from the deck passengers below. These were the third-class passengers, eating their meagre evening meal and preparing to sleep in the open space provided.

Lucinda was oblivious to wind, water, and fire.

Three hours earlier the doctor had confirmed her fear. She was pregnant. She and Lawton had made love only twice in the past month, and both times he had been drunkenly impotent. She knew for certain that she was carrying Wyman Ridgeway's child.

Her knuckles were white as they curled around the brass rail, seeking support. Not only did she have to endure the fact of her pregnancy, but she could not forget the scene with Ridgeway just before she had boarded the boat. He had been stunned when she told him that she was pregnant.

"But . . . Lucinda . . . I've thought myself . . . I've been told I was incapable of . . . being a father," he'd said. "You know my marriage with Rafaella is meaningless . . . and doomed."

She became hysterical as she insisted that there was no doubt that he was the father. Her sobs and hysteria convinced Ridgeway that it was so and that she was determined to have the child and raise it as Lawton's.

They had met in a café near the docks. Lucinda was certain no one she knew would be there. Ridgeway began to drink brandy and rapidly became intoxicated. Lucinda was silent and miserable. She sipped a glass of sherry, and he begged her to see him again. She refused. She was adamant. She would not discuss the matter.

"So, I'll never see my . . . the only child I'll probably ever produce," he said.

"Never," she said. "I can have nothing more to do with you. If you threaten me, I may . . . take measures."

"No!" he begged. His eyes were wild, his voice low. "No, by Christ, abort no offspring of mine!" Then his eyes grew softer. "Please, Lucinda, I know I have no rights. You owe nothing, but please have the child."

He drank a glass of brandy in two swallows.

"I believe I will," she said. "In truth, I want a baby, have long wanted one."

Ridgeway groaned.

"What kind of brandy is our landlord serving?" he shouted abruptly. "I do believe the fellow is poisoning me. Or else, why would I voice such sentiments about fatherhood? And why should I be bitter? Why, I can return home to my child bride. I presume she awaits me. Or look there, Lucinda. Those men are recruiting volunteers to fight in Cuba. Another filibustering expedition! Listen to their talk! Why, this lot wants to free the island, free the oppressed natives! How goddamn droll!"

She finally calmed him down, and he managed to escort her to the boat. She sent him off at once, fearing she would see people on the boat who knew her. And she had been right. She knew a score of passengers and had to decline their invitations to drink, to dine together.

Nausea had troubled her for the past two days. Now it was returning. She wondered if this resulted from her pregnancy or if it was another sign of her profound anxiety and melancholy. She had to regain her good spirits before she reached The Columns. She had to pretend to be perfectly content and normal, when actually she felt completely different.

She had made her decision and now she must implement it. She would have the child. There was no question of confessing her infidelity to Lawton. He would never understand. How could he? She did not fully understand herself. She had wanted to protect Lawton, and Wyman had said he would soon be leaving Natchez. She supposed she had wanted some kind of . . . of what? Retribution? Revenge? Because Lawton had let himself be involved with Raffles? But no, she reminded herself. The truth was that she had been irresistibly attracted to Wyman Ridgeway.

She would bear the child. She would pray it resembled her and not Ridgeway. And now she must return to The Columns and seduce Lawton, make love to him again and again, to make sure he thought himself the father. Lucinda's stomach ached. She gripped the rail tighter. Some kind of madness had surely possessed her, she told herself. Why, she loved Lawton. She loved the plantation and the people. And she had all but abandoned them for an evening of ecstasy.

She had been away too much, but now she was going home, and once more she was going to become mistress of The Columns.

58.

Gale winds shook the sodden branches of the sweet gum trees, and rainwater rolled off the leaves of the tall oaks marking the boundaries of the cemetery of the Benton Presbyterian Church. A light rain still fell, and Rafaella huddled under a huge black umbrella at the side of her father's grave. Lawton stood by his horse at the cemetery gate. He had come once more, because Rafaella had begged him to, but he wouldn't agree to stay.

The extremes of the Mississippi climate would never cease to amaze her. Here it was the middle of May, and the thunderstorm that had come out of the west without an hour's notice had left the day miserably cold. She shivered, pulling a black knit shawl more tightly around her shoulders. Lawton, she noticed with some satisfaction, had neither a jacket nor a hat. Perhaps he would take a chill, or even develop pneumonia. She hoped so.

"He can die for all I care," she told herself. Lawton had made her suffer, so she wanted him to suffer. If he continued to make her suffer, she wanted him to suffer more. If he continued to reject her, she would make him pay . . . in ways he had never even thought to fear.

She heard the primitive monotone rhythm of the gravediggers' chant as their shovels shifted the muddy earth. The four huge black men were excavating her father's grave. The regular gravediggers had refused to work in the thunderstorm, so she had brought four of her own slaves—slaves from Frannie Deavors's plantation.

Grady Weston had objected, at first, to Rafaella's decision to move her dead father's body into Natchez. Lawton hadn't understood her determination to do it, either, but Rafaella was damned if any of them would stop her. They'd all lied to her and probably schemed against her. She was really all alone, and so she'd do whatever she pleased, even if it pleased nobody else.

Her isolation was even more complete, now. Ridgeway was nothing at all to her. Their marriage was doomed. It scarcely existed, he was so often downriver. She no longer needed Wyman, for she had taken control of her inheritance by marrying. And she still could not tolerate him physically. To this day, she had never allowed him to consummate their marriage. The idea was disgusting to her, as horrid as the sight of his hand, or the way he laughed at her anger at Frannie and the Deavorses.

And Lawton. Lawton was so unsatisfactory it made her both miserable and furious. Except for that one instance when she had retreated, he absolutely refused to touch her, to kiss her, to give in to her, despite his obvious desire.

"Damn it, damn it, damn him," she muttered. She shivered and pressed her arms around her body; under the shawl she was clad in a lightweight blue silk dress. The wind had shifted and rain stung her face. The slaves were chanting louder now, trying to overcome their fear and abhorrence at disturbing a grave. Their song was low and eerie.

"Stop that wailing!" she shouted nervously. "Stop it, you hear me?"

The singing stopped.

Rafaella tilted her umbrella to deflect the swirling

rain and saw that Lawton was leaving the cemetery. How could she endure it? Each day was more miserable than the previous one. She had no friends, no interests, and she was worried sick that Lawton would ruin her, reject her; that one day he would decide to betray her, proving that Sarah Deavors was not her mother and that she was . . .

The hem of her blue silk dress was dragging in the mud. It was such a beautiful dress. Her father had had it made for her by the finest dressmaker in Rome. Oh, how she missed her father! None of this would be happening to her if he hadn't left her.

"Daddy!" she whispered, "I love . . . loved you so much. I know you only died because you loved me. But I'm so lonely, Daddy."

Fearfully, she realized that she was mumbling aloud. This had to stop. Why, they said that talking to oneself was a sign of approaching madness.

Lawton had mounted and was looking back at her. She longed to run after him. It was so frustrating, so infuriating, the way men were always leaving her. If it hadn't been for Lawton, her father would still be alive, and now Lawton was leaving her. Why wouldn't he at least stay and help her through this ordeal? If he were any sort of a gentleman he would; instead, he'd made some excuses about Lucinda being sick and being busy on the plantation. Wasn't she more important to him than a dull old farm and a skinny wife?

Oh, it made no sense. So much of it made no sense, unless Lawton despised her because he believed her the daughter of a slave. Unless the slanders weren't slanders at all, but the truth.

She choked. No! She would truly go mad if she allowed herself to doubt her father's word. But there were so many inconsistencies, so many doubts, so many loose ends.

The slaves were grunting and grumbling. One groaned, and she looked around, forgetting Lawton. She gasped. They were hauling up the coffin!

"Dear Lord in heaven," she gasped.

Rafaella took a step toward the grave. The rain was falling harder. The ebony coffin was covered with mud, dripping with slimy soil. And her father . . . her father was inside. She began to walk after the coffin; she stumbled momentarily, but kept moving.

The slaves had hoisted the coffin up on their shoulders. They were chanting again in low, fearful voices, glancing back at the open grave as though they expected something terrible to rise up and follow them.

Rafaella was crying uncontrollably. She began to shiver violently, and bile rose into her throat so that she gagged.

All around, the storm had quickened. Wind snapped limbs of the sweet gum trees and massive oaks, ripped free the clinging grey Spanish moss. The air was full of a sickening, sweet smell like something dying . . . a smell like rotting pineapples . . . or flesh decaying from the grave.

"Oh, Lawton," she whispered. She needed him so much. It swept over her like a fever. She could never totally destroy Lawton. He was her last hope. She could not stand to be alone.

One of the slaves lost his footing in the mud, and the coffin pitched off his shoulder. Another slave on the other side couldn't take the sudden shift of weight, and in his effort he, too, slipped. The coffin slid forward and slammed into the side of the wagon.

"Oh, God, don't hurt him!" she screamed. "That's my father, you clumsy damn niggers!"

Rafaella staggered through the deep mud and snatched the whip from the carriage box. She was trembling, and chills raced over her spine.

"Pick him up, damn you!" she screamed. She struck the nearest slave with the whip, and he yelped and let go of the coffin. It fell to the mud. "Pick it up!" Rafaella screeched. "I'll make you pay . . . you damn slaves. I hate you . . . all of you . . . niggers. You'll always be slaves. How can . . " The men were cowering from the whip. She lashed another man, but this drained her fury and she stumbled backward, sobbing.

She didn't hear the riders until they were nearly on top of her. Then she jerked her head up. There were eight of them, all armed. The leader had his rifle up to threaten the slaves.

"These niggers attackin' you?" the man asked. "They part of the rebellion, we'll string 'em up right here. They so much as laid a hand on you, Miss."

"What?" Rafaella asked. "Attacked me . . . no, no . . ." She brushed tears from her eyes. "Just clumsy . . . stupid . . . dropped my . . . dropped the coffin . . . they belong to me."

The leader dismounted. The other men were passing a jug around, as they surrounded the cowering slaves.

"Don't guess you folks out this far heard the news just come from up the Trace," the leader said. "Niggers risin' up all 'long the Trace, formin' armies, Yankees everywhere, they murderin' and burnin'."

Rafaella was too shaken to absorb much of what the man was saying. But she was grateful for his assistance in getting the coffin placed safely on the wagon. And she accepted his offer to have two of his men escort her back to Natchez.

"Nothin's happened south of Natchez yet, and they patrols all 'long the road," the man said. "But I couldn't rest easy if I let you go a mile alone with four niggero, Miʌʌ."

She let herself be helped into the carriage and waited while one of the slaves climbed into the box and took the reins. She sat without moving for a quarter of an hour. When she looked down, she saw that her dress was hopelessly ruined by the rain and mud. She sank back in the seat, incapable of crying any more, her restless spirit temporarily subdued.

59.

Rafaella dropped a red rose into the basket carried by Lossie, an obese, very dark woman. Lossie was one of the five slaves she'd taken from Frannie's plantation to work at her Natchez home—the home where she was Mrs. Wyman Ridgeway. Rafaella had already cut two dozen roses, but she wanted to take a whole armload to her father's grave. But the mid-afternoon sun was so hot she felt she would be sick if she stayed outside any longer.

"Pick another two dozen, Lossie," she said. "I'm going inside."

"How many, Miss Rafaella?" Lossie asked.

"Two dozen! Twenty-four, Lossie. Do you understand?"

"Yes'm," Lossie said. "I jess wanted to be sure."

"Be certain you are," Rafaella said.

Rafaella handed Lossie the scissors and walked toward the house. Much more of such incompetence and Lossie would find herself on a field gang.

Several horsemen were galloping past in the street. Rafaella idly watched them through a gap in the shrubbery. She wondered where this lot of poor white drunks was headed. Why, those wretched patrols had lynched a dozen valuable slaves, and all those rumors about an insurrection had been proved groundless. The fact was, three slaves had struck a white overseer and run away. That was all.

Honestly, she thought, runaways were an impossible problem, all the fault of Yankee agents and abolitionists. In the past month, seven slaves had run away from Frannie's plantation, and Frannie had been helpless to do anything. Each was worth a substantial sum.

There was something odd going on with Frannie. Her slave Tolver had again been accused of helping runaways, and for the second time Frannie had cleared him by saying he had been with her at the time.

Rafaella had long thought Tolver too independent and surly for a slave. When she was living on Frannie's plantation, she'd been appalled by the way Frannie consulted him, indulged him, treated him at times with . . . well, almost with deference! She recalled little gestures between Frannie and Tolver when they thought no one was watching. Odd gestures . . . implying something like intimacy.

Rafaella had a scandalous and delicious thought! It would be too perfect if Frannie Deavors were being intimate with a slave! The idea was horrible and yet . . . amusing. She wished it were true, but it was far too much to hope for. Even Frannie couldn't be *that* depraved. Still, it was something that needed looking into. She might try to spread some gossip about it. She would love to see Frannie humiliated.

The sun was reflecting on the windows and the tall, white Doric columns of the red-brick Greek Revival house. It looked like a huge box on fire. Rafaella hated the house. She had never liked it; Ridgeway had chosen it. The place reminded her of a courthouse. She shuddered as she crossed the gallery. A slave opened the door, and she walked into the empty foyer.

Unhappiness settled on her with the familiar sense of enclosure. The minute she ended her marriage, she would sell the place. She had never felt it was hers, anyway. When she had her own home, she told herself, it would be white and graceful, perhaps in the Spanish style. She had taken no interest in furnishing it, and would not. Let Wyman furnish it if he wished, but she wanted no responsibility for it.

The grandfather clock at the foot of the stairs was striking four. She hadn't realized it was so late. She hurried up the stairs. She planned to visit the cemetery and then get to the park at about six, in case Lawton was strolling there, as he often did when he was in Natchez. She was desperate to talk to Lawton. He had ignored her last note, but she was determined to reach him. This time she would have it out. She would be direct in her bargaining. She would threaten him with

Wyman's blade, anything, but she had to get the truth from him about her father's past and know how Lawton felt about it. The thought depressed her.

She sagged against the banister. With an effort, she forced herself up the stairs. She would be lost soon, unless she either won Lawton or destroyed him.

Rachel, her personal maid, was not in view. She rang the bell and called several times, but there was no answer.

"Lazy nigger," she said as she walked into the bedroom. She would begin to dress herself, but Rachel would pay dearly if she didn't come soon. Honestly, Frannie had not trained her people properly. They were lazy, slow, and stupid . . . just like Frannie herself. To think that Frannie might be mixed up with Tolver . . . The idea had fastened itself in her mind. It was disgusting and amusing. *That* would fix Frannie!

Rafaella saw her reflection in a large gold-framed mirror that had come to Mississippi from France. The anxiety in her wide, staring eyes frightened her. Did she always wear such a vulnerable expression? Could everyone see her fear? She was far too hot and discouraged to fight off the doubts that had been building from bits of memory about her father. The evidence had accumulated in her mind, and it made sense only if she accepted the unthinkable idea that her father had lied.

Rafaella shook her head, trying to clear it. "No!" she said aloud. She looked harder at her reflection. No. She leaned against the wall, her fingers trembling as she began to undress. But she lacked the will either to remove her garments or to resist the inevitable progression of her thoughts.

She recalled times in Rome when her father's past had come up. He had always preferred not to discuss it and had deflected all inquiries. When pressed, he became annoyed. She remembered that he had become irrationally angry one night when they first arrived in Natchez and she had mentioned his tale of hunting crocodiles in Africa. She knew he had traveled in Africa and the Orient. Why would he never discuss those places with her?

Rafaella wiped at her eyes. Her stomach was knotted with tension and her heart was throbbing. She was driving herself mad with this wild speculation. She must be logical, must stop tormenting herself to no purpose, and . . . and do *what*?

She shoved herself away from the wall and began to undress. This very day she would establish the truth with Lawton, she told herself. She would somehow force him to tell her everything he knew, to admit whether he had any proof. Dammit, she so fervently hoped that he had none; that all this was nonsense and would soon be over. She had an image of herself at her father's grave and tasted bile. She hated him for an instant; then she bit her lips so hard they hurt.

"It's not true," she mumbled. "Not my father . . . not me . . ."

She knew it was time to dress. She was stepping from her undergarments when she heard someone in the bedroom. "Rachel!" she called out crossly. "Where have you been? I told you I would be in a rush when I came in from the garden. Come in here and help me!"

But it was her husband, not Rachel, who came into her dressing room.

60.

"I'd be glad to help undress my child bride," Ridgeway said, "but in your delicate health, I'm not allowed to touch you. Since we've been married, your nigger maid has been more intimate with you than I have."

"Wyman, you've been drinking again," Rafaella said. She hated the smell. And she dreaded the way he stared at her body. It made her flesh crawl. She was especially apprehensive about being alone with him in her dressing room.

"Yes, but I found intoxication boring. It occurred to me that there might be other diversions."

"I thought you wouldn't be back until this evening."

"A logical thought. After all, I have no reason to come home, have I? Dear Rafaella, what pleasures await me at home?"

"I haven't time for your pleasures," she said. "Surely you have everything you need. You seem to have nothing better to do than drink all day, and I happen to be very busy."

"Yes, I know all about your business," he said. His sneer and narrowed, bloodshot eyes frightened her.

"Now, please," she said, "I have to dress. I'm late as it is."

"And where, may I ask, are you going?"

"I'm going out to the cemetery, Wyman. To visit my father."

"In the name of creation, Raffles, you were out there just this morning!"

"I won't have you mock my respect for my father," she said. "How could you ever understand? A man who holds nothing sacred!"

"By God, Raffles!" he said. "Grief, love, duty . . . all this would be normal. But you have an obsession with your dead father!"

"Damn you, Wyman!" she said. "Don't you dare talk to me in such a manner! Now, please leave me alone. I have to dress."

"I think I'll stay," he said. "I've been married for two months and I've never seen you undress, my dear. Of course, I won't be the first man, but being your husband puts me somewhere in line."

"You bastard!" she said. His words frightened her. They implied . . .

"I talked to the good doctor, my dear," he said.

For a moment, she was relieved that he had only meant the doctor, but then she realized what would follow.

"You had no right, Wyman."

"I have every right, Raffles. In that sense, we're very much two of a kind."

She ignored the remark. "If you won't let me change, then I'll simply wear the same clothes," she said. She picked up her undergarments. He tore them from her and threw them across the room. She gasped and shrank back.

"The doctor was hesitant, at first, to tell me the truth. But he was persuaded to confirm what I've suspected—that your illness has all been a sham."

She backed away from him. He was so ugly with his twisted lips, his liquor-reddened eyes, the venomous tone of his voice. He was capable of anything.

"Wyman, you don't understand," she said. "It wasn't a sham, darling. Not really. Let me explain . . ."

"Spare me any explanation," he said. "About your illness or your virginity. Or about your affair with Lawton Deavors."

Rafaella's mouth fell open. She trembled. He took a step and she moved backward.

"Wyman, I haven't . . . how dare you!"

"I suppose I should be grateful that I've been of use to you," he said. "The use of my blade, the right to claim your inheritance after our marriage. Yet, strangely enough, Raffles, I haven't derived the satisfaction you must have thought would be sufficient compensation."

Rafaella tried to compose herself. He was drunk and angry, yes, and bitter, but he seemed to be mocking himself more than threatening her. She sensed that she could manipulate him if she were careful. And she had to protect poor Lawton. She decided he was merely bluffing about Lawton. How could he possibly know anything? And after all, nothing had really happened.

"Save your self-pity, Wyman," she said. "If our marriage does not suit you, you must take as much blame as I. Your claim about the inheritance is absurd, as you would know if you were sober, while your accusation about Lawton Deavors is even more . . ."

Rafaella didn't finish the sentence. Something in his eyes, in the twisting of his face, told her she had taken the wrong approach.

"Oh, Wyman, what's happened to us, darling?" she asked. "Our marriage promised us both so much. And we can still make it succeed." If only she could extricate herself from his drunken menace now, she would find some way to divorce him without scandal and difficulty. "As for consummating the marriage, I promise you that it will be consummated shortly. If you like, why don't you watch me get dressed now. Then I'll explain why I had to lie about my illness. Once you understand that . . ."

"You're magnificent, Raffles," he said. "Christ, what a spoiled, self-centered little bitch you are! And to think how I wanted you, to think I considered you quite perfect, the ideal woman I thought I would never find. To think I was about to possess the loveliest, surely the finest, young whore in Natchez and abandoned her for you. Goddamn it! I actually fought a duel for your honor with the man with whom you're now having an affair!"

"I won't be insulted in this manner! And I won't have you threaten Lawton Deavors. He's my cousin, after all. There's not one word of truth in your drunken accusations, Wyman!"

"But my dear, I've seen you together," he said. "I've seen you look at him, try to kiss him. It's not difficult to imagine what else happens."

"You've seen us?" she said. "You've been spying on me!"

"Yes, my dear, that is exactly what I've done. It's helped to pass these long spring afternoons. It's been enlightening if not amusing. I've seen you scheming with that 'respected' barrister Hiram Cranston. I've even overheard some of your talk with Cranston in our parlor. You amaze and horrify me—an accomplishment of which I wouldn't have believed you capable. I can understand your desire to destroy your stepmother, but what seems to be a planned vendetta against the Deavorses makes me . . . well, suspect your sanity."

"I have my own reasons." What did he know about the slanders? she asked herself.

"Yes, I'm sure you do, Raffles," he said. "You always have your own reasons. Please spare me. I haven't the time. I've made a decision, as I stare at your lovely white flesh. I've decided to end this charade of a marriage. I do believe I'll take a trip to the Continent."

Rafaella could not believe her good fortune.

"After I conclude one piece of grim business."

"No, you can't, Wyman," she said. "You may mistake innocent kisses between cousins as intimacy. But that gives you no right to hurt Lawton."

"Oh, I don't intend to hurt Lawton Deavors in any way, my dear," he said. "Compared to you, he's a pillar of propriety. My only unfinished business is you, my dear Raffles."

"Me? But Wyman . . ."

"It amused me, this afternoon, to think I might come back here and put my blade to a useful purpose for a change."

She could not speak. Her legs began to give way. She groped behind her back for support and put her hand against the wall. She opened her mouth, but she could not even scream.

"Let me tell you a story," he said, moving closer. She stepped back but realized she was trapped against the wall. "About my hand. You've *always* wanted to know about my hand, Raffles."

Ridgeway told her about his first duel, when he was seventeen, a duel for the honor of a girl who later betrayed him. The duel was long and vicious, and though he had finally wounded his opponent mortally, the man's blade had cut his left hand in several places. Losing blood, he had gone to a surgeon. The surgeon was incompetent. He'd cut the wrong nerve in Ridgeway's wrist, and the hand had atrophied.

"I thought to kill her then," he said. "But I didn't. Oh, I have no special respect for death, Raffles. I wouldn't kill you. That's not what I had in mind. When I found her with her lover, I sliced off three of her fingers."

Rafaella curled her own fingers against her palms and whimpered. She bit her lips together and tasted blood. Her mind raced desperately, but she could think of nothing to say. Her fear was now terror.

"The affair was covered up, but when I was elected to Congress it hovered in the background," he said. "My family's name and influence protected me a long while. But I grew realistic and cynical about government and didn't care any longer. Men who could not face me in open debate, who crawled from the House with the shame of having been exposed as half-witted fools, these men joked of my hand behind my back. My cynicism gave birth to boredom. I left Congress, and my boredom grew to be a malignancy. It made staying alive barely worth the effort. To relieve this boredom, I took up dueling again and found that it amused me to play God and create—to leave an adversary in my own image."

"Wyman . . . oh, please, no . . ." she gasped. "I'll do anything you want, darling . . . please!"

"I swore that I would never again fight a duel as an affair of honor," he said. "And until I met Lawton Deavors in your behalf, I did not. All my duels were fought to relieve my boredom, and in the hope that some adversary would prove my superior and end this unlikely thing called my life."

"Wyman, don't hurt me," Rafaella pleaded. "Don't . . . cripple me, I beg you. I'll . . . when we . . . later . . . tomorrow . . No, now, Wyman, we can . . . consummate our marriage. Don't you want me to be beautiful when you come to me?"

"With all of your shrewdness, Raffles, you should have been shrewd enough to guess that, more than anything, I hate being made a fool of. And you've made a monstrous fool of me! You've used me! You'd promise anything now. But if I touched you, you would shudder."

"No, Wyman . . . No . . . If only you would allow me to explain . . . No . . . I swear I want you!"

"Then lie down on the floor and spread your legs," he said. "I respected you as a virgin. Now I'll take you as the whore you are."

"The floor?" she said. "Now . . . oh, Wyman, please don't humiliate me in such a way. At least . . . let's go into the bedroom, darling. You go in first and just give me a minute to . . . to freshen up." She saw a chance now. There was another door from the dressing room, leading out into the hall.

His laugh made her gasp.

"Make any explanations you will about our marriage," he said. "It matters not the slightest to me. Likely, you'll never see me again—after I finish with your body. You may do what you wish with your stepmother, but I warn you, Raffles, don't use the threat of my blade in your vendetta against the Deavorses."

"I won't. I won't, Wyman. I swear I won't."

"I don't like your vendetta, Raffles. One way or another you'll involve me, as you did in the past, and I won't have that. On your life, I warn you to do nothing to the Deavorses, to their children to come. Or I'll find out, Raffles, and I'll return, no matter how far I have to come. And I'll kill you, Raffles, I'll take vengeance on your beautiful body, bit by bit, with my blade."

"No! I won't. I swear I won't. Don't hurt me, Wyman. Please don't hurt me."

He grabbed her arm. In her panic, she stumbled and fell against the dressing table. The blow stunned her, and a crystal bud vase smashed to the floor. He fell on top of her.

"No!" she pleaded. "Oh, Lord, no, not this way."

At first she tried to fight him off. But she knew that resistance was futile and might increase his anger. She lay stiff, her eyes shut, her teeth against her bloodless lips. He bit her nipples. She groaned. A spasm racked her body. His fingers pinched her breasts. The strange

315

flesh of his left hand tormented her nipples, and her spasms intensified.

She tried to scream, but the sound died in her throat. She had to endure this so he would not cripple her.

But when his withered hand gathered up the flesh of her thighs, she could not control herself. She thrashed about and tried to crawl from his grasp. He threw her onto her stomach. She cut her arm on a piece of glass and cried out.

His knees dug into the backs of her legs, then her thighs. She struggled and flailed at him with her hands.

Then his hands forced a way between her thighs again. The left hand abused her vagina, and she heard herself whimpering.

But when his penis invaded her body, the sensation was so blindingly intense that it allowed her to open her mouth and scream. And the worst of it was that, probably because of her years of activity as a horsewoman, there was no hymen to be penetrated, no virginal blood to be shed, and Ridgeway never knew that his bride was truly a virgin.

61.

Lawton paced restlessly while Lucinda supervised the two female slaves who were packing his trunks. It was a hot afternoon in June. Lawton, Theron Sumrall, and five other Adams County planters were leaving for Liverpool the next day to arrange for the direct sale and shipping of their own cotton. The venture required an initial outlay of substantial capital, and since they would see no profit for perhaps two years, they wanted to investigate firsthand the situation in England.

Lawton had never been further from the plantation than New Orleans, and he had never been happy at school there. He had no desire to be away from home for so long. He felt none of the excitement at visiting England that had gripped some of the others.

"Lawton, you're fretting yourself again," Lucinda said. "I can tell by the look on your face."

Lawton glanced at her abstractedly. "No, I just . . . well, I suppose I was . . ."

"Why don't you go take a ride or do some work. You're no use here. In fact, to be honest, you're in our way."

"Maybe you're right," he said. He walked over to Lucinda. "How you feelin' this afternoon?"

"I'm feeling fine. So don't add me to your list of worries."

"I want to be sure you're over the last spell of sickness before I leave," he said. He looked at Lucinda. Pregnant, she was more beautiful than ever. There was new color in her cheeks and a sparkle in her eyes. He hated to leave her alone, although, of course, she would not really be alone. Theron Sumrall's father would stay at The Columns in Lawson's absence. It was not the custom to leave a lady alone with only slaves. If he had the slightest suspicion that Lucinda would have any troubles, Lawton would not go.

"Of course I'm over it," she said. "And it had nothing to do with my having a child, anyway. Now go on, Lawton, we'll manage fine."

Lawton kissed Lucinda's cheek before he walked out of the room. As he often did, he speculated on whether he wanted a son or a daughter. He had to admit he would prefer a boy. But he would also love to have a daughter. As he walked down the stairs, he asked himself how he and Lucinda could have gotten so estranged before. Now their marriage was everything it should be. They were in love and making love, and Lucinda was carrying his child. She was beautiful, glowing with the happiness of having her first baby, and taking on even more responsibility in running the house.

Lawton stopped on the gallery to talk to Cellus. Cellus was skeptical of the Liverpool venture, Lawton knew, and it was rare for him to go against Cellus's advice. But this time Lawton was convinced that he should take the risk. If it worked, it would be enormously profitable. Why shouldn't they make the huge profits that the middlemen were making on their own cotton? He arranged to have a final talk with Cellus about plantation business that evening after supper. Then he went out to the barn and had Lucius, the young hostler who was Ed's apprentice, saddle his horse.

As he rode off, he saw Cellus standing at the back of the gallery. He had no fears about the running of things while he was away, for Cellus was certainly capable of managing the plantation. Between Cellus and Lucinda, everything would go well. And Filch was equally capable of taking responsibility for everything in the fields. He would have a final talk with Filch, but first he decided to ride down and see how the carpenters were doing with the landing and cotton gin on the river. They were also building a small summerhouse, modeled after a Greek temple. It had been Lucinda's notion, and Lawton had been pleased to indulge her.

Lawton enjoyed riding through the newly reclaimed riverbank acres. Half of the land had been cleared by the Irishmen and was already planted in cotton. There was more clearing to be done, but Lawton didn't know when—or how—he would manage it. The project had been only partially successful. It was slow, murderous work. Before the Irish laborers had finally left, half their number had fallen ill with swamp fever, one man had drowned, and two others had suffered broken bones. And one man had been killed when he tripped over hidden roots and fell into a nest of cottonmouth moccasins.

Lawton had been glad to dismiss the Irishmen. Three times in their last weeks on the plantation there had been nasty scenes between the slaves and the white men, and a sixteen-year-old slave girl had been raped. The bitterness that the white men felt for the slaves had surprised and angered Lawton and had left him confused.

Long stretches of tall and dangerous bluffs lie along the Mississippi River, bluffs often covered with a tangle of vines and trees as thick as a jungle. But Lawton's holdings on the river were flat, lying between two ragged bluffs and providing a quarter-mile stretch suitable for a landing and a summerhouse with access to the river, as well as the cotton gin under construction.

Lawton talked to the eight carpenters who were at work. He was pleased with the quality of their work and their progress and he felt reassured that Amos, the senior carpenter, could handle the work while he was away. He sat in the saddle and watched a padwheeler glide by, leaving a trail of white smoke. In the very near future, he thought, such boats would stop at The Columns to pick up passengers or to load the cotton ginned by the plantation's own gin.

Lawton bade Amos farewell, then rode inland. He still had to talk with Filch. But there was no hurry. He rode slowly and aimlessly, away from the vast fields green with tender, young cotton plants, and took a narrow trail into the edge of the swamp. The good air and fine weather relaxed him, and he let the horse move along slowly until they were enveloped by the lush growth. The sun was by now obscured by the thick leaves and grey Spanish moss. Lawton heard creatures stirring in the undergrowth, heard something squeal, heard water splashing. Then the swamp was still except for the low din of insects. He thought of how long it had been since he had been hunting, or since he had taken a leisurely ride, just for pleasure, as he used to do so often.

He was glad for this opportunity to be alone on his own land. He savored it. He would miss the plantation when he was at sea and far away in England. Then he glanced up. He had come to a stream. Vines and moss hung out over its banks. He stiffened in the saddle.

Sexual excitement flowed from his loins through his body. This was the spot where Rafaella had offered herself to him . . . and it was also the place where he had watched Joleen bathe naked the summer that . . .

Lawton jerked on the reins so sharply that his horse whinnied nervously. He jabbed with his heels to turn the horse away and into a trot. Why had he come down here, he wondered? It was more than a leisurely and nostalgic ride. He wanted to forget everything that had happened at the damned stream. And he thought he had forgotten all about that summer with Joleen. They were little more than children then.

Thoughts of Joleen reminded him of that whole summer. That was the summer he had made love to Nettie, his first woman. After that, he had been sent to school in New Orleans, and his parents had given the pregnant girl her freedom. Nettie had promised that she would leave Natchez and never return. But she had not kept her word. He had seen her with his son in town. The boy was probably as white as Nettie was, as white as . . . as a Deavors, although he never got a good look at him. It tormented him: slaves should look like Negroes, not white people. If they looked white, how did they feel? Did he have a white-looking son, made in his own image, walking the Natchez streets?

And if so, what should he do about it? And what in hell should he do about Raffles?

He thought of Rafaella's dark eyes, the seductive twist of her lips, the sensation of kissing her; of her large, pale, unbearably beautiful breasts, the maddening touch of her fingers along his scar . . . His scar . . . now he had a scar. When they were young, it had been Joleen. Joleen . . . Rafaella . . . When he was abroad, he determined, he would somehow rid himself of his obsession with her. He was fed up with feeling guilty . . . and the woman was dangerous.

Lawton was finally out of the swamp. He began to gallop along the narrow road, leaning forward, savoring the wind after the smothering heat.

Rafaella was dangerous: it was the beginning of a familiar argument with himself. She had her own obsessions—grief and bitterness and hatred and fear. She was irrational; she'd accused him repeatedly of scheming with Frannie against her, and had even hired that scoundrel Hiram Cranston to root out evidence of this. Cranston was the sort who'd make trouble even if he didn't find it . . .

And though, finally, Rafaella seemed to believe that Lawton had never wanted the Price Deavors estate, she had not abandoned her fear that he would let out the secret charges against her father to humiliate and ruin her. Nothing he could say, nothing he could promise, would persuade her otherwise. He had met with her—twice—to convince her, but his chivalrous, hard-fought refusal to become involved with her romantically—sexually—only convinced her that he believed the accusations, believed them and shunned her because of them.

They were only accusations. There had never been any proof. Anson's agent had sent word that he could find no documents to validate the rumors he'd heard in Rome. Yet, suppose . . . suppose there had been some basis to those rumors. It was a disturbing thought. Then, like most thoughts of Rafaella, it became exciting. He was powerfully attracted to her. He longed to fondle her breasts, to possess her pale, exquisite body, even though he loved his wife, even though Rafaella was dangerous and unstable . . . and his cousin . . . a Deavors. Somehow, it all added to his excitement, just as the mystery of Rafaella's origins augmented her exotic attractiveness. She was foreign . . . admittedly, but not, could never be, servile. Why, she was so pure . . . so white.

And then Lawton remembered that with Nettie he had violated the strict family code. Unlike some other masters, a Deavors never had sex with a slave. Not only because it was wrong to force sex on a helpless slave, but because Deavors blood had always been kept pure. But he, Lawton, had succumbed, and what a mistake that had been. Nettie . . . the child . . . his guilt.

Lawton reined up in the middle of a field. To hell with women, he told himself. He needed a glass or two of whiskey to calm himself. Tomorrow he would go away and things would sort themselves out.

He galloped toward the house.

Lawton set down his empty whiskey glass. It was nearly ten o'clock. He had talked to Filch and Cellus. His trunks were packed. There was nothing to do but go upstairs to bed and to Lucinda and try to sleep. Soon it would be morning and time to leave. He knew he would sleep after so much whiskey, but after all his thoughts about Joleen and Nettie, and particularly about Raffles, he felt guilty about making love to Lucinda, though he wanted to lie with her, lie near her, near their child, this one last time for many weeks.

Adding to his uneasiness at leaving was some trouble with a runaway slave. The man had been missing for two days and had been returned earlier in the evening by a slave patrol. There had been a lot of talk recently about a slave uprising. Feeling was running high. The patrol had taken it on themselves to give the slave ten lashes when he tried to break away from them. Lawton hated to see it and he'd had a bitter argument with the patrol's leader.

Lawton dragged himself up from the chair. There was no more that could be done about the situation tonight. He was surprised at how weary he felt.

Upstairs, in their cool, breezy bedroom, Lucinda lay in bed reading a novel. She looked relaxed and pretty in a pink satin peignoir, but she was a little pale.

Lawton undressed and lay beside his wife. He put his arm around her, touching her pink satin shoulder. They talked of domestic matters. Soon the talk turned to their separation, and they both grew sad. Lawton wondered why he had agreed to leave Lucinda for so long.

He held her closer, gently kissed her cheeks, her

eyes. He rested his hand on her round stomach and stroked her neck.

They kissed and caressed, slowly, tenderly, for a long while, but when Lawton finally moved between her thighs, he felt very little passion. Love, respect, tenderness, but that was all.

He felt sad as he grasped her buttocks and tried desperately, whispering that he loved her. Finally, he gave up and kissed her lips. She kissed him back, and they both fell asleep, Lawton with unbidden thoughts of lying between Raffles's soft thighs, of loving her fiercely.

62.

Lucinda felt a bit dizzy after Dr. Stacey's visit. She was now three months pregnant and often felt so heavy and drowsy that she seemed nearly ready to give birth. Perhaps it was the heat. Everyone said it was the hottest July ever.

The doctor had visited her at the Delsanos' home. She always stayed with Juan and Consuela when she was in Natchez. The Delsanos were good friends—old friends of Lawton's family—and they had been kind and helpful while Lawton was abroad. She would see Consuela this afternoon—for now it would be good to be alone, and she didn't feel like resting, not just yet. There would be time enough for that when she returned to The Columns. With Lawton gone, her life there was very quiet and very solitary, except for the company of Theron's father, ancient Mr. Sumrall.

So she had Romulus drive her to the Arcadia Tea Room. Habitually, she took tea at the Blue Bird, but today she wanted a change, some time to think and see if she felt well enough to make the planned visit to the madhouse this afternoon. It was a curious destination for an outing, but it seemed quite worthwhile. As she sat in the busy tea room and sipped her steaming tea, she remembered what she'd heard. The project had been conceived, according to Consuela Delsano, at last week's meeting of the Natchez Eleemosynary Society. Most of the members of the music society also belonged to this group, as well as a dozen prominent Natchez doctors and lawyers. It concerned itself with helping the county's poor, helpless, mad, and sick. Natchez was growing fast, becoming a good-sized town, and it was high time for philanthropic institutions. Lucinda's friends were aware of their responsibility.

Except for the jail and the madhouse, there were no public institutions to care for unfortunate, impoverished newcomers and foreigners. As a result, many sane but destitute people had been placed in the madhouse, which was already overcrowded and understaffed. Worse, it had been discovered that not only were indigent free Negroes placed in the same wards as white people, but that in the absence of adequate staff, the madhouse warden, Ferrell Shanks, was using his own slaves, and at county expense, to confine and supervise white inmates!

What had caused the latest scandal and invited the investigation of the committee was that an impoverished and elderly man had been sent to the madhouse by a vengeful cousin who wanted what little the poor man had left in the world. The man came from an old and prominent Mississippi family, but by the time other relatives from out of town learned of his plight and secured his release, he was indeed almost mad, although he had been in the place less than a week. It was said that he might never recover from the abuse he'd received at the hands of the madhouse keepers.

Lucinda finished her tea. She was feeling a little better. She decided to have a second cup, then make up her mind about what to do. While she waited, she remembered what the doctor had said. Thoughts of that madhouse had driven her own troubles out of her mind. Dr. Stacey had warned her that, although she was in good health, her pregnancy did not seem to be normal.

She was too big too early. It might be a misplaced pregnancy, or perhaps it was twins. It was too soon to tell, but if things weren't better in a few weeks, he wanted her to go to New Orleans for further examinations and consultation with a specialist.

His gravity of manner had frightened her. She hated to leave The Columns again, even with Lawton gone. Oh, why couldn't it be a safe, normal baby?

Lucinda did not consider herself particularly religious or superstitious. But she couldn't help wondering if she were being punished in some way for the fact that she was carrying Wyman Ridgeway's child and not her husband's. Of course, she told herself, she did believe in God, and believed him to be just as well as stern. And God was good, for not only did Lawton assume the expected baby was his, but Wyman Ridgeway had sent word that he was leaving Natchez and would not trouble her again. He asked her to please take care of the child and said that if she ever needed his help, he could be reached through a New Orleans bank.

Ridgeway's note had also carried a warning: "Though I do not know what she is planning, you should be wary of my child bride, whom I believe capable of *any* desperate act."

Lucinda would have liked to discuss the warning with someone, but there was no one she could turn to. Ridgeway's advice troubled her. She disliked and mistrusted Rafaella, but had tried to forget about her. Lawton had not mentioned her in months, and nothing could have pleased her more.

Lucinda was glad to forget about Rafaella—and Ridgeway, too. It was good that Wyman had gone away, and she found that she now had very little feeling for him at all. Her marriage was much more important and had been especially satisfactory in the last weeks before Lawton left for England. She had practically forgotten her own infidelity, and she only hoped the child bore no resemblance to Wyman. But that was a worry for the future.

Lucinda finished her tea. She was feeling steadier and thought she might take that trip out to the madhouse, after all. Consuela was so anxious that she join the investigatory committee. Lucinda paid for her tea. When she stood up and turned to leave, she stopped short. She had heard someone come in and sit at a table behind her, but she had not turned to see who the person was. Now she was staring at Rafaella, whose face looked momentarily anxious, but then broke into a smile.

"Why, good morning, Lucinda," Rafaella said.

"Good morning, Raffles," Lucinda said. She hesitated, then walked toward the door, which took her past Rafaella's table.

"Won't you join me?" Rafaella asked.

"Thank you, but I have an appointment," Lucinda said.

"Only for a minute," Rafaella said. "I want to talk to you, Lucinda."

Reluctantly, Lucinda took a chair at Rafaella's table. "Only a minute," she murmured.

"So, it's true that you're expecting," Rafaella said.

Lucinda stiffened. Could Raffles know that Ridgeway was the child's father?

"Yes . . . I am."

"Congratulations," Rafaella said. "When is the baby due?"

"Around the end of the year," Lucinda said. The sweetness in Rafaella's voice seemed unmixed, but Lucinda was still wary.

"I'm sure that Lawton is proud," Rafaella said.

"Yes, he is, Raffles," Lucinda said. "Now, if you'll excuse me, I really must be going."

"May I ask where you're off to in such a hurry?" Rafaella said.

"I'm . . . a group of people are going to visit the madhouse," Lucinda said.

Rafaella laughed. "The madhouse! How curious."

"No, there's nothing curious about it. Conditions there are appalling, and a committee has been formed to try to improve the situation."

"It's hardly the sort of business I would want to involve myself with. No, no, please, Lucinda, I can tell how anxious you are to rush off to your lunatics, but you must spare me another minute or two."

"Raffles, I've been here too long already," Lucinda said. "And I can't imagine what else we have to discuss."

Lucinda saw Rafaella's mouth twitch slightly. Her eyes were narrow, and there were frightening wrinkles around them, wrinkles that did not belong on a girl so young. Lucinda thought of Wyman's warning.

"I've just come from visiting my father's grave," Rafaella said. "I miss him terribly, Lucinda, and I still blame you and Lawton for his death. I want you to understand that. My father wouldn't have killed himself if you—"

Lucinda gasped. "I understand how deep your grief is, Rafaella, but you mustn't blame us! I refuse to accept any blame. I won't sit here and listen to this kind of talk!"

"I doubt very much if you have the slightest idea of my grief, Lucinda," she said. "Nor of my loneliness. I tried to trust Lawton. I was wrong in some of my fears, about your scheming with Frannie, for instance. But I cannot blame my poor father, no matter what, Lucinda! And it's not true, I don't care how much . . . evidence there might be. And even if it were true, I'm not going to sit by and let myself be ruined."

"What on earth are you talking about, Raffles?" Lucinda asked. Again, she remembered Ridgeway's warning. The girl made no sense; she was ranting as though she had lost her mind. Lucinda was upset by her outburst, and she felt a swell of resentment, remembering that this woman had involved Lawton in that duel.

"You know very well what I'm talking about,"

Rafaella said. "Oh, Lawton has tried to convince me he told you nothing, but I know he's told you everything. And if he chooses to believe those . . . those hideous slanders, Lucinda, I'm quite sure you will, too. And even Joleen. You're all against me! You don't even want to be seen having tea with me, do you?"

"No, I don't want to have tea with you, Raffles," Lucinda said. "Not after the trouble and suffering you've caused." Lucinda stopped. She was hardly in a position to lecture, since Rafaella's husband was the father of her child.

"Don't mention suffering to me!" Rafaella said. "You Deavorses . . . you're so damn cold! You have no idea of suffering, or the constant fear you could be . . . that I could be, oh, God . . . branded . . . could be ruined . . . perhaps be sold. Oh, Lucinda, I know you hate me, but please, please, you must spare me."

"Spare you *what*? I still don't understand!"

"I should have known better than to ask your help. I know you just can't wait to see me ruined, subjugated . . . But you're wrong, Lucinda! I'll destroy all of you first. All! You and anyone else who knows. I swear it! You've had your last chance. By the time Lawton returns from Italy with his proof it will be too late."

"Raffles, Lawton has not gone to Italy," Lucinda said. "They've only gone to look over the Liverpool markets."

"Oh, yes, at first I believed it was just Liverpool," Raffles said. "Then I found out about France . . . and Italy. I'm sure . . . and I know why. . ."

"Yes, I forgot, they are going to Paris but . . ." Lucinda stood up. "Raffles, I really must go now. You make no sense. And frankly, I would suggest you take something to calm your nerves. You talk as though you have a fever of some kind."

"Go! Run on off and visit your precious lunatics!" Rafaella said. "I've given you your last chance to save yourself and your family. I'll punish you for being so . . . condescending with me! You think you can dismiss me as though I am a slave. You don't consider me a Deavors at all. Before you can ruin me . . . When I'm finished, all you Deavorses will be ready for the madhouse! So go have a good look at it, Lucinda!"

Rafaella jumped up, knocking over her tea. She ran from the room before Lucinda could speak.

Lucinda went directly home to The Columns that afternoon, without visiting the madhouse. She had been stunned by Rafaella's crazy threats. She was hurt by her suspicion that Lawton had kept a lot of things from her about which she should have known. From Rafaella's talk, it was obvious that Lawton had seen her recently.

Lucinda was exhausted after the drive home from Natchez. She went directly to her room to rest, but sleep evaded her. The encounter with Rafaella had frightened her. The girl was nearly hysterical. She was full of fear and hatred with her talk of revenge and madness. It was easy to believe she was indeed capable of anything.

Lucinda forced herself to dress and go down for supper. Old Mr. Sumrall talked continuously, as usual. Lucinda listened, nodded occasionally, and picked at her food. When she left the table, she felt weak and nauseous. She went out onto the front porch for some fresh air. By the time she reached the porch, she was scarcely able to stand. The encounter with Rafaella had made her physically ill. Her stomach hurt so badly she began to groan. She felt she would vomit. She sank into a chair. It was terribly hot. Sweat poured from her face. Her cheeks were feverish.

She tried to call Rubella or Ellen, but could not. When the maid finally came out to the porch five minutes later, Lucinda was doubled over in her chair, and the maid's cries were the last thing Lucinda remembered hearing before she lost consciousness.

63.

Rafaella was not yet ready to leave her father's graveside. She had brought him white roses and had just finished laying them in a meticulous pattern before the marble monument. Anger was her first reaction to Hiram Cranston's interruption, but the bad news he brought was enough to send her running to the carriage. She told her driver to keep the horses at full gallop all the way to the plantation.

"The bloody flux struck hard—a couple of days ago," Cranston said. "All the slaves on Frannie's place. And I just found out that instead of hirin' a regular doctor, Frannie Deavors's daddy, Slidell Runnels, is treatin' the sick ones. And from what I know of nigger doctors like that, more are likely to die than get well."

Rafaella sat rigidly in the corner of the racing carriage, torn between her dislike of her own lawyer and outrage at what Frannie was doing to property that was by all rights half hers.

"So far I haven't found out anything about Frannie and that uppity nigger Tolver," Cranston was saying. "But I swear I must agree with you, Mrs. Ridgeway. Somethin' smells bad there. Nigger's been accused of being with runaways twice, and both times Frannie was his alibi. And when I watched them a few times, well, they was little things between them that . . . well, that just don't seem right between a mistress and her nigger."

"Keep following them," Rafaella said. "Keep trying to find witnesses. Bribe the slaves. Get someone to talk. It's urgent, Mr. Cranston. I want proof, right away . . . real proof or not . . . of a relationship between them. Do I make myself clear, sir?"

"Yes'm, you sure do," he said. "And I'll have that proof for you right away. Soon's I can."

Rafaella twisted around on the seat. The heat was damp and stifling. Even Rome wasn't so miserable in

late August, she told herself. Just being in the same
carriage with Cranston made her want to rush home
and take a long, cool bath. Some people might have
thought Cranston attractive with his dark brown hair,
neat brown beard, and rather tall, slim body. But
Rafaella despised his servile manner and his small,
close-set eyes. They darted about, always furtive, wary,
and at the same time presumptuous. She felt his eyes
were invading her, undressing her.

Cranston was talking about some free Negro woman,
and Rafaella's attention wandered. Cranston was certainly hard-working, ruthless, and unscrupulous, but
so far he had not accomplished nearly enough. If he
didn't soon find some proof, or manufacture some, she
might as well dismiss him. The Tolver thing was a last
hope; it seemed a likely way to ruin Frannie. And she
desperately wanted Frannie ruined.

Lawton was due back from Europe soon, Rafaella
understood, and he might bring evidence about her
father. She squirmed again, remembering that he had
left without bidding her farewell. Wretched man! Even
with new evidence, she didn't know that Lawton would
slander her . . . but he might be careless. Or that
damned Lucinda might.

Just thinking of that scene with Lucinda in the tea
room made Rafaella angry. She would love to see that
proud Lucinda humiliated. She'd love to see her in her
own damn madhouse, abused by slaves! And Lawton,
too. *That* would humble the Deavorses. Then no one
would believe them and their rumors.

Next time she saw Lawton, she was more determined
than ever to manipulate him sexually, do whatever she
must. But would that be enough? What if he used her
body and then forgot her? She nearly despaired of
securing his love. She had been frantic with worry and
schemes for weeks, but all to no avail.

". . . Word I get about the free nigger is . . . Are you
all right, Mrs. Ridgeway?"

Rafaella sat up. "What? Yes, yes, I'm quite all right.

It's merely this oppressive heat, Mr. Cranston. Now, what were you saying about some free nigger?"

"Well, I been pokin' around like you wanted," he said. "Tryin' to find out what I could about the Deavorses. And like I mentioned, I've come up with two things. First is what I said about the free nigger, and the second is—"

"Mr. Cranston, I was distracted for a moment. Would you please repeat what you said?"

"Well, it may not be anything, Mrs. Ridgeway. But I paid out some bribe money here and there. And the fellow works in the county clerk's office, he remembered that to all recollection, the Deavorses only freed one of their niggers, woman name of Nettie, few years back. Sent her away from Natchez. Manumission procedures had to go through the court, you understand?"

"Yes, I understand about manumission. But I don't see of what interest that is." She glanced from the window. An alligator was crawling toward the green-slimed surface of a pond. She turned away quickly and dabbed at her damp face with her handkerchief.

"Yes'm, well I'm just gettin' to that."

Cranston mentioned that several people had seen this freed slave, Nettie, with a child, in Natchez recently. The child was said to be the spitting image of Lawton Deavors. It was even more obvious because Nettie was an odd-looking Negro; she looked completely white. And so did her son.

"So you see, I come to the conclusion that if she's the only nigger they ever freed, and if she got a boy look like Lawton Deavors . . . ."

Rafaella was so excited by the news that she felt a chill race over her back.

"Mr. Cranston, I want you to locate this . . . this woman, Nettie, and I want to speak with her," Rafaella said. "Now, what is the other thing?"

"Bein' family, I suppose you heard all about Lavon Deavors and his troubles," Cranston said.

"Yes, I've heard countless times how Lavon Deavors tried to destroy his family and take over The Columns, and how he and his nephew Tillman were burned to death," Rafaella said. "Please spare me that grim talk, Mr. Cranston."

"Well, then, do you know anything about the rumors circulating around Natchez at the time of Lavon Deavors's death, Mrs. Ridgeway? Or the reason Lavon Deavors took that slave patrol out to The Columns that night?"

"No, why?" She leaned forward. His ugly little eyes were obviously proud that she was interested. Cranston was smiling, an expression that seemed out of place on his lean, usually bland face.

Cranston told Rafaella that there had been fear of a slave uprising led by Yankee abolitionists in Natchez at the time. And Lavon Deavors had spread the word that Aaron Clauson, Joleen's husband, was one of the Yankee agents. He claimed the patrol would find proof at The Columns. But the patrol was drunk. They went crazy, killing and raping slaves, burning. They found nothing, and Lavon was shot and wounded by Clauson. The sheriff arrived during the carnage, and the patrol backed down.

"Word is, Sheriff Crandall was Lavon's man, owned hook, line, and sinker," Cranston said. "Now, what with Lavon Deavors hatin' his family and all, it was likely just tall tales he was making up. I'd heard some of those stories at the time but had forgotten about them. They died off quick. Guess folks was ashamed to think they could ever suspect the Deavorses, they being so old and prominent a family and all . . . or even anyone married into the family."

"I see," Rafaella said. "Well, sir, I would suspect them of anything." She had suddenly remembered Joleen's behavior the day of the horse race. It had never seemed right to her. "You look into it right away, Mr. Cranston."

64.

Rafaella soaked in a warm tub for nearly an hour that evening, sending a weeping Rachel downstairs before she began. The slave woman had annoyed her by singing. Everything annoyed her tonight. She felt tense, apprehensive. Gradually the warm water began to calm her, and she grew thoughtful. She admired her own body as she washed it. And she thought, with some distaste, of having sex with Ridgeway.

Thank God she had not gotten pregnant. Still, she felt . . . unclean . . . invaded . . . contaminated. He had made her feel pain and fear and self-hatred for weeks. He was vile. She would have killed him, given any chance at all.

Now, as she touched herself, she believed that her body had never been violated. She was still a virgin. She was still pure, still waiting for love . . . for Lawton. Absently, yet deliberately, she scrubbed herself between her thighs until it hurt and felt wonderful, and she cried out with pain and pleasure.

Feeling much better, she climbed out of the tub and dried herself. She dressed quickly in a pink silk gown. The ritual was over. She wouldn't think of Ridgeway or his assault again. He was well gone and would never return. His threats had been drunken threats, the result of his anger that she didn't consider him worthy to possess her. She need pay them no mind. She had manipulated him and then discarded him.

Rafaella went downstairs to dinner. Her dining room was huge and nearly bare. A chandelier with twenty-four white candles lit the room. The rising wind blew through the French doors from the patio, whipping the flames about and bathing the oak-paneled room in deep shadows.

She ate little of the simple, well-cooked food served her, but she drank two glasses of white wine and felt slightly intoxicated. William, her butler, hovered by the table, but she dismissed him and poured herself another glass of wine. As she sipped the wine, her eyes filled with tears and she choked back a sob. She refused to cry again, as she had last night at dinner. From behind the patio and beyond the trellis of scuppernong vines came the sounds of talk and laughter, a distant piano and violin. She had heard the same sounds the night before.

She couldn't remember when she had last been invited to dinner or a party. Even the Westons avoided her now. She supposed it was because of Wyman's reputation and conduct. Since his duel with Lawton, she had been shunned by Natchez society.

Suddenly a terrifying new thought came into her head. Perhaps Lucinda had already begun to spread the rumor that she was the daughter of a Moslem slave. Perhaps that was why people looked at her so oddly in the street.

No, no, she argued with herself. Nothing would happen until Lawton returned from abroad. After all, it was Lawton who controlled her fate. But she was too strong for him, she told herself. Wine rose in her throat. She swallowed hard. She would destroy him . . . destroy them all . . . somehow.

Thoughts of Lawton made her feel lonely. She hated him, but she wished he were here tonight. She hated being alone. And she wanted Lawton, she had to have Lawton, make him obsessed with her, dependent on her in every way. "Damn you, Lawton," she mumbled.

She was further tormented by the memory of the hideous scene out at Frannie's plantation that afternoon. She'd arrived with Cranston to view dozens of dead and dying slaves, vomiting, bleeding, screaming, all with cholera, or what people called the bloody flux. And that fool Slidell Runnels had been treating them with potions made from rusty nails, opening their veins and bleeding them with leeches, sticking funnels down their throats and force-feeding them nasty draughts.

Rafaella had left after a short but bitter argument with Frannie. She had sent Cranston into town to find a proper doctor and to try to get an injunction to stop the slaughter of her property.

"Miss Rafaella!"

It was Rachel, calling from the side gallery that Hiram Cranston was at the door.

"I got the injunction and the doctor," he said. "And that's not all, Mrs. Ridgeway. I paid out some money to some slaves, and I got proof now that not only is that nigger Tolver and Frannie Deavors intimate, but he's a conductor on what they call the Underground Railroad!"

Rafaella smiled triumphantly and told Cranston to sit down so they could make plans.

65.

Lawton returned from Europe the third week in September to discover that Lucinda's pregnancy was far from normal. She had been seriously ill and had nearly suffered a miscarriage. Furthermore, the cholera epidemic had killed twenty-three slaves, and cotton prices were low, lower than ever. Everyone said there was financial panic all over America.

After dinner on the evening of his homecoming, Lawton and Lucinda sat on the front porch of The Columns. The weather was hot and damp, the front lawn and gardens obscured by a misty ground fog. Lucinda was enthroned in a wicker armchair, her feet on a stool. She was wrapped in voluminous knitted shawls. Her face was pale, her forehead beaded with sweat. She had smiled bravely and tried to play down her troubles, but Lawton had learned the truth from Cellus. Two doctors had recommended that she consult a New Orleans specialist, and Lawton wanted her to go downriver right away. He was distraught that he was too busy to accompany her.

"Are you sure I shouldn't come?" he asked her.

"Absolutely sure," she said. "I'm not really sick, just expecting. Ellen and Rubella will travel with me, and if you worry about me, I'll be angry, Lawton."

She took his hand and smiled. He kissed her cheek, frightened at its pallor and waxy texture. Lucinda's hand fell away. She closed her eyes a moment.

"Are you all right?" Lawton asked.

She opened her eyes and smiled. "Just a little tired," she said. "I'm better now that you've come home. Oh, Lawton, I'm so glad you're back. I've missed you so much."

"And I've missed you, dear," he said. "I never knew how much I loved you until I had to endure such a long time away from you. Now I'm goin' to carry you upstairs and put you to bed."

"I'll go soon, but there's something I have to talk to you about first—something that's been on my mind."

Lawton listened with increasing anxiety as Lucinda described her encounter with Rafaella in the tea room. When she'd finished, she demanded that he explain what Rafaella had been talking about.

"I think I should know, Lawton," she said seriously. "I think you should have told me."

"I just wanted to spare you the worryin' and all," Lawton said, upset by the strained look on Lucinda's face but thankful that Rafaella hadn't mentioned anything intimate happening between them. "And I've been worried about any of this goin' any further, since there's no proof it's true."

Briefly, Lawton explained what Anson had said about Roger Blaine.

"Why, that's incredible," Lucinda said. "Poor Raffles. Now I can understand. You're quite right, Lawton. No matter what we think of the girl, we must protect her. The consequences would be too absolutely devastating. And yet . . . it could be true, couldn't it? I've never understood Roger's suicide. This might explain it."

Lawton nodded.

"What do you propose to do?" Lucinda asked. "Raffles frightened me with her wild talk of vengeance

337

and destroying people. She seemed almost crazed, Lawton. I'm inclined to think we must do something."

"What can we do? We tried to help her."

"I guess you're right," Lucinda said. "But there's one more thing, Lawton, and though I've hesitated, I have to ask it. I feel so vulnerable in my present condition. Lawton, you haven't become Raffles's lover, have you?"

Lawton felt a painful stab of guilt. He'd never thought Lucinda could be so bold. He was thankful she wasn't looking into his eyes, glad for the dim twilight. He feared his face would betray his feelings.

"No, Lucinda, on my oath, I haven't become Raffles's lover," he said stiffly. He was glad she hadn't asked him if he loved Rafaella. He wasn't sure now whether he did or he didn't, but at least he could say with a clear conscience that he had never been her "lover."

Lucinda kissed his cheek. "Please forgive me for asking," she said. "I knew it was impossible. But I had to hear you say it."

"I understand," he mumbled. "After the duel and all. I understand."

Lawton picked up Lucinda and carried her upstairs, filled with relief, vowing that he would never have another rendezvous with Rafaella.

Two days later, he again carried Lucinda, this time to a pallet installed in the back of a wagon. Very slowly and cautiously, they rode into Natchez with Rubella and Ellen and Dr. Stacey. The two slave women were accompanying her to see the special doctor in New Orleans. Lawton was worried about Lucinda, but she was cheerful and confident that taking the trip was the best thing.

After seeing Lucinda and her maids safely aboard the *Natchez Star*, Lawton visited his banker and attorney, and then met Theron Sumrall and some of the other planters involved in the Liverpool venture. It was a solemn group. They had all made heavy investments in a plan that could show no profit for at least two years. They had returned to find the worst financial crisis in recent memory. Talk was that cotton prices would be the lowest in ten years.

Lawton drank two whiskeys he did not want, then left the group. He missed Lucinda already, and the melancholy demeanor of his business associates had depressed him. In an attempt to lift his spirits, he went out for a walk in the city. He thought of the letter from Joleen that had arrived just that morning.

Joleen had written that Aaron had to travel to the island of Cuba on an extended business trip, and that she'd decided to return to The Columns for a visit while he was gone. Lawton was very pleased with this news, but it didn't erase his gloomy mood. He stopped at a tavern, hoping to distract himself with drink, but the rough whiskey only released further anxieties.

After an hour or so, Lawton left the tavern and took a room at the Parker House Hotel. He was too drunk to return to The Columns, and far too drunk to notice that the man who had been watching him from a corner of the tavern had followed him into the lobby of the hotel.

In his room he loosened his linen and slumped into a chair. He closed his eyes, but they were both there in his mind: Lucinda and Raffles, Raffles and Lucinda. He got up and paced the room, thinking of the long weeks in England and France, of his feeling of alienation and his boredom with everything there. And he thought of the Moslems he had seen on a London street. Most of them were swarthy, dark-haired men who dressed in strange robes. But one . . . he'd been startled to see one who was tall and had fair skin and eyes.

Something had compelled Lawton to ask about him, and he'd been told the man was a kind of Egyptian slave called a Mameluke. Typically, he learned, they were fair, and at one time such slaves were quite common in Egypt. Lawton's thoughts were interrupted by a knock on the door.

"Mr. Deavors? A message, sir!" someone called.

66.

Lawton groaned with guilty pleasure as Rafaella touched his tongue with hers. His hands trembled as they caressed her breasts through the soft, thin silk of her dress.

When he had received her summons at his hotel room, he had immediately succumbed. He had hired a carriage and had driven out on the madhouse road to meet her. She was sitting in her carriage—alone. Lawton had made no attempt to rationalize his action. His obsession had overwhelmed him, despite his fears of detection, of losing control. And he also feared her. Feared . . . what? It made no sense.

Rafaella was only a beautiful young girl, timid but happy to see him. She begged him never again to leave her for so long. They sat side by side now in her carriage, and they talked very little. It was a hot, windless night, and Lawton knew he would never forget the scent of Rafaella's perfume in the closed carriage. Blood pounded in his head. Before he knew it, he was kissing her, kissing her hungrily and uncontrollably.

For a few moments he forgot everything—lost all sense of time and place and even her identity. He was conscious only of her mouth and her breasts, and he was sweating and groaning with arousal.

Then Rafaella pulled away. "Lawton, I've never had a lover," she whispered. "Not even my husband. My body is untouched . . . waiting for you, Lawton . . . if you want me."

"Yes, I want you, Raffles," he said. "I want you very much, Raffles."

"Tell me what you want, Lawton."

"Your breasts . . . so lovely, Raffles . . . so exciting . . . you're so beautiful . . . beautiful."

Lawton trembled with longing as Rafaella loosened her bodice and slid the silk from her shoulders. He stared at her breasts. They were hazed with perspiration. Little drops had collected on her red nipples. Her breasts were so full, so soft, the loveliest breasts he had ever seen, as lovely as . . . Joleen's breasts. The thought stunned Lawton, and he fought for breath as he anxiously, awkwardly caressed her bosom.

"You've waited so long, Lawton," she said into his ear, each word a damp kiss. "You've been so aloof, Lawton. But I know you love me, Lawton. I always knew. Tell me why you've lied to me."

"No, I haven't." He stroked her breasts and squirmed to relieve his aching penis. He touched her nipples and gasped for breath. "I don't know, Raffles . . . I'm sorry that you think I've been hateful. But I couldn't . . . I was afraid to give in to my feelings for you, Raffles."

"And Lawton," she whispered, her tongue teasing his ear, "admit it, Lawton. You could ruin me, darling; in one angry moment you could destroy me with those rumors . . . and you do believe them, don't you?"

"No, no . . . Raffles, I don't. I wouldn't hurt you anyway . . . not for anything." He strained to kiss her, but she twisted away and put her hands on his neck as she leaned to his ear once more.

"Yes, you could ruin me, Lawton," she said. "And I could hurt you, too, darling. Though I don't want to. But you must be honest with me and admit you believe those rumors about Daddy. Admit you have found some proof."

"No! I haven't, Raffles! I swear I haven't."

Rafaella leaned back and cupped his face in between her small hands. Moonlight shaded her face, but he could see the frightening smile on her lips.

"You think you can deceive me about everything, Lawton," she said. "But you're only honest in one thing tonight, darling; that you want to be my lover."

"Yes, it's true. I want to be your lover, Raffles," he gasped, as he fondled her breasts. "I'll do anything to be your lover." He had been faithful to Lucinda in England, and since his return she had been too ill for sex. He had never been more powerfully aroused.

"Yes, Lawton, your desire has the better of you now," she said. She held her lips an inch from his. "Before, you didn't want to touch me because you thought me a slave's daughter, unworthy . . . even when I offered myself to you. Now you can't control your desire, and you think of me as some chattel to be taken on a deserted road at night. You want to take your pleasure with my body and you'll discard me as unworthy when you're finished with me."

"No, Raffles, that's not true!" The shadows shifted, and her dark eyes held him, weakened what was left of his resistance. He felt her eyes penetrating him, seeing that despite his lust he also felt . . . a sense of distaste . . . felt . . . almost a revulsion at the thought of impure blood.

There was silence between them as she stared at him while he twisted and his loins ached. He sucked in her perfume and stroked her breasts and nipples.

"You wouldn't use me and then discard me, would you, Lawton?" she asked.

"Oh, no, no! I wouldn't discard you! I'll always . . . love you and take care of you. Please . . ." he begged. His fingers were clumsy at the tight sash of her silk dress. They tore at the fragile silk, then moved to stroke the silky softness of her body, up to her full, firm breasts. He was so hot, so hungry for her. He knew he would pay any price, agree to any terms, to make love to her.

Coolly, she moved to tuck her legs under her. Her thighs were outlined in the thin silk, and his hands began to stroke them. She moved to loosen her bodice, and her dress fell open to below the waist. His hands ripped the dress aside. Her thighs shone in the moonlight, dappled with shadows. He touched them with trembling fingers. Her skin felt warm, firm, yet soft, and slightly damp.

He groaned again as he rubbed her thighs with one hand and stroked her breasts with the other.

"You're so beautiful, Raffles," he gasped. "I've wanted you for so long! I'd do anything for you . . .

always . . . I want to kiss you and touch you and worship you . . . your body . . . Raffles. I would never hurt you, never leave you, please believe me!"

"Lawton, remember when we were . . . together . . . before, how you called me Joleen?" she asked, tracing his scar with her fingertip.

Lawton's stomach knotted. Thinking of Joleen made his lust even more powerful, and yet . . . how could she know how to manipulate him like this?

"Yes . . ." he whispered. "No! I didn't mean to!"

"I think you did, Lawton. I've been thinking about it . . . about you and Joleen, you and your sister. I've been thinking how you called out her name."

Lawton's head was reeling. He was drunk and dizzy with desire, and now he dreaded what she was leading up to. How could she know? She didn't know! No one could know. "Please, Raffles," he whispered.

"Tell me about Joleen, Lawton," she said. "Tell me what you did to your sister. Tell me what happened between you. Were you and Joleen lovers?"

"No! No, Raffles, we . . . we never did. I swear it, Raffles."

"Lawton! You promised you wouldn't lie to me, darling."

"We were . . . never . . . lovers." He put his hand to his forehead, trying to steady himself. This was dangerous, too dangerous. How the devil could she know? His stomach was churning, and he felt an awful sense of fear, and yet he was more excited than ever.

"Don't lie! I know what you were to each other, darling. You don't have to be ashamed. Not with me, Lawton. Talk to me . . . I won't betray you. Tell me about Joleen, Lawton."

"There's nothin' . . ."

She interrupted his protest with a kiss, completely distracting him as she touched the roof of his mouth with her tongue, caressed him through his linen shirt, moved his hands back to her breasts. Slowly, she spread her thighs. His fingers slid higher on the intimate flesh . . .

"Tell me the truth, Lawton, if you have any hope of being my lover."

Some small part of Lawton's thoughts was still rational. Some part of his brain warned him to get away from Rafaella, even now, but it was a feeble impulse against his overpowering desire for her.

"And when you tell me, Lawton, I'll be Joleen for you. If you like," Rafaella purred, "you can call me Joleen, and we can . . . do what you did with her. No, don't pull away, Lawton. Don't be afraid, darling. I know anyway, Lawton. Don't resist what you want to do with me. No one will ever know."

And how did Rafaella know? Lawton wondered, as he remembered it all, powerfully, painfully . . . with the guilt and shame and excitement that always accompanied the memory.

"Tell me," Rafaella insisted. "Tell me how it happened."

He told her, then, and the telling was even more exciting than just remembering. He told her how he had been excited and aroused by Joleen's budding sexuality that long-ago summer. She had teased him, and they had both known their feeling was as forbidden as it was powerful. He had treated her badly all summer —to punish her for teasing him. But secretly, he had hidden and watched her swim naked in the creek and he had masturbated, hiding in the bushes.

Then one night at a party, they had walked out together to the back garden and he had confessed to her his feelings and his desire. And, incredibly, she had wanted to lie down with him on the damp grass. They had kissed, and he had kissed her beautiful breasts and undressed her. She had made him beg her and apologize to her for his meanness and tell her over and over again how much he wanted her.

He had wanted her . . . but in a special way. Though he had never thought of it before, he had licked up her smooth, damp, salty thighs and buried his face deep between them and he had kissed and licked at her vagina for ever so long . . . so long that Joleen had cried out in ecstasy. And then she had run away from him, and he had masturbated.

"But nothin' else . . . ever happened between us, I swear, Raffles," Lawton mumbled. "Nothin' else."

"I'll be Joleen for you," Rafaella said. "Just like Joleen. Just like that summer night. And you can . . . kiss me the way you kissed her . . . and you can call me Joleen, Lawton."

"No . . . I can't . . ."

Rafaella slid across the carriage seat and spread her thighs. Moonlight bathed her damp, milky skin, her silky black hair, the moist pinkness of her vagina.

Lawton stared a moment and he was lost.

"Yes, I'll call you Joleen. I want you so much, Joleen. I worship you . . . I can't think of anybody but you."

He lowered his head and he licked her thighs. He rubbed his face higher and higher along her thighs, he felt her pubic hair, and he inhaled a musky odor laced with the sweet perfume. He moaned as his lips touched . . . moistness. His tongue licked the forbidden flesh of her vagina. He pressed his mouth over her mound and into the moist, soft crevice.

Rafaella laced her fingers through his hair and squeezed her thighs together to deny his mouth what it sought. He looked up the length of her pale body covered with rivulets of perspiration, up to her triumphant smile.

"I'll let you do this if you want me enough, Lawton," she said. "But I won't let you make love to me tonight. You'll never make love to me, Lawton, until you admit how you feel about me . . . and make amends for it. And until I know I'm . . . safe from what you know."

"Raffles," he began, but he could not speak. He was trembling. He felt so weak that his arms and legs seemed to lack bone and muscle. He tried to kiss her. Her thighs barred his mouth.

"Pretend I'm Joleen, Lawton. Tell me what you really think about Raffles, Lawton, and I'll open my thighs for you."

"Joleen . . . Raffles . . . I want her so much. She's so beautiful. I'm mad about her . . . but . . . her father was . . . could have been . . . Moslem slave . . . I don't know if . . . there's no proof . . . I swear it . . . no proof . . . Joleen . . . please, Joleen."

Rafaella opened her thighs.

"Shhh, stop whining and try to control yourself, Lawton," she said. "You may stay there . . . all night . . . why not? We have so much to talk about."

Lawton looked up at her taunting smile. Then his face was imprisoned by her thighs and vagina.

67.

"Oh, Lawton, it's so good to be comin' home!" Joleen sat beside Lawton in the carriage bringing them out from Natchez. The drive had never seemed so long to her, so anxious was she to arrive at the plantation and see everything again.

Lawton was happy, too, and he had tried to spare Joleen some of the troublesome news that awaited her. Joleen herself was anxious and unhappy that Aaron had gone with the filibusters to Cuba, but she had put the worry out of her mind for the time being. For now, it was wonderful just to be coming home.

After a fine supper, Joleen and Lawton sat together on the front porch. Lawton's mood was very somber, and he drank a good deal of whiskey as he described the troubles of the past few months. Lawton told her a rambling, disjointed story that, coming from anyone but her brother, she would not have believed. He said there was strong, if not conclusive, evidence that Roger Blaine had formerly been a Moslem slave. Rafaella was terrified that this would get out. She had first believed that Lawton schemed to deny the Blaines the Price Dcavors estate, then that Lawton was scheming with

Frannie to cheat her out of her inheritance. Now, though she had no proof that this was true, she was full of hatred, blaming the whole Deavors family for her father's death, talking of revenge, threatening terrible retribution if a word got out about her father's past.

"But what can she actually do to hurt us?" Joleen asked.

Lawton sat up and sipped his whiskey. He sighed. "I don't know, Joleen," he said. "But I'm worried. Lucinda thinks Raffles is a little crazed at times . . . and so do I. A crazy person is dangerous. Oh, I don't guess she can really hurt us. I don't know. I have so much else on my mind."

Lawton glanced at Joleen, looked away, drank whiskey. She was certain there was more to his story, but he refused to respond to her prodding. Finally she gave up, concerned about his mood and the amount of whiskey he was drinking.

They talked of harmless, nostalgic things for a while. Joleen was tired from her journey. They both went to bed early, but Joleen lay awake half the night.

During the next few days, Joleen spent many hours alone, riding in the fields and along the river. She hadn't had another good conversation with Lawton, who seemed depressed and distant. When he returned from Natchez one evening, he was half-drunk and so despondent that Joleen was alarmed. For her part, she was frantic to hear from Aaron, although she knew it was still too soon. She was worried about him, so worried that she became openly angry with him. She told herself she would never forgive him for going on such a foolhardy expedition. Nor could she ever really trust those firebrand abolitionists. She was thoroughly disillusioned with them all.

Then, on her fifth day back at The Columns, she received an urgent message from Tolver. Immediately, she suspected some trouble, but she did not hesitate to ride out and meet him in the forest near the village of

Benton. She was surprised at how much Benton had grown. She remembered it as one muddy street with a cotton gin, a church, a general store, and two or three houses. Now there were an additional dozen houses, three stores, and two taverns.

And at the end of Benton's main street was a sight that made her go cold and then hot with outrage: a slave was suspended from a sweet gum tree. A white man was ripping the slave's shirt from his back. The man held a vicious-looking whip. Some two dozen people were gathered around the tree, including two young boys.

Joleen reined in her horse and trotted off the street between two stores. As she turned off, she heard the first scream. The sound made her tense, and a chill ran down her spine. Her eyes filled with tears of anger and helplessness.

The village of Benton ended abruptly, and she rode into a thick forest of loblolly pines. Dense bushes and vines made riding difficult. She had the odd feeling that she was the first person ever to enter this wilderness. She felt very much alone, and yet she could still hear the screams. She rode faster, trying to get far away from the sound, but she encountered Tolver, no more than a quarter mile from the Benton road.

"Mornin', Miss Joleen," he said. "We got to talk fast."

"Let's ride further back."

"Don't have time," Tolver said. "And might be some trouble back there a piece." She realized he held a pistol in his right hand. She could not make out his face clearly, but his voice showed anxiety and anger. " 'Sides, if Luther can suffer like that and not talk, surely we can stand to listen. And if he does talk, I'm ruined anyway."

"What in the world happened?" she asked. She could hear the man screaming again. She glanced around at the deep shadows moving lazily, ominously in the meagre sunlight that filtered through the pines. The sounds from the shadows were alien and menacing, punctuated by Luther's screams.

"Luther and me had things goin' good," Tolver said.

"Helped lots of slaves escape. I got a fine . . . situation, bein' Frannie Deavors's driver and all. I can get away with most anything with that gal. She done lied twice to protect me when I was nearly caught. But somebody talked. Don't know who. Somebody done named Luther but not me."

"What did you mean about trouble back there?"

"I had the feelin' I was bein' followed," he said. "Had that feelin' a few times lately. Wouldn't have asked you to meet me here, but I thought they was takin' Luther into Natchez." Tolver shook his head. The anger drained from his voice. "Poor Luther. It'd be more merciful if I was to put a bullet through his head. I could do that and get away, but they's no way to rescue him. They got too many armed men there in Benton."

"I . . . Tolver, what can I do?" She did not think she could endure another scream. Then she realized with horror that the screams were growing fainter. She also realized the danger she was in.

"Even if Luther don't talk, I got the feelin' I'm in a lot of danger and it's time to get away. I'll try to help him escape, if he lives through this beatin' and the brandin' they's sure to give him. But it's like the last time, Miss Joleen. I got to have some cash money or I'll never get away. You're the onliest one I can turn to."

They quickly decided on arrangements for Tolver to pick up a parcel of money that Joleen would leave in an abandoned house just outside Natchez. Tolver himself insisted on this arrangement, saying she would be in far too much danger were she to meet him again.

There were no more screams as Joleen rode back toward Benton. She reached the edge of the forest but decided to avoid the town. She did not think she could stand the sight of Luther's bloody, branded body. And there was no way she could help him.

She circled a bayou covered with flat green lily leaves. Suddenly a man on horseback loomed in front of her. Joleen reined away from the man and galloped out of the forest. The man followed. Once in an open field, with a horse and people not far away, she turned and faced the rider.

"Beg your pardon, ma'am," the man said. "Just wanted to apologize for scaring you like that."

"Yes, you did give me a fright, sir," Joleen said. "And I appreciate your apology."

Joleen rode away from the man, haughty, feeling safe again now, but still disturbed by his small, close-set, nervous black eyes.

68.

Rafaella looked down the street to the lawn of the Natchez jailhouse where Tolver was being forced into a set of stocks that enclosed his neck and wrists. A crowd of spectators was gathering. A man selling nougat and lemon ice was doing a brisk business.

Hiram Cranston had arranged for Tolver to be ambushed as he tried to free a Negro named Luther. Cranston had done his work very well, Rafaella told herself, as she motioned for her driver to pull away. He had bribed a fugitive slave who had been captured in Ohio and returned to Natchez, and whose testimony had made Tolver's conviction certain.

Tolver would be held in the stocks for two days, given a hundred lashes, and branded in the palms of his hands. Then he would be hanged, because he had seriously injured a white man when he was captured.

Rafaella was gratified to see Tolver punished severely. He had robbed her of many thousands of dollars' worth of slaves. On the other hand . . . She smiled, thinking that perhaps he shouldn't be killed. He should be rewarded for being the instrument of Frannie's undoing.

"Damn you, watch those ruts!" Rafaella shouted at

her driver. The idiot was making her nauseous with the carriage's jostling. And she had already been sick that morning. Thinking how Frannie could ruin her if Frannie learned about her father always made her ill.

But she would soon be safe from Frannie. This very afternoon she and Hiram Cranston would confront Frannie with enough real and forged evidence to fix her for good. Rafaella didn't doubt that Frannie would do as she was told. No, after today, Frannie would be no threat. And she, Rafaella, would be the sole mistress of a vast estate.

Then why did she feel so ill? Perhaps it was because she had slept very little the past few nights. She had been plagued by nightmares. She had lain alone and frightened in her enormous bedroom, and all the thoughts she could keep away during daylight now came back to her. All those threads of evidence persisted in weaving themselves together into an all-too-convincing pattern of her father's past.

Rafaella's head throbbed. She shouted at the driver to slow down and threatened him with a whipping. She was getting dizzy again. And people on corners seemed to be staring at her. What did they know about her? Why hadn't they invited her to the pageant—some elaborate fake medieval pageant they'd been setting up near the Natchez jailhouse. She'd seen the preparations and heard talk about it all week. How did they dare not invite her?

Damn them all. They would all be sorry, everyone in Natchez, in the whole damned county. She would destroy the Deavorses and she would be enormously rich and she would have Lawton as her own, and then no one would dare exclude her or whisper about her and she would be safe.

The carriage was pulling into the driveway of her house. She hoped that Cranston wasn't late. After dealing with Frannie, she had to meet Clement Storey, a banker she thought might help her contrive Lawton's financial ruin during these hard times.

Lossie came from the house to meet Rafaella as she got out of the carriage. The black woman was carrying a basket and a pair of scissors.

"You want to cut them roses now, Miss Raffles?" Lossie asked. "Though, Lord knows, not good to cut flowers with the sun shinin' on 'em this way."

"No, I haven't time to cut roses today," Rafaella said. "Has Mr. Cranston arrived?"

"They been no callers," Lossie said. "You busy, you want me to cut them roses?"

"I won't need any roses today," Rafaella said.

"But you didn't go out there yesterday, Miss Raffles, and you ain't never before missed two days in a row and you—"

Rafaella got so angry she very nearly slapped the woman. Instead, she grabbed the basket, threw it in her face, and ran into the house.

That night, Rafaella was huddled in the corner of her carriage, wrapped in a shawl but shivering as she stared out at the crosses and gravestones. She had decided to come out to the cemetery on a sudden desperate impulse.

She'd known it was a mistake at the cemetery gate. The caretaker, a toothless old man who reeked of whiskey, was reluctant to open the gate. He muttered something about her being "mad as a coot, comin' out at ten o'clock."

Now she supposed he would spread the story in taverns, and people would think she was indeed mad.

What did it matter? Natchez already snubbed her, thought her so . . . so much an outcast that her madness would hardly surprise them.

A dog howled mournfully. Rafaella shifted around in the carriage seat and avoided Lossie's eyes. The woman sat without speaking. Rafaella wondered if the slave, too, thought her mad.

And Lawton? Did he think her mad?

He had been rather strange, distant, and preoccupied when they met yesterday, she recalled. She warned herself she must not push Lawton too far. Particularly in their rather . . . unusual erotic games. She had played him slowly. He was resigned to meeting her, but she knew he felt tremendous guilt, felt he was crazy to love her, as she knew he did. He'd said, in fact, that he thought they were both mad, and it had made her very angry.

She enjoyed having him long for her, worship her, and thirst for her body. Indeed, she thought she could drive him to distraction, if she so chose.

But she did love him as well as hate him, and she must be kinder to him, must be cautious and deliberate. Lawton must be led along by his obsession and his love for her, blinded by his guilt and uncertainty, until it was too late. And by then the Deavorses would all be ruined, penniless, homeless. Then, she planned, Lawton would be hers forever, and she would take care of him and he would take care of her.

Everything had gone well during the brutal confrontation with Frannie, better even than Rafaella had hoped. Frannie had been white-faced and trembling as they laid out proof, both real and forged, that Frannie had been intimate with Tolver and carried his child. Dr. Roberts, who was also Frannie's doctor, had been quite cooperative in that matter, after Rafaella had paid him a long visit. They accused Frannie of being active in the Underground Railroad and had even showed her what she believed was Tolver's confession.

Frannie had no choice but to sign the documents Cranston had drawn up. She agreed to stop contesting the marriage contract, had given Rafaella control of ninety percent of the estate, and actually begged for the chance to flee Natchez and have an abortion downriver.

But just seeing Joleen had spoiled Rafaella's pleasure. Joleen had snubbed her cruelly. She'd never liked Joleen, but now Joleen was even more arrogant than usual, and her slaves had giggled and whispered and stared at Rafaella.

To Rafaella, this meant that she had been permanently banned from the Deavors family! It was as simple as that. Oh, they had no proof against her poor father. Lawton had convinced her of that. But they *believed* her to have tainted blood. If she visited the plantation again, one of their arrogant slaves would most likely order her to call at the back door! The idea made her stomach tighten with rage.

Oh, no, they wouldn't slander her now. They wouldn't want to tarnish the Deavors name. She had been wrong about that. But some day one of them would say something to someone. It was inevitable, now that they all knew . . . And she could not and would not live in that kind of fear and danger.

"What did you say, Miss Raffles?" Lossie asked.

"What . . . I didn't say anything, Lossie."

Had she been talking to herself again? This had to stop.

Rafaella comforted herself with Clement Storey's statement that through his manipulations The Columns could be ruined by spring. Cranston was convinced they could trap or frame Joleen. That left only Lucinda.

And from what Rafaella had heard, Lucinda was very ill. Her pregnancy might very well kill her. Rafaella was very pleased about this news. Lucinda had no right to carry Lawton's child. She, Rafaella, was the woman who should do that, for it was she whom Lawton truly loved. And if Lucinda died, she would be mistress of The Columns by summer.

69.

The first light of dawn touched the north coast of Cuba as Aaron and twenty-three other men were rowed ashore. A small advance party had landed at the Bay of Pinar del Rio two hours earlier and had returned with reports that there were no Spanish troops nearby and that the Cubans were rising in rebellion at the news of the group's arrival.

Most of the men in the longboat ignored the wind-whipped spray and choppy water and boasted about the inevitable success of their invasion. Several men drank from flasks of rum. They talked of the fear they had put into the Spanish soldiers, and one old man, who boasted he had fought the Spanish on several occasions in the Caribbean, expected only a token fight. They would break and run, he predicted, under the return fire.

But Aaron shared neither the rum nor the optimism as he stared at the massive royal palms along the flat beach. Though he was buoyed by the reports of the uprisings, he was skeptical of both the men's fighting ability and the officers' competence. And he knew that no matter how successful their military operations might be, serious trouble lay ahead.

He and some seventy abolitionists had sailed down-river from Cincinnati with high spirits, arms, and money some weeks earlier. But few of the men who had joined them at a secret base south of New Orleans shared their antislavery beliefs. They were a mixed and motley bunch of adventurers—disgraced men of quality, filthy river rats, greedy dandies, fugitive criminals, soldiers of fortune, and deserters from the Spanish army.

Though they were landing with nearly four hundred men, Aaron would not depend on a quarter of them in a hard fight. He brushed the salty spray from his face, and his eyes met those of his friend Charlie Duffy. Duffy was only twenty-four, but he had served in the British army for six years before his strong pro-Irish sentiments led him to desert and flee to America. He had been a valuable member of the Underground Railroad in Ohio, and he was a man Aaron would trust in battle.

"If the ride ashore were any longer, the men would be too drunk to fight," Duffy whispered. "Or even run."

"At least there are no Spanish near to challenge us

now," Aaron said. "And once ashore we must take steps to end this drinking."

"That we must," Duffy said.

Aaron had come to depend on Duffy. He liked the young Irishman whose dark features bore an uncanny resemblance to Aaron's own. Since they both now wore full beards, the resemblance was particularly striking, and at odd times Aaron had looked at Duffy as if he were seeing himself as a younger man.

The sound of rifle fire pulled Aaron from his thoughts. He strained forward to check its source, but there was only the lonely beach and the range of mountains beyond. The men in the boat had hushed abruptly, and one old man paused with his flask at his mouth. His suddenly twitching lips and frightened eyes revealed all too clearly that he was unaccustomed to gunfire.

No more shots came. The men settled back and returned to their drinking, but their talk was subdued now.

Ten minutes later the boat touched sand, and the men scrambled through the pounding surf, holding their rifles high as they went ashore. Aaron was reassured to see that two of the advance party were waiting behind a low sand dune. The shots, he learned, had come from a brief exchange with half a dozen Spanish soldiers who had wandered onto the beach. The Spanish had fled quickly when fired upon by an unexpected enemy. The men's good spirits were restored as they moved inland a hundred yards and began to set up camp under a stand of coconut palms.

An hour later the officers met to confer on strategy. Aaron and Duffy cautioned that they should spend time in reconnaissance and in fortifying their base, and that they should keep their force together. But the others disagreed. They insisted the force be split into several groups, each to use the elements of surprise and to push on inland, staying in touch through runners and relying on the Cubans to rise up and support them.

"These kind of men won't sit still for no garrison

'duty or no slow, soldierlike movin'," a one-eyed captain argued. "They got to see the Spanish tuck tail and run, got to smell success and booty and see some enemy blood."

Aaron and Duffy glanced at each other. They argued further, but they were outvoted. As he returned to his men, Aaron knew for sure that even if this venture succeeded, the officers would be at each other's throats long before they reached the walls of Havana.

With Duffy and ten men, Aaron marched to the nearby town of Bahia Honda, fifty miles from Havana, to reconnoiter and recruit. It was a small, poor town of frightened, sullen peasants, who seemed far from revolutionary and certainly unready to take up arms.

As they marched back along a narrow, vine-choked jungle trail, dense with mosquitoes, they heard gunfire. The men broke into a run, and the man on point suddenly jerked up and fell over, taking a bullet through his forehead.

Aaron deployed his men into the scrubby undergrowth. They advanced slowly and killed two Spanish soldiers. Proceeding to camp, they found it under attack by a large Spanish force. A dozen men of the assault party were already dead and many were wounded. Their position was desperate—enclosed by Spanish forces on three sides, with the sea to their backs. Already some of the men were whining in fear and begging to make a run for the ships anchored in the bay.

Aaron and Duffy worked to tighten their perimeters. They tried to force some discipline and order. The men were frantic and firing at random. Duffy and a dozen of the abolitionists made a successful flanking move to the Spanish left. Alarmed, the Spanish commander took men from his center to reinforce his left flank. Aaron then led fifty men in a frontal attack just as the Spanish were shifting their forces.

The Spanish, confused, their ranks broken, fell back nearly a quarter mile before they reformed their lines.

Aaron killed or disabled four Spaniards. A bullet grazed his left arm. Three of his men were killed and eight wounded.

Aaron worked quickly to set up new perimenters, but when he returned to the beach he learned that nearly forty men had deserted in the longboats and were making a run for the ships. Aaron, Duffy, and two other officers were holding a quick conference when Aaron heard an explosion and looked up to see one of their longboats blown out of the water.

A Spanish man-of-war was moving toward their ships. Another longboat burst into flames. A fusillade toppled the mast of one of the ships. The American ships returned fire, but their cannons were no match for the range and firepower of a ship of the line.

Aaron had been told by the Spanish agents that there were no Spanish warships in these Cuban waters. They had been betrayed or . . . It was too late for conjecture. They now had to fight their way clear of the beach. They could be of no help to the ships, and quite soon the man-of-war's forty guns would be turned on the beach and they would all be slaughtered.

The sight of the man-of-war spread panic among the remaining men. Some of them tried to hide in the thick undergrowth, but shots and screams indicated this tactic was hopeless. The previously arrogant and confident officers had lost all enthusiasm for command. They were as frightened and indecisive as their men. Aaron and Duffy assumed command. Already the man-of-war was bombarding the beach, the first shots falling too short, then too long, and far to the right and left as the gunnery officers worked out the range.

Aaron sent Duffy and his men toward the Spanish center with a feint, while he led another group to the Spanish right. Resistance was fierce. The Spanish held for one desperate charge, then another. Aaron's casualties were high. All around him, men he knew from Ohio lay dead or dying among the bloody brown and green uniforms of the Spanish regulars. Aaron heard the agonized screams of a middle-aged Cincinnati druggist with his right leg blown off. Mercifully, he put a bullet through the man's head.

On a third charge, which cost a score of lives, Aaron's men broke the Spanish flank, but the soldiers fell back only a dozen yards. The warship's cannons, now on target, were slaughtering Aaron's men. Panic immobilized them just when the Americans might have finally broken the Spanish line.

Duffy had forced the Spanish back with four bloody charges, but the right of the American line was giving way to a furious Spanish assault. Fighting close together, Aaron and Duffy led their exhausted men in one final charge and breached the Spanish lines, only to see fresh Spanish troops arriving through the jungle. The Americans fought to the left, away from the new troops, and a score of them, bleeding and desperate, broke free into the jungle.

Aaron had been hit with a bullet in his left arm, but it was a clean flesh wound that bled little. Duffy had been bayoneted in his right wrist. They staggered on into the jungle with their men, with no plan except escape, for there was nothing they could do to help the others. By now they were hopelessly cut off from the sea by new Spanish troops on their heels.

The little group finally lost the soldiers by splashing across a vine-choked stream into a mangrove forest. They paused to tend their wounds. A young carpenter from Baltimore was bleeding heavily and died as they watched. It was smotheringly hot, and the air buzzed with insects. Aaron knew many men would die unless they could treat the wounds at once.

Beyond the forest, they stumbled into a tiny village of thatched huts, but the people fled at their approach and refused all help. At another, larger village, the men who did not flee were sullen and hostile, and Aaron had to force an old woman at gunpoint to give them some cotton cloths.

As they were stumbling through the street of the village, a little boy hit Duffy in the shoulder with a rock. Half an hour later, they heard the first bloodhounds.

They ran faster and lost the dogs in water for most of the day. But by early dusk the wounds, the running, the heat, and the insects had drained the men of any will to resist.

When they heard the dogs again, only Aaron and Duffy could stagger to their feet. They were able to get just a quarter mile into a banana grove before the dogs caught them. Duffy killed one soldier with a clean shot through the heart; then he was clubbed to the ground. Aaron shot one Spaniard and tried to bayonet another, but he was too weak. He was already falling—his only thought was of Joleen—before the rifle butt smashed against his head.

70.

Joleen considered the whole idea of the medieval jousting tournament as silly as grits, but she had a good reason for agreeing to wear a costume and tie her colors to Lawton's lance. The tournament was being held in a field adjacent to the Natchez jail, and it might give her a chance to free Tolver.

The ladies who had organized the tournament had objected to the sight of Tolver in the stocks; they had also felt that he might scream and interrupt the affair. So the sheriff had moved the stocks out of sight into a patch of shrubbery behind the jail and postponed Tolver's whipping and branding until the next day. A single deputy was posted to guard the slave.

Now at half past three on a warm afternoon at the beginning of October, Joleen sipped sweet Malmsey wine and smiled at her reflection in the small mirror of the ladies' dressing tent. She was dressed in a rich burgundy brocade gown with trailing, funnel-shaped sleeves—in the Byzantine manner, she'd been told.

The committee had erected a dozen tall, round tents with striped, peaked tops in an open field. A score of slave artisans had been shown illustrations of French medieval tents in a book printed in Paris, and had been ordered to duplicate them. Other slaves had been ordered to construct suits of armor from similar illustrations in the books, but the results had not been particularly successful. Despite the ladies' thirst for authenticity, chain mail was unavailable. Finally, it was agreed that the suits would be made of tin and cotton dyed to resemble metal.

Absentmindedly, Joleen listened to the ladies talk about the symbolism of a new age of chivalry in Mississippi. They called it the dawning of a golden era of refinement, high ideals, and elegant manners. Joleen thought it all a bit exaggerated. Certainly her family and the other planters lived very well, but with her new sophistication Joleen could see that Natchez society was very isolated. She found this pseudomedieval fair rather funny, for example, but there was no one with whom she could share the joke. Before her marriage, and her new feelings about slavery and the system, it would have been Lawton. But Lawton hadn't been himself lately.

Joleen, too, was worried about Aaron. She had nearly consulted the Delsanos, who had family in Cuba, but to do so might endanger Aaron. So she waited, day by day and hour by hour. She was confused and felt helpless. All these people were so foolish, so shallow compared to Aaron, but where was he? How could he have left her, even for a noble cause?

The ladies' talk seemed even more inane now. They were becoming intoxicated on imported wines. Claret and port as well as Malmsey were being poured liberally.

She was taking a terrible risk, she knew. She had promised Lawton she would never again involve herself in anything dangerous or illegal. Yet she could not abandon Tolver to torture and death.

Joleen bought a marzipan strawberry, bit into it, and threw it to the ground. She walked on, nodding and speaking to people she had known all her life—and now mistrusted. She swore this was the last time she would do the Railroad's work in Mississippi. She could never forgive the abolitionists for sending Aaron to Cuba, nor could she forgive him for going, as much as she loved him. Oh, what was she to do? Sometimes she felt so much at home with these people, and on the plantation; much more at home than in Ohio, even with Aaron there. Yet she hated slavery, and she could not watch idly while someone like Tolver was killed.

Against her better judgment, she accepted another glass of Malmsey, presented by a knight in grey cotton. She intended to drink very little, to remain steady, but now she felt she must calm herself. She wandered over to a raised platform, bedecked with red and blue pennants, where seven black musicians in tight-fitting silken page costumes and caps were playing what the ladies assumed to be medieval music.

She was enjoying the simple rhythm when she looked up and saw Rafaella's lawyer, Hiram Cranston, a few feet away. He turned away too quickly, and she knew he had been watching her. She told herself she had nothing to fear, but she was becoming quite nervous about his spying on her.

Why had Rafaella dismissed a reliable attorney like Grady Weston and hired a common man like Cranston? Joleen hadn't really credited the accounts of Rafaella's maliciousness until that afternoon she'd met her on the street. Why, Rafaella had looked so fierce and frenetic it was nearly frightening. Rafaella was probably capable of anything. What kind of hold did Rafaella have on her brother? She had been stunned when Cellus told her Lawton's duel was fought over Rafaella. Lawton had never sufficiently explained why. Angrily, he had denied being the girl's lover. Yet it didn't make much sense . . .

The hideous face of a gargoyle loomed up out of the shadows. Involuntarily, Joleen gasped and shrank back. A burst of drunken laughter came from Carlos Delsano as he pulled off his mask. Joleen forced herself to smile forgivingly. She stood with Carlos at the edge of the field near the jail.

Some of the stands and gaming tents had been cleared from the field and a huge open-sided tent raised for the ball to honor Lawton, who had won the knights' ring tournament. Most of the medieval revelers still wore their elaborate costumes and had also donned masks. Joleen's mask was that of a grinning parrot, but she had concealed a lion's mask in a deep pocket of her brocade gown. She touched it nervously as Carlos Delsano surprised her.

Joleen let him escort her back to the tent. They passed pheasants, quails, rabbits, sides of venison, and suckling pigs roasting in open barbecue pits—all foods the ladies thought ideal for a medieval feast. Music was playing and Joleen danced with Carlos, grateful to avoid conversation with him. Her heart began to pound rapidly. It had taken all her courage to set out on her mission. Carlos had interrupted her at the crucial moment, and now she had to force herself to wait—and then find new courage.

She could not remember ever seeing more of the good folk of Natchez drunk. They had at least successfully emulated the flamboyance of a medieval extravaganza. The dancing was fast and dizzying. Men had gorged themselves on the food, and many lay sprawled on carpets on the ground. Women giggled hysterically, and both men and women played drunken games of hide-and-seek. Joleen had hoped the fair and feast would be sufficiently gay to create a distraction from her mission, and so far she was satisfied. She was also relieved to see that the deputy sheriff had been persuaded to empty several glasses of whiskcy.

The dancing grew gayer and the music louder. Each time Joleen tried to leave the tent, someone else insisted she dance with him. She was anxious to slip away. Then Lawton asked her for a dance, and there was no way she could refuse him. She was relieved that he had thrown himself into the mood of revelry and seemed less sad.

When she finally reached the tent's edge some five minutes later, a man with an ape's mask intercepted her. She tried to refuse him but he insisted, so she danced with him, her fear and anxiety growing. When the dance ended and she found she was dancing with Hiram Cranston, she nearly gasped aloud. His little pig eyes sent a shiver down her spine.

Whirling away, she nearly fell into the arms of Theron Sumrall, who pulled her into a game of hide-and-seek. Gratefully, she ran to hide, but her courage nearly failed her.

It was the time. She forced herself to put on her lion's mask and crept to the edge of the shrubbery behind the jailhouse, relieved that the deputy had left his post to accept another whiskey.

Despite the music and laughter from the ball, Joleen could hear a dozen small noises nearby. Was someone following her? She stopped twice and glanced back frantically. Sweat stung her eyes behind her lion's mask. Blood pounded at her temples.

Frightened and almost without hope, she forced herself through the shrubbery, taking awkward, stumbling steps. A crunching sound in the darkness nearly caused her to bolt and run. But she went on and reached the stocks. Tolver did not look up. He seemed to be unconscious, and Joleen felt sick as she saw the agony etched into his face. She wondered if he were capable of straightening up, of walking. Then his eyes opened slowly. He seemed to have difficulty focusing, but he was conscious.

His mouth opened but he did not speak. Saliva dribbled from his lips. His body convulsed in a sudden gesture that made Joleen gasp. She heard another sound and looked around. Again, her fear nearly overcame her courage.

She moved to the stocks and removed the bolt that

held the two pieces of wood together. For a moment, Tolver still didn't move; then he tried to lift his head. He groaned and his lips quivered.

"Get away . . . go on," he muttered. "I'll be all right now."

Joleen turned and ran through the shrubbery. She was sure she heard someone coming after her. She glanced around. Hiram Cranston's face loomed in the leaves. She stumbled. She fell. She was lost.

As Cranston moved toward her, another figure emerged from the darkness. Tolver's body was jerking uncontrollably as he stumbled forward, but he was on Cranston before the man realized what was happening. Joleen climbed to her feet and ran out of the shrubbery.

She discarded her lion's mask and retrieved her parrot face, but as she turned toward the tent a hand touched her shoulder. She gasped and shrank back.

"You're it, I caught you!" Theron shouted.

Joleen's knees began to fail her. Theron became concerned and helped her to the ladies' dressing tent, where she collapsed on a chair while half a dozen ladies hovered about and fanned her.

Half an hour later, Joleen sat at the edge of the dance floor and sipped a sherry. She declined invitations to dance. Though people were still drinking and dancing, the mood of the evening had changed. Word that Tolver had escaped and had seriously injured Hiram Cranston spoiled the festivities. Two dozen men had gone off to join the sheriff's posse and the slave patrols.

Joleen tried to reassure herself that Cranston could not have recognized her, but she was very frightened. She nearly found herself hoping that he would die. As soon as she felt strong enough, she rose to excuse herself and have Romulus drive her back to the Delsanos'. When she stood up, a man without mask or costume approached her. At first she did not recognize him. Then, with a stab of anxiety that knotted her stomach, she realized that he was a friend of Levi Coffin, the Ohio abolitionist leader who had opposed the Cuban invasion as strongly as she had.

"What happened?" she asked. "What—"

"The news is grave," the man said. "The invasion failed. And I . . . I will be blunt, Mrs. Clauson. We fear there were no survivors, though there is still some small . . ."

Joleen fell to the ground before he could finish the sentence.

71.

That fall, the increasingly severe financial panic brought ruin, anxiety, and despair to all parts of the United States, touching Natchez as well. But it seemed nothing could dampen the Mississippians' enthusiasm for their good life or alter their assumption that a new golden age was at hand.

Everyone at The Columns was caught up in this optimism and in the hard work of harvesting cotton. Lawton had his worries, financial and otherwise, but he was determined to live life as usual, to uphold tradition. He still visited Lucinda as often as he could. He had been relieved on his last trip to learn that Lucinda was considerably improved and still set on returning to The Columns in time to give birth at her own home. Then, as was customary, they would hold the annual Harvest Ball at the plantation.

As he climbed wearily from bed before dawn each day and joined his slaves in the fields at first light, Lawton's thoughts strayed from the mechanics of getting the cotton out of the ground and down to his new riverbank gin. As he crossed and recrossed the hundreds of acres and sat on horseback at the stations where each slave's pickings were weighed, he tried to think clearly about Lucinda and Joleen and Nettie, who was still in

Natchez, as if to haunt him. And he brooded most desperately about Rafaella.

Joleen was miserable. The news of Aaron's probable death had nearly killed her. Though Lawton had never really liked Aaron and had blamed him for Joleen's involvement with the Underground Railroad, he was bitterly sorry, for Joleen's sake. Nothing he could do raised her spirits. She was grieving terribly, sitting in her room or taking long rides alone. She ate little and had lost weight. Nothing in the world seemed to interest her except the faint prospect of further news from Cuba. But no news came, and Lawton felt she had to accept what seemed to be the inevitable: Aaron was dead.

As for the financial panic, Lawton sensed dangers in every direction. The cotton harvest was a fine one, but he had visions of a warehouseful of cotton bales rotting, and of being forced to sell the cotton at a ruinous price.

Lawton's expenses had been heavy in the past year. He had paid for the new land and for the construction of the summerhouse, the dock, and the gin. He was badly overextended and must soon seek financing for next year's planting. Lawton's wealth was in slaves and land, and his family had never considered selling either, no matter what the crisis.

But his most persistent, guilt-ridden worries concerned Nettie and Rafaella. The unofficial existence of his first-born son, the product of his youthful indiscretion, tormented him. His relationship with Rafaella was even more shameful. He longed to rid himself of his passion for her, but he could not. They had fallen into a pattern of meeting outside of town.

He had not made love to a woman in months, and each time he met Rafaella she led him to believe that she would finally become his lover. Each time, he praised her beauty, kissed her, fondled her breasts, and then knelt with his head between her thighs in the hot, close carriage. As he did so, he became nearly irrational with desire.

And each time, he gradually realized that she still

refused to give herself to him. He could have raped her, but he would not; he only tried harder to please her and arouse her to passion. The extent of their secret erotic games frightened Lawton. Later he would curse himself for being weak, particularly after the nights when they acted out his scene with Joleen. He could hardly face Joleen the next day, and shame overwhelmed all other feelings he had for his sister.

Rafaella's ability to arouse, manipulate, and humiliate him was frightening. Just when he thought her mad and so dangerous that he must end his affair, she became sweet and tender, yielding and sympathetic. She could convince him of her isolation and loneliness and fear, and hint strongly that soon, very soon, perhaps next time, she would become his lover.

She no longer made wild threats of revenge. She never mentioned her father or her husband. And she no longer talked about Nettie and the boy. What a shock that had been, to discover that Rafaella knew of his indiscretion!

But one part of Rafaella's behavior had not changed. She was half-crazed with bitterness and fear because of his confession that, although he had no solid proof, he suspected that her father was a Moslem slave. By now Rafaella was a past mistress at wringing the truth out of him, and he could not conceal the fact that the idea of her heritage repelled him. She never spoke of her father, only of herself, of living in fear that the secret would come out and ruin her, of being thought nothing better than a chattel, to be used and discarded after his pleasure. She complained that she had been banned from the Deavors family as something inferior, untouchable, impure. It made her cruel. She taunted him and manipulated him. She mocked his lust and obsession, and the look of bitter triumph on her lovely face was chilling. Four nights earlier, this had gone on longer than usual. Lawton had praised Rafaella, begged her, and licked every part of her damp body. She had hurt him with her thighs and crooned that she would show him who was the slave. Then, suddenly, she burst into tears. She cried a long time as she hugged and kissed him, and she promised that she would become his lover within the week.

So Lawton rode the endless rows of cotton plants and lived with visions of Rafaella's face and breasts and thighs and the hope of becoming her lover. And he lived with his aversion to it all, with the same aversion he felt toward Nettie, who was a slave, who should never have been given his seed, should never have been used for his pleasure to carry his son, and then abandoned.

Lawton believed desperately that once he had made love to Rafaella, his obsession would end as surely as it had ended with Nettie.

72.

Rafaella picked at her dinner and thought about how closely her life was tied to Lawton's. She had no other friends, and she seldom visited her father's grave any longer. During her last visit, she had started trembling violently. The caretaker had seen her and shaken his head. She doubted that she would ever visit the grave again. She could no longer bear to think of what her father might have passed on to her, particularly when she saw slave auctions in the streets or was confronted by the servility of her own slaves.

"No," she mumbled. She bolted up from the table and nearly knocked over the paraffin lamp. No, she wasn't like that at all!

No matter what, she had to make her own life. And she had Lawton now. She had to have Lawton. He was everything she wanted and needed. And he was a Deavors! When Lawton was known to be hers, then she would once again be accepted as a Deavors. She would have no fears of being exposed and ruined.

But did she have Lawton? Although he adored her

and spoke of their future together, Lawton knew of her father's past and despised it even as he longed for her. Thinking of this twisted her love into a bitterness so violent she began to tremble.

She heard a sound and glanced over her shoulder. Lossie was walking toward her.

"You want your coffee now, Miss Raffles?" Lossie asked.

Rafaella nodded and tried to stop the spasms as she stumbled to the table and sat down. Lossie held the cup and saucer in one hand as she poured coffee. The spigot of the pot missed the cup. The hot coffee splashed onto Rafaella's dress, and a drop stung her arm.

"You clumsy idiot!" Rafaella screamed. "You've ruined my dress! Clumsy, stupid slave." Rafaella looked into the frightened eyes. "I hate you!" she shouted. "How could I ever be like you!"

Rafaella tried to stand up. She nearly lacked the strength and grabbed the table for support. Her elbow knocked over the coffee pot, and coffee soaked her dress and burned her arms.

"See what you've done, you fool!" she shouted.

"Miss Raffles, this time it wasn't none of my doin'."

"How dare you talk back to me! Get out of here! I'll see you whipped. You're nothing but a slave. That's all you'll ever be . . . nigger . . . no . . . No!"

Lossie was turning to leave. Rafaella choked back a sob and snatched up the paraffin lamp with trembling hands. She hurled the lamp at Lossie. The lamp broke, and the scalding paraffin poured down Lossie's back. She was screeching and trying to claw at her back as Rafaella ran from the room.

An hour later, Rafaella paced the patio and drank sherry. When the doctor finished treating Lossie, he had given Rafaella a sedative, but it was already wearing off. During that hour Rafaella had tried desperately to convince herself that this nightmare would end soon.

Lawton would be hers. She would be a Deavors, mistress of The Columns.

But what if this nightmare just continued as it was . . . on and on and on? She knew that, despite his obsession, Lawton could not be manipulated and humiliated much longer. And despite her pleasure in their erotic games and her fear of being hurt by another man, she knew she would never replace Lucinda unless she gave Lawton what he wanted. She had often calculated that if she carried Lawton's child, his attitude might change drastically and he might love her even more . . . but she always remembered how quickly the Deavorses had disposed of Nettie when they learned of her pregnancy.

And didn't Lawton think she was the same as Nettie, really? And if he had a profound aversion for her father's past, how would he react to the thought of having another child that wasn't all . . . that wasn't pure?

The thought made her shake with anger and misery.

She ran into the dining room and took sherry from the sideboard. She poured a glass that overflowed before she realized what she was doing. She glanced around, but no one was watching. She gulped the sherry in quick little sips as she returned to the patio.

She assured herself that once Lawton became her lover, he would be overwhelmed. He would worship her totally. She would bind him to her in another, stronger way. Lawton *would* be hers, just as surely as her father should have been hers . . . hers alone!

The last time they sat in the carriage, he had begged her more ardently than ever to be his lover. Yes, she had only to surrender herself to him and then, somehow, she would get rid of Lucinda and Joleen . . . Rafaella grew furious when she thought that Lucinda was about to give birth to Lawton's child. She should be the one to give Lawton an heir. And once Lucinda gave birth, it would be far more difficult to get Lawton away from her.

"But I'll get him away!" she promised herself. "And

if Lucinda survives that pregnancy . . . I'd rather see the baby dead . . . lying dead . . . I swear it!"

Rafaella realized she was talking to herself. She glanced around. Three slaves were staring at her from the dining room window, as though she were in a cage, on exhibition.

"After tonight, they'll all think I'm quite mad," she mumbled. "Oh, Lawton . . ."

The next evening, Rafaella again drank alone on her patio as she thought of her business activities that day. The panic that was ruining so many people was having far less effect on her, since in addition to land and slaves her holdings included stocks, bonds, and investments abroad. And the banker Clement Storey, whose passion for gambling had left him deeply in debt, had promised that he could show her a way to destroy The Columns financially. When the time came to finance spring planting, Storey said, he would arrange it so that Rafaella would end up holding all of Lawton's bank notes. She would be able to call in the notes early, and Lawton would be ruined.

Yes, she told herself, soon she would own Lawton financially, as well as sexually and every other way!

She realized that two slaves were staring at her from the windows of their shacks behind the patio. She nearly shouted at them but held back. They had all acted strangely toward her since Lossie's stupidity had provoked her last night. They would put a dish on the table, then practically run out of the room. They whispered as she passed, she was certain.

She supposed they had mentioned her behavior to neighbor slaves. Now Natchez society would have one more tale about Rafaella Ridgeway. At times she felt so tainted that she despaired that even having Lawton and being a Deavors could save her. If only Lawton himself could be tainted in some way! Certainly, having a bastard son by a slave was so common it wouldn't do. Even Lawton's relationship with Joleen . . . there was no way to prove it.

Rafaella sipped her sherry and decided Lawton must be tainted in such a way that it was public knowledge. She drained her glass and recalled a recent talk with Ferrell Shanks, the madhouse warden, who was interested in buying some of her land adjacent to the madhouse. In a moment of anger and despair, she had imagined all the arrogant Deavorses howling like dervishes in the madhouse, for all the county to see. Then she would save Lawton, and . . .

Rafaella shook her head miserably. She could never get a Deavors into the madhouse. She felt helpless, because earlier she had resolved that at their next meeting she must surrender to Lawton.

Joleen had been outdoors alone, riding all afternoon. She was still overcome with grief and worried about Lawton and the plantation, about Lucinda, about Rafaella's threat to the family. She returned home to find she had a caller.

He was the same man, the friend of Levi Coffin, who had brought the bad news of Aaron and the invasion. Joleen stared at him a moment as though she did not believe he was there. She had to steady herself with her hand against the wall before walking down the gallery and out to the front porch.

"Are you all right, Mrs. Clauson?" he asked. "Here, let me help you."

"No . . . what news . . . please."

"The news is . . . good but not promising," he said. "We've had word that a number of prisoners were taken. Aaron was one of them."

Joleen let herself be helped into a chair.

"Not promising . . . in what way?" she mumbled.

"I'll speak frankly, Mrs. Clauson," he said.

The Spanish, he told her, had imprisoned the Americans under appalling conditions. Many had died of their wounds or disease or the brutal treatment in the Havana prison. And each week, several of the prisoners were publicly executed by garrotting.

Joleen asked what garrotting was. He was reluctant

373

to tell her but gave in when she insisted. She was sorry she had asked. The garrote, he said, was an implement like an iron collar that was tightened and squeezed until the victim died of strangulation.

"But Aaron's alive," she mumbled. "How do you know he . . . he hasn't been . . . garrotted yet?"

"We can't know for certain," he said. "But it's been the practice in Havana to execute such invaders in a public plaza, as a spectacle, a few men each week. The leaders are usually the last."

Joleen stood up. "What are you doin' to free him— to save him?"

"There's little we can do," he said. "The Cuban governor would certainly accept a bribe, but it's difficult to raise money."

"A bribe?" Joleen began to hope, began to believe that Aaron could be saved. She would raise his ransom, any sum at all, no matter what it took. And she would get in touch with Governor McNutt and the senators and congressmen and have them use their influence to delay Aaron's execution.

"Please sit down and make yourself comfortable," Joleen said. "I'll send someone out to see after your needs, and then I want to have a long talk with you."

Joleen ran down the gallery, calling for a slave to look after the visitor. She ran to the barn, mounted her horse, and galloped out to the fields to find Lawton.

73.

Lawton's obsession with Rafaella had always been fueled by his frustration. The longer she denied him, the stronger his lust became. Their long, hot, perfumed sessions in her carriage, when he was permitted to touch and kiss and lick her but not become her lover, had created for him a world of exotic eroticism. His lust and continued humiliation fed his fantasy, and he came to believe Rafaella was an ideal, virgin goddess, a perfection beyond mere flesh and blood.

He had nearly lost any hope of having her on the cool November night when Rafaella lay back on the carriage seat and drew Lawton to her naked body. She spread her thighs as he fumbled to take off his pants. The moment had come.

Her mouth was quivering but her body was rigid. She felt no desire for Lawton. She told herself she must seem excited, somehow appear passionate, but at the first thrust of Lawton's penis, bile rose in her throat. She could barely control her fear and distaste. He seemed so hungry, so intense, so demanding. It was disgusting. She bit her lips until she tasted blood. As his hands ran along her body, she stiffened even more and dug her nails into her palms.

Lawton knew at once that something was very wrong. She seemed so stiff, so cold. Very quickly, her erotic hold on Lawton loosened. The truth came suddenly and awesomely to him: Rafaella was simply flesh and blood like any other girl. Her face looked strained and not very pretty, her vagina was too dry, her body was wooden and unfeeling, and even in the moment of his triumph, the moment he had long dreamed of and would have sacrificed anything to get, he was disappointed.

They had kissed and petted so long that almost before he could enter her fully, he reached a climax. He could not believe it was over, as he lay panting and gasping on her small, unresponsive body, unable to look into her angry, dark eyes.

"You hurt me," Rafaella whimpered. "Move . . . damn you, Lawton, you're smothering me."

He got off her and scrambled across the carriage. He sat hunched over, his head drooping. He had been so aroused and his release had been so sudden that he felt drained, his stomach hollow and aching. He watched Rafaella as if she were a stranger as she sat up, shivering and trembling, and huddled with her arms wrapped around herself. After a minute, she seemed to remember she was naked and pulled on her dress.

Fretfully, she demanded that he talk to her, thank her, praise her, but when he did she cursed him and accused him of lying. He was upset and guilty, but even as he was protesting, it was as if the scales had fallen from his eyes. Lucinda was due from New Orleans in two days. And, after all, Rafaella was only a girl, like any other. He'd thought her a beautiful, mysterious, and awesome virgin goddess, but once between her thighs, he realized she was inexperienced, stiff, uncaring. How very different she was from Lucinda, all warm, soft movement and delight . . .

Perhaps sensing the threat of Lawton's thoughtfulness, Rafaella crawled closer to him. She tried hard to change her mood, but her tactics were transparent. She praised Lawton's forcefulness and pleaded her fear and lack of experience. Anxiously, she tried to arouse him once more, but she could not reach him.

Then she became abusive again. She talked about being rejected, and they had a short but bitter argument. She grew sweet and persuasive before Lawton left the carriage, promising that next time she would be a much better lover, promising that they could play any games he wished, do anything he wanted . . .

But they both knew the relationship between them had changed drastically, and that Lucinda would be coming home before they met again.

74.

Aaron's fingers trembled as he picked maggots out of his ankle. The filthy, rancid flesh had been abraded by an ankle iron. He retched at the stench; the pain was intense but he knew he had to fight infection. He refused to die from disease, as had so many men in the confines of this Havana prison.

When he could no longer bear the pain or the feel of his own rotting flesh, and when the screams of the prisoners dragged out to the courtyard for execution began to drive him half-mad, he scrambled to the wall and began to dig at the decaying brick that held his chain. His nails were cracked and his fingers bled, but he worked at the brick as often as he could. His friend, Charlie Duffy, who was sleeping fretfully on a pile of straw across the cell, did the same. It seemed their only possibility of escaping the garrote that would kill Aaron's last two remaining men today.

The men had stopped screaming. Aaron didn't think he could watch another death, but in an odd way he felt he owed it to these men. They were Ohio abolitionists, both in their early forties, like him gulled into this futile expedition by idealism and the urge to correct everything by taking up arms. His bitterness passed quickly. It was a luxury he could not afford. He thought an instant of Joleen, but that, too, he resisted. He saved her memory for the long, sleepless nights on his straw pallet.

Aaron heard the drum roll. He pulled himself up and scraped his hand along the rough brick as he stumbled to the window. The sun hurt his eyes. He shielded them and squinted.

His eyes adjusted to the bright light. A sob caught in his throat as he looked down on Carl Shays and Derek Sanders, seated on stools and strapped to wooden stakes. Iron collars attached to the stakes had been fastened around their necks. Black-hooded executioners held the collar screws while the drums rolled and a priest mumbled from a Bible. After they were strangled, the men's heads would be cut off and displayed on poles.

Shays had been a teamster, a big, brawling man who liked to drink and hated slavery. He had a young wife. Sanders was a sober, serious man, a notary with a wife and four children. Shays sat as though already dead. Sanders was jerking and crying.

The priest finished. He made the sign of the cross. The drums rolled louder and the hooded men began to turn the screws. If Shays and Sanders were lucky, the iron collar would cut off their life quickly. If they were unlucky, death could take many agonizing minutes.

The men's bodies convulsed. They screamed. The executioners were in no hurry today. The iron collars would be tightened very slowly.

Aaron fell back from the window at the next gurgling scream. He covered his ears with his hands and cried.

75.

Lawton received two frantic notes from Rafaella in the next few days. He ignored the first but responded to the second and met her for a brief afternoon rendezvous. He refused to sit in her carriage but stood stiffly beside it as they spoke. She tried to be sweet, gentle, and appealing. He was aloof and cold.

Lawton said he was sorry if he had made her suffer in any way. He said he would always be fond of her, said she need never fear that he would spread any rumors about her. As he talked, Rafaella's heart pounded wildly. His cool blue eyes reminded Rafaella of Joleen's. Rafaella was overwhelmed by a sense of panic.

"It may seem I've taken advantage of you," Lawton said in an emotionless voice. "But you're far from innocent in the matter, Raffles. Far from innocent. It was . . . we both gave in to lust. Now it's over. Lucinda is back. I won't be unfaithful again. Please don't send me any more notes."

"But you . . . you talked about our future, Lawton," she pleaded. "And I *was* innocent. No man had ever had me! And what if . . . if I have a child . . . your child?"

"I used a French letter," he said. "You'll have no child. As for our future, any talk of our future, I'm sorry, Raffles. I was . . . am quite fond of you, of course. And perhaps some time in the future, we can be friends. But that's far away. We both must accept the reality that our relationship has ended."

Rafaella clung to his shoulders and tried to seduce him with wet kisses. She begged for one more chance and promised that she would be a better lover, that she would do anything he wanted.

Abruptly, as coldly as if dismissing a field hand, Lawton pried her hands loose and mounted his horse. She cursed and shouted threats as he galloped away. She knew it was stupid to act that way at so critical a moment. Her curses would hardly bring him back. But she was too angry and frightened to control her emotions.

Rafaella returned to her house in despair and went directly to bed. Though the day was mild, she huddled under two quilts, her body racked by chills that became convulsions. Her mouth was dry, and she swallowed again and again to relieve the dryness. She had no strength at all and found it difficult even to twist around on the bed.

She felt she would surely die before she ever got out of bed again. All that sustained her will to live was her hatred of Lawton. If she couldn't have him, she truly wanted to die . . . but first she would destroy him so that no one else could have him.

No, no, she mumbled to herself, she would destroy Lucinda and the child. Then Lawton would be hers. In her misery, she became convinced that she was pregnant, despite the fact that Lawton had used a contraceptive. From hour to hour, she changed her mind about bearing Lawton's child or seeking an abortion.

Her schemes for destroying Lawton and Lucinda grew imaginative, often wild, but none of them lasted more than a few minutes. When she could no longer endure her misery, she rang for Lossie. She rang a dozen times but there was no answer.

Finally she willed herself out of bed and stumbled to the hall door. She was startled by her high-pitched, feeble voice as she shouted for Lossie. Several minutes passed before Rafaella saw Bonita, a young kitchen slave, creep up the stairs.

"Where's Lossie?" Rafaella asked.

"Lossie, she done run away," the girl said. "Lossie and two others. Oh, Miss Raffles, don't look at me that way. I'm a good girl. I didn't run away. Don't hurt me like you done to Lossie, *please*, Miss Raffles."

Rafaella turned slowly, swayed once, and barely reached the bed before collapsing.

By the next day, the worst of the weakness and nausea had passed, though Rafaella still had periods when she was consumed by a flushed, weak feeling that left her short of breath. But she knew she was doomed if she gave in to this feeling. She had to act, immediately, had to . . . to do something desperate, but clever. Yet beyond ruining Lawton financially she could think of nothing.

On the very day that Hiram Cranston brought word that Joleen's husband had perhaps survived the Cuban filibustering expedition, Rafaella encountered Joleen in Natchez. Rafaella would have turned away, but Joleen would not let her.

Joleen said that Lawton had told her about the affair. She said that Lucinda was home now but still quite ill. She warned Rafaella to end the affair with her brother or suffer the consequences. She didn't define the consequences, but a miserable, frightened, and lonely Rafaella looked into Joleen's clear, imperious blue eyes and knew Joleen meant it.

"You would, wouldn't you?" Rafaella muttered. Her legs grew weak. She thought of the three hundred slaves on Joleen's plantation. Joleen was talking to her as though she were simply one more chattel, a worrisome nuisance whose usefulness was at an end and who must be disposed of. Lucinda was back, and Rafaella was to be discarded by the Deavorses.

"But you won't . . . I swear you'll pay for this, Joleen," Rafaella said. "How could you be . . . You've always hated me, from the very first. But do you think I'll let myself be ruined? I'm far from helpless."

And yet she felt very helpless, felt Joleen could just turn to people passing them in the street and tell them about her father and the word would spread. She would be ruined, disgraced, stripped of her wealth; she could be dragged to the auction block and sold.

"Nobody wants to hurt you, Rafaella," Joleen said, her voice weary and impatient, as though dealing with a slow-witted slave. "But Lawton's been . . . vulnerable. He's had a lot of problems. I know . . . I know it takes two people to . . . to have an affair, but that's over now. Lawton wants no more of this. You have your own life. You're a wealthy girl now and you . . . surely you'll want to remarry."

"I'm no girl, damn you, Joleen," Rafaella said. She felt tears in her eyes. "I'm nearly as old as you. Yes, Lawton has had me and now, like the arrogant scoundrel he is, he intends to discard me, just as he discarded that nigger, Nettie. Did he send you to finish up his dirty work? He'd never have the courage himself. He never had courage for anything. But I'll have him back, anyway . . . And I'll be a Deavors again, I swear it on my father's grave."

"No, you won't have him back," Joleen said quietly. She sighed. "I can promise you that. And if you cause any more trouble, there are ways to deal with you, Rafaella."

"Yes, to ruin me, to see me as a chattel. But there are ways to deal with *you*, Joleen. Oh, I know all about your precious husband and your disgusting abolitionist activities. I'll see you in prison for that, Joleen! And that's not all I know." She was so angry she very nearly mentioned what she knew about Joleen's sexual relationship with Lawton, but she dared not make Joleen any more dangerous an adversary. "I . . . you can't even stand to talk to me on the street, you think me so low . . . so untouchable."

"That's nonsense," Joleen said. "I think you're spoiled, arrogant, selfish and a little crazed with self-importance. As for the other, I couldn't care if you were a Hottentot or a Chinaman."

Their encounter ended on that note. Rafaella rushed home, swearing that she would have Cranston trap Joleen or forge evidence about her, that she would see the hateful bitch in prison.

She was so angry that when one of the yard slaves stepped on a rosebush that afternoon she took her riding crop to the man.

Lawton and Joleen had not been closer in years. Their constant bickering over slavery was ended at last. They were truly very dependent on each other, and since Lucinda was now bedridden, it fell on Joleen to plan and preside over the traditional Harvest Ball, which she brought off with great success.

When the hopeful news of Aaron arrived, Lawton put aside his dislike of his brother-in-law and agreed that, of course, he would do anything he could to raise the ransom money.

But raising the money was a great problem. The sum of fifty thousand dollars had been mentioned as being required to buy off all the officials that would be involved. Banks in Natchez, as everywhere else, were failing or had already failed. The Deavorses' holdings were all in land and slaves and in the cotton itself. Joleen grew frantic, desperately trying to put together enough cash. Finally, when she felt helpless and defeated, Lawton said he would do something that no Deavors had ever done: he would sell part of their land, sell part of The Columns to ransom Aaron.

Joleen knew how enormous a sacrifice this was for Lawton, but she accepted it. Once it was decided, the land was put up for sale, and it would surely be bought; but she feared, even so, that the money would arrive too late, too late for Aaron.

She was panicked about getting the money safely to Havana. Who could be trusted? Finally, she resolved that she would take it herself.

76.

Lawton was so strongly opposed to Joleen's going to Cuba with the ransom money that, even as they said good-bye in the lounge of the *Memphis*, he tried to stop her. But Joleen was adamant and insisted that she would do all right. She would be safe. After all, Juan Delsano was sending his son, Carlos, to escort her.

Lawton had wanted to go with Joleen, but it was impossible. Lucinda's condition and the requirements of the plantation made it necessary for him to remain in Natchez. Two more banks had recently failed, and Dr. Stacey said that a premature—and dangerous—delivery was quite possible. So Lawton reluctantly kissed Joleen good-bye, shook Carlos's hand and thanked him again for going with his sister, and left the boat with the Delsanos. He was both depressed and frightened.

On the docks, he told Juan that he had business on the river. As soon as they parted, he headed for Under-the-Hill. He had realized that he was not free of his lust for Rafaella but that anything was better than succumbing to her again. He would find a prostitute and indulge himself with her. Even a prostitute was better than giving in to his recurring longings for Rafaella.

Water oozed through the cracks of the wooden sidewalks Under-the-Hill. The water was putrid and slime-covered; fishheads and dead rats bobbed to the surface. Though the day was cool, the humidity on the river was stifling. A stench rose from the water and from the warm red mud on the nearby banks. Pigs rooted in the mud and fought dogs for garbage.

Hundreds of shacks and shanties stood in this huge mud flat under the bluffs that rose two hundred feet off the river. Crumbling wooden buildings on stilts lined the wooden sidewalks on one side, and on the other a jumble of barges and flatboats knocked together with the rise and fall of the river.

As Lawton picked his way along the swaying sidewalk, he thought of his talk with Cellus and Joleen and of his decision to cut his losses by abandoning the Liverpool venture. He hoped he would not regret the decision, but he had little choice.

Thank God, he had at least taken Cellus's advice to finance the spring planting through a source other than a bank. By coincidence, the day before, he had talked to W. A. Britton, an old family friend who owned a lottery and exchange brokerage. Britton, who had not yet been hurt by the panic, had mentioned that he was extending financing to some of the older families. An hour later, Britton and Lawton had agreed that the broker would lend Lawton the money for the spring, even though his rates were higher than bank rates.

It was not only the possibility of ruinously low cotton prices that made the banks hesitant to loan money to The Columns, or that Lawton was already deeply in debt. The banks themselves were short of cash. Both the Agriculture Bank and the Planter's Bank had already failed, and more bank closings seemed inevitable.

Lawton thought of the land he had sold to raise Aaron's ransom. He could have sold more land to finance the spring planting. But that would be different: to do so he would have to admit that he was incapable of maintaining his family's status and traditions. To sacrifice the family's land because he loved his sister was one thing. To sell land because of his own mismanagement was quite another. And he'd had to sell the land for Joleen at a price far lower than its true value.

But as Lawton moved deeper through Natchez-Under-the-Hill, he was distracted from his financial worries. He passed gambling dens and dim, foul taverns, where pimps and criminals and polemen threw dice, drank Monongahela whiskey, broke into fistfights at the slightest provocation, or banded together to rob or murder unwary outsiders. All his life, Lawton had heard lurid stories of this district, and he began to realize his mistake in coming here alone.

Black whores lounged on the deck of a long barge. They called to Lawton in soft, sexy voices. A skinny teenage girl licked her lips and made sucking sounds. Another opened her dirty red dress and fondled her breasts. It was just one of many whore-barges where black and mulatto women offered themselves and bared their bodies.

A drunken man staggered toward Lawton and cursed him. Lawton stepped back and nearly fell into the water. A few steps farther along, he saw two black men fighting with knives, and in the shadows between two stilt-taverns he saw the shine of steel and heard a scream that ended so abruptly he caught his breath. He stopped. He felt sick. His desire had long since fled. What was he doing here? He glanced around. The sun was setting. Ominous shadows moved all around. He would be fortunate if his throat weren't slit.

Lawton turned and hurried back toward the docks. These people were more desperate than ever in these hard times. He'd heard tales about them falling on any-one with a coin, a watch, or a gold tooth. He'd heard that in recent months men would commit murder for the price of a bottle of whiskey.

Lawton finally reached the docks. He hired a carriage, anxious to reach the Parker House and take a long, hot bath.

77.

On a raw, wet afternoon in early December, Rafaella and Hiram Cranston drove back to Natchez after talk-ing with Ferrell Shanks, the madhouse warden, who wanted to buy some of Rafaella's land. Normally Rafaella would have left the matter to Cranston or one of her bankers, but she was so miserably depressed that she felt she had to get out of the house.

First, Cranston had brought news that Lawton was financing his spring planting through a broker who could not be bribed. Then she learned that Lucinda had given birth to twins!

A strong wind slapped the leather curtains against the side of the carriage. Rafaella shivered in her silk dress and light cape. Cranston was smoking a nasty black cigar, and its smell turned her stomach.

At her demand, he discarded the cigar. But he rattled on with his dull, self-important talk. She glanced at the ugly little eyes. How she hated Cranston! He was vulgar and provincial and stupid. And yet he was her constant companion. There was no one in her life but her slaves, Cranston, and a few recent, boorish suitors. She hated Cranston and those suitors! She hated all men! They all betrayed and hurt her. Her father. Her husband. And now Lawton.

Yet despite her hatred, she loved Lawton as much as she loved her father. And in the two or three hours that she was able to sleep each night, she dreamed constantly of them both. The dreams were always memories. Often she would dream of a scene with Lawton, but the face would be her father's. Or she would dream of her father, but Lawton would be there instead.

The most frequent dream the past few nights was the incident in her locked bedroom with her father at Frannie's that day. But the man was usually Lawton and not her father. Rafaella would wake from the dream shivering and perspiring, and she would cry as she waited for the dawn. She had very nearly won her father that time. If only she had been bolder . . . Again and again during her lonely hours in bed, her thoughts slipped back to that scene, and she remembered the odd, exciting feeling, a kind of triumphant sexual excitement, which she had not known before or since.

She might hate Lawton to sickness, but she still loved him desperately. He was hers, dammit! She had lost her father but she must never lose Lawton! Never! Lawton had ignored her recent notes, but he was badly mistaken if he thought he would live many more days without her. She would . . .

Fighting a wave of nausea, Rafaella put a hand to her temples. They were throbbing. She had been ill constantly of late. She talked to herself, and the slaves whispered among themselves and avoided her. And now three had run away.

Now that Lucinda had given Lawton children, he would feel even more that he could abandon her, Rafaella. In his stupid blindness to his real feelings, he still thought her the same as Nettie!

But all those nights in the carriage . . . that was how he really felt about her! She should never have given herself to Lawton! That was her mistake. If she could have him alone again, she would rekindle his hopeless weakness, his obsession. Her mistake was in not going far enough in their erotic games. She had a vivid imagination. She would devise even more bizarre games that would fascinate Lawton, bind him to her, show him that he was the chattel, the inferior one, not she, not Rafaella.

Rafaella sniffled and tucked her arms tightly against her chest. At times it all seemed so hopeless. She didn't doubt that in time she could enslave Lawton once more. But she had to act quickly. Joleen had run off to Cuba before Cranston could trap her. At least, she was no threat for now. And Lucinda had nearly died in childbirth. She was still quite ill. Obviously Lawton had had no sex with her. Yes, she would force Lawton to see her again, no matter what threat or deceit she had to use. When he came to her—and it would be to her house—she would give him one final chance. She would wear the beautiful white silk wedding dress she had refused to wear for Wyman. It would be their wedding day.

She would be so desirable, so lovely, so imaginative that Lawton would not be able to resist her. She would not lose Lawton, as she had her father! She would win by using his obsession to show him who was the slave . . .

And if he again rejected her because of her father, she would have him destroyed, so help her! And his wife—and children! He would have one final chance to show his love and worship, or she would send him to hell! But how could she ever kill Lawton? Unless she killed herself also. She could not live without him. The others, yes, but not Lawton.

Cranston was bragging of his cleverness in bargaining with Shanks. Cranston had been clever, it was true, and he had run the price up. Shanks was desperate to have the land quickly but seemed to lack the money. He was obviously willing to do anything to get that land.

With the silhouette of the brick madhouse on the grey horizon and the howls of the inmates on the rising wind, Shanks had explained that he was using his charges to work his private cotton acreage, so the acreage had to be adjacent to the madhouse. Of course, he was quick to explain, this was only to provide the inmates with meaningful work, not for profit. Rafaella dismissed his explanation. She recognized greed as quickly as anyone, but it was no concern of hers. Shanks finally said he needed to think the matter over and that he would get in touch with them.

Rafaella squirmed in the seat and tried to stop shivering. She thought of the howls. She could not have Lawton killed, not ever. But if he rejected his final chance, she could give Shanks the land . . . and have Lawton secretly committed to the madhouse!

The thought excited her. Only she would know he was there! She wouldn't let him out until he agreed to everything she demanded. He would be tainted then, weak, his spirit broken. He would never again be able to think her inferior and untouchable; not a man who had been in the madhouse.

And if Lawton were there, she could ride out and tell Lucinda that she and Lawton were living together. Rafaella smiled at the thought. Lawton would have his one last chance to be enslaved in a more personal way, though. Rafaella twisted around on the seat. She closed her eyes . . . She and Lawton were in the bedroom at Frannie's . . .

Her heart began to thump. Blood rushed to her head. She squeezed her arms against her body, her thighs against each other, as she imagined each detail, spoke each word to herself.

"I won't stop," she would say to Lawton. "I want all this settled now. I swear I won't spend another night in this house alone. Tell me, would it have been different if I had been real nice to you? I did everything else for you, didn't I? If you had asked me, I'd have done that, too . . ."

Minutes passed. Finally Lawton was between her thighs . . .

". . . After this, Daddy, you'll be mine, won't you? We'll stay together always, just us; we'll belong together, won't we? No one will ever be able to come between us, Daddy . . ."

78.

Joleen and Carlos stood on the deck as the *Alcazar* sailed through the narrow entrance into Havana harbor. It was nearly nine in the evening. Joleen was consumed with fear and the recurring image of the garrote. To banish the image, she tried to think of something else, anything else—Lawton, Lucinda's pregnancy, even Rafaella. She also recalled her encounter with Wyman Ridgeway in a New Orleans park a few days earlier. She had expressed her anger at the man for wounding Lawton, but Ridgeway's appearance was so appalling and his manner so changed that she almost felt compassion.

Ridgeway seemed to have aged years since she had last seen him. His hair was speckled with grey. There were deep lines under his eyes. Worst of all, he bore a deep red scar along his cheek. And the tip of his right ear had been cut off!

Her anger vented, Joleen would have left him immediately, but he had begged her to stay a minute longer. He had said he was sorry for the suffering he had caused Lawton. He had asked about Lawton and Lucinda in a quiet, weary voice, then added that a recent Natchez visitor had mentioned that Lucinda would soon give birth.

"Yes, the baby is due soon, Mr. Ridgeway," Joleen had said. "Unfortunately, it's been a very difficult pregnancy. Other than that my family is fine. No, no, actually, your wife has caused no end of trouble, and trouble is the last thing Lucinda needs in her weakened condition."

"Raffles?" Ridgeway had asked. "She is . . . her actions endanger Mrs. Deavors and the baby? Before leaving, I warned her to end her vendetta."

"Then your warning did no good, sir," Joleen said.

His voice chilled Joleen: "You may be sure, Mrs. Clauson, that my child bride will cause no more trouble for your family. Good day."

He had turned and left abruptly.

Carlos was chattering about the sights of Havana. He pointed out the Morro lighthouse to their left and behind it the grey-white walls of El Castillo del Morro and the Cabañas fortress. On the right, loomed another fortress, La Punta.

"And there, on the bay side of the city, is the oldest of the forts, La Fuerza," Carlos was saying. "And look, up there on the hills, you can see other forts, Príncipe and Atarés. Then soon you'll see the Chorrera fort, and there is also San Lázaro . . ."

Joleen knew Carlos was only trying to divert her from her worries, but already she was afraid of Havana, this foreign city filled with ominous-looking forts. A sudden splashing startled her. She turned to see a boat pulling a heavy chain across the harbor entrance. She tensed as a cannon went off.

"*El cañonazo*," Carlos said. "Don't be alarmed, Joleen. Each night at nine the harbor is secured by the chain, and a cannon signals that the port is closed until morning."

Joleen felt trapped now. She tried to assure herself that the chain was indeed routine. At least their ship was docking. There were only formalities with the police and customs and then . . .

And then what? she asked herself miserably.

Carlos and his cousin Hermano hurried Joleen from the customs shed to a waiting carriage. It was necessary to declare the purpose of her visit, and the officials had been rude, almost threatening, when they learned of her reason for coming. For several minutes she feared they would not let her stay. But a few gold pieces smoothed the matter over.

Hermano had had no word of Aaron for two days, he confessed. As they drove through the cluttered docks, Joleen sensed that he knew more than he was saying. Or that Carlos was not telling her everything, for Hermano spoke no English.

They had left the port area and were driving along the Prado, the principal avenue that led to the heart of Havana. Normally Joleen would have been impressed by the gracious buildings of West Indian white coral and limestone, but her only thoughts were of the endless night ahead. Despite her pleas, Hermano insisted that it was unthinkable to disturb the Governor at this hour.

"And Hermano assures me that executions are never held at night," Carlos was saying as they drove through a square fronted by government buildings. "Please, Joleen, calm yourself. My cousins have a fine chef and a good wine cellar. You must give in to their hospitality, for form's sake if not for your own good."

But Joleen did not hear the rest of his sentence. As the carriage halted at a busy intersection, she saw several poles to her right. The light was dim. She could not quite make out the bulges on the top of each pole. Surely they weren't human heads!

"Carlos," she whispered. "Oh, Carlos . . ."

Hermano spoke sharply. Carlos grabbed for Joleen's arm, but she twisted away and stumbled across the cobblestones.

She stopped and screamed.

On the last pole was a head that looked like Aaron's!

79.

Lawton was watching his slaves chop cotton plants when Rafaella's note arrived. It could not have come at a worse time. The day before, Lucinda had suffered a relapse.

"Damn her!" he said. She had written that if he did not come to her Natchez home, she would ride out to The Columns and "confront Lucinda with all the sordid details of our relationship, including our little games about Joleen."

Such a shock might kill Lucinda! Why in hell hadn't he found the strength to deal with Rafaella? He had been stupid to think she would give up so easily. She was capable of anything. But this encounter would be different.

A young slave girl answered the door and led Lawton to an upstairs parlor. Rafaella was sitting on a dark blue couch. She was beautiful in a white silk dress.

"Hello, darling," she said. She stood up. "Thank you for coming. I must apologize for my terrible note. I could never do anything like that to hurt you."

"Dammit, Raffles, I believe you're capable of doing anything," he said. "That's why I'm here. I intend to end the affair today, dammit!"

"Please, Lawton, pour us some champagne," she said.

She indicated a silver ice bucket. Lawton poured two glasses. He tried to collect his thoughts and control his anger. His fear for Lucinda's health gave him the determination to do whatever was necessary, no matter what! But except for threatening to expose her father's past, he could not decide what to do.

They sipped champagne and did not talk for a minute.

Rafaella was shadowed by the candlelight. She had never looked lovelier. Her full, pale breasts strained against the delicate silk of her low-cut bodice. The milky white silk accentuated her dark hair and eyes. The eyes looked different, though he didn't know exactly how. They were . . . almost hypnotic, as if she were a bird of prey, able to hypnotize its game.

Lawton drained his champagne and put the glass down. He had to get hold of himself, be adamant, ruthless!

"Shall we sit down?" she asked. "Help yourself to another glass of champagne."

"No, dammit," he said. "No more champagne, thank you. And I'll remain standing. Raffles, I won't have my future and that of my family constantly jeopardized by your threats. I made a mistake in . . . in becoming involved with you, promising you . . . some future with me. But that's all finished! I swear to God, this is the last time I'll see you! And don't underestimate my determination."

Rafaella stepped toward Lawton and silenced him with a finger against his lips. The smile twisted on the corners of her lips, and the lips twitched several times. She had moved out of the shadows. Lawton was startled by the deep lines beneath her eyes. And the eyes . . . They were wide, frightening, something beyond mere black.

"Oh, we'll resolve everything today," she said. "Your future will be settled in this very room, darling, I promise you that. This is my wedding dress. I didn't wear the dress when I married Wyman. That wasn't my real wedding. Daddy had this dress made for me. And once . . . I put it on for him. Do you like my wedding dress, Lawton?"

"It's very pretty, Raffles," he said. "But dammit, it has nothing to do with us. I'm only here to end this affair! And I won't be distracted. Can't you understand? I'll do anything to protect Lucinda. Please stop this nonsense."

Again, her finger touched his lips. He sucked in his breath and smelled the familiar, sweet perfume. Rafaella closed her eyes a moment, and when she opened them, they held a faraway look.

"I won't stop," she said suddenly. "I want all this settled now. I swear I won't spend another night in this house. Tell me, would it have been different if I had been real nice to you? I did everything else for you, didn't I? If you had asked me, I'd have done that, too. I'd have done anything for you. I let you watch me undress, let you watch me bathe; I posed for you. Though lately I haven't, have I? Is that it? Do you want me to undress for you? Right now? I believe I can please you better than that woman!"

Lawton was puzzled. Her words made no sense at all. But she was offering herself to him again. That was obvious. He decided it was just another of her games.

"Spare yourself the trouble," he said. "Keep your clothes on. Your promises of sex won't—"

"No, I expect I've failed you," she said, as though he hadn't spoken. Her voice was high-pitched. He realized she was nearly hysterical. "If you had to turn to someone like Frannie, I failed you miserably. If I'd been bolder about undressing and posing and all, I could have bound you to me. None of this would have happened. Lock the door, and I'll make it up to you. I'll get undressed. And pose . . . in all kinds of ways. And you can . . . touch me . . . and all. . ."

"What in hell are you talking about?" he shouted. "Frannie? Will you shut up a goddamn minute and stop trying to seduce me?"

Her head snapped. She shuddered. "What? Oh, Lawton . . . You *are* Lawton. Of course . . . It will be so much easier if you tell me that you love me, that we'll always be together, without her . . . because we will, I swear it, darling. Here or in hell together. There *is* a hell for you, Lawton . . . or paradise here with me. On our wedding day. And I've got Daddy's best suit all laid out for you."

"Rafaella, what in hell's wrong with you?" he asked. "What kind of game is this? Talkin' about hell. And wedding days!"

Lawton was terribly uneasy. This was no game. Her voice, her eyes, her words. She talked as if she were losing her mind. He was becoming desperate. He turned toward the door.

Rafaella ran past him. She turned the key in the lock, shutting them in her upstairs parlor, seized the key, and tucked it into her bodice.

Her eyes were wild with a glowing, luminous excitement. She lifted her skirt to unfasten her stockings.

"I love you," she said. "And I want to do everything for you."

"Dammit, no!" he shouted. "So help me, I'll kick the door in if I have to!"

"Oh, yes, I will! I can't stand to have you . . . prefer *her*." Rafaella kicked off pink satin slippers and unrolled her long white silk stockings. As he stared, she lifted her full, pleated silk skirt and bared her knees. Her face was flushed, but the skin of her legs was pale, unblemished, delicate.

Suddenly Lawton was flooded with an excitement beyond control. His heart was pounding. He turned to the door, fought with the handle. It was securely locked.

Rafaella moved toward him. Desperately, he reached out to grab the key from her, as she turned round and round in a display of legs and silk petticoats. She stopped suddenly and tugged open her bodice. The key fell to the floor, and Lawton's hands were full of her heavy breasts.

"Oh, yes, please, touch me . . . kiss me . . . oh, tell me I'm beautiful. Tell me I'm prettier than she is . . . that we'll always be together."

Before he could speak, she pulled away and fumbled at the hooks that held her petticoats to the cinched waist of her corsets. Her breasts swung free and Lawton stared at them. He could not look away. He was fascinated, fevered, sick with guilt and desire. He knew by now that he would be taking advantage of a deranged woman, but he could not help himself.

Lacy, filmy silken sashes and slips dangled for a moment on Rafaella's round, white hips, then slid to the floor. She was naked.

"See . . . all for you. Do I please you? You'll have to show me how. You'll have to teach me what you want me to do . . . what I need to do to make you happy. I'll do anything you want . . . anything."

Her voice was a whisper, sibilant and sinister. There was not a drop of innocence in her crazed words or in her beautiful, twisted smile. Lawton groaned. He was reeling with desire and guilt; he wanted to die and he wanted to touch her. He knew, finally and terribly, how far his obsession with Rafaella had gone. It was out of all control. His fingers ached to touch her skin. His arms tingled with longing to hold her. He was sexually excited in a way that he had never been before.

"What are you waiting for?" she asked. "Isn't this what you wanted? Isn't this what you raised me for? Don't I please you anymore? I always used to please you. You brought me up to please you, didn't you? What's the matter? You look funny. Why are you turning away from me?"

Lawton scrambled on the floor for the key. He felt waves of dizziness, felt perhaps he would black out.

"You can't mean to leave me!" she said. "You can't leave me now. I love you . . . you love me. I can't live without you. I won't! Give in to your obsession . . . so I can be gentle. Don't force me to send you to hell."

She ran over to the kneeling Lawton and spread her naked body over his clothed one, her legs on either side of his back, her arms and hands clinging to him, her breasts and belly spread against his back.

He felt her soft weight with a sickening pleasure. She squirmed. He tried to rise, and she fell alongside him, grabbing at him with astonishing strength. Her mouth fell open, twitching at the corners, and her eyes were luminous and frenzied. He could not help but stare at the soft planes of her body, the curves, the silken mound of her stomach, and the perfect triangle beneath, where her legs joined the core of her sex. Her skin shone with a fine, transparent beauty. He had to touch it. His fingers trembled, reached out, stroked her torso to the swell of her hip.

Rafaella whimpered. "Yes! Yes . . . I want you to. I always knew you would be the first man to make love to me. And I want it now . . . Oh, no, no, you don't want to make love, you want to play games . . . no . . . oh, please, please kiss me." She wriggled under him, and his fingers felt the satiny resilience of her belly, then felt the softness below.

"Kiss me there . . . but first tell me that you want me more than her. Tell me that you belong to me . . . only me . . . that you're the chattel, not me."

"I want you more than her," he heard himself whisper. His eyes were shut against what he felt himself about to do. "Yes . . . I belong to you. For always."

"Kiss me! And look into my face! Know it's me . . . your baby, who always loved you best."

Desperately he forced himself to open his eyes, to look into her face, even as his lips touched her vagina.

"After this, Daddy, you'll be mine, won't you? We'll stay together always, just us; we'll belong together, won't we? No one will ever be able to come between us, Daddy. And we'll destroy her, together, Daddy."

Lawton stared into Rafaella's face, and what he saw stopped his heart.

"No! No!" he muttered as he fought to free his face from the vise of her thighs. He wrenched her thighs apart and crawled away. He found the key and scrambled to the door.

Rafaella was crawling after him. She clutched his leg as he unlocked the door.

"You are mine!" she crooned, her face distorted. "You belong to . . . you . . . chattel . . . not me . . . beg me . . . Daddy . . . know what . . . means to be . . .

alone . . . tainted . . . frightened . . . destroy her . . .
babies . . . I . . . free you . . . be mine . . . no one else
. . . want you . . . broken . . ."

Lawton finally kicked free of her hands and lurched
from the room. His legs could barely carry him from
the house. He was nauseous with the horror, the excitement, the guilt, the insane threats.

At the sidewalk, he bumped against two men standing by the gate, and as he muttered apologies and
stumbled away, he looked into one of the men's tiny,
dark eyes.

80.

Joleen was under sedation the next morning when
they informed her that it was Charlie Duffy's head on
the pole. Aaron was still alive, but an execution was
scheduled for that very morning. Joleen drank black
coffee, took a cold bath, and paced her room, trying
to overcome the effects of the medicine. Word had
already been sent to the Governor that the ransom
money had arrived. He had replied that Joleen would
be received in the warden's office of the prison at ten.

Joleen's nerves were near the snapping point, despite
the sedation. Each minute seemed an hour. And it was
only half past eight. Everything oppressed and offended
her in this hot, lush, alien city: the curious dress and
customs, the elaborate courtesy that masked cruelty,
the grim forts. And most of all the strange language
that totally excluded her and made her feel that she
and Aaron were being discussed, that terrible things
were being said to her face. And second by second,
minute by minute, there was the fear that, despite
everything, there might be a blunder or an act of
treachery, that she might pay the ransom and be given
Aaron's bloody head in return.

Joleen was seated in the carriage ten minutes before

it was time to leave. Finally, Carlos and Hermano joined her. The hacienda gates opened. They drove out into the street. Joleen huddled in the corner, her hands gripping the bag that contained the money. She had concealed a small pistol in her dress. She vowed that if the Governor did not deliver Aaron to her un-harmed, she would kill the man on the spot.

The massive prison gates slammed shut behind the carriage. They drove along a low arcade filled with menacing shadows and faint mutterings in Spanish. There was a shout somewhere ahead, a scream. Joleen glanced around. What if this were some kind of trap, to get the money? What if Aaron were dead? She might never leave this terrible place. She forced herself to be rational. After all, she was with Carlos and Hermano.

The arcade curved sharply, and they drove around a huge courtyard surrounded by grey stone walls and barred windows. Suddenly, a tableau loomed up: wooden stools, wooden poles, iron collars and screws . . . the garrote!

Joleen shuddered and looked away.

The carriage stopped in front of a low arched door. Carlos helped Joleen out. They climbed steep stairs and passed two ominous-looking soldiers with rifles and bayonets. They entered a cool, low-ceilinged room that contained a broad desk, two high-back wooden chairs, and a rack of rifles.

Hermano talked to an officer. The man went into another room. He came back and demanded the money. Joleen hesitated. Reluctantly, at Carlos's insistence, she handed it over.

The officer disappeared again. Minutes passed. There was an unreal silence in the prison. Joleen paced the room, sat down, stood up.

She was sitting down again when the door opened. Aaron stood there, an emaciated, haunted-looking man with hideous wounds at his ankles and wrists. Joleen choked back a sob. She bolted across the room and hugged Aaron. He gasped and collapsed in her arms.

81.

Six whiskeys in two taverns had soothed some of the horror, guilt, and fear Lawton felt after his visits to Rafaella and Nettie, but he could not erase the images of Rafaella's crazed face or the mirror-image face of the boy Nettie insisted "will grow up here as Randall Deavors."

Lawton had found Nettie in a small wooden house at the edge of town, where she took in sewing and laundry. He felt no nostalgia or longing for Nettie as he looked at her white features, her large breasts pressing against the muslin dress. He felt only guilt and discomfort.

She had been a field hand on The Columns. He had hardly known her at the time she seduced him. He never saw her again. He went away to school, and when his parents learned what had happened, they gave Nettie her freedom and some money on the promise that she never return to Natchez.

"But I don't feel bound to no oath like that," she had said as they sat in her parlor. "Didn't have no choice. And I done spent all the money. I come back, been waitin' for you to know I'm here . . . was 'bout to let you know. Not for me, it's for Randall. He don't have to grow up a free nigger. He ought to be white; got lots more white blood than nigger. He's a Deavors . . . and I intends to see he lives here like a Deavors."

Lawton had tried to reason with Nettie, but reason was impossible. There had never been the slightest reason in any of it; certainly his taking her that day by the creek was no act of reason, nor was his running away to school instead of facing what he had done. He had offered her more money, an annuity, and said he would see that the boy went to fine schools, so long as they left Natchez. Their talk was turning into a bitter argument when Lawton heard a sound and looked around.

He had stared into a face that could have been his at that age . . .

In the tavern, Lawton gulped whiskey and glanced around the noisy, smoke-filled room. Two men were sitting at a table across from him. One of them had small, dark eyes, eyes that disturbed Lawton. Hadn't he seen the man before? Yes, as he was leaving Rafaella's, he remembered.

For a moment he wondered if he had been followed. He shrugged and turned back to the bar. He shouldn't imagine things. He had enough to worry about as it was. He drank more whiskey.

Once more, he saw the boy's face as he had stood there in the door, framed in sunlight. There was no hint that he was Negro, nothing in his pale face, his blue eyes, his straight blonde hair to indicate that he wasn't . . . pure.

"Randall, come here," Nettie had said.

The boy did not move. Nor did his eyes leave Lawton's eyes.

"You want to pick him up?" Nettie asked.

"I . . . no . . . Hello, Randall."

Randall didn't say anything. He stuck a finger in his mouth.

"Come on, say hello, Randall," Nettie coaxed. "Give him a kiss, Randall."

Lawton's heart pounded. He wanted to hold the boy, yet the thought of being kissed disturbed him. This was his son, his first-born . . . but he could never be a Deavors, never bear the Deavors name. He must be taken care of, given adequate funds for his education. He should have a fine education, and if he wished, live as a white man. But not in Natchez . . . never in Natchez . . . never as Randall Deavors.

And still the blue eyes held him. He had to . . . to hold the boy, at least, just one time. He stood up. Randall stepped backward. He glanced at his mother.

"He's not goin' to hurt you, honey," Nettie said. "This here's your daddy, the one I been tellin' you 'bout, and now that he's seen you, he's goin' to be your daddy for real."

A chill shot up Lawton's spine. No, no, he wanted to cry out. He would insist they leave town, would force them out if necessary.

Randall took his finger from his mouth. "Papa?" he asked.

Lawton moved toward the boy. Randall burst into tears and fled into his mother's arms.

"He won't hurt you none," Nettie said. "He's your daddy. He goin' to take care of you."

Lawton sank back into the chair. Randall wouldn't come near him, and though he wanted to hold Randall, he didn't know how he would respond to a kiss.

He and Nettie began to talk. Again Lawton tried to explain why the boy could never live in Natchez as Randall Deavors. As they argued, Randall began to cry.

Nothing was resolved. Lawton finally stood up. He mumbled that they would have to leave; then he would see Randall well taken care of. Nettie grew bitter. Randall cried louder. Lawton stepped toward the door. He paused, looked over his shoulder. He bent down and kissed Randall's cheek, then walked out.

As Lawton drank whiskey in another tavern, images floated in his hazy thoughts: Rafaella's face, Randall's face, the tiny, red faces of his infant son and daughter. He felt such sorrow, such guilt, such happiness, such fear. Tears formed in his eyes. He sipped whiskey. Several drops fell over his chin. Drinking any more is stupid, he told himself. He must return to The Columns. He was worried about Lucinda and anxious to see the twins.

But he finished his drink. He felt wretched, and he had resolved nothing with either Rafaella or Nettie. As for Nettie and the boy, he wasn't sure what he would do, though it would be simple enough to force two free Negroes out of town.

Rafaella had indeed lost her mind. She was danger-ous—and yet all the whiskey in the county couldn't hide the memory of how close he had come to yielding to his obsession with her. Lawton did not doubt that she would follow up on her threat about Lucinda and the twins. The thought put him into a rage. He would talk to his lawyer! He would see the sheriff! The girl was a deadly menace. People were sent to jail for making the kind of threats she had made.

Lawton shoved himself away from the bar. He stopped. He thought he saw those same two men on the other side of the bar, but in the dim light and thick smoke he could not be sure. It hardly mattered. He would soon be on his way back to The Columns.

A mist was falling. He walked two blocks, savoring the sting of rain even though he was cold. The street was deserted.

The footsteps were almost at his back before he realized what the sound was. He stopped and looked around.

He saw the dark, close-set eyes at the same instant he was smashed to the ground.

Lawton was aware of being carried through the rain. Hands were holding him, strong hands that hurt him. His eyes wouldn't focus. He tried to speak but didn't think any words came out. His head ached. He realized he had vomited. He tasted blood.

He had nearly lapsed back into unconsciousness when he heard a door creak open. The smells of vomit, ammonia, and urine stung his nostrils. He shuddered and blinked back his vision, and in the same moment he was fighting free of the hands.

He stumbled to his feet. He was in a long, dim hall. Groans and sounds of crying came from the darkness at the back of the hall. The two white men he had seen earlier, along with four Negroes, stood around him.

"See, I warned you he'd be violent," the pig-eyed man said. "He'll fight like hell and make up any wild story, just like he did earlier when he attacked his own baby."

"Get him down to the cellar," the other white man said. "If he gives you any trouble, put him under the pump, give him an emetic, and shackle him."

Lawton heard the words but did not believe this was really happening. The four black men were moving in on him.

"Dammit, I'm Lawton Deavors!" he said. "Keep your hands off me!"

"This afternoon he was Governor McNutt," the pig-eyed man said and laughed.

"I *am* Lawton Deavors and you'll pay . . ."

Lawton was able to knock the first Negro away, but he was no match for the others. Fighting, screaming, retching against the smells, he was carried down the hall into a world of crying and screaming, of drooling, grinning, toothless faces that stared from iron cages and cells.

82.

Lucinda awoke from a fretful sleep. Her first thought was of the babies. She glanced over at the crib. The twins were both asleep. She looked at the clock; it was nearly midnight.

"Has Lawton come back?" she asked Rubella, who sat beside the bed.

"Not yet," Rubella said. "Carriage stoppin' out front. Can't make out who it is."

For a moment Lucinda thought it was Lawton. Then she heard voices down the hall. She didn't recognize them and couldn't understand what was being said, but one of the speakers was a woman. The voices were coming nearer. Blood rushed to her temples. She wasn't allowed any visitors. And who would call at this time of night?

The door flew open. Rafaella and a tall man with small black eyes stood there, arguing with Beatrice, who was trying to keep them out of the room.

"You can't go in there," Beatrice said. "Miss 'Cinda, doctor say she too sick to be disturbed."

"Get out of my way, nigger," Rafaella said. "Lucinda, I want to talk to you. Our situation with Lawton must be settled . . . and Lawton insists that I be the one to discuss it with you."

"Lawton?" Lucinda asked. Her face was hot. "What about Lawton? Please, Raffles, I fear I lack the strength for this."

"Then *find* the strength!" Rafaella cried. Her eyes were wild, her cheeks scarlet. "Because unless you do, I promise you'll never see Lawton again. I own him! He belongs to me now. I want you to know that! He's the chattel now, not me. I'll never take abuse from the Deavorses again. Lawton and I . . . We're living together."

Lucinda could not speak. She could barely breathe. One of the babies awoke and started to cry. The crying woke the other.

"Lawton wants only me!" Rafaella said. "Not you, Frannie! Only I can save him! Go away, Lucinda! Take your damn babies! They'll never inherit The Columns! I . . . He always loved me best."

There was a sound in the hall. Cellus ran into the room. "Miss 'Cinda!" he said. "You, Rubella, go find Dr. Stacey. And you, Miss Raffles, you and that man leave. Miss 'Cinda, she too sick to see anybody."

"I pay no attention to what niggers tell me," Rafaella said. "I'll soon be your mistress, Cellus. Remember that. I want to talk to Lucinda and I will. Why, your babies are crying, Lucinda. What kind of mother are you?" She walked toward the crib. "If you don't want them, leave them. We'll see that they're taken care of, Lucinda . . . if you go away now."

Lucinda shrank back against the pillows. Her body ached with fever. She gasped for breath. Her throat was dry. She had difficulty swallowing.

"I won't tell you again," Cellus said, moving closer to Rafaella. "You and that man, you leave right now!"

"Oh, I want to hold these bastards of Lucinda's," Rafaella said. "Mr. Cranston, discipline that arrogant nigger."

Cellus grabbed Rafaella's wrist with his left hand and swung her away from the crib and out the door. Cranston hit Cellus in the face, but Cellus wrapped his arm around Cranston's waist, lifted him up, and hurled him across the hall. Cranston hit the far wall and slid to the floor.

The door closed. Beatrice was mumbling prayers and fanning Lucinda. The twins were crying fretfully. Lucinda's small reserve of strength began to fail her. She groaned with her pain and fever.

She was barely conscious when Dr. Stacey reached her.

Lawton came awake violently and stifled a scream. All his senses rebelled. His legs were fettered with iron rings. His ankles ached. The stench of vomit, urine, and excrement made him gag; the overpowering smell brought tears to his eyes. A score of chained, wild-eyed men hovered about him.

Lawton glanced around frantically, trying to calm his terror, to organize his thoughts. He dared not rebel or threaten the keepers again. Three times since he'd been thrown into this dungeon he had tried to fight his way out, screaming curses, and each time he had been held under a pump of freezing water until he nearly drowned, then force-fed calomel and jalap, emetics that violently drained his body as though he had a virulent form of cholera.

The first night, he had feared the madmen would attack him and tear him to pieces. He crouched on his filthy straw, fighting away the sleep that his brutalized body demanded. Then he came to realize, with even sharper horror, that there was no violence in those pathetic, half-dead eyes. The creatures lacked the will for violence. Their minds were gone, their spirits broken.

He had tried to convince himself that help would come. They couldn't leave him here forever. Whoever had done it couldn't . . . Whoever . . . In his heart Lawton realized that only Rafaella could be responsible for a deed such as this, but he couldn't stomach the thought.

When his mind turned to Lucinda, so fragile after her confinement, and to the helpless newborn babies, he was driven to frenzy. What would Lucinda think of his absence? She needed him so much! What if Rafaella went to The Columns? The shock might kill Lucinda.

He tried not to think of Lucinda at all, fearing utter madness would come over him. He lay on his filthy straw pallet, enduring the pain and stench and the convulsions that the emetics had caused. He tried to plot some escape. By the second night he began to lose hope. It was cold, and all the inmates shivered in their rags.

"A fire, please give us some fire!" an emaciated spectre pleaded with one of the black keepers.

"What you need fire for?" the keeper asked. "What does a crazy man need with fire? You hot enough with your madness!"

Lawton couldn't keep down the gruel that arrived twice a day in filthy bowls. He began to lose strength and to spend more time on his straw pallet. He had fits of crying that he couldn't control. He drank too much water when he had the chance and presently lost all control of his bladder. He slept in fits and had terrible nightmares. Time took on odd new dimensions. Hours were weeks, then months. When he thought of Rafaella, he went cold with hatred. Rafaella and that pig-eyed man. Lawton had never realized he was capable of such hatred. With all his feeble strength, he hated and ached to punish her when he was freed.

When he was freed . . . He huddled in the corner to relieve himself, now a painful act. His scalded brain seethed with desperate plans for escape. But, as always, he ended up collapsed on his pallet, shivering, crying, his hope gone.

On the fourth day, the warden came to his cell. Lawton listened as the man told the inmates that he wanted to provide them with meaningful work, to give them the chance to get outside for a time each day. The warden instructed the keepers to attach iron bars to the fetters and herd the men outside.

Lawton hobbled over to the warden. He tried to remain calm as he talked to the man, tried to sound reasonable, persuasive, as he begged the man to send a note out to The Columns, promised that there would be an immediate response, that the man would be amply rewarded.

"So you're one of the Deavorses again, are you?" the warden asked. "And tomorrow you'll be askin' me to send a message to the capital, I suppose, 'cause then you'll be Governor McNutt."

Lawton began to shake. "I *am* Lawton Deavors!" he screamed. He reached out for the man, but a black keeper quickly shoved him away.

The threat of the pump and the emetics quickly ended his rebellion. He let himself be herded out behind the madhouse with the other men. He knew he lacked the strength for real work, but anything was better than being confined. He was assigned the task of chopping down cotton plants. His hands blistered, and the blisters split. The air was raw and wet and smelled of sulphur. Lawton constantly glanced around for some means of escape. But he could hardly drag himself along with the weight of the iron bars. Two black men on horseback rode along the cotton rows, huge bullwhips curled in their hands.

"You the sorriest field hand I ever seen," one of the keepers shouted at Lawton. He had been working for two hours. "I'm goin' to teach you how to work a cotton field, you hear me!"

The man lashed Lawton's back. With his last strength, Lawton grabbed the whip and pulled the startled man from his horse. Only his fetters kept him from choking the man before the other keeper pulled him off.

He fought desperately as he was dragged to the pump.

83.

Rafaella sat in a mound of silk dresses on the floor of her bedroom. She had taken all her clothes out of the closets as soon as she had decided she must flee Natchez immediately. Now, two hours later, she huddled in the tangle of rich fabrics, shivering and so flushed and weak that it took an act of will to stand up.

No, she told herself, she must change her plans. She could never leave Natchez! And she must free Lawton! He had suffered enough, surely. If she left him in the madhouse any longer, he might never recover.

She stumbled about the room, knocking down dresses that slid to the floor, only to be trampled on. She mumbled to herself about Lawton, about her father, about her new plan. She would not leave, but people would think she was leaving. Then they wouldn't blame her or punish her when Lawton was freed. She would get Hiram Cranston out of town. How she loathed that pig-eyed cretin! Since putting Lawton into the madhouse, Cranston had demanded more and more money. And he had assumed an air of such confidence and intimacy that she knew he would soon approach her sexually. And he'd had the audacity to mention that she was acting strangely.

She would rid herself of Cranston. She would promise him a substantial sum of money to go away, and she would hasten his departure by saying that Wyman would soon return and take his blade to Cranston. As for Shanks, he might as well howl at the wind as accuse her. Without Cranston, there was no one to back up his accusations.

So she would insist that Shanks free Lawton, and the

man would have no choice, really. Lawton would suspect she had a part in what had happened to him, of course, and he would be furious when he learned that she had gone to The Columns and confronted Lucinda. But he would be weak and lack the will to do anything. Particularly if he thought she was leaving town.

She kicked aside a yellow silk dress and wiped perspiration from her face. She had made a mistake in confining Lawton. Oh, she was glad to have him punished, to have him learn what it meant to be helpless, to be thought inferior, to be tainted. But she had come to realize he would never be really tainted . . . not him . . . not a Deavors. He would get nothing but sympathy from his planter friends. And the wrath of God would fall on Ferrell Shanks.

At the start, she knew too that Lawton would think he hated her. He had suffered and would be angry, especially that she had gone to Lucinda. But in time, he would surrender to his ultimate obsession, his hopeless love, the love as deep as that of her father. He would be hers because all those who had influenced him against her—Lucinda and Joleen and Cellus—would be dead.

Rafaella looked at the clock. Clement Storey was coming at eleven. He had gotten in touch with her the day before, fearing for his life at the hands of gamblers to whom he owed huge notes. He would do anything for money, and he had access to The Columns.

An hour . . . She had time to . . .

Rafaella ran down the stairs, shouting for her carriage to be prepared.

"That was my first mistake, Daddy," Rafaella said as she stood in the graveyard, staring down at the marble headpiece. "To ever believe that you were anything but an English gentleman. But even if those despicable rumors had been true, if it had only been Lawton who knew after you gave your life for me, it would not have mattered. That was another mistake, Daddy. I should have destroyed the others then.

Lawton would have become . . . Daddy, he loved me so much and fought a duel for me. He would have married me and worshipped me, and I would have posed for him . . . and let him touch me and kiss me all over. Lucinda and Joleen and Cellus . . . they're to blame for all that happened, Daddy. I must save him now. Oh, I know he won't want me for a little while . . . but he will when the others are all dead. Then he will belong to me. And the babies, the two little babies . . . they won't be dead. He would never forgive me for that. I'll raise those two babies. Then I won't have to give him any of my own. They're so little . . . we can think of them as our own babies . . . if only they don't cry and I don't have to hold them. Yes, Lawton, and Daddy will accept me as . . . wife . . . He will, Lawton . . . my love, my husband."

When Joleen and Aaron returned to The Columns they heard that Lawton had run off with Rafaella. Then Lawton had appeared at the door, sick, hollow-eyed, unshaven, emaciated, and bruised.

Lucinda had been asleep, and they were able to clean Lawton up and fortify him with soup and whiskey before Lucinda saw him. Then Lawton had been put to bed.

Lucinda, though still weak, had come out of bed with a vengeance. She had suffered the hurt and humiliation of thinking her husband had left her for Rafaella, and she felt guilt for believing Rafaella's story. She expressed a hatred of which Joleen would have thought her incapable.

Lucinda summoned the sheriff, two judges, Juan Delsano, and Theron Sumrall. They were all outraged. Lawton told them what happened, and warrants were issued for the arrest of Hiram Cranston and Ferrell Shanks. The sheriff promised that as soon as there was any shred of evidence, as soon as either man talked, Rafaella would also be arrested.

Cranston could not be found. Shanks was caught at the county line, trying to flee with the slaves he had used as madhouse keepers. They were all locked up and were certain to be severely punished. A committee of Natchez doctors took over the madhouse.

Shanks claimed that Rafaella was behind Lawton's imprisonment, but he could offer no proof. And Rafaella, surprisingly lucid during this crisis, angrily denied any part in the affair. She retained a new lawyer and threatened libel if the accusations went any further. She also said that she had decided to take her father's remains back to Italy for burial, and that in a month, probably less, she would leave Natchez and never return.

Joleen and Lucinda agreed that Rafaella was directly responsible for what had happened to Lawton. And they did not believe that Rafaella would leave. But, lacking evidence, they did not know how she could be arrested for her part in the madhouse incident.

And Lawton refused to press the matter, once he heard she was leaving town. He seemed almost desperate to believe that indeed she would go. At times he spoke bitterly about Rafaella, but it was obvious that he only wanted the matter to end. And he was still so physically and emotionally debilitated by his confinement that Joleen and Lucinda dared not argue with him.

Lucinda stole away from the Christmas party to check on Clayton and Cynthia. Both babies were asleep, and Rubella said they hadn't stirred. Lucinda knew it was irrational, but since her confrontation with Rafaella she feared being away from the twins for more than a few minutes.

Lucinda kissed the babies and left the room quietly. She knew her fears were unfounded. Tiny Clayton and Cynthia were certainly safe enough here with Rubella. But thinking of Rafaella troubled her, set her nerves on edge. Like Joleen, she took Rafaella seriously and was quite certain she had been responsible for what had happened to Lawton. Rafaella's crazed look the day she came out to the plantation and lied about Lawton's living with her had convinced Lucinda that the girl was deranged. Surely, she was capable of anything.

Lucinda also doubted that Rafaella would leave Natchez. But Lawton was still not fully recovered, and if he found comfort in believing she would leave, Lucinda dared not alarm him by trying to force him to take immediate action against their cousin.

But if Rafaella didn't leave . . . Lucinda reached the bottom step vowing that if the girl wasn't gone within a month, she would force her out of town, no matter what harsh methods she had to use.

Lucinda accepted a glass of punch from Ambrose and joined a group of women making polite conversation. She was glad to see that both Lawton and Aaron were mingling with people, talking, drinking. It was splendid to see them enjoying the guests. Perhaps she could hope everything would work out.

Lucinda excused herself from the women and moved to straighten a flickering candle. She found herself talking to Clement Storey, a Natchez banker she had never liked. Lately he had ingratiated himself with Lawton, though in fact Lawton could not remember inviting Storey to the party.

"I understand Captain Chalmers of the *Biloxi Maid* has offered to stop by Deavors Landing and pick up a gala New Year's party," Storey said.

"Yes, there's been some talk of it," Lucinda said. Actually, the riverboat party up to Natchez had already been arranged, but she didn't want Storey to know it. He might try to join the party, and he was not the sort of man she welcomed at The Columns.

Unpleasant rumors hovered around Storey, a poor man who had married into a Natchez banking family. His gambling bouts Under-the-Hill were a minor Natchez legend. More than once, his father-in-law had paid the money he lost at cards. Now the bank he worked for was nearly ruined by the panic, and word was out that half a dozen gamblers were ready to kill

Storey if he didn't pay them the large sums of money he owed.

But tonight Storey talked genially of the party aboard the *Biloxi Maid*, and Lucinda was relieved that he made no direct effort to have himself invited to the affair. She did find it curious that he asked so many questions concerning the boat's schedule, but she finally assumed it was merely another aspect of his fawning, unpleasant nature.

Lucinda was relieved when Storey thanked her for the evening and said he had to go. He was in a cheerful mood when he left, as though his brief stay at The Columns had somehow been of some value to him.

84.

Alone, Rafaella drank champagne to toast the new year. It was near midnight on New Year's Eve. She swirled about in her candle-lit parlor in a white silk dress. Soon it would be time to drive out to the bluffs overlooking the river and watch the *Biloxi Maid* explode.

"And then they'll *all* be dead," she whispered to herself as she sipped the cold champagne. "Lucinda and Joleen and her husband and Cellus . . . but not Lawton. Clement Storey will keep him from getting on the boat, and he'll live and he'll come to me and he'll be mine for always."

Storey had bribed a debt-ridden mechanic on the boat to throw lard into the boilers and then jump overboard. The mechanic had been shocked and indignant at first, but the sum offered to him by Storey was so generous that he soon succumbed to the temptation. The *Biloxi Maid*'s captain liked to race and had a reputation for overtaxing his vessel. Riverboat explosions were common, and this one would not seem suspicious.

"No one will ever know I'm responsible," Rafaella murmured as she picked up the hem of her dress and danced around the room.

Four orchestras played dance music for the hundreds of guests who milled about the lavish suites, salons, and dance halls of the *Biloxi Maid*. Lucinda sipped a gin fizz and turned to speak to Lawton. "I'm so glad you came aboard at the last minute, darling," she said. "You've been working too hard . . . and it's New Year's Eve. Clement Storey and his urgent business be damned!"

"Yes, that's what I told him, in so many words," Lawton said. "Strange man. He was so frantic that I thought I'd have to knock him down to get on board! But, my dear, you're so beautiful tonight . . . prettier than ever."

Clasping hands, they drank more gin fizzes and then moved out among the others to dance. Both were struggling to hide the special fears and apprehensions that beset them.

Lucinda had not wanted to leave her small babies at The Columns. Of course, they were with their nurses, being well cared for. She was too protective, she told herself. She had responsibilities to Lawton, too. And she must not spoil this time with her husband by letting him know her silly fears.

Lawton smiled and complimented Lucinda, danced and drank, determined that she shouldn't suspect his own dark mood, his own deep fears. Foremost among them was the dread that Rafaella would not leave Natchez as she had promised. If she did not leave, he would be compelled to drive her out. He had sworn it as he relived those hellish days in the madhouse and remembered the look on Rafaella's face that last time, remembered his horror as he stared into her burning eyes. She *had* to go away. She could not stay among them, for she was obviously capable of any act of cruelty and madness. Oh, she would leave! Surely she would leave of her own accord. That would solve everything. But if she did not, he would have to act—to use the rumors of her father's past, or anything else, to drive her out.

Lawton cleared his throat, coming back to the present. After all, it was New Year's Eve. He kissed Lucinda's cheek and smiled at Joleen and Aaron across the floor near the orchestra.

"Oh, come out on deck!" someone shouted. "Come, everyone! You can see Natchez in the distance!"

People streamed out to the starboard decks. Lawton, Lucinda, Aaron, and Joleen stood in the happy crowd and watched the hazy lights become distinct lamps and lanterns and buildings under the hill. But suddenly it was as if the *Biloxi Maid* were trying to set a new speed record. The boat moved faster and faster and began to rock crazily in the water as its velocity increased. A murmur of apprehension swept the crowd on deck.

"I hope the captain doesn't get carried away," Lucinda said.

"He's a competent fellow," Lawton said. "We'll be safe enough." But he was beginning to worry.

The *Biloxi Maid* was bucking over the water outside Under-the-Hill when the passengers heard the first rumblings from her boilers. The din of drunken chatter and laughter stopped abruptly. The huge craft trembled. Masses of red and gold sparks, like fireworks, shot up from the two enormous white funnels.

Suddenly, there were more rumblings, more sparks, as though they were riding a floating volcano. Steam hissed out from the back of the boat. Women screamed.

"Get up forward, away from the boilers!" Aaron shouted. He dragged Joleen through the screaming, confused crowd. Lawton and Lucinda followed close behind.

The first explosion knocked Aaron and Joleen to the deck. Lawton and Lucinda were slammed against the rail and nearly fell overboard. Steam enveloped the back of the boat. Sparks fell like rain and burned screaming, panic-stricken passengers.

Aaron scrambled to his feet. His head ached and he was still weak from his Cuban ordeal, but he jerked Joleen up and moved forward again.

"Get up front!" he called to Lawton, who was shaking his head as if stunned and wiping blood from a cut over one eye. "It's our only chance!"

They had fought their way another few feet forward through the crowd when the second explosion lifted the boat and tilted it sharply to one side. All four of them were thrown into the cold water, along with dozens of other passengers.

For a minute, they were separated in the darkness. Then a third explosion lit the sky with brilliance, and the *Biloxi Maid* began to burn. In the bright light of her flames, they caught sight of one another again. Gasping for air, they clung together in the debris-cluttered water. The current was swift. They awkwardly swam toward shore, along with Cellus, who had somehow found them. Chunks of debris—much of it on fire—smashed against swimmers' heads. Some were killed at once.

A greasy oil slick was flowing out from the boat's ruptured boilers and spreading in erratic rivulets over the water. The fire found this fuel and skittered over it hungrily, devouring frantic swimmers. There were hideous screams, and the smell of burning flesh filled the air.

Near the shore, someone called Lawton's name. He glanced around. In a flash of light he recognized Lissy, a slave from The Columns.

"Can't swim, Mist' Lawton!" she gasped.

"Go on, I'll help Lissy," Lawton said.

"No, Lawton!" Lucinda begged. But he was gone, and a minute later she lost sight of him in the dark water and the smoke.

The survivors stumbled ashore and were greeted by the leering, drunken, murderous faces of men who had just come from the Under-the-Hill taverns and gambling halls. They were men who would kill for a bottle of whiskey. Now they gazed in astonishment at the half-drowned, helpless people, soaking wet and exhausted, wearing diamonds and jewelry and rings and watches and bracelets.

"And I thought we'd already had Christmas!" a gap-toothed giant shouted as he pulled a knife and fell on a shrieking fat woman who wore a necklace of huge pearls.

Another man reached out for Joleen's emerald ring as though he would bite off her finger to get at it. Aaron knocked the man to the ground. He had just taken Lucinda's hand to pull her closer when two thugs attacked them. Both had knives. Aaron wrestled with one man. The other reached for Lucinda. Cellus took the man's wrist, snapped it, and hurled him aside. Aaron was still struggling, his strength failing him. Cellus locked his arms around Aaron's attacker, jerked him from Aaron, raised him up into the air, then dropped his limp body into the water.

"Let's get out of here!" Aaron shouted.

"Lawton . . . in the water . . ." Lucinda sobbed.

"Lawton!" Joleen gasped. "Oh, God, where is he?"

"We'll be murdered here," Aaron said. He seized a pistol from the belt of the first attacker's trousers.

"We can't leave Lawton," Joleen said.

"You all go on," Cellus said. "I'll go back to the river and see if I can find him."

Cellus was gone before anyone could move. Joleen and Lucinda were stunned by what they could see around them—desperation, murder, hideous carnage, as men sliced off fingers to get rings, leaving their victims screaming. Aaron dragged the two women toward the docks, away from Under-the-Hill. Twice he had to drive off thugs with his stolen pistol. At last they reached a safe area at the edge of the docks. Men who had not dared to rush into the Under-the-Hill section to rescue them, now offered coats to Joleen and Lucinda. They both huddled beside Aaron and waited.

Half an hour later Cellus returned, wet and exhausted. Joleen knew as soon as she saw Cellus's face. Lucinda was slower to read the truth in his expression.

"He's dead," Cellus said. "I pulled his body ashore . . . but I was too late." There were tears in Cellus's eyes.

Joleen and Lucinda held each other and sobbed violently.

Rafaella's eyes had glowed as she watched the three explosions destroy the *Biloxi Maid*.

"Now we'll be together for always, Daddy," she crowed as she climbed from her carriage and paced along the edge of the bluffs. The hem of her white silk wedding dress trailed in the mud. "Just us . . . she won't come between us any more. No, she's dead now . . . and Joleen and her husband . . . and that nigger Cellus. Now there's just the two of us!"

The minutes passed, a quarter hour, half an hour. She was anxious to have Storey confirm the deaths. Then she would drive home and have another bottle of champagne to celebrate the last night she would ever be alone.

"We'll be together always, Daddy." She shivered. "No, I mean Lawton! It's Lawton . . . my darling Lawton . . . you're dead, Daddy, but Lawton is alive and he's mine. And he'll always love me, be my husband, my father . . ."

The sound of a horse startled her. She glanced around to see Clement Storey riding up.

"You've kept me waiting far too long, sir!" she said as he dismounted. "I watched the explosions. You'll have your money tomorrow as I promised. Why are you looking like that?"

"That idiot on the boat," Storey said. "He did something wrong. The explosions . . . many people escaped."

"You assured me no one would survive! *You're* the idiot! Did any of the Deavorses survive? Which ones?"

"Well, all but one. Mrs. Ridgeway, you promised me that money first thing tomorrow. I'll be killed if I don't have it. Now, I did what you wanted, and it's not my fault if that mechanic made a mess of things! If you don't give me the money . . . so help me, I'll tell everyone what you made me do!"

"You won't get one cent if any one of them is alive!" Rafaella said. "Who lived? And . . . they wouldn't believe you. Even Lawton wouldn't believe you. He loves me too much and he belongs to me. And he would never—"

"Lawton's dead. Lawton's the only one who's dead!" Storey said. "I couldn't stop him from getting on board. And I'll make sure they believe me. I've *got* to have that money!"

Rafaella felt a sick rush of fever. A chill shot up her back. She trembled so violently her knees nearly buckled.

"Lawton . . . dead?" she gasped. Her throat was dry, and she choked on her words. "You goddamn . . . you're responsible. You killed my father! Oh, no, no, I can't stand it! I can't live, then. Him dead, too? No, oh, no, please . . ."

"Not your goddamn father!" Storey said. "Lawton Deavors! And I want my money, or so help me . . ."

Rafaella's face began to contract. She could not control her muscles. Her lips twitched and she bit down and tasted blood.

"There's no help for you!" she shouted. "You killed him . . . you're responsible!"

Rafaella stumbled around and grabbed the carriage whip. "You killed him!" she screeched again, as she flailed at Storey with the whip.

Storey stepped back to escape her assault. His feet reached the edge of the bluff. For one instant he seemed to realize his danger, but a blow across his neck made him jump, and he stepped backwards and fell two hundred feet to the mudflats. His mangled body, buffeted repeatedly against the side of the cliff as he fell, disappeared under the water.

Rafaella ran to her carriage. If her father really

were dead . . . all was lost. They would punish her for certain now . . . Lucinda and Joleen and all the rest. She whipped up the horses, gasping with excitement. If they were still alive, but he was dead.

She had to run! She would flee to Europe! She would still have her money here . . . they couldn't take that away. Soon she would return and ruin them all. But first . . .

"Those babies," she whispered. "The little babies. They're out at The Columns alone. Why, that's it. Daddy, I'll smother those little babies . . . that will be my revenge for your death! I'll put the little babies in Lucinda's bed, where you slept with her, not that you ever really loved her. You loved only me and you died for me!"

The carriage lurched as she drove the horses faster and faster, cracking the whip over their sleek backs. Rafaella was half aware of a single horseman behind her, but she was too involved in her plan to pay any attention.

At The Columns, Rafaella left the carriage on the house road. On foot, she crept up the big front lawn, shivering with the cold. She sensed that she was being followed, as she had on the frantic ride out from town.

The big house was dark and quiet. She crossed the verandah and passed through the huge white columns. After one creaking step in the front hallway, she was about to move upstairs without making a sound. The nursery door stood partly open. A black woman was sleeping on a cot near the double crib. Rafaella slipped into the room. She snatched up a vase and smashed it against the woman's head.

Then she picked up a down pillow and moved toward the crib. The twins were fast asleep . . . Clayton and Cynthia, Storey had said they were called. They should have been named after her father and mother: Roger and Sarah.

As she lowered the pillow, she heard a voice.

"Raffles!"

The voice chilled her. She dropped the pillow and wheeled to face him.

Wyman Ridgeway stood in the doorway. His face was hideous, twisted, scarred. Part of his left ear was missing.

Rafaella shrank away from the sight of him. "Wyman? My God! What are you doing? Oh, Wyman!" Involuntarily, she stared at the ever-present sword in its scabbard at his side.

"You were going to kill the children."

"Yes, yes, so I was . . . but why should you care? A man like you?"

"I'm their father, Raffles! And I told you you'd pay with your life if you tried to harm them."

"Their father! You . . . and Lucinda! Oh, God!"

Ridgeway made a swift movement. His naked rapier suddenly glinted in the candlelight. "I had hoped the last swordsman would kill me. But the scoundrel lacked the ability. How appropriate. Now we can die together . . . beloved husband and wife."

"No!" Rafaella screamed. "No! I won't . . . I'll do anything. I didn't know. Oh, Wyman . . . they killed my father!"

He moved toward her, his rapier high. She screamed again and threw a silver vase at his head. He ducked, laughing.

Rafaella ran into the hall, down the stairs, screaming incoherently. Ridgeway followed. She ran out the back door of the house, oblivious to the voices from the quarters, to the lights blinking on in the small cabins.

"No, no!" she screeched as she reached the edge of the swamp. "No . . . Daddy . . . save me, Daddy!"

Rafaella turned to beg Ridgeway. He cut off her right thumb. The index finger dangled by a thread.

She lurched, screaming like a wounded animal, into the swamp. He followed.

Neither of them was ever seen again.

SPECIAL PREVIEW

Here are opening scenes
from the first novel in
this sweeping series

THE PLANTATION

Prologue

Natchez, Spring, 1831

There was the sound of horses in the darkness. The mob strained forward. There were shouts. Several guns were fired into the air. Two white men dragged a Negro out of the darkness. They forced him to lie between two green pine logs on the ground. Green pine burns with a low flame and slowly roasts a man instead of flaring up and killing him quickly. The Negro's lips quivered. He cried softly but said nothing. The men tied loops of wire to his ankles and wrists and fastened these wires to the logs. Then they stepped back. A hush fell over the mob, a hush so total and sudden it seemed almost religious.

A man whose left forearm ended in a wooden stub dipped a cup into a vat of paraffin beside a woodpile and poured the paraffin over the logs. The paraffin flamed up; then the logs caught fire and burned with a low blue flame.

There was not a sound from the mob. On the Mississippi River, a few yards away, a paddle-wheeler blew its whistle. The logs began to crackle. Termites crawled from cracks and fled the heat. Thick smoke rose up. Crickets chirped in the hot shadows. A night bird cried from a catawba tree.

At the first inhuman scream, several men slipped away from the mob. The Negro screamed again and again. Wind blew up from the river. The smell of burning resin and flesh swept over the mob. A redheaded boy on the edge of the crowd vomited. Several more men fled the scene. But the others stood quietly. They drank from jugs of Monongahela whiskey and stared into the flames.

The fire now grew white. The smoke was white

and gray. The Negro screamed one last time. Then he was silent. The wind shifted back toward the river. A murmur passed through the crowd. The men began to talk softly and pass their jugs around as they waited for the second slave to be brought up.

It was a hot April night on the mud flats beneath the Natchez bluffs. The men drank more whiskey as they became restless. Several men debated whether the two charred logs should be used again or whether two new logs should be taken from the woodpile.

Two fresh logs were laid out on the ground as the second Negro was brought into the faint light from the fire. He struggled against the cords that bound his wrists behind his back. He was a big man and much younger than the first. Blood trickled into his left eye from a cut on his forehead. Flies buzzed indolently at the blood.

The slave's resistance aroused the mob's fury. Men shouted and cursed, and guns were fired into the air. The one-armed man stoked the fire, and another man prepared several torches. The Negro fought his cords, but he only caused his wrists to bleed. The mob surged forward several feet as the men drank and watched the struggling slave. Those nearest to him saw the hatred and defiance in his face change to fear as he looked at the charred corpse of the first Negro.

A man dressed quite differently from the rough clothes of the mob stood hidden in a vast canebrake a few yards behind the slave. This man wore the ruffles and high-fashioned clothes of a gentleman. Only minutes ago, in a mansion high on the bluffs, his foppish manners and cynical wit had amused the planters who drank sherry and port and whiskey and pretended they did not know that, down on the flats, a mob of rednecks and rivermen was lynching two slaves accused of attacking a white woman.

The man took a lace handkerchief from his sleeve and patted perspiration from his face. He wore two pistols, and there was another pistol in the saddle of the horse he had tied a hundred yards back in the cane. He carried a long cloak and wore a hat pulled down to shadow his face. Now he slipped into the cloak.

The fire was roaring. The mob backed off. A strange hush fell over the men. Blood dripped from the Negro's head and from the cord cuts in his frantically twisting wrists.

The man in the cane bent down and took out two flints. He struck them together. Sparks leaped against the dry cane. A brittle cane stalk began to smoke. The man crept forward several feet to the edge of the clearing. The cane flamed up, and the fire instantly spread. The mob was startled by the sudden fire and thick smoke. Under this cover of smoke, the man ran the few feet to the woodpile. He kicked over the paraffin vat. It soaked several logs. The man snatched up a torch and ignited the wood.

The paraffin blazed like an explosion. The one-armed man ran blindly from the flames. The mob retreated in panic. The men holding the Negro released him and stumbled from the heat and smoke. The man in the cloak ran to the Negro. He took a knife from his coat and sliced through the cords.

He motioned to the cane. The Negro followed him through the smoke. As the man had calculated—and risked—the wind had fanned the flames toward the river, enabling them to stumble through the smoke and run toward the horse that was rearing up in fright.

But the mob's panic had now passed, and the men realized what had happened. Cursing and shouting, they chased through the smoke and into the cane.

The man in the cloak steadied his horse. He mounted the horse and gave his hand to help the slave climb up behind him. A shot snapped past them. Another. They galloped through the cane, coughing from the smoke.

A dozen men stopped and fought for breath. They cursed and coughed.

"What in hell was that?" a man asked.

"Couldn't be but one thing," another man gasped. "That goddamn Underground Railroad again!"

Chapter 1

There had never been another place in America like Natchez-under-the-Hill. In all his travels on the Continent and in Morocco, Lavon Deavors had not seen anything like it. It stretched along the Mississippi River for over a mile beneath bluffs that rose two hundred feet to the parks and mansions of Natchez. Shacks and shanties and lean-tos hugged the mud flats below the bluffs, while houseboats and barges crowded the wharves. They housed the indigent and fugitive, who had been swept up and down the river and had finally ended in Natchez, and also provided space for hundreds of whorehouses, taverns, and gambling dens.

On a hot May afternoon Lavon stood on the dock beside the paddle-wheeler *Kentucky*, which had just brought him upriver from New Orleans. He looked from the bluffs to the mud flats and wondered if anything had changed in the years he had been away. His friends in London and Paris had romantic ideas about the plantation South of Georgia, Virginia, and the Carolinas. A few of these friends had visited famous plantations and cities such as Charleston, Richmond, and Savannah. But they knew nothing of this part of the South. This was wilderness. This was frontier country. There were a few large plantations outside Natchez, and the little city thought itself sophisticated, but the real nature of this land was condensed under the bluffs to Lavon's right. Or has it been tamed? he asked himself. He walked from the dock and decided to have a look before hiring a carriage for the last leg of his long journey.

Water lapped through the cracks of the wooden sidewalks. The humidity was stifling. Heat mirages shimmered up from the brackish water, and a stench rose from the warm red mud. Pigs rooted in the mud and fought dogs for the garbage.

Lavon stepped inside a tavern that crouched over the river on wooden stilts. He ordered whiskey and paid with one of his few remaining coins. The whiskey tasted good, but the tavern depressed Lavon. It was a small room hung with cigar smoke and filled with sullen men who, from their talk and clothes, Lavon took to be minor functionaries from the port and clerks from the chandleries and warehouses.

He left and walked along another sunken sidewalk. He passed gambling dens where dandies in outlandish clothes threw dice and talked horse racing with well-dressed pimps and hustlers. In other dens polemen played cards and drank from jugs. These men were giants, and their drinking and fighting ability were legend along the river. Their arms and shoulders bulged with the muscles built up from years of poling heavy flatboats down the Mississippi.

Lavon paused to watch a cockfight in a mud pit. A rust-colored rooster sank its talons into its opponent's skull and ripped out an eye. Blood-splattered men shouted and clapped and hurried to take their winnings from the loser's owner.

While drinking whiskey at an open stand on a mud flat, Lavon heard distant music from a spinet. Claire Devonshire, his last mistress before he ran out of money, had played her spinet in her little house in London's Stewart Park. How odd to hear such music under the hill, Lavon told himself. The music's source became an idle quest.

Lavon pushed along a crowded sidewalk. Old women in tattered dresses hawked crawfish. Trappers thrust stinking, bloodstained pelts at Lavon. Negroes idled in gloomy doorways and talked with immigrants, marked by their language. Emaciated children played with fish heads and dodged drunken polemen, whose weight sank the sidewalks deeper into the water.

On a half-sunken barge a dozen Indians in ragged buckskins thumped cane drums and performed a pitiful dance. These Choctaw and Chickasaw had once ruled this land and had inflicted a humiliating defeat on the French. But first the French, then the Spanish, the English, and the Americans had subjugated and demoralized the Indians, and now this group did their dance and the leader held out his palms to Lavon and begged, "A bit, sir . . . some whiskey, sir . . . me good boy . . . you like war dance. . . ."

Black whores lounged on the deck of a long barge. They called to Lavon. A teen-age girl licked her lips and made sucking sounds. Another opened her green dress and fondled her breasts.

Lavon walked on. The spinet was being played on the next barge. It was a huge red barge. Its windows were shuttered and its door was shut. The red barge was famous, and Lavon remembered visiting it when he was in school. In its perfumed rooms of plush carpets and red draperies and crystal chandeliers were beautiful octoroon and quadroon whores brought up from New Orleans. They were skilled in music and dancing as well as sex. The barge's owner was a six-foot-eight-inch-tall mulatto named Annie Easter. Annie opened her door only to the most select of customers.

Lavon forced himself to move on. He would have liked to lie on the silken sheets and make love to a beautiful young quadroon, but he didn't have enough money to tip Annie's servants, much less pay for one of her girls.

The sidewalk was two inches below water now. A man was lying across the sidewalk, his face in the water. He'll drown, Lavon told himself. He pulled the man's face up. Empty eye sockets stared at Lavon. He dropped the head and stumbled down the sidewalk, past more barges where white and black and yellow whores displayed themselves.

Two black men were fighting at an intersection. They fell into the water. Nobody stopped to look. The water grew red. Lavon walked faster.

He stopped abruptly. He was nauseated from the stench and filth and heat. There might be a thousand taverns, whorehouses, and gambling dens ahead. He could walk under the hill for hours, and it would only get worse as he got farther from the docks. And he realized he was only procrastinating because he was hesitant to face his family at long last.

Lavon decided to return to the docks by a route that took him along the mud flats directly under the bluffs. He told himself he was glad he had taken this walk because it made him realize to what level he might have fallen if he had remained on the Continent without money.

Two slaves, haltered by a rope around their necks, were being led into a building.

"What's that building, boy?" Lavon asked a black man who was selling catfish.

"That there? That be a nigger pen there, sir."

"A nigger pen? What's that?"

"For slaves just brought down from Virginny or one of them North places."

"A slave trader?" Lavon said. "When I lived here they weren't allowed to set up permanent quarters in the city."

"The man there, he sells niggers, yassuh. Folks say he be here permanent. He just come back with a new load, from what I hear tell. Them two niggers yoked up, I 'spect they part of the new ones just arrived."

Lavon decided to have a look inside. He broadened his step to avoid a pool of mud, but looked at his wretched boots and planted his next step in the mud. Better they look soiled than out of repair, he told himself.

The building was ramshackle but had recently been whitewashed. Lavon thought he remembered the place, but he could not recall why. He passed a pen of dogs that snarled at him. A few feet away was a set of stocks.

Lavon paused at the door and studied a notice stuck to a pole:

REMSON COLLINS JUST ARRIVED FROM VIRGINIA WITH A CHOICE LOT OF NIGGERS, INCLUDING SEAMSTRESSES, IRONERS, WASHERS,

MECHANICS, CARPENTERS, COOKS, BLACK-
SMITHS, AND PRIME PLANTATION HANDS, AS
WELL AS PRIME NIGGERS FOR BREEDING. IN-
TENDING TO ESTABLISH MYSELF HERE PER-
MANENTLY, I WISH TO ANNOUNCE THAT
THROUGHOUT THE SEASON MY STOCK WILL
BE CONSTANTLY REPLENISHED WITH CHOICE
NIGGERS.

Lavon shook his head. So slave traders had indeed descended on Natchez and begun to set up permanent quarters instead of selling on the streets. Well, he
reminded himself, he had been away eight years, and
anything could have happened in this godforsaken
wilderness.

He walked through the open door and down a
hallway that led to a courtyard, which was dominated
by an oak tree draped with moss that touched the
ground at the ends of sagging limbs. Along the left wall
were a dozen fig trees, and the mud was purple with
the pulp of fallen figs. Some thirty slaves milled around
the trees or sat on pads of moss. There were a half-
dozen black men stripped to the waist. Their bodies
glistened with sweat. Except for two middle-aged
women who fanned themselves with banana leaves, the
other slaves were all young women or teen-age girls.

A white man was releasing the slaves Lavon had
seen outside. They rubbed their wrists and flexed their
shoulders. One man mopped his face with a cloth. The
other drank from a gourd. The white man motioned the
two blacks to a table. They sat down and ate from a
bowl with their fingers.

Another white man came from a door in the right
wall. He was followed by two girls who were no more
than eighteen. One was short and black, with a body
that was just shy of plump. The other was tall and slim.
Her skin was yellowish. Both girls took hesitant steps
and stared at the ground. The man's head bobbed as he
talked. He shook his head and fussed with the shorter
girl's calico dress.

Lavon told himself to be on his way. He turned to
leave.

"Sir, you lookin' to buy yourself a nigger?" the man called.

Lavon stepped back into the courtyard. The man was hurrying over. He stopped abruptly as he got a good look at Lavon's clothes.

"What you want here?" he asked.

Lavon sometimes forgot how shabby his outfit was, and when forced to take note of his appearance by someone he considered inferior, he had difficulty controlling his anger.

"I was looking over your niggers," Lavon said. "Good day."

Again he started down the hall, but his exit was blocked by a white man with a wooden arm, who was dragging a sack along the floor. He and Lavon looked at each other, and, like the buildings, the man hovered in Lavon's memory. He would not have remembered him but for the wooden stub.

"I know you from somewheres," the man said. He squinted up into Lavon's face. "I know I knows you, but I ain't seen you in a coon's age. You used to come drinkin' when I had me the alehouse here."

"That's correct," Lavon said. "I have come here, though, on only a few occasions, and that was years ago." He recalled drunken nights in the alehouse. The man's name was Chunky, and he loved to demonstrate how he could punch open an ale barrel with his wooden stub.

"You're a Deavors, I swear," Chunky said. "The one that went off, went north to New York, or Paris, France, or one of them places. I'd know a Deavors anyplace. But they done said you're dead."

"It would seem they're wrong," Lavon said. "Now, if you'll get out of my way, I must leave."

"Just a minute, Mr. Deavors."

Lavon looked around. The other man was walking toward him.

"I'm new to Adams County, sir," the man said. "Just bought this place from Chunky last year. But, of course, everybody knows about the Deavors family. How can I help you, Mr. Deavors? My name is Remson Collins."

"We have no business to conduct, Mr. Collins," Lavon said.

"I noticed you lookin' at the two girls, Mr. Deavors," Collins said. "I picked 'em out special up to Richmond. I got me a fine eye. Why, I used to trade cattle 'fore I took to niggerin'. Would you like a closer look at the girls?"

"I wouldn't be interested," Lavon said.

But he was interested. He had not touched a woman for nearly a month.

"Well, sir, why not come on back to the shade and at least have somethin' to drink," Collins said. "If you headin' out to the plantation, you got a long ride."

"I am thirsty," Lavon said.

"Then you come right on back here," Collins said. "Chunky, you better look after the stock."

"Sure thing, Remson," Chunky said. He walked away.

The stock. . . . What a disgusting way to refer to the slaves, Lavon told himself as he followed Collins across the courtyard. He thought of leaving. Word might get back to his family or their friends. Someone might see him. He was back so short a time, and already he was consorting with the lowest sort of men.

His shirt was matted to his back. Sweat stung his eyes. His boots creaked in the mud. He wanted the whiskey desperately.

Chapter 2

The two girls looked up as Lavon passed. They were even younger than he had realized, no more than sixteen or seventeen. Collins escorted Lavon around the oak, past an auction platform, and seated him at a table covered with white muslin. The table was crowded with ledgers, bottles of patent medicine, spoons, links of chain, a Bible, shackles, rope, a leather whip, two vases of nasturtiums, a jug, and two cups.

Collins sat down. He poured whiskey into the cups. Lavon nodded thanks as he accepted the cup Collins offered. He took a swallow. The whiskey was terrible. It hit his disbelieving stomach like a rock, but he drank again and wiped his mouth with the back of his hand.

"Well, now, Mr. Deavors," Collins said. "From what I heard, it would appear you been away. Doin' some travelin'? . . ."

"I've been on the Continent," Lavon said. "And in Morocco." He was amused at Collins' effort to understand how any Deavors could find himself in such wretched garments.

"That a fact?" Collins said. "Me, I do a lot of travelin', but it's always here in this country. I come down from Richmond couple of days ago with a load of stock. October to May's the season, and I'm pushin' it here at the end, but business been so good, I plumb near sold out. You ever been to Richmond, Mr. Deavors?"

"My ship stopped in Richmond harbor, but I didn't go ashore," Lavon said. He sipped whiskey and looked around the courtyard. The slaves were lounging in the shadows. The two girls sat on a barrel, their heads tilted together as they talked. They held hands. The men who had just arrived stood naked while Chunky measured them for clothes.

"Did those two niggers come down from Richmond?" Lavon asked.

"No, no, I bought 'em off a fella down to Woodville. Off the sheriff, in actual fact. Fella had him a little farm and couldn't make a note after he'd put up the niggers for collateral."

"How do you get your niggers down from Richmond?" Lavon asked. "Bring them on a coastal steamer?"

"Why, no, Mr. Deavors, matter of fact, I don't. Costs too much, among other things. No, I shackle 'em together and make up a coffle and march the niggers overland. This time I come down the Natchez Trace from Nashville."

"How do you go about buying the niggers?" Lavon asked. He had never talked to a slave trader before, and despite his repulsion at the man and his trade, he was curious.

Collins bolted down the whiskey and leaned forward. His head went up and down as the words poured out. He said that on a buying trip he staked out an area. On the last trip it was a few counties around Richmond. He attended plantation and courthouse sales, sheriff's auctions, foreclosures. He advertised in local journals. It seemed he specialized in mechanics, which were scarce in Mississippi, and especially in women who would make good breeders.

"I see," Lavon said. He drank whiskey. This bastard was not only a trader, but was actually going to breed his people as though they were cattle.

Collins seemed delighted to have found a man of quality to hear his complaints and problems. He said the local planters did not understand the hazards and expenses of his trade. They were angry because he charged seven to eight hundred dollars for a prime breeder or mechanic. Actually, he said, if these folks knew the trouble, expense, and danger of bringing the niggers down from Virginia . . .

And by God, he gave fair measure. He didn't do like some, buy old men and tint their hair dark and pull out their whiskers. He didn't buy sick niggers and give them rum so they would look sprightly for a buyer. And he didn't go to some sheriff and take his murderers and thieves for a song and sell these criminals to unsuspecting farmers.

Lavon watched the clever eyes dart about. Collins wore two ruby rings. A planter who boarded the ship in Richmond had mentioned that prime slaves there were selling for two or three hundred dollars. So Collins was making a handsome profit, obviously.

He watched Collins pour whiskey into his cup. "Thank you," he mumbled.

Collins' head began to bob again as he talked of

the dangers on the march down. They came through savage country, he said. The slaves tried to escape. There were bandits at every bend of the road, and a gang of slave rustlers up near the Tennessee border.

"Man's got a right to make a little profit after risks like that, Mr. Deavors," Collins said, but Lavon barely heard him.

He was staring at the girls again. Chunky went over to the black girl and said something to her. He poured whiskey from a jug and gave her the cup. She hesitated, then drank the whiskey. Chunky talked to her again. She drank whiskey, and it spilled over her chin and wet the front of her dress. Chunky smiled. The girl nodded and unbuttoned the dress. She discarded the calico and knelt on the moss. Chunky gave her more whiskey. Lavon stared at her black skin, glistening like wet velvet. She was so young and ripe, and perhaps even a virgin. Her breasts were large and uptilted. Beads of moisture fell from the long nipples. One of the new black men crawled over to her and took the cup and drank whiskey. The man put his hand on her leg and leaned over and kissed her. She lay down beside him. Lavon glanced around. The couple lay in a sea of black and brown flesh that seemed to undulate with a common sexual stirring. The other young girl, the high yellow, was watching the kissing couple with wide eyes. Lavon drank whiskey. He thought of the firm breasts, the lean, strong legs. He hadn't touched a Negro girl in years.

"They sure are fine-lookin', Mr. Deavors."

Lavon turned around. He had forgotten Collins for a moment. He drank more whiskey than he wanted. It rode in his throat, and he forced it down. The silence stretched. He wanted no more talk with this man. His stomach protested even the smell of the whiskey. He shifted on the wooden seat. Despite the shade, the heat was weighing him down as surely as if he had been covered with wet sheets. He sucked in his breath and smelled figs rotting in the sun.

He did not want to stay, but he could not bring himself to leave. He had to say something. "How did you get into this business?" he asked without interest. He would hear the man's answer and then be on his way for sure.

"Well, sir, I saw some years ago that tradin' niggers was goin' to be worth more'n tradin' cattle," Collins said. Once more he began to speak rapidly. "The farms up to Virginny and Maryland, why, sir, they bein' farmed out. And there's no new land left up there. Not like out here in the West, where a man can farm out his lot and move on down the road and find untouched soil rich and cheap as can be. Well, now, what you think's goin' to happen in them states up there, Mr. Deavors?"

"I wouldn't know," Lavon said. He looked through the moss. The slaves were naked, and Chunky was washing them down with buckets of water. The black girl and the man were walking into a little open cubicle directly opposite Lavon and Collins.

". . . become one big breeding pen." Collins' voice caught Lavon's attention again. "Folks already floodin' in here for this rich land. And folks up there, they findin' it lots more profitable to breed their stock and sell the surplus niggers than to work new acreage with 'em. Uh, you goin' to be stayin' for good out to the plantation? . . ."

"Yes, Mr. Collins, I'll be staying for good at the Columns," Lavon said. He shoved back his stool and stood up. "But I can forestall your next query. It has always been my family's policy neither to buy nor to sell slaves."

"That's not what I was leadin' up to, Mr. Deavors," Collins said. "Though you might change your mind in the future. Man's got to change with the times, sir." And to Lavon's annoyance, Collins rattled on again. "Why, in Alabama they outlawed slave tradin' for three years, from 1827 until last year, and it didn't work out. You know, I've never been able to follow the logic of them as owns slaves and gets rich off 'em on a plantation and yet opposes them as do the tradin' and breedin' of slaves." Collins was whining. "One feeds off the other, sure as fat dogs fart, and it's all a natural part of slavin'. . . ."

"No, Mr. Collins, it's not the same thing," Lavon snapped. "Hell, there's no need to argue it further." What had come over him, sitting in this courtyard, arguing with a slave breeder?

Lavon turned, and stopped. The girl was lying down on a bed in the cubicle. She was naked. Her lush body was silhouetted in the dim light. She opened her thighs wide. The man lay between her thighs. The girl lay still a moment while the man writhed around. Then they began to move together. The girl squeezed her legs across his back. Lavon heard the squeak of the bed and the sounds of their lovemaking.

His penis began to stiffen. He shifted his weight. He thought of the girl. She would be bred again and again for the rest of her life. But now she was so young. She would be tight. All this sex was new to her. Lavon stared at her heaving body. She was groaning now. He could almost sense the damp heat of her vagina.

"Now, Mr. Deavors, it was more a discussion than an actual argument," Collins was saying. "Why don't you sit back down and have some more whiskey. And tell you what. Maybe you'd like to mount the nigger while the buck's got her all worked up. Never been fucked before, and see, she takes to it like a pig to the sugar house. She's one fine piece of 'tang." Collins no longer whined. He spoke with the confidence of a man who knows he has finally found merchandise that is irresistible to a buyer.

"I must be going," Lavon said.

"Now, please, just a minute, Mr. Deavors," Collins said. "Chunky! Chunky, bring Moselle over here for Mr. Deavors to examine. Now, Moselle, she's the high yellow you was lookin' at. She's still a virgin. You can be first. I done picked her out special for breedin'. But like as not, 'tween times with the bucks I'll put her up as a fancy lady for white men." . . .

ABOUT THE AUTHOR

A Mississippian by birth, GEORGE MCNEILL graduated from the University of Mississippi and worked as a journalist on various Southern newspapers. As a free-lance writer he has written magazine articles as well as a number of paperback originals (under a pseudonym). He is the author of the very successful novel, *The Plantation.*

DON'T MISS
THESE CURRENT
Bantam Bestsellers

RELAX!
SIT DOWN
and Catch Up On Your Reading!

Bantam Book Catalog

Here's your up-to-the-minute listing of every book currently available from Bantam.

This easy-to-use catalog is divided into categories and contains over 1400 titles by your favorite authors.

So don't delay—take advantage of this special opportunity to increase your reading pleasure.

Just send us your name and address and 25¢ (to help defray postage and handling costs).